Black Wind

by Ron Baird

Order this book online at www.trafford.com
or email orders@trafford.com

Most Trafford titles are also available at major online book retailers.

Note for Librarians: A cataloguing record for this book is available from Library and Archives Canada at www.collectionscanada.ca/amicus/index-e.html

Printed in Victoria, BC, Canada.

ISBN: 978-1-4269-1378-5 (sc)
ISBN: 978-1-4269-1379-2 (dj)

Library of Congress Control Number: 2009931990

We at Trafford believe that it is the responsibility of us all, as both individuals and corporations, to make choices that are environmentally and socially sound. You, in turn, are supporting this responsible conduct each time you purchase a Trafford book, or make use of our publishing services. To find out how you are helping, please visit www.trafford.com/responsiblepublishing.html

Trafford rev. 8/24/2009

Cover art by Ray Geier.com

www.trafford.com

North America & international
oll-free: 1 888 232 4444 (USA & Canada)
phone: 250 383 6864 • fax: 812 355 4082

Dedicated to wounded warriors everywhere, and to the kids of the Shiwi Messenger newspaper, Zuni Pueblo, N.M.

Acknowledgements

The following people have been absolutely critical to this book's publication:

Gurney Steele, for moral and other support, critical reading and editing

Barry (Bear) Tobin, for extraordinary editing, advice and encouragement

Dave (Luke) Lucas, for critical reading and suggestions

Jethro McClellan, for eagle-eye editing the final draft and saving me much embarrassment

Margaret Morrell, for critical reading and support

Nancy Morrell-Baird, for critical reading, editing, love and support

Jannette Taylor, for critical reading, support and comments

Greg Morrell for author photograph

Ray Geier for cover art

C.J. Box, for proving that successful authors can be nice guys

Each and every one of you were critical to this story's publication. All thanks.

Vietnam, Ia Drang Valley, 9/Nov/1970

Just a routine patrol, Lt. Wertheimer said, ticking off his reasoning like he was pitching vinyl siding instead a meander into the dark heart of Victor Charles' country: No hostile contact for a year, too poor to harbor troops, and so on and so forth. "Just go check it out," he said. "Think of it as a picnic in the country."

But nothing was routine for a platoon that had lost six grunts in nine days without ever engaging—even seeing—the enemy.

What Wertheimer really wanted was to get these psycho motherfuckers out of camp before they started fraggin' cherry-assed, second lieutenants like himself for kicks.

The frustration was worse than jungle crotch rot, ringworm, poisonous jumping spiders, leeches, vipers that killed you in a heartbeat, terrier-sized rats that chewed on you while you slept, perpetual dehydration and diarrhea collectively, because it festered impotence in men trained to kill.

No, we weren't looking for a day at the beach. We were looking for blood.

The trouble started before we ever hit the ground when the pilot realized we were putting down in a valley too close to the ville. We said, "Fuckit, doan mean nuthin. Roll on."

I looked around at the sorry sonsabitches in the squad. The machine gunners, Flatt and Scruggs, still had Cro-Magnon-like hangovers from drinking rice brandy and smokin' opium joints (OJs). Our point man, Stoney, had been up three days on a Dexie binge. He had sworn the night before that Tricky Dick was dry humping Kissinger in the next bunk. We'd made him remove the clip in his M16, fearing he would go into convulsions and start hosing his own squad.

Squid, a 6-7, half-breed Bible thumper from Oklahoma with arms and legs too long to be human, was our radio man and convinced that his height would single him out to a VC sniper. Consequently, he carried the radio like the Hunchback of Notre Dame, his upper body at a 90-degree angle to his legs. Chopper Medina, who carried the M79 grenade launcher, had passed out in his own vomit the night before. Doc Gatewood, who humped full combat gear as well as his medical kit, walked along going "eenie, meenie, miney, mo" trying to decide which toe to shoot off so he could be sent back to the world.

And then there was me, Cpl. Aaron (Hillbilly) Hemingway, a gung-ho, half-wit cowboy who wanted to save his country from the evils of falling dominoes.

Yes-siree-fuckin'-bob, the cream of the American war effort.

In charge of this scabrous crew was Sgt. Oscar (Rock) Santanilla, a battle-hardened lifer who was nearing the end of his third tour in Vietnam, and who hated everyone and everything because he finally realized the war was, and always had been, a sham. And that all the soldiers who had died under his command had been lost in vain.

As we came down the hill through the waist-high grass, the squad spread out into a raggedy-assed skirmish line. The shabby hooches, emerging through the mist in the valley floor, looked occupied but there were no villagers about—a BAD sign.

Rock raised a fist, then flattened a palm and pressed downward, and everyone crouched deeper in the grass. In a harsh whisper, he said, "Flatt, you and Scruggs find a spot with a clear line of sight and set up."

He motioned everybody else forward, at a crouch. When we had gone about 20 yards, an AK-47 clacked out a short burst, and half of Squid's face dissolved in a pink mist. We dove into the grass. A figure in black bolted from behind one of the huts, zig-zagging crazily toward the treeline on the far side of the valley. The M60 roared and churned up the ground and trees and a water buffalo— everything but the target. Stoney was banging the wrong end of the clip into the receiver with the heel of his hand. Rock's greasegun, with its short barrel, was notoriously inaccurate at that distance, but he was firing anyway. I rose on one knee, aimed and put a burst into the VC's back, throwing him forward into the dirt.

With the kill, something elemental had changed in the atmosphere, like the flood of ozone in the aftermath of a lightening strike. The sky darkened and what we called the black wind moaned across the valley. According to grunt superstition the black wind blew away all vestiges of humanity.

Rock, his face flushed and eyes shooting sparks, yelled, "OK, boys, we've been eatin' motherfuckin' gook shit for two months and it's time for a little payback. Put everything you've got into those huts, left to right. I want nothin' and nobody left standin'." The relief was almost orgasmic.

The previous night's debaucheries burned off in the pure adrenalin rush. Flatt and Scruggs opened the 60 up, in chorus with an M79 grenade launcher, three M16s and Santanilla's Swedish K greasegun. The grenades went through the bamboo like rice paper, blowing out whole walls when they exploded. Moving bodies were visible inside the collapsing hooches until the sustained fire from the machine guns finished the job.

The squad had just turned the first hut into a pile of straw when people started streaming out of the other four, running, stumbling, crawling in every direction but toward us. We let go with everything we had. Their screams were drowned out in the deafening gunfire.

From my position, I could see a ditch with elephant grass on both sides leading up the hill directly behind the third hut. There were two figures, hunched over, sneaking up the ditch. I snapped a shot into the ditch, which brought the figures upright, and then put a three-shot burst into them before I saw it was a young girl leading an old mama-san to safety. It was then I realized that none of the fleeing villagers were wearing black and that we had taken no more fire from the ville. Holy Mother of God! We were massacring civilians.

I stopped shooting and screamed into the raging gunfire, "HOLD FIRE, HOLD FIRE. THEY'RE CIVILIANS." Nobody looked at me. They just kept shooting. I sprinted toward Rock, who swung the greasegun around. His eyes looked like the black wind had swept through and sucked out his soul. The veins protruding from his forehead were ghoulish. There was no hint of humanity there. Just a lust to kill, to erase the fear and frustration that had been driving us all mad.

Finally, the shooting stopped as everyone turned to watch the confrontation. Most of the squad even stood up, with weapons pointing at the ground in mute testimony to the fact that no fire had been coming from the village. Everyone knew and had kept shooting anyway.

Rock squinted, then smiled. "Hillbilly, you turnin' on us?" I could see his finger tightening on the trigger—knowing it was a guy like me who blew the whistle on My Lai. My squad's guns were raising in a slow arc toward where Rock and I stood, leaving no doubt which side they had taken.

I thumbed the fire selector to full auto and jerked the barrel upward just as the hillside behind the ville erupted with the thundering roar of a cyclone. Rock's mouth moved and his eyes widened in surprise as his chest blossomed like a huge red chrysanthemum. Something mule-kicked me in the side, spinning me so I could see the bodies floating in the rice paddies, littering the hillside, tangled in the wreckage of the huts.

And my comrades, like marionettes performing a macabre dance with limbs being flung wildly in the air, held aloft not by strings but by 7.62 mm slugs—a movie seared into the deepest reaches of my being as the world went black.

Chapter 1

June 6, 1997

Aaron's eyelids snapped open and he wrenched upright, tangled in a blanket wet with the stench of fear. His heart was like a hammer fist, trying to pound its way out of his chest. Like a Chinese handcuff, the more he wrestled with it, the more it bound him. He looked around and instead of the steamy jungles of Vietnam, he saw the dim interior of his mountain cabin. He lay still and took many deep breaths and relaxed, finally snaking an arm out of the folds and the sheet fell away like magic.

It was little consolation. For 27 years he'd lived with the horror of that morning and for the last three it had gotten steadily worse. He flopped back onto the bed and closed his eyes.

I can't do this for one more day, one more hour, one more minute, he told himself. He had accrued a load of karmic debt that couldn't be paid off in this lifetime. How much worse could a hundred lifetimes as a cockroach be? What was the point in delaying?

His hand crept toward the nightstand, slid open the drawer and felt for the gun. He wrapped his fingers around the grip, slipped a finger through the trigger guard and lifted it out. He slid the barrel into his mouth, pressed it against the roof and thumbed back the hammer. The unholy cocktail of nitro solvent, light oil and old cordite flooded his taste buds. The gun sight cut into the thin skin on the roof of his mouth and blood began to trickle down his throat. He closed his eyes and imagined the sweet relief that awaited him. Then, as he tightened his finger on the trigger, he heard the clickety-click of toenails across the bare wood floor. He looked to his right, where Roscoe stood, his big eyes wet. His splotchy purple tongue lapped Aaron's face from ear to ear.

Aw, shit, Aaron thought, sagging, there's the point right there: my best friend in the whole fucking universe. If Aaron followed through, he would be deserting the one creature on the face of the planet who still *really* needed him. Roscoe was a one-man dog. Aaron had left enough casualties in his wake. He released pressure on the trigger, pulled the barrel out, eased down the hammer and put the Colt Python back in the drawer. The phone rang. It was Pete Magpie, a Lakota shyster and the primary source of Aaron's meager income. He had some legal papers he wanted Aaron to serve. "It might be a little tricky," he said.

"Give me an hour," Aaron said and hung up the phone. He got up, showered off the stink of fear, fixed some strong coffee, loaded Roscoe into the car and drove down the mountain to Boulder. He still hadn't come to grips with what had happened that morning. The coffee woke him up but did nothing to clear the turmoil churning in his head. He didn't know whether to be happy or even more depressed, as if he had the choice. He was just numb, as he had been more and more in recent months.

This slide into nothingness had begun three years ago when his daughter, Cassie, had been taken hostage by a murderer and then saw three people die violently during her rescue. Her mother had taken her away and disappeared. He hadn't heard from either one of them since. Between Nam and Cassie's abduction, Aaron's partner in the Denver police had been gunned down by a drug dealer they were chasing down an alley. There were other—lesser—incidents. Each of these events was ordained by a confluence of forces and circumstances, which, while not totally predictable, did not seem to be random either. The unifying factor was Aaron's presence. It was just history: Bad shit happened to people when he was around. The worst shit. The situation with Cassie confirmed it in his mind. So he went to ground, associating only with a small group of shady lawyers and the lowlifes, scofflaws and ne'er-do-wells they did business with. His rationale was that if anything happened to any of them because he was around, well, they probably had it coming anyway. He decided he simply had to stay away from people he cared about. But the vacuum that decision created took a heavy toll as time went on.

One result was that the memory of what happened in Nam returned and with time grew like a metastasized cancer in his soul. Dying was *an* answer. Any other seemed, at this point, beyond his grasp. He just had to take things one step at a time until he figured out a way to take care of Roscoe, not take him down too.

Chapter 2

After two years of watching Pete Magpie part with greenbacks as if each were a dirty family secret, Aaron would have been more suspicious, had he not been so preoccupied, when the Lakota shyster offered to double his usual fee.

"It might be a little tricky," Pete Magpie had told him again. After the morning he'd had, he didn't give it a second thought.

"Whatever," he said, and stuck out his hand for the summons.

One of his mother's favorite adages was trying to wiggle its way into his consciousness just as the barbecue joint, on a quiet stretch of the Ute Highway west of Longmont, came into view. A finger of smoke wafted out of the stack above the building—little more than a grungy house in need of a paint job. If the place had a name it wasn't obvious from the road. Aaron pulled his '93 Subaru Legacy wagon into the parking lot, then turned it around to face the street. Still thinking tricky, he left the keys in the ignition.

He got out, started toward the front door, stopped and turned back to the car.

"You comin'?" he asked. The car creaked and Roscoe's head, the size of a small grizzly's, appeared in the window.

"Let's go and get this over with," Aaron said, slapping his palm on his thigh. The dog squirmed through the opening and landed in a huff on the ground.

They walked together and climbed up to the unpainted porch, Roscoe's nose twitching at the odors leaking from within. The front door was open so they went in. Roscoe flopped down just inside. His nose continued to twitch. He laid it on crossed paws, as if in prayerful benediction that some of the source of those tasty odors would find its way to his jaws.

The carpet was stained from years of dripped sauces, spilled beer and God only knew what else. The checkered oilcloth table coverings were faded, cracked, and pitted with enough cigarette burns to make them look like a microscopic slide of a virulent throat culture. The dented metal garbage can in the corner was overflowing with sauce-encrusted paper plates and beer cans, with dozens of cigarette butts sprouting from uneaten food on the plates.

No wonder the guy couldn't pay his bills, Aaron thought, the place has all the ambiance of a truckstop restroom.

The likely owner—Vurle Gaddis, according to the summons—emerged from the kitchen wiping one hand on a blood-soaked apron and carrying a meat cleaver as big as Rhode Island in the other.

Gaddis was short with simian-like arms that could probably let him scratch his knees without bending over. His face was creased and greasy, a battlefield where exploded capillaries fought to take over every clear patch of skin. Thin strands of gray hair were plastered across his balding head. As if that weren't enough, a filtered cigarette hung from his mouth, a long ash just waiting to fall into a bubbling pan of sauce or a bowl of bright yellow potato salad. Aaron's stomach rumbled at the thought.

"No dogs allowed," Gaddis said in a whiskey-scarred voice, raising his stubbled chin toward Roscoe.

Maybe it was just the mood Aaron was in but everything about Gaddis infuriated him. He wanted to ask, "What, you afraid he'll catch some fatal disease from being in this pig-sty?"

Instead, Aaron acted as if he hadn't heard, sat his briefcase down on the faded counter top and offered his hand, "Mr. Gaddis?" Aaron sported a full, short beard, dark hair parted in the middle and cut to collar length and pulled back in a ponytail. Today, he wore a white shirt, a brown corduroy sport jacket with elbow patches, Wranglers and a pair of beat up work boots. Pete Magpie once told him he looked like an ex-con selling magazine subscriptions, somebody you might buy a subscription from just to get them off your porch.

It was his process-serving uniform, and often he had the paper served before the target had figured out quite what was coming through the door. Not today, it seemed.

Gaddis's beady eyes flicked from Aaron to Roscoe, narrowing to suspicious slits. "Yeah. Who wants to know?"

Since Gaddis had identified himself, Aaron dropped his extended hand and pulled a summons-to-appear from his back pocket with the other.

"Pete Magpie, Esquire," he said and held the summons toward him. When Gaddis continued wiping his hand on his apron, Aaron dropped the summons on the counter.

Without taking his eyes off Aaron, Gaddis swung the cleaver and, with a thud, chopped the briefcase nearly in half. Fortunately, there was nothing in it. It was a prop.

Roscoe jerked his head up, then his ears. A low growl escaped as his purple lips were pulled tight against his teeth. With murder in his bloodshot eyes, Gaddis wrenched the cleaver free, bellowed like a wounded bull and started around the counter. Roscoe was up, his ears flat, a rumble forming in his massive chest.

"Roscoe, stay!" Aaron said, in a voice that left little room for doubt. Gaddis hesitated, then went for him. Like an old-time gunfighter, Aaron drew the grizzly-strength pepper spray from under his sport coat where it was clipped to his belt and shot a spurt in Gaddis' face.

Gaddis came upright like someone had hit him square in the face with a cast-iron skillet, dropped the cleaver and pawed at his eyes. His legs buckled and he dropped, retching, to the floor.

Aaron stepped wide around him and grabbed the briefcase. It wasn't going to be much use as a prop anymore. But it might come in handy as evidence in case Gaddis decided to file assault charges.

Gaddis gurgled as a spasm shook his body. "Go! Go!" Aaron said, as he rushed Roscoe out the door. He decided to call the sheriff's office from the pay phone in front of the place to report what happened—just to cover his ass. He searched his pocket for a quarter, dialed 911 and listened to a series of screeches and clicks. This continued for what seemed like a minute but was probably five seconds and he was getting antsy to be gone. Just as he heard a voice start the 911 litany, Gaddis burst through the screen door, staggering blindly around the porch like

Joe Cocker, but with a stubby pump shotgun in his hands instead of a microphone.

Aaron dropped the phone, sprinted for the car, and wrenched open the door, twisting the key as he slid into the seat. Taking the cue, Roscoe launched himself through the side window.

Keeping his head as low as possible, Aaron gunned it, with all four wheels spraying gravel until they hit the asphalt and squealed into the road. Gaddis must have heard the car and fired at the sound. Shotgun pellets thwacked the back of the car and covered the back window with pimples of frost. Aaron flinched and reflexively hunched over the wheel, his heart trying to climb out of his throat.

About a hundred yards down the highway, he still had a death grip on the steering wheel but he finally whooshed out the breath he'd been holding and let off the gas. The deep-throated turbo quieted. Another shot sounded faintly in the distance but they were well out of range.

Roscoe, no stranger to the business end of a gun, was still panting hard so Aaron reached back and scratched his woolly head. As he did, something bloomed slowly in his chest, like a giant sunflower raising its bowed face to meet the sun of a new day. And he realized it was a revelation: he was glad he was alive; he didn't want die.

Just outside of Lyons, he turned south on U.S. 36, headed back to Boulder. A couple of miles down the highway, the sunflower began to slump, as if a cloudbank covered the sun. And another thought crept in: So what. Nothing has changed.

Within minutes, Aaron was in Boulder and backing into the parking space next to the old single-wide that served as Pete Magpie's office and home. It was in a small mobile-home park behind an upholstery shop, a garage and a greasy-spoon restaurant on north Broadway. The street people called the area "Dogpatch"—for those old enough to remember L'il Abner's "hood." For a short time Aaron had lived across the gravel driveway, before the noise and congestion of the city got to be too much and drove him back to the mountains.

Magpie's car, a mint-condition, copper metal-flake 1978 Chrysler Brougham, was parked on a white, concrete slab next to the mobile home. It was clean and waxed, and stood out like an expensive hooker on east Colfax.

Running a law office out of a trailer park was a zoning violation, but since the rest of the residents were generally heroin addicts, alcoholics, transients and fugitives from justice, Magpie's using it as a law office was probably ignored as a beneficial—if non-conforming—use. Of course, his clientele didn't look much different from the neighbors, so it was possible nobody knew. Besides, the whole shebang was scheduled to be torn down and a bulldozer would be coming soon to scrape away the blight, the unwashed and the code violators in one fell swoop.

Aaron opened the door without knocking. Pete Magpie was leaning back in the chair with his feet propped on the desk, eyes half-closed and long fingers laced behind his head. A tape by the Indian rock band Red Thunder was playing in a boom box on his desk.

"So, you made it, huh?" A slight twitch tugged at the corner of Pete's mouth.

Exhausted by the events and mood swings of the morning, Aaron could barely muster enough annoyance to set the briefcase on Magpie's desk with a little more drama than was necessary.

Eyes opening a little wider, Pete said, "What the heck happened to that?"

"The greaseball chopped it with a meat cleaver, then came around the counter after me. I hit him with pepper spray."

"No shit?" Pete said, the corners of his mouth twitching like he was suppressing a grin.

"And that's not the best part," Aaron said, "Take a look at my car."

Pete shrugged with the imposition of it all but managed to stand up and peer out the window. There wasn't much damage. The rear window looked frosted and the hatch door looked like it had a mild case of acne. Pete might have hiked an eyebrow a millimeter or two, Aaron wasn't sure.

"That's why I couldn't send a college student. The guy's a known psycho," Pete said.

"What about the damage to my car?" he asked, the tension rising in his voice.

"I'll cover it and triple your fee," Pete said, with a shrug. Now Aaron was really getting suspicious. This kind of generosity was unheard of, and Pete picked up on Aaron's thoughts. "My red-skinned brothers know you have to have the chips to play in the white man's poker game, in this case known as county court." He handed Aaron $150 in cash, a proof of service and a receipt to sign. "Get me an estimate on the damage."

Another tense silence settled in the room until Pete said, "You're lucky it was birdshot."

"What?"

"It was birdshot, lots of little pellets. If it was double-aught, you'd have a headache."

"I've got a headache now," Aaron said, rubbing his temples.

For Pete Magpie, this was a deep conversation and both men were a little startled at the direction it was going. When Aaron took it no further, Pete flipped over a scrap of paper on his desk.

"Oh, yeah, Harlan wants to see you. He said he has some work for you."

"Work? What the hell's he talking about?"

Pete unfolded a newspaper. "He didn't say, but it could have something to do with this."

"ATV rider decapitated," the headline all but screamed. Aaron grabbed it and scanned the first three paragraphs. The victim, who was not identified, "apparently hit a thick wire stretched between two trees while driving at a high rate of speed" on land the town of Jack Springs had recently annexed. Harlan Silbaugh was the town's Marshal and one of Aaron's few friends.

Normally, the Boulder County Sheriff's Office handled major cases in the town, the story reported. But the sheriff's investigators were tied up in two high-profile murder cases. The Jack Springs Marshal's Office would be in charge of the investigation for the time being.

Aaron was stunned by the implications. "You think he wants to hire me as a cop?"

Pete shrugged. "Call him and find out."

On one level, it made no sense at all. Aaron hadn't worked as a cop since he was quietly drummed out of the Denver Police Department seven years earlier. And he hadn't stepped into the town of Jack Springs since losing his job as a reporter for the local newspaper three years earlier.

On the other, Harlan had tried to lure him back to town on a variety of pretexts. It hadn't worked but they had kept in touch.

Yet Aaron had been a cop for 15 years. And despite getting ushered out of the Denver Police Department, he had no felonies or serious misdemeanors to his credit. So it kind of balanced out.

What he didn't know was whether he had it in him to exist on that level anymore, or whether he could face the town where his life had most recently come apart.

All this time, he'd been standing in front of Pete's desk. When he came out of his reverie, Pete looked as unconcerned as if no one had been there. Aaron shook his head. "I gotta think."

Pete Magpie put his size-sixteen Tony Lamas back up on the desk, leaned back and said, "Good idea," as Aaron left.

A few steps from his car, Aaron told himself, no, I don't have to think. What I've got to do is drive up there and talk to Harlan, see what he wants.

And of course, on the way to Jack Springs, the past flashed before his eyes like the last moments of a dying man.

Chapter 3

Aaron crested the hill at the 17-mile mark in Boulder Canyon and was greeted with what seemed a fairy-tale setting: a deep, blue reservoir with a light chop fracturing the reflection of sky and sun; a small town nestled into the far end of the valley beneath an amphitheater of snow-capped peaks.

Passing through, a visitor might see the eclectic architectural styles, the neat green patches of lawn, window boxes filled with flowers and stacked piles of firewood and think it would be a funky, mellow place to raise a family.

But slow down, shed the rose-colored glasses, and they'd see aging piles of toxic mine slag sprouting twisted, stunted growth, the vicious dogs restrained behind six-foot woven-wire pens, the rusting hulks of old VW buses, vans, and trucks stuffed with trash or hazardous materials.

For all its quaint façade, violence lurked just beneath the veneer of civilization in these old mountain towns and Jack Springs was no exception.

In its time, men had been killed over gold, cards, women, a bottle of whiskey or a dirty look. If the act was judged to be egregious, the good townsfolk would get together and throw a necktie party with the offender as the guest of honor and then display the body on First Street in a cheap, open casket for all to see.

The land itself was unforgiving and could turn simple lapses of judgment into fatal mistakes. Madness, simmered in alcohol during bitter winter nights, erupted with the light-speed slash of a broken beer bottle, a knife slipped silently from a boot, or the hellish explosion of a large-caliber bullet.

Three years ago, an upstanding citizen had murdered two people and blown up a number of buildings trying to stop a mining operation he feared would reveal the victim of a murder he had committed thirty years earlier.

Now, a dirt bike rider had been beheaded, BEHEADED, in the town's 4,000-acre mountain park.

Yet here he was—he who had been avoiding old friends and the town itself like the plague, who knew what lurked beneath the veneer of this town—entertaining the thought of plopping himself smack dab into the middle of the goddamn lunatic asylum that passed itself off as a town.

Aaron drove a few blocks into the heart of town, turned right and parked in front of the small, stuccoed building that served as the Jack Springs Marshal's office. As he drummed his fingers on the steering wheel, doubt came on like a runaway truck on Vail Pass. He looked around, got panicky, started the engine, put the transmission in reverse, then back in park. He goosed the accelerator a couple of times, turned the engine off.

And nothing happened. Nobody came at him with a gun, nobody pointed at him, screamed and ran away, or worse, laughed. Maybe the time and space had dulled the feelings to the point where he could admit he missed the easy familiarity, the comforting wackiness of the town. After all, for three years he had felt right at home here, and in the end had proven himself one of the crazier inmates in the asylum.

Moments later, a stout oak of a man stepped from the marshal's door and ambled toward Aaron's car. He wore blue jeans, cowboy boots, a gray Stetson and a red and blue flannel shirt that barely closed over his beer-keg belly. As he reached Aaron's car, he rested his hand on the roof and lowered his head to the window. "Oh, hell, it's just you. I was beginning to think I had a suspicious character lurking out here, plotting some mischief against the good folks of the town."

"Howdy, Harlan," Aaron said.

"Come on in," Harlan said.

Harlan's office was just as he remembered it: cramped, worn out, threadbare but neat as a pin. Like an old widower on social security who just wouldn't give up the ghost. By contrast the old town meeting hall, which had adjoined the marshal's office, had been remodeled into an annex, with a half-dozen desks, new computers, and a holding pen at the rear—20th-century modern instead of a relic of the previous one.

"The town has changed," Harlan said. "We got about three hundred more residents, thanks to those subdivisions up in the hills over the reservoir and up in the Dark Angel valley. Business is good, what with the ski area expanding and the gambling down in Black Hawk." He paused. "We got more crime, but nothing like…" Harlan's face flushed momentarily. "Otherwise, not that much I guess…until this," he waved toward the newspaper headline Aaron had read earlier. "We paid for the new equipment with a half-mil grant from the state's gambling taxes. We got two new vehicles and two more officers. It's been a good year for the marshal's office."

"How about you, Harlan? Is the town taking care of you?"

"Let's just say it's better than it was."

Harlan brought his can of Skoal out, tapped it against the palm of his hand to pack it, grabbed a wad and stuck it between his cheek and gum. "What you been up to?"

Aaron told him about the incident at the barbecue joint. Harlan nodded and listened patiently, his forehead wrinkling in concern as Aaron described Gaddis hacking the briefcase.

When he told Harlan about Gaddis staggering out onto the porch and letting go with the shotgun, Harlan said, "Whoooeee," sucked some tobacco juice down his windpipe and began choking violently. His face flamed red and then purple as he tried to both clear the juice out of his lungs and take a breath—a feat akin to breathing under a toxic sludge pond.

Aaron jumped up and pounded Harlan on the back a couple of times, and Harlan's coughing finally subsided to a rattle in his lungs. The flush in his face faded to a splotchy pink.

"That, my friend, was not a pleasant experience," he said, mopping his tear-streaked face with a blue bandanna.

"I'll take your word for it," Aaron said.

Still shaky, Harlan swiveled around, filled a couple of mugs with coffee and set them on his desk. Aaron sat, too, raised the mug and took a sip, expecting the battery acid Harlan used to serve. This coffee wasn't bad, not bad at all.

Harlan said, "You know, I could have filled you in over the phone, but I'm glad you came. It's been too long."

Aaron was suddenly overwhelmed with affection for this good man and felt more than a little guilty for staying away so long.

"Yeah, well, you got me here, so fill me in," he said, feigning gruffness to cover up the too-familiar feeling.

Harlan said, "I reckon you've figured out what this is about. Earl can't free up any investigator in the near future—they're all tied up in the task force handling that little Rainey girl's murder. So I promoted Tobias to detective. He was ready for it anyway, been taking classes and such down at Arapahoe Community College.

"The problem we got is that I'm going to be out of town for a few days next week, our new-hire has only been on the job a week and Tobias will be on this full time, at least for the present. I want you to fill in on patrol…and maybe help him from time to time on the investigation since you're familiar with the territory. Rich Kuchera is going to be the acting marshal. You remember I told you about him? He was a police chief in Blue Springs, Missouri. Retired and moved here, then decided he was bored. So I hired him."

Aaron nodded, vaguely recalling Harlan's mentioning it at some point in the past year.

But he was curious. "Where'd you get this crazy idea?"

"Of hiring Kuchera?" Harlan looked puzzled.

"No, of hiring me," Aaron said.

"Earl suggested it," Harlan said. If Aaron was surprised before, he was floored at this bit of news. Earl McCormick was the chief of detectives for the Boulder County Sheriff's Office and also a friend and former colleague. But he rarely let on that Aaron was anything other than a troublemaker and a huge pain in the ass. It was almost unthinkable Earl would recommend him for the job.

"It just doesn't make any sense," Aaron said.

"Well," Harlan said, grinning like a shark, "it's not that you're our best choice. You're our only choice."

Aaron let the remark slide, not sure if it was meant to box him in a corner or if it was the truth. Probably both, he conceded. Then he realized he had to put a stop to this nonsense. "Uh, Harlan, listen, I'm, uh, not doing too well these days. I don't think I'm in any shape to be working as a cop." He could not elaborate on this because nobody—except himself and the Army honchos who covered it up—knew what had happened in Vietnam. He'd never told a soul. He'd awakened in a hospital in Hawaii with a Purple Heart, a medical discharge with honors, and a ticket home. It took a while to figure it out, but it was the best way to shut him up short of dropping him out of a chopper.

Harlan undoubtedly thought what was bothering Aaron was the situation with Cassie, which was true, but he didn't know the HISTORY.

"Well, it's no goddamn surprise to ME that your state of mind is poorly," Harlan said. "You've shut yourself away from anybody who cares about you. That's no way to live." This was said kindly, except for the profanity. That one word said more than anything else about the way Harlan felt, because he almost never cursed.

"But you know why..."

"And I don't buy it, never did. None of that business with Cassie was your fault. Hell, it was more my fault than yours. But I've thought on this more than you know, and I can't think of one thing I would of done differently." He sighed. "Look, blame aside, I need your help. Give me a week. I can't send this new-hire out by herself. She's going to be good but she needs someone to keep an eye on her. If, after a week, you still feel this way. Fine. Go back to your hidey-hole and I won't bother you again."

It was one hell of a hole card Harlan was playing, Aaron thought, showing confidence in him to do the one thing he most feared. It wasn't as if any deputy in Jack Springs had ever been killed in the line of duty. All he'd have to do was keep her—her?—safe. Just for a week. One hour, one day at a time.

After what had almost happened this morning, maybe this day-by-day thing would give him an answer he could grasp. Maybe it was worth a try. And maybe he was fooling himself.

Feeling the noose tightening around his neck, Aaron asked, "When do you need an answer?"

Harlan sat back in his chair and drummed his fingers on his belly like he was thumping a watermelon to see if it was ripe. It sounded ripe. "Right now," he said.

Damn Harlan anyway. He knew if he gave Aaron time to think it over he could find plenty of excuses to back away from the offer. And there were still plenty if he thought about it. But Verle Gaddis had shown Aaron that he really didn't want to be dead. He wanted to be alive, to feel alive again.

Damn Harlan anyway. He'd found the key to break the psychological dam by dangling exactly what he needed: a carrot of hope.

Why, then, he wondered, do I have this feeling of standing upon a precipice with homemade wings, thinking: maybe this time I can fly.

Chapter 4

On the drive back into town that night, the breeze carried the scent of moisture even though no clouds were visible. The sky was dusty with stars; a sliver of crescent moon hung over the peaks. Aaron wondered if the wind had just blown the pollution out onto the flatlands, leaving the sky preternaturally clear, or if the stars were always so plentiful, only he hadn't raised his eyes to the heavens in a while.

In the intervening hours, he'd shaved his beard down to a thick goatee, trimmed his hair to a respectable length just below the ears, and cleaned up as much as he could in the cabin. He had changed into newer denims, a white western shirt and his favorite work boots, which were light enough to move quickly in. It had been unusually warm all day but driving with the window down he was glad for the coolness to help him stay awake.

He had hoped to get a couple of hours of sleep but a surge of panic had squelched the possibility. He had accepted Harlan's offer but then felt like a rip tide was carrying him helplessly out to sea. The idea that he could, after all those years, put on a badge and gun and operate at the level of competency he had before seemed foolish. Hell, he was only about nine hours past thinking about blowing his brains out. His heart rate and blood pressure had elevated to the point that the blood rushing through his carotid artery sounded like a Ginger Baker drum solo in his brain. His chest was so tight he felt like he was slowly being crushed beneath a concrete slab.

It was fear for himself, not only that he would somehow look as foolish as he felt, but also that he would overreact and hurt or kill an innocent person. Even worse, he feared his slower reaction time if the shit went down.

What had finally lifted the slab was remembering that Harlan had shown no doubt about Aaron's capability to handle the job, and that Earl McCormick had recommended him for it. Harlan's judgment could be clouded by sentimentality, but not Earl's. There wasn't a sentimental bone in his body when it came to police work. But there was no way, after that, Aaron could sleep.

So here he was, still nervous but only rationally so, enjoying the cool mountain breeze coming through the window, glad he'd brought the Carhartt fleece-lined vest. And thinking about what lay ahead.

Harlan had explained there was no uniform available, that Aaron would have to do with the black ball cap with the gold-encircled star insignia for now. Of course, he'd be with the uniformed, mysterious new-hire. So that should eliminate any confusion. His Colt Python .357 was in a cut-down, padded duck holster on the passenger seat because, concealed or not, carrying a big pistol was uncomfortable as hell. But if you're working patrol, people need to see a gun that shows you mean business. The Python .357 with oversize Pachmeyer grips looked like serious business.

The holster mounted on his belt, above his hip but below the vest for all the world to see. He hoped it would stay there because he was a terrible shot. Aaron pulled his car into the parking lot across the street from the office. He grabbed the gun and jacket and got out of the car.

Someone was lounging against the Jeep Cherokee parked beneath the streetlight in one of the spots reserved for patrol cars. The other spaces were empty and he figured it was the new deputy. As he approached, there was something familiar about the person and he realized it was a woman—a big woman.

She turned and shot right into his brain with laser blue eyes and said, "Fishboy, is that you? Say, you clean up purdy good. Haw, haw. They told me you got hired, but I said I wouldn't believe it till I saw it." She thumped him hard on the back.

"Lila June, holy shit!"

She beamed a lighthouse smile at his surprise. She called him "Fishboy" because he had, not long after she arrived in town, offered to give her fishing lessons and she accepted. To his dismay, he realized it really *was* fly-fishing lessons that she wanted, but they had remained friends and she had called him "Fishboy" since.

Lila June had operated a beauty/barber shop out of her home in Jack Springs for several years. She was what everyone meant when they said a woman was 'big-boned.' When Aaron last saw her she had big hair, blonde, piled high in an artful demonstration of her craft, the same blue eyes and a little extra flesh that did a lot of jiggling when she moved, but only in the right places.

She had always projected the Southern Belle mentality that physicality was for men, not women. But that had apparently changed. Now, even standing in the street, he could see broad shoulders and a narrower waist beneath the tan, khaki uniform shirt, subdued breasts and sturdy thigh muscles inside the tailored uniform pants. Some serious physical effort went into the new Lila June. And her hair was cut short, what Aaron thought of as a pixie hairdo back in high school although he couldn't imagine what it would be called these days. She certainly didn't look like a pixie.

"Lila June, what the hell…?"

"Not now, Fishboy," she said, laughing, her voice still whiskey-rough with a faint southern twang. "We can't stand here jawing all night. The shift starts in 10 minutes. Let's just say I had a life-changing experience. There'll be plenty of time to catch up if things are quiet tonight."

Still shaking his head in amazement, Aaron walked into the office to get his baton, cap, portable radio or "PAC" set and handcuffs. A striking Latina was at the dispatch desk idly leafing through a magazine. She wore the tan Marshal's Office uniform shirt with short sleeves. Just below the right sleeve was a tattoo of blue barbed wire circling her biceps. "*Mi Vida Loca*" was written below the barbed wire. A slightly wavy mane of dark hair was parted on the left and pulled back into an unruly bun secured with an inlaid enamel and pearl chopstick. Her face was speckled with faint acne scars. Dark, Toltec eyes, high cheekbones, a generous mouth and a little bump on the upper bridge of her nose gave her a severe, almost dangerous look. Until she looked up and a big smile changed her into something altogether different.

"You must be Aaron," she said. "I'm Belinda Mondragon." Pronouncing it *Moan-drah-goan* with the accent on the final syllable, she extended her hand—long, dark fingers, short nails, no polish—and Aaron took it. It was warm, dry and firm. "Nice to meet you."

"The same," Aaron said, wincing at the female contact but captured by her flashing dark eyes.

"So, uh, anyway, if things are slow, we just communicate normally, but if something develops, we'll switch to codes. Anything that goes county wide is green channel and requires radio codes. You may be a little rusty but Lila June has it down." Aaron realized he was still holding her hand and dropped it quickly, a flash of heat enveloping his face. Belinda Mondragon's smile never wavered, though.

"Sounds good," he said, wanting nothing more than to get the hell out of there.

"The equipment locker is through the door in the back. Lila June already got the shotgun, so just grab your personal equipment."

"Thanks, I will," he said.

As he walked away, Belinda looked at her hand, felt a tingling warmth there. She was tempted to look over her shoulder at the old guy but quickly dismissed it. Look out, chica, she told herself. This one is trouble and you don't need no more of *that*.

When Aaron got back to the Cherokee, Lila June was behind the wheel and the engine was idling. He slid into the passenger seat.

"You gonna wear that peashooter or just leave it in the seat where you can stare at it?" she said, glancing down.

"All right," he said. "Pull over to my car. There's something I almost forgot."

She stopped the Jeep behind the Legacy. Aaron got out, opened the rear Jeep door and then the Legacy rear door. Roscoe bounded out, took two steps, leaped into the Jeep's seat and stood, thwacking his tail like a baseball bat into the seat back.

"Roscoe, you darling boy, how the hell are you?" Lila June boomed. He put his head over the seat back and gave her a big slurp. "Ack," she said, then laughed.

"Down," Aaron said and Roscoe, with great effort, lay down and let go a big sigh. Lila June laughed again.

"I don't know what we're going to do if we have to transport a prisoner," she said, looking at Aaron.

"Don't worry, Roscoe's better than handcuffs," he said.

Lila June picked up the mike, said, "OK, base, K-9 one is on patrol."

"What? Repeat that," came Belinda's confused response.

"Never mind, Belinda. Just a little joke, dear. We're clear," Lila June said.

There was a time when graveyard patrol in Jack Springs meant sitting in the street in front of the Jackass Inn, particularly on weekends. During the week, a deputy could sit in the office, which was a half-block away. Ninety-five percent of the trouble went down in the street in front of the bar.

These days, with the developments in the hills above the reservoir and the valleys above the town, officers swung through these areas regularly. But after one in the morning, it was back to First Street. After three a.m., it meant parking on the highway looking for drunks coming from the casinos in Blackhawk.

It was a weeknight and still early, but Lila June swung through town anyway then doubled back and headed up into the hills. Her command of the routine indicated a familiarity that surprised Aaron, because Harlan had mentioned he wanted Aaron to show the "new-hire" the ropes. He told her as much, which brought a chuckle.

"*He* told *me*," she said, "that I was supposed to keep an eye on *you*. I rode along with Toby or Rich Kuchera on my days off from the academy. The other officer works days because he has another job in the evening. Don't run into him much."

His curiosity at Lila June's transformation was driving him crazy, as she probably well knew, but they were five minutes into the shift and she had yet to volunteer anything. So he asked, "What was the life-changing experience that got you into this new line of work? By the way, whatever it was, I approve of the outcome."

She batted him on the arm. "Haw, you are a silver-tongued devil, Fishboy, just like always."

It was difficult for Aaron to envision himself as ever being a silver-tongued devil, but he wanted to hear the story so he kept his mouth shut.

She watched the road and started talking; her normal exuberance toned down a notch. "I was nearly raped a couple of years ago," she said. "A guy came into the shop at closing time, wrestled me to the floor and put a knife to my throat. Told me he'd kill me if I resisted. A friend pulled into the lot before he could do anything and the guy run off out the back and got away. I was so scared, I would have let him do it. So I decided nothing like that was *ever* gonna happen to me again."

Whatever Aaron had expected to hear, it sure as hell wasn't this, and it was difficult to know what to say. Finally, he said, "It's nothing to be ashamed of, Lila June. There's a lot of sick fucks wandering around looking for prey. Most women aren't strong enough to physically resist an attack."

Lila June looked at him and smiled. "Think that's still true, Fishboy?"

Aaron looked at her arms. "No, probably not. But why in hell become a cop?"

"Because I had to get strong, learn to defend myself and…" she hesitated, "I get to carry a gun."

"I guess that covers it then," Aaron said. He was still impressed that she'd taken it so far. They were cruising a loop through a row of mansions that were perched along a ridge directly above the reservoir. Million-dollar mountain mansions.

"There's a house up here where we've had some trouble. Some college kids live there. One of their fathers actually bought the house for his son to live in while he went to school. "It's up here on the ri—" Before she could finish, a long chokachokachoka of automatic weapon fire ripped apart the night. "Aw, crapola, that's got to be them."

She accelerated. Aaron froze up for a few seconds, needing to say something but unable get anything out. The sound of that gun, which had to be an AK-47, was the same sound that haunted his nightmares. It was etched into his conscious, subconscious and unconscious like a diamond cutting into glass. But where the fuck is there room for irony in the concept of karma? Unless karma IS the ultimate irony: we actually do get what we deserve. It was exactly what he was afraid of—that Lila June was going to get burned by his karma. He knew they could be speeding to disaster and time was running out. Finally he found his voice and croaked, "Lila Jean. Pull over and let's get on the mike. Call for backup." From the rear, Roscoe let out a low whine. Aaron reached back and scratched his head. "Easy, boy."

"Good idea," she said. "My mind went blank there for a second." She pulled over, switched to green channel. "Boulder Comm, this is Patrol One, Jack Springs Marshal's Office."

"Boulder Comm, go Patrol One."

"We've got a 10-57, possibly full-auto."

"10-4, Patrol One, any casualties?"

"Don't know, just heard the shots."

"What's the 10-20?"

"Uh, 3 Lake Ridge Drive, south side above the reservoir." Three short bursts cracked. "Requesting 10…uh, get us some backup, quick!" Lila yelled into the mike.

"10-4, Patrol One." The call went out.

"Now what, Fishboy?" Lila June asked, voice husky with fear. "I think I musta been absent the day they dealt with this at the academy." Aaron reached over and turned down the radio.

"Any vests in the car?"

"Yeah, just Harlan's."

"Put it on."

She did.

"OK, let's try to get close enough to see exactly where the shots are coming from. No flashers. Go real slow." He unlocked the Ithaca pump action 12-gauge, put the barrel out the window, jacked a round into the chamber and locked the safety.

They heard the dispatcher mutter something, then say, "ETA 12 minutes."

"Copy," Lila June said shaking her head. "Shit, 12 minutes. That's a big help. Maybe we should wait." They were creeping up to the driveway when another burst erupted. Lila June looked at Aaron with dread in her eyes and said, "Guess not."

Aaron couldn't believe this was happening but she was right: It was too late to back out. But he knew that only one thing mattered: Lila June had to walk away from this alive and unscarred. He looked at her hands white-knuckled on the steering wheel, staring into darkness up the road, and knew that this was all on him now. If he showed any hint of doubt, the situation could become, using an old-but-apt Army acronym—FUBAR—fucked up beyond all recognition. Strangely, the thought comforted him. "We'll be alright." He only half believed it.

As they closed the distance, they could hear loud music and voices coming from the house. Lights were coming on in the neighboring houses, which, fortunately, were not all that close. "Sounds like they're partying," Aaron said. "At least we don't have a rip-off coming down." The Jeep glided to a stop about fifty feet from the house.

"What the hell do we do now?" Lila June asked. "I'm forgetting everything I learned."

Aaron was remembering. "Open the door and get behind it." He reached over and grabbed the mike, switched to loudspeaker. "Tell me Harlan's loudspeaker works."

"I don't know," she said. "No, I remember. It works." Whoops and yea-haws were coming from the far side of the house. Aaron opened his door, held the shotgun in his right hand and keyed the mike with his left. "THIS...IS…THE…POLICE. PUT DOWN THE GUN AND COME AROUND THE HOUSE WITH YOUR HANDS IN THE AIR."

The message was loud and clear. The laughing and whooping stopped. The music was turned off. He repeated it: "THIS...IS…THE… POLICE. PUT DOWN THE GUN AND COME AROUND THE HOUSE WITH YOUR HANDS IN THE AIR."

It was quiet for a moment, then someone yelled belligerently, "Fuck that. We're just having' a lil… lit-tle fun." The voice was slurred.

"Great," Aaron said. "We've got a drunk with a machine gun." But he could hear other voices imploring the guy to put the gun down.

He keyed the mike again, said in what he hoped was a calm voice, "Listen to me. Right now we've got a *little* problem here. But if you don't do what I told you to do, we're going to have a real *big* problem. In a couple of minutes, this house is going to be surrounded by cops. And most cops don't cut people with automatic weapons any slack like we're doing right now. Come out single file around the east side of the house with your hands raised in the air. NOW!"

"Lila June, put the spotlight on my side of the house but watch the doors and the west side. These guys might not be smart or sober enough to know which side is east."

They could hear the voices rise again. Someone said, "Fuck it." Then someone volunteered, "We're coming."

Aaron triggered the loudspeaker again. "I repeat, the east side of the house. That's to your left. Get out here with your hands in the air. Now!"

After a few moments, one emerged into the spotlight's beam. He lowered his hand to get the spotlight out of his eyes.

"Keep them up!" Aaron said. "Walk forward ten steps and get on your knees, facing the light." Two more emerged, eyes big as dinner plates. "Please don't shoot, we were just—"

"Shut your fucking mouth. GET ON YOUR KNEES, NOW!" Aaron said, his leg muscles quaking.

They dropped. Finally, a fourth stepped into the blinding light. His hands were barely raised, and he had a defiant look on this face.

"This sucks," he said. "We were just shooting into the lake. We didn't hurt nothin'."

"There's our punk," Aaron said. "Watch him." The kid, barefoot, dressed in cutoffs and a muscle shirt, stopped, but he didn't go to his knees.

"GET ON YOUR KNEES, NOW!" Aaron said. He jacked another round into the shotgun, for effect, then squatted, picked up the loose shell and shoved it back into the shotgun.

"All right," the kid whined, like an angry mosquito.

"Now, I want you all to put your hands out in front, lie down and keep your hands visible." The first three did as they were told, but the whiner moved in slow motion until he was prone. Let him have his little protest, Aaron thought. The sounds of sirens were beginning to bounce off the canyon walls.

"Lila June, are you okay?"

"Yeah, I'm better, now. It was just the excitement," she grinned over at him. The fear had tapered off now that the situation appeared to be under control but her adrenaline was zooming.

"We're going to cuff whiner first, then I'll walk him to the Jeep and search him. Just keep your gun on these other three until we get help."

Then Aaron thought of something. "Are there any more people in the house?" he asked them. A couple of muffled "nos" came from the group. He hoped it was true. It seemed likely that the bad actor in this drama was the petulant one lying on the ground.

"Now I want you to put your hands behind your backs."

Predictably, three complied quickly.

"Sorry, dude, my muscles are too big. I don't think I can do it," he snickered.

"Please try," Aaron said and he did, slowly of course. Aaron and Lila June came out from behind the car doors, walked forward with their guns up.

"I got them covered, Lila June. Cuff this one first," he waggled the barrel at the whiner. She holstered her gun, grabbed the cuffs and snapped one on. Grabbing the other, she pulled his wrists together.

"Ouch, that hurts, bitch!" he said and started to struggle. Aaron touched the cool barrel of the shotgun to his ear.

"Whoa," the whiner said, and stopped resisting.

"Loosened those muscles right up, huh?" Aaron said, His confidence back but his legs were still shaking. "Just don't shit your pants."

"You think you're funny but you ain't. You're in fucking trouble, fuckwad; my father is a fucking lawyer and you're gonna be fucking grinded up into fucking dog food."

"Nice vocabulary they teach you down at the university," Aaron said. The kid started to say "fuck" again but Aaron stepped on the back of his head and pushed his face into the gravel. It came out as "Fugbug," then "booowwww."

Two patrol cars, one from the Boulder County Sheriff's Office and another from the Colorado State Patrol, skidded to a stop behind the Jeep. Lt. Earl McCormick, Aaron's benefactor, got out of the Sheriff's cruiser with a 5-cell Maglite in his hand. He was slapping it into his palm as he walked. A deputy and the state trooper also got out and walked to where Lila June was kneeling.

Aaron lifted the troublemaker to his feet, walked him to the Jeep and leaned him over the hood, where he conducted a pat search.

"Jesus Kee-ryst, Hemingway," Earl said, shaking his head. "Seven years off the job, then 10 minutes into your first shift you run into a moron with an automatic weapon. You are a goddamned magnet for trouble."

"Next time, Earl, I'll wait at the bottom of the hill until the S.O. gets a car up here," Aaron said. When he looked at Earl he saw him smiling.

At that moment, Harlan pulled up.

Earl shook his head. "Well, we're all here now. Just one big happy family."

Since Aaron and Lila June had to search the house and secure it for a more thorough inspection tomorrow, Harlan and Earl transported the troublemakers to the town lockup for processing.

When the search was done and the crime-scene tape was in place, Jack Springs' new deputies slid into the Jeep to go back to town. Lila June looked over and saw Aaron chuckling.

"What's so funny, that we couldn't find the gol dang machine gun?" she wanted to know.

Aaron shook his head. "I was just thinking of something I used to do when I was at North Metro. I had a tape player in the car and when I had to transport a suspect, I'd play some of these whiney old country songs. If they were high, and most of them were, the music would fuck with their heads so bad I could sometimes get a confession for promising to shut it off. I was just thinking I'da liked to get muscle boy back there and throw George Jones "He Stopped Loving Her Today" at him. If that didn't work, I'd play Eddie Arnold's "Lonesome Cattle Call." That yodeling just sends 'em over the edge. Play it three times and they'll be back there confessing to shit they *didn't even do.*"

Lila June looked to see if Aaron was pulling her leg. When she decided he wasn't, she said, shaking her head, "Fishboy, you *are* a corker!"

It was about 3 a.m. and Aaron sat in the Cherokee in the Super Foods parking lot yawning deeply, the kind of yawn that cracked like a dislocated jaw. He'd been up about 20 hours and was as tired as he could ever remember being, even in Nam. Bone-weary came to mind. His nerve endings felt sanded by 40-grit paper. Even his hair hurt.

Aaron had given Lila June the bust, which also left her at the office filling out the reports. They had been unable to find the machine gun in the dark. He suspected it had been tossed into the reservoir. But they had found a stash—reefer and some white tablets that could have been ecstasy or ketamine, also known as Super K, an animal tranquilizer that produced a dreamy, psychedelic nod in humans. That was the kind of shit these rich pricks were into. Lila June was going to be busy.

Roscoe was sitting in the front seat, his big head tilted against the headrest. Aaron scratched him lazily under the ears, eliciting a series of pleasurable sighs.

"Told you it would be okay," he said. "Was I right?" Roscoe rolled his eyes and sighed again. He had recovered well. At least this time no one had been shooting at *them*. He wondered if he should leave Roscoe at home. But they'd been together so long, it felt strange when Roscoe wasn't with him. Like they were twins or something. Especially after this morning.

What a fucking day. He was still shook from the freeze-up. But he was also feeling pretty good somewhere beneath the fatigue. He knew he'd handled the situation after that first moment just right. Not bad for being off the job seven years.

It was one small but good step up out of the state he'd been in. He hoped he could sustain it.

The car phone buzzed. "Hey Fishboy, bring it on home. We got 'em booked, let them have their phone calls and packed them off to Boulder County Jail. I'm done with the paperwork, and since I slept this afternoon, I'm going to finish out the shift and let you go home. You've had all the fun you're allowed for one day. Oh, by the way, you know the noisy one who said 'fuck' a lot? His father is so pissed at him he said he was going to let him sit in jail for a while. So I guess you won't be 'grinded up into dog food' after all." She laughed.

"Bless you, Lila June. You are truly a saint. I'm on my way."

"Yeah, that's me, Fishboy—the Virgin Mary," she laughed.

Chapter 5

June 9

After the somewhat atypical excitement of that first night, the next three nights had been typically uneventful, and Aaron was relieved because he was having a hell of a time adjusting to the graveyard shift. He felt like he was jet-lagged by three non-stop trips around the globe. He yawned so often that Lila June took pity on him and told Harlan she was ready to go solo. But it had given them time to catch up and Aaron learned that her son, Billy Bob, was now 14 years old and something of a computer whiz, in fact was in some trouble for "hackin', or crackin' or some such crap." Her daughter, June Bug, was "15-going-on-21," Lila June said, and already becoming a handful. Aaron wasn't surprised, remembering that even at 12 years old, you could already tell she was going to be a looker, a willowy version of Lila June with curly blond hair and those same enormous blue eyes. Both kids were with their father for the summer.

Aaron had, with some difficulty, told her about Cassie and her mother's disappearance from Kansas City, his trip there to look for them and his realization from the reactions of her mother's coworkers that she'd just skipped town, in all likelihood to keep him away from his daughter. He wanted to, but didn't, tell her of his prayer every night that Cassie was safe, normal, even happy. It wasn't one of those kneeling-down-at-the-bedside-with-interlaced-finger prayers, just saying aloud to whomever might be listening when he lay down to sleep, "Baby, I hope you're okay. Please be okay." How could he explain something like that when he didn't even believe in God?

Instead, he described a little of the past three years of his life, leaving out the morning when he nearly ate his gun.

"My poor Fishboy," she had said. "I'm glad you're back to the land of the living."

In any case, there was a message from Harlan when Aaron arrived for work on the fourth night that he could change to the swing shift the following day. But he asked Aaron to come in at noon the next day and talk to Toby about the murder case.

But the most remarkable thing about the past three nights was that the Vietnam nightmare had not returned. He hoped it stayed that way.

Albuquerque, N. M.

The driver was uncharacteristically jumpy, as if the synapses in his muscles were misfiring. His right leg was bouncing, making it difficult to maintain an even speed. A vein in his temple throbbed. His neck muscles were jerking his head from side to side. A light sheen of perspiration covered his face.

All around him, Central Avenue was putting on its nightly, high-desert version of the Festival of Caligula. Hookers lined the sidewalks, bustiers, tube tops and bikini tops, satin short-shorts and miniskirts revealing a rainbow of flesh tones, teetering and wobbling around on six-inch patent-leather heels or platform sandals, leaning into car windows, watching the action on the street. In dark alleys intersecting the street, knots of young men in baggy tan pants, wife-beaters and hundred-dollar high-tops and sporting red and blue do-rags, hair nets or angled ball caps lounged in the shadows carrying out another of the world's older forms of commerce.

The carnival atmosphere was repeated on the street, where low-riders, cowboy Cadillacs, exotic sports cars, SUVs and drab rental cars all cruised at low speeds. Throbbing bass notes pummeled the hot night air. Brake lights winked incessantly, as the vehicles' occupants checked hot prospects, as dictated by their particular tastes.

The flush of sexual excitement permeated the night. There was a time when the driver would have been caught up in it, but this night he watched as if from inside a thin membrane. He pictured himself a baby bird—no, that wasn't right—a hatchling tyrannosaurus forcing his razor-sharp beak against the leathery sheath of the egg, fighting for that first breath of fresh air, that first taste of flesh. His breathing became labored, his guts heaved with the effort.

As he drove up the next block, the sight of a black and white Albuquerque police car, nose out in an alley, broke the spell. The cops were just sitting there as the maelstrom of crime swirled around them. Nevertheless, it brought him out of his bizarre state of mind. It wouldn't do to be noticed now, no, it wouldn't do at all. So, another time.

He was driving east on Central, heading back to the car rental agency when he spotted a gaggle of young girls standing beneath a bright streetlight. It was several blocks from the main prostitution scene but that really didn't mean anything, so he slowed. Their clothes were more typical of teenagers than whores but only by a matter of degrees. These little Mexican girls learned how to strut their stuff as soon as they had any stuff to strut.

Three of the four had miniskirts, revealing blouses, heels and big hair with ludicrous bangs that were lacquered straight up. But one had a low-cut, frilly white blouse that showed unusually perky breasts and a band of flat stomach. Cutoff jeans hugged her thighs and long dark pigtails draped over her shoulders. She wore unlaced high-top basketball shoes and had the face of a brown Madonna.

The driver's heart almost lurched into his throat when she smiled and threw a demure wave his way. "Lord God, Almighty, thank you!" he said aloud, nearly slamming on his brakes right there, but deciding to circle the block. He wheeled his car into successive right turns around the block and closed in for the kill. The girls were still there. As he approached, the white blouse stood out from the more garish clothes of her friends, and the driver's heart started beating wildly. His leg was shaking again and he almost missed the brake, panicked and mashed it too hard, causing the tires to squeak.

The girls were laughing and the driver could feel the heat of embarrassment on his face. He almost kept going, but the Madonna had detached from the group and started walking toward his car. She was a little thing, maybe five feet tall. My God, the driver thought, she looks so young. But his growing excitement dispelled any qualms he might have had, in fact, her youth and beauty were making it almost painful.

The driver lowered the passenger window, and the girl leaned down and put her forearm on the window rest. "Hey, mister, you looking' for a date?" The driver's excitement turned sour: the ease of her approach belied the innocence she projected. Then the driver noticed some discoloration on her forearm so he grabbed her wrist and pulled it towards him, exposing fresh needle tracks, bruises and some scarring from old tracks.

Realizing his Madonna was really a junkie whore, he jerked her arm so hard it pulled the top half of her body through the window. Before she could scream, he had his left hand at her throat, so furious at being deceived he could barely speak. "You…you…" Her friends were moving toward the car, screeching, "Hey, you leave her alone, asshole. Call the cops," and the clincher, "Get the creep's license number."

The driver snarled through clinched teeth "You diseased little cunt, I should kill you." Instead, he launched her head like a shot put back through the window and out onto the pavement. Her head disappeared from view, followed by a sickening thud. He mashed the accelerator and squealed away. In the mirror, he saw that the three girls were gathered around their friend, not trying to see his plate number.

The driver breathed a huge sigh of relief. He didn't quite know what had gotten into him tonight, but he could still feel the tingle of excitement when he thought he had found the perfect little beauty.

It was time to head back to the hellhole where, after the close call in Colorado, he'd sought sanctuary from the past—blacklisted from academia, disowned by his family (Thank the Episcopalian God that the trust fund, though shrinking, was inviolable) and hounded by enemies. At least he had a new crop of college students arriving to work the dig. And with them came new possibilities, but he feared none would be as exciting as the one he thought he had found tonight.

Chapter 6

June 10

A wall of gauzy gray clouds blocked out the peaks at the head of the valley as Aaron pulled into one of the parking spaces reserved for the marshal's office. Gusts of wind were blowing debris across the parking lot. Despite only five hours of sleep, he felt good and was looking forward to working a more civilized shift. He snugged his coat against the chill wind and headed for the door.

Once inside, Tobias Echohawk, who everyone but Harlan called Toby, waved through the doorway of a cubicle with tall dividers. Aaron stepped inside as Toby rose from the desk and offered his fist. They bumped knuckles.

"Hillbilly," Toby said, nodding, smiling, dredging up an old nickname he'd given Aaron after learning something of his past, unaware that that had been his handle in Nam. Toby, a Jicarilla Apache, had shaved his head sometime in the past three years—a big surprise in that he used to say half-jokingly that he took the job in Jack Springs because Harlan wouldn't make him cut his long hair. His once-wiry frame was now thickened with muscle. With his tight black T-shirt, snug jeans and shoulder holster, he looked like the prototypical movie cop. Although he was 28 or 29 , he still had a teenager's face.

"How's it going?" Aaron asked.

"It's all good," Toby said grinning. "And it's good to see you, man. Things have been kind of quiet since you left. Until this…" he shrugged toward a wall full of pictures, notes and diagrams. Aaron glanced up and was dying to look closer at some of the pictures, which even from a short distance he could see were of a body on a four-wheel motorcycle.

Something was distinctively odd about it. Well, shit, it was *headless*, for Christ's sake.

But another seemingly unrelated picture entered his head: Wiley Agnew, a crazed, wounded survivalist, bringing a big black semiautomatic pistol to bear on Aaron as a bullet cut his spinal cord and blew out the side of his throat.

Aaron owed Toby his life and maybe his daughter Cassie's life as well, because Toby had fired that shot after Aaron sneaked into the Agnews' old mining claim, which had been turned into a militia compound, to try and get his daughter away from the kidnapper who had taken refuge there. Aaron realized he had bailed out of town so quickly after it happened that he had never even thanked him.

But Toby seemed to harbor no hard feelings, saying, "It's good to have you on board."

"Yeah," Aaron said. "So far so good."

"Well," Toby said, whisking fingers along his chin line as if checking for beard stubble, although there wasn't a trace of whiskers anywhere on his dark face. "There's something I'd like you to do for me. We need to talk to a guy who lives up there near where the murder happened. I'd go, but I had to bust his head a few months ago when he got drunk down at the Jackass, so I'm thinking it might go a little smoother if someone else did it."

If Aaron hadn't known him so well, he might have thought that Toby was avoiding a confrontation. But Toby was a 4th-dan Kendoist, the equivalent of a black belt in Karate, graduated top of his class from the New Mexico State Police Academy and was a certified sharp-shooter. But more important than any of those things, he knew Toby, despite his youth and sometimes joking manner, was absolutely fearless, and that he was simply making a good decision concerning the investigation.

"I guess you better fill me in on the murder," Aaron said.

Toby looked at Aaron, appraising, "How much do you know?"

"Believe it or not, the only thing I know is what I read in the newspaper that first day. Man, I've been so beat from working the graveyard shift, I've been too tired to wonder or to read."

Toby nodded. "That's good, then. I'll start from the beginning." He shuffled some notes on the table.

"Two years ago, Mac McKendrickson donated about 4,000 acres of his mine claim to the town for use as a park. We annexed it and opened a few trails. Of course, we don't have the manpower to patrol it, so the ATV crowd showed up. At first, most of the folks were local and minded their manners. Then, last summer, a wildlife biologist discovered a population of genetically pure cutthroat trout in a creek in the middle of the valley. A few weeks later, after some heavy rains, she noticed the creek was filling up with mud from the dirt bike and four-wheeler tracks. These fish are on the Endangered Species list, so she called the Fish and Wildlife Service. They pissed and moaned but finally banned motorized vehicles from the area.

"Jeter, our victim, announces on a talk show that he's organizing a protest and will lead some dirt bikers into the area. The feds were waiting and arrested Jeter and five other riders, who pulled their guns on the feds. It was a real Mexican standoff until the black helicopters arrived."

"No shit? Wow. I guess that put a stop to it."

"Not hardly," Toby said. They just got sneaky and came in at night, tearing up the creek bottom and everything else they can ride up or down. It was wanton destruction and it was pissing off a lot of people, even some of the ATV riders who had been lobbying to reopen the area.

"Then somebody started spiking the roads so their tires would blow out. Shots have been fired at people who were riding in there illegally. Things quieted down over the winter.

"The valley opened up about a month ago and early last week, when the biologist went to check on the fish, most of them in the main stretch were dead, poisoned most likely since we found two empty two-gallon containers of chlorine bleach right there by the creek. Six days ago, some hikers found a headless body on a four wheeler, its hands gripping the handlebars, about 50 feet into the meadow where the fish were killed."

"Fucking bizarre," Aaron said.

"Bizarre doesn't do it justice," Toby said. "When the hikers called us, we called the Sheriff's Office but Earl handed it back to us. Earl sent some evidence techs up, though. Before the crime techs arrived, we secured the scene and I found the victim's head in the creek, right in the pool where the dead fish were found."

Aaron pictured the scene and grinned at the ludicrousness of it. "The newspaper story said the booby trap was some kind of wire stretched across the trail."

"Piano wire," Toby said, with a grim smile.

"Piano wire," Aaron said, the answer raising a nasty buzz in his head. This was not going to be a simple investigation, Aaron suspected. He absently scratched his temple. "That is either one hell of a coincidence—somebody sets a random booby trap and just happens to get the main guy in the controversy—or a very ballsy murderer with a highly refined sense of irony. "

"I'm leaning toward the latter," Toby said. "We've sent everything from the crime scene down to the Colorado Bureau of Investigation lab. The bad news is that they're swamped with stuff from the murders down in Boulder. The good news is that our stuff is fairly straightforward. The wire, footprints, tire tracks, a little trash in the vicinity of the booby trap, finger prints on the machine."

Aaron asked, "What else do you have on Jeter?"

"He owned an ATV dealership in Denver. He was also the leader or maybe the main mouthpiece for the Free Riders, since they appear to be kind of loosely organized, not a formal club. Jeter was a regular on those AM talk shows, threatening environmentalists and 'jack-booted government thugs', as he liked to call them. These guys are always packing some heavy heat when they're in the woods, right out where everyone can see, so it's legal. They'll run hikers and bicyclists off the trail, shit like that. Forest rangers or wildlife officers, forget it. They look at those guys as targets."

"Was he strapped when he was killed?"

Toby nodded. "A Desert Eagle .44-magnum semi in a shoulder holster."

Aaron felt like he hadn't taken a breath since Toby began talking, so he gulped a big one and let out a long, low whistle. "Shee-*it*," he said. "Sounds like this guy could have had a long list of enemies." He frowned, realizing he was missing something, then took a stab at it. "Have you got any leads on who was spiking the trails or shooting at them?"

Toby looked up and put a fist to his mouth like he was suppressing a cough, which turned out to be a chuckle.

"Well, yeah," he said, a gleam in his eyes. "The guy we want you to go talk to."

Chapter 7

Following Toby's map an hour later, Aaron got on an old mine road so bad he feared the Legacy would bottom out, so he pulled over and hiked the rest of the way with Roscoe. It was good because, on foot, he got a better look at the area. The park the town had acquired was in the wide valley below the road. Odd rock formations jutted from the thick timber clinging to the slopes. Narrow swaths of dungy snow still lay in the swales beneath the budding aspens. It had been a century since any actual mining had gone on in the valley and the test holes and sluice operations had been reclaimed by nature. Faint traces of old roads still latticed the level areas of the valley and zigged their way up the steep slopes. Aaron could see the attraction for ATVers.

As he came around a bend in the road, Aaron saw an old, fairly large cabin nested against the scarred side of a hill. Next to it a freshly boarded up mineshaft entered the mountain. Behind the cabin was another building, what might have once been a hay shed but currently had a battered pickup truck bed sticking out of the door. Old mining equipment was strewn about the yard, dead weeds had grown up to the front door steps, which didn't enjoy the protection of a porch roof. It was a hard-bitten kind of place.

Still, the peaked metal roof was fairly new and the chinking between the logs was solid. The windows, filled with multi-pane glass, looked clean and sturdy. Thin gray smoke leaked out of the large, black metal chimney, which rose several feet above the roof. And a well-stacked pile of firewood, the size of a small shed, stood beside the south end of the building. The front door was cracked open but no one was moving around inside.

"Hello," he said loudly. Within seconds a shadow seemed to fill the doorway. Then the screen door slapped open and a great bear of a man took the top step. He was squinting behind a gray-shot, red beard that climbed thick and bushy out from his cheeks and all the way down to his chest. Above the beard was a massive tangle of reddish gray hair that appeared to be pulled back. He wore threadbare brown coveralls over a red union suit and cradled an M1 carbine loosely against his belly, the barrel in the crook of his arm.

A black wolf-dog as large as Roscoe slunk silently into the yard from behind the firewood pile and lay at the man's feet. His pale eyes were locked on Roscoe, but he appeared to be well in hand.

With probably 250 pounds of testosterone-laden canine flesh between them, Aaron thought a fight could prove lethal. Instead of hostility, however, he noticed Roscoe's curlicue tail wagging. The wolf-dog remained still.

"Can I help ya'?" the man said.

"Sam Hite?" Aaron asked.

"I be the same," the mountain man said.

Roscoe was now standing stiff-legged, trying to restrain the rumba he did when excited. "Roscoe, no! Sit." He stayed in place, but his body twitched as he wrestled with self-control.

"I'm Aaron Hemingway, with the Jack Springs Marshal's Office. I'd like to ask you a few questions."

Sam Hite's gaze hardened for a moment before seeming to relax a bit. "Say, I recognize your name. You were the newspaperman who got into that fandango with them Agnew brothers a couple of years back. Come on in."

"Roscoe, stay!" Aaron said.

"Your dog's intentions seem honorable. Let 'em play. Sadie gets a little bored up here with only an ol' fart like me for company."

If that's a female, I'd hate to see the male, Aaron thought. "Sure. Roscoe could use some exercise."

"It's okay, girl," Sam said with a fondness in his voice. "Go on."

Roscoe was about to come apart at the seams until he saw Sadie approaching. He rushed forward and slid to a stop with his forepaws wide, his butt stuck up in the air, wiggling like a can-can dancer. Roscoe froze as Sadie carefully pranced up for a sniff. He jumped sideways and she tried to nip his shoulder. Then they rocketed into the trees.

"I guess we don't have to worry about those two," Aaron said.

"Naw, it 'pears a famous friendship has been consummated." Growls, yips and the sound of breaking limbs emerged from the trees. Sam Hite held the door open. "I got some coffee on. Yer welcome to join me." He leaned the carbine next to the door.

Inside, the log house was warm and dark. And clean. Completely different from what Aaron expected. The kitchen area, with a rough wood counter, heavy table and cast iron cook stove, sat in the middle of the back wall. A blackened metal coffeepot rested on the stove. To the left were a comfortable armchair, a desk and a large bookcase filled with books.

A large cedar-framed bed, covered with Indian blankets, dominated the opposite end of the room. Kerosene lamps were spread throughout. One was lit on the kitchen table and another was throwing light on the desk where a large, leather-bound book lay open.

"So Hoss, let me guess. If yer working for the marshal, ya prob'ly want to know if I killed that cretin on the 4-wheeler," Sam surmised as he placed two blue enamel metal cups on the table.

Aaron never responded, waiting to see if the old man would fill the silence with information. The soft light from the kerosene lamp danced on his weather-beaten face and gave his washed-out green eyes a devilish look. But he didn't take the bait.

"Well, anyway, have some coffee," he said and poured the bubbling brew from the coffee pot into both cups. "Ya take it black?"

"Black's fine," Aaron said, wondering how long the stuff had been on the stove. It smelled wonderful but looked lethal. Sam almost had to coax it out of the pot.

"Let it cool down some, now. I wouldn't want ya to burn yerself," Sam said and gave an amused smile.

"Right," Aaron said. Sludge or not, the aroma was maddening. The two men locked eyes across the table. "I hear that you keep a close watch on the land down there and have even had some run-ins with this bunch. So you may have had some dealings with the guy that was murdered."

"Not personal, I don't believe," Sam said. "Least ways I didn't recognize the picture from the newspaper. But I've prob'ly seen him and his gang from a distance. And I didn't care for what I saw. They weren't just riding. I don't have a thing about riders. Got a four-wheeler and a snow machine myself. But there is something off-kilter about that outfit. All they want to do is tear things up.

"You show me where in the Constitution or in *any* of the goddamn law books it says just because you got the money to put a goddamn $5,000 machine under your ass, you got a *right* to ride it any goddamn place you please, without regard to the con-se-quences to God's good Earth and His creatures!" His voice had risen throughout and he punctuated the last 11 syllables by punching his thick, stubby finger into the tabletop like a blunt-nosed woodpecker. "You show me that and I'll kiss your ass," he said, slapping his palm on the table so hard it nearly sloshed coffee out of the cups.

"I'll confess to one thing, though: I ain't sorry to see the sonofabitch dead."

Aaron believed him, but it was obvious he was quick to anger. Still, the piano wire was not an impulsive weapon. It took planning and knowledge to murder someone like that, and maybe a little luck. And if Jeter was the target, it took something that Sam Hite obviously did not have—a line of communication to the outside world.

"Did you see or hear anything unusual that night?" Aaron asked.

Before Sam could answer, a crack rang like a shot from the trees where Roscoe and Sadie were playing, and Sam jumped up and moved to the door. Then the sound of what could have been a small tree crashing to the ground followed. Through the window, Aaron saw the dogs dash into the road as Sadie tackled Roscoe. They both tumbled several times and came up running. Then they were gone.

Sam looked down the road, shook his head and laughed. "A couple of years ago two bull moose were tangling down in the meadow. You could hear 'em a half mile away. Tore up about four acres of ground and snapped off pert near twenty trees. I hope those two tire out before they do that much damage. Anyway, you were saying?"

"Did you hear or see anything unusual that night?" Aaron repeated.

"Naw, I din't hear nothing. I was feeling a little poorly, so I turned in early, had me a couple of shots of bourbon whiskey, too. But from the trail he was on, he would have come in from the top of the valley. That's where they found his truck, and it's a far piece from here. So I prob'ly wouldn't have no how. Besides, most people are too damn smart to go riding around the woods at night. I guess that Jeter feller wasn't one of them, though." He chuckled.

Aaron wondered if Sam was telling the truth about not hearing anything that night, especially if he could hear bull moose fighting a half-mile away. He made a mental note to have Toby check the muffler on Jeter's machine to see how loud it was.

The metal coffee mug was cool enough to hold so Aaron held it up and took a sip. Lulled by the relative coolness of the cup, he had taken a decent swallow before his stomach registered a low-level nuclear detonation. He wasn't sure if the stuff was going to stay down, but it did. A fierce band of sweat broke out across his forehead to fight the fire that smoldered on his scalp. Then he got the hiccups, big, breath-robbing hiccups. Sam sat there, his eyes dancing with humor while Aaron's internal organs went through meltdown and threatened to genetically rearrange themselves.

Finally, the spasms subsided, his scalp cooled and Aaron believed he could take a large enough breath to be able to talk. He picked up the cup, nodded and said, "Damn fine coffee, Sam." A warm glow and a feeling of wellbeing inexplicably flooded his body.

"A touch of ginger and cayenne and a couple things I picked up in the valley do give it a kick, I believe," Sam said, smiling hugely. "Nothing in there'll hurt ya none, though." Then, his eyes dissecting Aaron like twin scalpels, he said, "You done good, Hoss."

Aaron felt the mild buzz level off, so he raised the cup to his lips, took another swallow, and said, "Someone's been spiking the trail and taking potshots at Jeter's gang."

"Are ya investigatin' those…incidents?" Sam wondered.

"No, I'm not. And I don't give a damn unless they're connected to the murder. But there are some who might think that's a logical connection."

"In that case, I'll not burden ya with an answer," Sam said, and finished the coffee in one gulp. He drew the back of his hand across his mouth, got up, took the cup to the sink, and hand-pumped some water into it before he shook it out and sat it on the wood counter.

"I've got to be getting back," Aaron said. "Let's see if we can find the dogs." Sam held his hand up to stop Aaron from talking. He cocked his head, listening to something Aaron couldn't hear. Then he smiled. "'Scuse me a second."

Sam went to the door, picked up the carbine and stepped outside. Aaron could now hear the drone of a dirt bike. As the noise grew louder, Sam raised the gun and pointed it across the road. Aaron wondered if he was going to witness a murder. He lowered his hand toward his gun.

"Sam, listen here, you know I'm..."

"Shush now," Sam said. "I ain't gonna shoot nobody in front of a lawman." The drone was growing louder. Sam let off a round, which was followed by a loud clang and a screaming 'whaaaannng.' He quickly repeated the process. Again, a slug ricocheted angrily into space. The noise of the dirt bike tapered off, then picked up again. Only this time it was moving away.

Sam Hite clicked on the safety, put the carbine on two pegs over the doorway, and sat back down with a satisfied look on his face. "Works ever' time," he said.

"How'd you do that?"

"Well, Hoss, I jest hanged an old cast-iron frying pan in a tree on the road. When I hear a biker coming, I pop a couple of .30-caliber, copper-jacketed slugs into it."

"Why not just shoot a few rounds into the bank?" Aaron asked.

Sam said, "Gunshots around these parts ain't no big thing, might even stir somebody with a gun up enough to look for a fight. But when somebody hears a ricochet, that sound jest grabs 'em by the testicles, runs a cold finger up their ass, and shuts off all discussion."

"It does, at that," Aaron said, and shouted for Roscoe. From the continuing yelps and growls, it was apparent that his testosterone-inundated companion was ignoring him and not freaked out by the shots for a change.

"Goddamn dog," Aaron muttered.

Sam put both little fingers to his lips and whistled. The commotion stopped and moments later Sadie came loping into the yard. Roscoe followed and he had mud, grass and tree branches matted into his fur. Sadie sat beside Sam and appeared unscathed by their romp.

Roscoe pranced, and when that didn't work he feinted an attack. Sadie gazed into Sam's eyes and ignored Roscoe. Then he whined and reluctantly joined Aaron in the road.

"Thanks for the coffee," Aaron said.

"Yer welcome, Hoss," Sam said. "Come back anytime."

Chapter 8

When Aaron pulled up to the office, Toby and Harlan were sitting in the window of Fat Jack's Deli and Ice Cream Parlor, next door to the marshal's office. Harlan waved him in. Aaron took a quick glance at Roscoe. Only whimpers and a heaving chest told Aaron that he was alive. With all the mud, leaves and twigs sticking to him, he looked more like the Swamp Thing than a dog. Shaking his head with a fond grin, Aaron went into the deli.

Harlan was finishing a large cone, licking the drips that ran down the side, and Toby was drinking coffee.

As Aaron sat, Harlan did a quick scan of the room but no one was close enough to overhear. "What did the old fart have to say?"

"He didn't confess, if that was what you were hoping. And he wouldn't deny that he was the mischief-maker up there."

"No shit?" Toby said.

"He didn't admit it, but he asked me if I was investigating those incidents. And when I told him no, he said he wasn't going to 'burden' me with an answer. The only other thing he said was, 'I ain't sorry the sonofabitch is dead.' And he was clearly angry about what had been going on up there."

"Means, motive and opportunity," Toby said. "The big three."

Aaron shook his head. "Except for one thing: How would he have known Jeter was coming when he did? And who would have told him?"

"That's two things," Harlan said.

Toby nodded. "Yeah, and that's enough to keep us from getting a warrant."

Harlan shook his head. "We had to try, I guess."

Aaron looked at his watch. "Time to go to work," he said, pushing the chair back and walking to the door. At the doorway, he turned, "Do you know if that machine of Jeter's is loud?"

Toby shook his head. "No, I'd have to say it's fairly quiet."

Aaron remembered another question he had. "Did you talk to Jeter's widow?"

"Nope." Toby said, shaking his head. "Her sister said she's too upset to be interviewed. They still got her under sedation." He rubbed a hand over his buzzed hair. "You know, for somebody who was as big an asshole as Jeter was supposed to be, he must have been a wonderful husband." He winked and grinned. "Either that or the widow *really* does not want to talk to me about him. Maybe I'll show up down there tonight and see how sedated she really is."

Next door, Belinda was in deep conversation on the telephone and rolled her eyes at Aaron as he walked by. Her hair was twisted into a knot on top of her head and impaled by the chopstick. A strand of hair had worked itself loose and fell across her left eye. A light fringe of wavy hair hung down to her collar. So far, he hadn't seen her hair fixed the same way twice. How she could make it look so casual but enticing was beyond him. Maybe she worked hard every morning to achieve the effect, he thought, but dismissed the possibility almost before it formed. More likely, she couldn't be bothered.

Maybe it was because the chaotic style was such a contrast to her personality, which was anything but chaotic and casual. He shrugged, mentally—it was truly a mystery. Aaron checked his in-box and saw two requests to investigate dog-at-large complaints—the daytime bread and butter of law enforcement work in Jack Springs.

When he walked out to the marshal's office patrol car, a black Ford Crown Victoria, he felt eyes following him and, glancing around, saw the knucklehead they had arrested five nights earlier. A dive team from the Jack Springs Fire and Rescue had found a Chinese knockoff AK-47, known as an SKS, in ten feet of water just below the deck the day after the incident. He was sitting in an expensive-looking Toyota SUV in the parking lot across the street.

The punk kept his eyes locked on Aaron as he moved. So Aaron opened the patrol car door, set his PAC radio and jacket on the seat, and walked over to the SUV. He tried and failed to remember the knucklehead's name. He stopped next to the driver's door and said, "Are you looking for me?"

The kid had an almost handsome face, but the shaved head, the thick neck pocked with steroid acne and wise-guy smirk ruined any chance he'd be considered so.

"No fucking way. I'm just sitting here. Thinking. It's still a free country, ain't it?"

"Sure, it's a free country. Speaking of free, your old man finally popped for the bail, huh?"

The kid's mouth tightened, then relaxed into a grin. "Must have, or else I broke out of jail. Did you hear anything about that? Me breaking out?"

"No, I didn't."

"Well, then."

Aaron nodded, turned and walked away. He was about four steps away when he heard the kid say something under his breath.

Aaron stopped in mid-stride and turned. "Say what?"

The kid smirked. "I said, 'watch out you don't step in any dog shit.'"

Aaron tilted his head a bit, as if trying to get a fix on a distant sound. Then a smile like a broken beer bottle crossed his face. He strolled back to the college boy's vehicle.

"You know, those pills you take have convinced you that you can do some things that you'd be much better off not trying. I'm sorry to be the one to tell you, but it's best if you find out now than later." He raised his finger like a pistol and let it lift with a slight recoil. Then he turned back to the patrol car, where Roscoe sat waiting.

Instead of getting into the patrol car, he went back into the annex. The kid was trying to intimidate him, as if some muscle-bound, punk-ass kid could do that by staring at him or reminding him of the threat that night that his father "would grind you up into dog food." He needed some information about the kid and his case. Inside, Belinda was now reading a mystery novel at the dispatch desk.

Not that he minded having an excuse to see her again. Coincidentally, he was sure she had switched to swing shift a day before Aaron did. He'd managed to chat with her a little at the end of his second night on the job but was too out of it to say very much.

"Hey Belinda, you got any information about the kid we picked up with the machine gun the other night?" She had tucked the wild strand behind her ear.

"Hey, yourself, Deputy Hillbilly," she said, put her book down, arched a brow slightly and asked, "Like what?"

Aaron was taken aback at hearing her use Toby's nickname for him until he realized that they'd been talking about him. He wasn't sure how to take that so he put on his game face. "A name or a rap sheet would be a start."

"Hold on a minute," she said, digging through a stack or reports on her desk. She found what she was looking for. "Michael Wentworth, age 21, no sheet, but the ATF is trying to trace the gun since it is a full automatic. I guess they want to know where he got it, but they haven't filed charges yet. Maybe they're enlisting his help."

"You think?"

She shrugged. "It's just a guess."

"Thanks," Aaron said, wondering, too, where young Michael had come up with an SKS submachine gun.

"Any time," she said, with a ghost smile crossing her lips. "Why do you want to know, anyway?"

"Just curious," Aaron said. He turned and walked toward the door, his step a little springier than before. It had been a long time since he'd experienced that sensation.

Chapter 9

June 11

The streets had been quiet so Aaron took a break, bought a corned beef on rye from Fat Jack's and went into the annex to eat it. Toby was still working and Aaron carried his sandwich to his cubicle. Kuchera was covering the streets so Aaron stopped and asked Ida, a sharp-tongued, banty hen of a woman who filled the dispatcher desk as needed, to let Kuchera know where he was. She snorted, put down her bodice-ripper novel, and got on the radio.

Toby was leaning over the table with his head in his hands, staring at some papers. "What's up?" Aaron asked. "I thought you were going down to the widow Jeter's to stake the place out."

Toby looked up slowly and shrugged. There was a look in his eyes Aaron had never seen before. "I feel like I've run into a mental brick wall. It's been seven days and we have no leads. You think our best suspect is innocent. And I'm not sure I'm up to this detective shit. You know, out on the street, where everything is *right there*, I'm on top of that, I'm all over that. But you give white people time to think, I'm way behind the curve. With Indians, they'll usually tell you what they think you want to hear, even though you know the truth and they know you know. Or if you give them time and approach it slowly, they'll tell you the truth and suffer the consequences. But white people, the more time they have the more twisted everything becomes."

Aaron had never really thought about it like that, probably because his mind worked the same way.

"You're right. People will lie and lie until you catch them lying once or contradicting themselves. Then, for 95 percent of your suspects, the whole shebang starts to unravel. After a while, they can't even remember their lies. So they'll either tell the truth, or if they're savvy, they'll clam up and ask for a lawyer. But they can do themselves a lot of damage before they get smart."

"If you don't mind my eating while we talk, we can hash it out a little," Aaron said. Toby nodded. Aaron sat and unwrapped the sandwich.

"As far as the old man being a suspect, you know my reasoning. Until we can hook him up with one or more of the Free Riders or Jeter's wife, there's no way to explain the timing. Another is that he's such a logical suspect, he'd have to be a lot more stupid than he seems to put himself in that position."

Aaron took a bite and chewed thoughtfully while watching Toby's mind working. "So, what's the next step?"

A little spark came into Toby's eyes as he started putting things together. "We've already agreed that whoever strung that wire knew Jeter was going up there that night and exactly where he was going. Whoever strung the wire, somebody close to Jeter had to alert the wire guy—either some of his Free Rider buddies or his wife, or maybe both. None of them have been willing to give me the time of day. And no evidence ties any of them to the crime, so I can't make them talk to me."

"Which makes your idea to stake out… what's her name?"

"Mona Jeter," Toby said, a shadow of a grin crossing his face.

"Staking out Mona Jeter's house for a few nights to see if she's up and around, or better yet consorting with any of these guys, is a good idea. Get some pictures, record any license numbers, that sort of thing. Then ask to see her again. If they give you any of that heavy sedation bullshit, pull out the evidence. If she still won't talk, threaten to take her before the Grand Jury. If she *still* won't talk, drop a subpoena on her ass."

Another idea came to Aaron, a follow-up on something Toby had mentioned earlier. "What's on Jeter's sheet?"

"There wasn't much recently—a couple of DUIs, drunk and disorderly, third-degree assaults in the past two years. About 15 years ago he was into some biker shit in California and had the kind of record you'd expect: assault, brawling, possession. He didn't serve a lot of time on any of them."

"Any domestics?" Aaron asked.

"No arrests or convictions," Toby said.

"Where's his house?"

"It's in Wheat Ridge."

"You might try calling the P.D. down there and see if they've been out to that address on a domestic. It sounds like Jeter has had a tendency to get out of control. What's the chance that his wife was spared from that?"

A look of relief swept Toby's face. "Thanks, Hillbilly. I may have gotten in a little over my head. But what you said makes sense. At least it will get me moving again."

"Don't worry about it. I owed you one, a very big one, in case you had forgotten."

Toby looked puzzled for a moment, then he understood. "Hey, I was just doing my job."

"Yeah, well..." Aaron said, pausing, "Belinda called me Hillbilly."

Toby looked a tad uncomfortable. "Uh, we were talking about you. I must have let that slip." Aaron wrinkled his forehead in a question. Toby shrugged. "You know, just shop talk," he said as he gathered some papers off the table, stuck them in a briefcase and left.

Aaron looked down at his sandwich, said "Shit," a little too loudly.

"What?" barked Ida.

"My sandwich is cold." He re-wrapped it and stood.

"Poor baby," Ida rasped in mock sympathy.

Aaron stood and walked toward the door, discreetly flipping her the bird whereupon she cackled like a rooster with a three-pack-a-day habit as he left.

Chapter 10

June 12

The morning broke with a leaden fog covering the meadow. Aaron built a small fire in the woodstove to ward off the chill. As his high-country cabin warmed, he brewed a pot of coffee, and plopped in his reading chair, which was strategically located beneath a broken skylight, with James Crumley's *The Last Good Kiss* open on his lap. Tiny drops of mist settled through the crack, making it necessary to lean this way and that to keep the pages of the paperback from getting damp. He vowed once again to crawl up there as soon as the weather improved and slap something over the hole. Typically, as soon as the sun came out, he forgot all about it.

A couple of hours later the phone rang. "So, how are things going in the little kingdom of diminished capacity?" asked Lt. Earl McCormick.

"Hey, I fit right in there," Aaron told him.

"Yeah, I guess you do at that," he said, without his usual sarcasm. "Are you still working the case you were telling me about—looking for that professor at the university?"

"Not actively. I hit the wall a few weeks ago trying to find someone to talk to me. I guess I don't blend well with the university crowd, at least the science geeks that I need to talk to."

"Yeah, but you'd fit right in with the hippies."

"Earl, the hippies are dead, haven't you heard? It happened in 1968."

"Not at the university, they aren't."

Earl paused and Aaron could tell that his banter was forced.

"Okay, what's up? Your comebacks are even lamer than usual. This case with the Rainey girl's murder got you down?"

"No way," Earl chuckled. "The police department has pretty much got the case now. We're tied in knots over that woman we found murdered up in Left Hand Canyon, though, so the manpower is still short. The Rainey Task Force has been dissolved but the announcement hasn't been made. I guess the P.D. wants all the glory. They're welcome to it if it ever comes." He paused. "The case is down the toilet. They blew it when they failed to haul the parents in for questioning that first day."

"So, who do you like for it?"

"Somebody real, real familiar with the house," he said, leaving it at that.

"If it's not that, what's bothering you?"

Another pause. "I got a phone call from Maya Rexford," he said with uncharacteristic emotion in his voice. "You remember that Tyrone's military police reserve unit was called up and sent to Saudi Arabia during Desert Storm?"

"Yeah, I remember," Aaron said. Every cop who worked with Tye was shitting bricks, worried about the chemical weapons that Saddam had waiting for U.S. troops. "I heard he came back OK."

"Well, he did. I guess there was an incident while he was there, but he would never talk about it. About two years after he got back, he had a seizure of some kind. It left him totally paralyzed and he's, well, not gotten any better. The fuck of it is that the VA denied him benefits because the seizure came too late to be designated a service-connected disability. The family is struggling financially. I was thinking about the guy you're looking for and realized you didn't know...about Tye."

Jesus Christ, Aaron thought, totally paralyzed for what—four and a half or five years? Aaron could only imagine what that would do to anyone, but the thought of it happening to Tyrone was beyond comprehension. Earl and Aaron had both worked with Tyrone in the North Denver Metro Drug Task Force in the late '80s, and Tye was one of the most vibrant human beings Aaron had ever met. He'd climbed out of the L.A. ghetto, where gangbangers had killed both his older brother and his little sister in a drive-by. He'd played linebacker at the university in Boulder and graduated in four years. Now this.

"Man, that is fucking sad," Aaron said. "Give me the phone number. I'll go see him."

Chapter 11

June 13

Aaron scanned the houses along South Pearl Street in Denver until he found Tyrone's address. Tye's home was red brick with white shutters, a picket fence and a small, well-trimmed lawn surrounded by flowers. A bicycle lay on its side in the grass, but everything else about the house looked orderly and cheerful. He found a parking place three doors down and sat for a while, gathering his thoughts, steeling his emotions.

Aaron's legs felt leaden as he contemplated seeing his old friend. At the same time, dread and guilt fought for the upper hand in his guts. It was going to be tough. But he knew it was time to move or to leave, and he was going in because he had told Maya he was coming, and Tye was expecting him. He swung out of the car and walked toward the gate. As he opened it, a young boy, wearing an oversize Broncos jersey, baggy shorts and high tops, darted into the yard then stumbled to a stop as he saw Aaron at the gate. The lad was stocky, with a short 'fro, light-complected skin and huge brown eyes.

He looked to be about six or seven years old. Aaron remembered he'd been born just before Aaron had left the Denver Police Department. "I'll bet you're Preston," Aaron said, and the boy's frame relaxed visibly, but his eyes stayed wary as he nodded.

"Are you a friend of my Daddy's?" he asked.

"Yes, I'm an old friend of his," Aaron said.

A change came over Preston's face and his eyes were like dark pools concealing a terrible secret. "My Daddy is sick," he said, flexing his small, chubby hands as if he were looking for something to hold on to.

"I know," Aaron said. "Is your mother home?"

Preston turned and bolted toward the front door. "Momma, Daddy's friend is here," he yelled.

Maya Rexford appeared at the front door wiping her hands on a plaid apron. She was still beautiful, Aaron thought, but thinner. Her smile was as wide as a river but when she stepped onto the porch, there were dark circles under her eyes.

"Aaron, it's good that you came," she said. "Tye's going to be so happy to see you. Not many of the guys come by any more." But her smile broke into a thousand pieces and she wrapped her arms around herself. Then the moment passed and the steel returned to her carriage. Her eyes darted to the bicycle.

"Preston, you put that bicycle around back where it belongs, young man," she said with fragile resolve.

Preston shuffled to the bike, lifted it and pushed it sullenly around the side of the house. Maya stepped forward and embraced Aaron as a shudder ran through her body. "It's so hard," she said, "even after four years. I can read his thoughts but he still can't move anything but his eyes. He's in no physical pain, of course, but…" she choked, "the pain in that man's heart at what was stolen from him is almost…" And she broke down, completely, sobbing deeply in Aaron's arms. In his peripheral vision, Aaron could see Preston staring from the corner of the house. Maybe Maya sensed him there, because she straightened again, holding Aaron's arms, and said, "Give me a minute and we'll go see Tye. I told him you were coming. He has probably been remembering the good old days with you maniacs on the task force. Lord how I hated those days, but right now, you don't know how bad I wish they were back." She turned and went inside, closing the screen door softly. Preston had disappeared around the house.

Aaron sat heavily in the swing on the porch and noticed the neighborhood, which looked tidy and cared for. A couple of blocks up, there appeared to be some modest businesses, and Aaron remembered there was a coffee house, a mystery book shop and some kind of folk music hall along the street. A pleasant, civilized place, just a couple of blocks from the seedy South Broadway district and the rail yards.

A steady stream of cars drove slowly up the one-way street. Some people smiled and waved. Whatever misfortune had befallen the Rexfords, they could have landed in a worse place, Aaron realized, and wondered how they had managed it?

Maya reappeared, wearing a skirt, white blouse and spotless Nike walking shoes, her curly locks pulled back in a scrunchy. Her mouth was set and her eyes were rimmed with pink, but there was no evidence of the tears. It was the game face she used to keep her family together.

"Come on in," she said. "Tye's ready. Remember, when he moves his eyes up and down it means yes. Side to side means no." Aaron, too, put on his game face as she led him into the cozy living room, but it lasted only until he saw his friend. Tye was strapped into the wheelchair, which was really more of a mobile bed. His once-thick frame and wide face were now just bones with a thin, ashen skin stretched across them. Aaron's heart was close to meltdown. Fucking war, he thought, mother-fucking war.

"Tyrone, here's another one of your fool running buddies," Maya said, a smile now stretched across her teeth.

Maybe it was Aaron's imagination, but he thought he could see Tyrone Rexford's eyes smiling.

"Hello, my friend. I'm sorry I haven't been down sooner but I got exiled from the P.D. right after you left. I've been out of touch. It's been too long, but I thought you were maybe ready to bust some chops out on the street. You still got your Louisville Slugger?"

Tyrone's eyes flicked up and down like a TV screen gone bad and Aaron thought he was saying, 'Yeah, let's do it,' like when the squad would roll out after briefing. Seeing Tye's excitement, he knew that talking about the good old days was what was needed here. But after about a half-hour, Aaron decided to bring Tye up to speed on what had been happening for the past five years in his life.

When he recounted shooting up his wife's lawyer's office, Tyrone's eyes went wide and moved side to side in an exaggerated "No!" of disbelief. When he related the events in Jack Springs three years earlier, Tye's eyes just stayed wide. Likewise the shooting at the barbecue joint. By the time Aaron was done, Maya was staring intently at her husband.

"Oh, my sweet Lord!" she said, choked with emotion. "He's smiling. Look at his mouth." Indeed, the corners of Tye's mouth were turned up just a fraction of an inch. Tye's eyes were flicking up and down, signaling, "Yes!"

From the back bedroom, Preston inched out and looked at his father. Tyrone's eyes moved to his son, but Preston just stared. "Is Daddy happy, Momma?"

Tyrone's eyes went up and down. Maya leaned over and gave her husband a huge hug and Preston joined them. What they couldn't see was the tear running down Tyrone's cheek. Aaron's composure had fled and he knew it was time to leave.

"I got to run, my man, but I'll be back soon. And that's a promise."

Tyrone's eyes went up and down, and crinkled a little at the corners, with tears now streaming incongruously down his face. As Aaron stood and moved to the door, Maya tore herself from Tyrone, grabbed Aaron by the shoulder and spun him around. She wrapped her arms around his neck and whispered in his ear. "You best be telling the truth, Aaron. Don't *make* me come up there to Jack Ass Springs to jerk a *knot* in your honky ass."

Maya walked him to the door. When they stopped, Aaron asked, "Do they know what happened to Tye?"

She shook her head. "Officially, no. But one of doctors we talked to, a guy who treated the veterans independently of the Veterans' Administration, said it sounded like encapsulated aflatoxin, something they had seen in other vets."

"What's encapsulated aflatoxin?"

"It's a neurotoxin that's covered with a protein that hides it from detection until it's ready to go off—like a time bomb." She hesitated and Aaron saw something dark in her eyes. "I haven't told this to many people, but we found Tyrone unconscious in the back yard. He was in a coma for two months and his breathing wasn't supplying enough oxygen to his brain. They wanted to put him on a respirator but he'd told me before he went over there that if something happened he didn't want to be kept alive by a machine. So I told them no. A week later, his breathing had improved and three weeks after that he came out of the coma. To live like that," she nodded her head toward the back of the house.

Aaron could think of nothing to say. He just shook his head in dismay. They hugged again and he left.

Outside Tyrone's house, burning with anger at what had happened to his friend, Aaron decided to start digging into the case again. It wasn't much, but it was something he could do, for Tyrone and all the sick vets who had been sold down the river by their government.

Aaron found Earl that afternoon at his office in the Boulder County Justice Center. As one of the top cops in the S.O., his office had a view of the creek. It wasn't surprising, as Earl was an avid fly fisherman, but Aaron suspected that since he had been promoted to the head of the detective squad, he probably didn't get to stare at the water for any extended periods of time.

Most of the time these days he wore a white shirt and tie with a sport jacket. He was a big guy, about six-foot five, and weighed about 245. He was solid but not fat. Recently, he had grown a thick but well-trimmed mustache. It didn't look that good on him, but he doubted anyone had the guts to tell him so—nobody but Aaron.

"Earl, you got to shave that mustache," Aaron said. "It looks like a big, black woolly worm crawled up on your lip and died."

"Coming from such an excellent example of tonsorial self-art," he snorted, eyeballing Aaron's still-shaggy hair, "I should worry? Besides I'm cultivating a less threatening look, not so much a hard-ass cop." He paused. "I'm thinking about running for sheriff."

Aaron's surprise was so profound that what would have been a snort actually came out sounding more like a fart. "What, have you lost your mind? Why would you want to subject yourself to that?"

"Because I'd make a good sheriff," Earl said. "And I want to tell you it's a good thing you don't have sinus problems because if you did I'd probably be calling in a HazMat team to clean your brains off my desk."

Aaron shrugged, conceding the point. "Yeah, you probably would—make a good sheriff, I mean." Then, remembering where he'd been, he sagged like a blown-out tire.

"I just came from Tye's, Earl, and I feel like a world-class asshole. I knew nothing about it, while Tye had been lying there wasting away for years."

Earl said, "Tyrone had the attack after you left Jack Springs, but I didn't find out about it for awhile. When I did, I just didn't think you needed any more weight on your shoulders at that moment in time."

Aaron considered, nodded. "You were probably right. Anyway, I talked to the lawyer and told him I'm going back to work on the Gulf War vets' case and I'm going to recommend to Maya that Tye apply for status as a complainant in the lawsuit. Mahoney, the lawyer, said go ahead and try to find this guy, if he exists. But I don't have a clue about how to crack the wall at the university. There are so many intrigues going on already, an obvious outsider doesn't have a prayer."

Earl steepled his fingers and appeared to be considering something. "I might have somebody you can talk to. He's with the University Police, been there for 25 years, and he's a wealth of information about that place. This guy is gossip central. His name is Tom Delorio. He's kind of an odd duck but he's the guy who'll help you if he can. I'll give him a call."

"Thanks. Let me know what he says," Aaron said and got up. "I'll let you get back to your administrating, or polishing your political image, or whatever you do in this fine office." He walked to the door and paused. "Hey, let's go fishing one of these days…." Before Earl could speak, he continued, "cause I've got this new fly I'm dying to try out." Earl knitted his brows, always a sucker for a new pattern. "It's a big, black woolly bugger."

Earl casually reached for a thick law book that was setting on his desk, backhanded it and nailed the wall next to Aaron's head with a loud thud as he ducked through the door. Two of the detectives in the squad room were coming out of their seats and reaching for guns when Earl stepped into the doorway, laughing.

"And you might try calling the HazMat to get that thing off your lip," Aaron said. The detectives snapped their eyes back to their work, sat back down shaking their heads.

Earl closed the door. As Aaron walked past the detectives, he heard one say something about a "crazy motherfucker." He kept walking, unable to decide if it was an insult or faint praise.

Three hours later, Aaron was on patrol near the reservoir, checking out five dread-locked hippies with three dogs, two cats and two hamsters who were living in an old mail truck, when Earl raised him on the radio.

"The subject will meet you tomorrow at 11:30 in the open space parking off Baseline and Cherryvale," he said.

"Thanks," Aaron said. He walked back to the mail truck, handed the hippies their IDs. "Okay, you guys, just don't sleep in town in this truck and I don't think anybody will bother you."

"Thanks, dude," said an old, bald-headed hippie with a leather cowboy hat, muttonchop sideburns, a leather vest and plaid kilt. "You're okay—for a cop." Sniggers belched from inside the van.

Aaron looked over his shoulder, shook his head, reached in the Jeep and keyed the mike, "Belinda, I'm clear."

"OK," she said as the phone rang. Aaron keyed off the mike. As he was pulling the patrol car out, she was back on the radio. "Aaron, could you swing by the park? Some tourists called complaining that a dog grabbed their package of hot dogs and ran off."

"Sure, Belinda, can't think of anything I'd rather do; well…, maybe one or—" A screech blasted out of his radio, and Belinda was back on. "Sorry 'bout that, it must have been feedback, or *some-thing*."

"Yeah, right," he said to a dead radio, not knowing where that had come from or how he felt about attempting such a trite flirtation. He thought maybe the wise course was just to pretend it never happened, or if she mentioned it, to pretend she had misunderstood. The odd thing was that she picked up on it so quickly. Hmmm.

When he stopped in the office to get a cup of coffee, Belinda looked over at him and said, her voice abandoning her professional dispatcher delivery for Latina sing-song and a half-octave lower than normal, "You know how many people listen to our radio transmissions, *eh?* You say things like that, an *peo-ple* are going to be *talk-ing*." She tried to look cross but the wild lock of dark hair had worked loose and hung over her left eye, where she tried to blow it out of her vision.

He raised his palms to her in mock surrender, knowing any dissemblance was bound to fail. "OK, OK, I'll watch myself. But if you'd go out with me…"

"In your dreams, funny man," she said, picked up her book and ignored both him and the lock of hair. He decided against the coffee and was going to leave when Toby came in, smiling. He motioned for Aaron to follow him back to his work area.

"Man, you were right on. I caught Mona Jeter up and around, with no lingering effects of any heavy sedation. She even got in her car and went to the supermarket. I called down there today and got her sister. She tried to run that same bullshit by me and I told her I got Mona on film coming out of the market. So she tells me Mona 'just don't want to talk about it.' I said, 'Fine, I'll be sending a Grand Jury subpoena down.' Eeeiii, you shoulda heard the cuss words coming out of that telephone. But," he said, grinning, "I'm going to meet her in her lawyer's office tomorrow."

"She's lawyerin' up, huh? That's interesting. But, it's a start," Aaron said, "Any luck with the Free Riders?"

"Not yet. I've got the list of arrestees from that mess up in the valley, when they were having their protest. I'll run their sheets and see what kind of history we're looking at. If anything looks interesting, I'll try again and threaten them with the Grand Jury if they balk. If that doesn't work, I'll go to the DA and ask for subpoenas and let the Grand Jury have them."

"Sounds like you're rolling."

Toby nodded, hesitated and asked, "Say, if I go down to talk to some of these Free Riders, you want to tag along? They're pretty hostile and, well, it wouldn't do me any good to get into it with these guys. Having another officer there might make it go a little smoother."

"I could do that," Aaron said, feeling a tingle of excitement. "In fact, it sounds like fun."

Chapter 12

June 14

Late the next morning, the trailhead parking lot was nearly full when Aaron arrived, but he could see a white unmarked Crown Vic with discreet antennas, a spotlight, and a state tag, so he figured it must be Delorio. He eased the Subaru into a tight spot as Roscoe rose from the seat where he'd been sleeping. There were a half-dozen people standing in the lot with at least that many leashed dogs sniffing each other's butts or tugging to hit the trail. Roscoe whined to join in the fun. "Not this time," Aaron said. "This is business." Roscoe huffed and flopped back down. Aaron got out and walked over to the idling white car. The window slid down and the cop nodded. "You Hemingway?" he asked.

"Yeah," he said.

"Let's go for a walk," Delorio said, picked up his portable and got out. He was a fireplug of a man, a little red in the face with a sheen of perspiration, wearing slacks and a plaid sport shirt. He wore a substantial-looking belly pack, which probably held a gun, as none was visible. They walked along the creek.

Delorio spoke first. "Earl asked me to see you, so I'm not worried about doing so. And I remember that fiasco you got into up at the mine camp, so your bonafides are solid. Tell me about what you're doing that I might be able to help you with."

Aaron explained that it had nothing to do with the marshal's office; it was a private matter he had been working on before Harlan had hired him. Delorio nodded as if the information jibed with what Earl had told him.

"It's a class-action lawsuit against American companies and some individuals who sold equipment and technology to Iraq in the years before the war. Most of it was legal at the time. Years earlier Reagan had signed a secret memo relaxing the restrictions on exporting dual-use technologies to Iraq and Bush had guaranteed a $750-million line of credit for the purchases from U. S. companies. It was really the President generating some very lucrative business for his friends and campaign contributors—nothing particularly new in that.

"But the thing is that dual use," Aaron hesitated, "is probably easier to understand than explain. Say chemicals or equipment that can be used to manufacture pesticides can also be turned into nerve gas, which is, in fact the case. Prior to the new policy, that technology or material could not be sold to Iraq, which had been gassing Kurds and Iranians for five years. Then it was legal, based upon the assumption that Iraq would keep its promise and only manufacture pesticides.

Delorio sniggered. "I guess we know how well that worked. What is it, 50,000 Gulf War vets are saying they're sick?"

"Yeah," Aaron said. "About that. You believe them? The government says they're all psych cases, caused by stress."

Delorio looked at Aaron as if he were speaking in tongues. "And the government always tells the truth. Just like pigs can fly and pig shit don't stink."

"Since we seem to be on the same page, I'll cut to the chase. Tim Mahoney, one of the lawyers representing about 2,000 sick vets, asked me to track down a rumor that a microbiology professor at the university sold something, some biotech process to Iraq, got rich, and disappeared from campus. What I'm trying to find out is if it happened and who did it, so I can serve papers on the guy."

Delorio stopped and looked off across the field. About a hundred feet out, a red-tailed hawk sat in a tree watching a fox rooting in the tall grass beneath the tree for mice. He rubbed his hand on the back of his neck. "What's the time frame we're talking about here?"

"Probably '86 to '89," Aaron said.

Delorio watched the hawk and the fox a while longer, grimaced and said, "We had a big-shit microbiology professor—he wasn't one of ours; he was a visiting professor from Princeton—pull up stakes pretty fast in '87 right after a graduate student he had knocked up committed suicide. I don't know anything about any research he was working on. The issue never came up, anyway." Delorio pulled a folded white handkerchief from a rear pocket, mopped his face and neck. "I think the guy's name was Carrington, Trey Carrington. Yeah, I remember ol' Trey, when we checked into it, we found out the reason he was *visiting* from Princeton is that he had been pulling the same shit there, maybe gotten a little rough about it. He's from a prominent, wealthy Boston family so they used their influence and money to protect him. The last time, the victim's physical injuries and evidence precluded any denial. So they sent him to us. That's the kind of shit you learn to live with working for the university. Let's head back."

They did.

"Listen, Delorio, thanks for the help. Walking cold into that place trying to get information—well, for a guy like me—didn't seem like it was going to pan out."

He stopped, looked over and grinned. "Yeah, the CIA ain't got nothing on the university." He rubbed his neck again. "You know, there was a graduate student around back then. He was the ex-boyfriend of the girl who killed herself. He's an assistant professor now. I'll try to get his name and give you a call. I don't think I can get into the personnel records without an active investigation, though. You got a card?"

Aaron chuckled. "You mean like a business card? No. Just call me at the marshal's office. I work the swing shift."

"Okay, the Marshal's Office then. Keep me informed. I'll add it to my files."

When Aaron raised his eyebrows, Delorio said, "Hey, I work for the university. How do you think I survived the Sports Illustrated scandal?"

Aaron remembered the story. It was about all the crimes committed by football players at the university. One cop was quoted saying that all patrol cars were issued a copy of the football program to aid in the identification of criminal suspects. Needless to say, university officials were not happy with the quote, although it turned out to be true.

"That was you?" Aaron asked, breaking into a grin.

Delorio nodded, grinning as well.

"Those files of yours must have some good shit in them."

"That's a fairly safe assumption," Delorio said. "I told them if they fired me I was going to write a book."

That night, Toby was looking at a sheet on his desk, turning it one way and then the other. Aaron sat down.

"So, did wifey come clean?" Aaron asked.

"Well, yes and no. She said she had a headache that night, took something for the pain and went to bed early. She said Jeter hadn't come home before she fell asleep. Also, Wheat Ridge P.D. has had five calls at their house on domestics in the past two months, but she wouldn't press charges, claimed they were just arguing. There was no sign of violence so there wasn't much they could do."

"How about the sheets on the Free Riders who were arrested?" Aaron asked.

"Not much in there," Toby said. "For the badasses they come off to be, their criminal records are pretty clean. I've got one, though, Henry Drusky, that has a big blank space in it from 1970 to 1990. He'd entered the Air Force in 1969, got sent to Vietnam. Then he's gone. He's a scary-looking fucker, too."

Toby handed over the sheet he'd been looking at.

"Is this his current address?" Aaron asked.

"Yeah, Commerce City, about two blocks from the Rocky Mountain Arsenal."

"This is a guy we should definitely check out," Aaron said.

"I'll go down and watch his place for a couple of nights, then we can brace him," Toby said.

"Let me know when you're ready," Aaron said.

Toby nodded, "Will do."

Chapter 13

June 15

At 10:30 in the morning, there was a lull in business at the coffee shop on University Hill, which meant it was only three-fourths full. Nevertheless, it took Aaron only about five seconds to find Ted Fuller, who had said yesterday when he agreed to meet, "Look for the tall, skinny guy with glasses." Even slouched down, he was still a half-foot taller than anyone else in the shop---probably six-five, maybe 180 pounds, with thick, wire- rimmed glasses. He wore a scruffy sport coat, blue sport shirt and khakis.

Aaron walked across the room and stopped at his table. "Dr. Fuller?"

Fuller looked up. "Ted, just Ted if you don't mind."

Aaron nodded. "Ted, I'm Aaron Hemingway."

"Sit down and have a cup of tea. Somebody'll be by shortly to take your order," Fuller said. As Aaron settled into his seat, a cute blonde, with dreadlocks twisted into a knot on top of her head and a long India print top with no back whatsoever, stopped. "Can I get you something?"

"Sure, how about some tea?"

"Okaaay…" she waited. When nothing was forthcoming, she raised an unplucked eyebrow and asked, "Any particular kind?"

"How about some Lipton's?" Aaron asked.

"Uh, we don't have any Lipton tea," she said, brow furrowed, tapping her pad with the pen. "That's really a brand name, not a type of tea."

"Where I come from, Lipton's is the only kind of tea. You mean there's others?"

"How about I bring you some *black* tea?" she said, getting the joke.

Aaron noticed Fuller was not amused at their banter.

"Black tea sounds good," he said, and she left.

Fuller got right to it. "So, why the interest in *Professor* Carrington at this late date?" he asked, snarling the question.

"His name has come up as a possible respondent in a class-action lawsuit," Aaron said.

"What's the case?" Fuller asked. Aaron gave him the standard rundown of information about the Gulf War veterans, the lawsuit and dual-use technology and the rumor.

"And Carrington's connected to this?" Fuller asked.

"Not necessarily. It was just a rumor that somebody decided to follow up on," Aaron said. "I didn't even have a name until yesterday." He saw the dawning of recognition on Fuller's face. "So tell me about Carrington." Clouds of pain swept across Fuller's face as he considered the request. Finally, he sighed.

"Missy found out she was pregnant and told Carrington he would have to marry her. She wouldn't admit it but I always thought he had raped her. When she told him, he laughed. She overdosed on pills a few days later. By the time the story got sorted out, Carrington was gone. She was a Latter Day Saint, you know, Mormon. I was in love with her, but she just wanted me for a friend. I could live with that. I mean, she didn't have any boyfriends and we spent a lot of time together. Until she fell for Trey-fucking-Carrington." He looked to be on the verge of tears.

"Right before he disappeared, a computer I had the research for my dissertation on burned up. I lost most of it. I was suicidal myself for two years after that. Man, I came that…" he held his thumb and index finger about an inch apart "…fucking close."

"And you think the two things are linked?"

"I don't know. I always assumed he split to get away from the situation with Missy. But as far as I know, no one has seen or heard anything about him since."

"Could you tell me a little more about the research?"

"Oh yeah. You want the short version?"

"The short, simplified, Microbiology For Idiots version," Aaron told him.

"It was about how HIV builds its protein shield so that it can remain undetected for so long," Fuller said.

The answer hit Aaron like a jab to the solar plexus. "Are you familiar with aflatoxin?"

"I am," Fuller said. "It's nasty stuff, very nasty."

"Could you use this protein sheath to encapsulate it?"

"I guess you could…" he was saying when all the blood had drained from Fuller's face. "That bastard stole my research," he said. "And then he destroyed the computer it was stored in to cover up the theft.

"That bastard!" he said, pounding the table, "I'll kill him!"

Aaron stood and put a hand on his shoulder. Everyone in the coffee shop was staring.

"Easy, easy, you want to go someplace else?"

Then, as if Fuller realized what he had done, he slumped down and covered his pale face with his hands, put his elbows on the table. Finally, he took several deep breaths and straightened a little. "They' re finding encapsulated aflatoxin in some of the veterans?"

Aaron nodded. "Would you be willing to talk to the attorney who hired me?" Aaron asked, nearly bowled over by what and how much he had learned.

"I'll talk to him, but I'll go you one better. I can give you the DNA print for the sheathing. I went back and duplicated my research and wrote my doctoral dissertation about it. A paper will be published in a medical journal on it next year."

"How will the DNA print help?" Aaron asked.

"Because if it matches the DNA they're finding on these organisms in the vets' blood, it's better than a fingerprint. And Carrington knew all about it. He was supervising my research."

Well, well.

"So, no idea where Carrington is these days, huh?"

Fuller shook his head. "He got blacklisted after Missy killed herself… well, really after her parents threatened to sue the university." Another cloud swept behind Fuller's eyes. "They reached an out-of-court settlement with the university, and the whole thing was swept under the rug—as usual," he said, his voice a knife-edge of bitterness cutting through the air.

Aaron nodded with an effort at sympathy. He'd certainly helped Fuller dredge up a closet of old ghosts.

"So, Carrington's been out there eight or nine years. Any rumors about what he's been doing?"

Fuller waved a hand as if he were trying to shoo a pesky fly. "I don't know for sure, but I'll bet it has something to do with young women. That's the pathology for a sociopath: they never stop, voluntarily. He used to talk about a place his family had in Wyoming, probably an enclave for wealthy rapists." Fuller pushed his chair back, stood and walked away. But he stopped, turned and said, "I'll ask around and see what I can come up with."

If it could be proven that Carrington had done something to put Tye in the situation he was in…well, that was down the road.

Later that evening, Aaron was on patrol when Toby radioed him and asked when he was due for a break. It was still early and busy in town but nothing reported as criminal, so Aaron told him that now was as good a time as any.

Toby said he'd meet Aaron in the shopping center parking lot. "Give me ten."

"You got it," Aaron said. Toby pulled up in the other Cherokee nine minutes later, parked next to Aaron, got out and slid into Aaron's passenger seat.

"What's up?" Aaron asked.

"I been staking out Drusky's place, yesterday evening and most of today. He's in there but he doesn't do much. He went to the liquor store last night, right after I got there. He went back home and stayed there, at least until I left at two a.m. I'm going to go down tomorrow evening and question him."

"You like some company?"

"I'd appreciate it," Toby said. "I've already squared it with Harlan. He's going to finish your shift for you. Said it's time for him to get out and rub elbows with the unwashed masses."

"It'd do him some good," Aaron said.

"So we're good to go?"

"Rock and roll."

"Lock and load," Toby said.

Zuni, N.M.

While Aaron and Ted Fuller were having tea, Trey Carrington sat before the make-up mirror and meticulously brushed and trimmed the fuzzy mat of hair—so thick the canal was entirely covered—in his left ear. It was painstaking work. He realized he probably could let the hair grow into a wild thatch and it would have the same effect, but that just wasn't his way of doing things. He supposed he was a bit obsessive, but then, he was a detail-oriented guy.

He angled the mirror so he could see his right ear and went to work.

From time to time, he'd let his gaze wander through the smoky window of the Paradiso motor coach and linger on the grad students working the dig—in truth imagining the young women's bodies beneath the baggy clothes meant to keep them cool in the sometimes blistering heat, which didn't completely hide their physical attributes.

The redhead, however, wore cut-off jeans and a sleeveless v-necked T-shirt, as if the sun and heat didn't bother her a bit. Of course, she used loads of sunscreen; kept a bottle in her back pocket. Even through the tinted glass, he could see the reddish tinge of her heavily freckled arms and throat and chest. Her head was covered with a blue bandanna, leaving just wispy curls dangling down her neck.

After a few days of her presence, he had decided: Yes, indeed, she's the one. He felt himself stir at the thought. After the debacle in Albuquerque, he decided to fall back into his old ways. He didn't really understand what had gotten into him that night. But he had always known the importance of patience and planning—and the resultant sense of heightened anticipation—so here he was back in his comfort zone.

Having finished with the right ear, he moved down to the hairs sprouting from his nose, pruning the long ones or the occasional unruly gray one. When he finished he would go outside and circulate, imparting kernels of wisdom and approval to keep morale high. Maybe a little pat on the shoulder for the redhead, just to keep things loose, followed by a word of caution about sunburn and dehydration. Of course, he hoped she wouldn't change into less revealing clothes, but he thought it was important that she feel he was looking out for her best interests.

After snipping and brushing, Carrington turned his head and admired the look he had cultivated since his college days at Princeton when a beautiful young lass remarked that the hair sprouting from their biology professor's nose and ears was sexy. The professor, while a relatively young man, did not cultivate the look like Carrington had. He was simply a charismatic field researcher who was too caught up in his work to be concerned with such things. Or at least that was the attitude he projected. Which didn't stop Carrington from adopting the old khakis and scuffed boots and floppy hats the professor wore. And finally, when age allowed, the elfin nose and ear hair.

The overall effect did seem irresistible to some of the pretty young students. And the rest never said anything about it, at least within his hearing. After all, he controlled them when they were on the dig. A bad word from him and they thought their futures would be down the drain.

What they didn't know was that Carrington also set up the foundation that funded their participation on the dig, as a way to corral fresh blood for his conquests; that his opinions in the world of archeology were worse than worthless. They were scorned. Nevertheless, the ploy often worked. If it didn't, he would hide his disappointment and wait for the next group. Even when it worked, though, the experience had paled. It was amusement—no more.

Since that night in Albuquerque, he wanted to temper his darker urges.

Now he was wise enough to know that if he kept his cool there would always be another, somewhere not too far down the road. When the next thing came along, well, he would know it when he saw it. It was out there, waiting for him. Of that he was sure.

He trimmed the last few unruly nose hairs and stopped to admire himself, thinking again that he looked like a younger Robert Redford—ruddy complexion, cleft chin and thick, sandy hair. Yeah, not bad, not bad at all. He smiled.

From the side, however, the self-satisfied smile looked like the desiccated grin of a gut-shot coyote.

Chapter 14

June 16

Henry Drusky sat at the chipped Formica kitchen table in the dingy Commerce City cinderblock house, walking a Tarot card over and over around his long fingers.

His hair was thick and oily, combed straight back from his broad forehead. It was well-trimmed in the back and around the ears. His face was clean-shaven, with bushy eyebrows overhanging hard, brown eyes. He wore a workingman's outfit—gray cotton work pants and shirt and steel-toed, black work shoes, not much different from about every other adult male living in Commerce City—which of course was the whole idea.

The house, two blocks from the Rocky Mountain Arsenal, one of the most polluted spots on the planet, was painted mustard yellow, set back from the street with a lot of untrimmed juniper bushes around the windows and doors. About half the population of Commerce City was transient, and the remainder had lived in the same house for a lifetime. The mix almost assured that people living there minded their own business.

Drusky had been sitting in the house for two hours without lights, television or radio to bother the gloomy silence as he executed the card trick he had learned in Vietnam 25 years earlier. With the fading glow of the evening sky, there was just enough light to see but not be seen. Just the way he liked it.

With his free hand, he shook two flat blue tablets from the brown plastic pill bottle, pinched them between his thumb and forefinger and placed them in his mouth. He chewed them for a few seconds, until the taste hit the back of his throat. Then, before he gagged, he washed them down with a shot of Smirnoff's finest from a glass that was almost opaque with oily fingerprints and hard-water stain. He sighed, knowing the actual relief was minutes away but imagining the warmth that would spread from his groin up his backbone, finally flowering in his chest and brain and wrapping a warm, soft blanket around the pain in his bowels.

Drusky knew he had to start treatments within the week if he had a chance, also that it might already be too late. But these corporate faggots were still stalling on his money and the fucking doctor wanted money up front, since Drusky had no insurance.

Not that any insurance company in the world would give him a policy after what his body had been through for the past 25 years: gassed with Agent Orange, shot, stabbed, and gang-raped in a Colombian prison, among many other desecrations. If there was any consolation in it, he'd wreaked much more havoc than he'd suffered. But that consolation had worn thin years ago.

Drusky knew they were stalling on delivering the cash but didn't know why or at least wasn't sure. None of the possibilities were good, though. Time was running out. He knew it was close to the time to play his hole card.

As he considered this, he heard a vehicle coming up the drive and reached for the 10-mm Glock lying on the table beneath a copy of the Rocky Mountain News.

When the automatic garage door started up, he relaxed, knowing only two people had a remote opener for it. He pulled his hand out from beneath the newspaper and started rolling the card again.

The door to the garage opened and a man wearing jeans, cowboy boots, a blue T-shirt and a light jacket snapped on the light and walked into the room. His name was Karl Hoest, and he was carrying a scuffed but solid-looking briefcase. A flicker of hope bloomed in Drusky's breast, but he had no intention of letting down his guard.

"You got my money?" Drusky asked.

The man's face darkened beneath the blond crew cut and the piggy nose. He set the briefcase on the table, pulled out one of the kitchen chairs and straddled it.

"I got your money, Henry. I told you I would." Hoest started to unsnap the briefcase but Drusky said, "Stop. Turn it this way so I can see inside when you open it."

"Goddamn, you're touchy today," he said, and turned the briefcase so that it would open toward Drusky.

"No, not touchy," Henry Drusky said. "Tired is what I am. And sick of being jacked around by these clients of yours. Or maybe just you." He knew that Hoest worked for a security outfit that "managed" crises for corporations and other entities and sometimes employed the skills of mercenaries like himself.

"You going to open it?" Hoest asked, his brow furrowed.

"No, you open it," Drusky said.

Hoest wagged his head like he was losing patience, reached over, unsnapped the latch and raised the lid. Inside were packs of crisp hundred-dollar bills. At the same time, Hoest, thinking the lid to the case would shield his move, dropped his other hand and pulled a small, chrome, semi-automatic .380 from his jacket pocket. Drusky saw the move, flicked the Tarot card toward Hoest's eyes, and knocked the newspaper off the Glock.

Hoest flinched but brought the small pistol up at the same time Drusky reached the Glock. At that point it was a draw but Hoest's hand was still moving when he fired the .380 into Drusky's left shoulder. Drusky, seasoned warrior that he was, fired while the gun was still almost flat against the table and shot through the briefcase lid. The .380 barely shocked Drusky, but the 10-mm slug, exponentially heavier and faster than the .380, took Hoest through the lower spine and sprayed blood, tissue and bone against the cabinet and wall across the room. His body doubled like a puppet with the strings suddenly cut and tumbled back against the cabinet.

Drusky looked at Hoest, grunted, and set the gun down. He ripped the shirt open and off his shoulder, then inspected the damage. The adrenaline had shotgunned the fentanyl/vodka cocktail into his brain, and the pain seemed like a faint abstraction. But a sense of extreme weariness, as if he had yet to take the first step up a mountain he knew he couldn't climb, pressed upon his body. Just then, someone pounded hard on the door. Drusky heard the shouted word "police" float through the mist surrounding his brain.

Nearly two weeks into the job and Aaron had been, since getting off the graveyard shift, feeling infused with a peculiar energy. No one thing stood out as being responsible, but today the feeling was particularly acute. He thought it was likely because he was getting into the puzzle-solving side of the job. Toby liked the street, but Aaron liked the cerebral—liked figuring shit out.

So he was psyched about the chance to brace someone whose past suggested he might know something to help figure out the puzzle of who decapitated Paul Jeter, that once-shining star of American manhood in the radical, anti-government galaxy.

Toby, in full uniform, was waiting in front of the office in the Crown Vic when Aaron pulled up. Two minutes later, they were headed to Commerce City. Aaron could barely keep from tapping his foot on the floorboard as adrenaline stoked his leg muscles. Toby, however, was somewhat subdued, or at least seemed that way to Aaron.

On the way down the canyon, they talked about the job, how each of them got into it, and where they came from. Toby surprised Aaron by telling him that, while he was born on the Jicarilla Apache reservation in New Mexico, his father was Pawnee. "I just tell people I'm Jicarilla because it's easier to explain," he said. "There's still a lot of bias among the tribes, which is kind of strange. An awful lot of Indians today have parents from different tribes."

He related that law enforcement on the reservation was pretty boring, that DUIs and domestic disturbances took up most of an officer's time. Of course, there were the fights and petty thefts.

But he said the main reason he left was that he was tired of pulling dead kids' bodies out of car wrecks. A year with the New Mexico State Police didn't change that situation very much.

Aaron reminded Toby why he'd left the Denver P.D.: He'd been working undercover narcotics and got strung out, first on speed, then on heroin. At the time, he'd been in the middle of a nasty divorce and one day he snapped, walked into his wife's lawyer's office and shot the place up. Earl had referred to the "incident" as every cop's wet dream, right before he'd told him no charges would be filed if he resigned immediately. Which Aaron did, but not gladly. Facing the possibility of charges on top of the nasty divorce and custody battles, all the fight had gone out of him. Following that, Aaron and Roscoe traveled the West, hopping from bar to bar. When he sobered up, he found himself working as a reporter at the local weekly newspaper. He loved the job but it, too, ended in a hail of bullets at the mining camp where he found Cassie and her abductor.

For a few moments as they drove south on the Boulder turnpike Toby was quiet, but he kept glancing quickly at Aaron and then back to the road, as if he were nervous about something. Aaron decided to ignore it for now, expecting Toby would tell him what was going on when he was ready. He was right.

Finally, after a deep exhale, Toby said, "I been meaning to ask you, and you can tell me if it's none of my business, but did seeing Wiley Agnew die that way when I took him out fuck you up? I mean, it was long distance for me and it was what I was trained for in the New Mexico State Police. You know, it was unreal, almost like a video game. But you were right there, man. That was the first and last guy I ever killed. And it kind of got me down for a while. I had counseling and it helped. I think. But, man, you were in the room. Is that why you left town?"

Aaron stared at the highway and the traffic while he considered. "I don't know if I can explain exactly why I took off, but I can definitely tell you that watching Wiley die was never even a consideration. He was seconds away from killing me and maybe even my daughter when you shot him. I've never been anything but grateful, as I mentioned a few days ago. The only nightmares I've had about it was that you might have missed."

Toby nodded hesitantly, as if being reassured. But Aaron could tell there was more.

"Have you ever killed anyone?"

Aaron tried to think how to answer. He didn't want to lie. Toby deserved better than that. And he didn't want to dismiss the question for the same reason. But neither did he want to get into a discussion. He'd never talked about serving in Nam to anyone. The things he'd seen, the things he'd done. Maybe that was part of his problem. Almost certainly it was. But there was just no way, now, to make the leap. Too much scar tissue. Too many fresh wounds.

"Not with the cops but, you know, I was in the infantry in Vietnam," Aaron said, leaving it at that.

Toby turned and looked, his eyes wide. "I didn't know."

"I don't, uh, say much about it."

"Ah, I shouldn't have... I'm sor—"

Aaron raised his palm. "Hey, it's okay. I understand. The thing is that if you're a normal human being, you never get over killing someone, completely. But if it was a righteous shoot, you learn to live with it. And *taking Wiley out* was a righteous shoot."

Toby nodded, hearing what he needed to hear. That was okay with Aaron, it just kind of slipped out. They drove the rest of the way in silence. But for the first time ever, Aaron realized he was tempted to tell someone—or in any case Toby—about the atrocity/ambush, which is how he thought of it.

His silence about what had happened in Vietnam was not necessarily the result of some macho military code. The truth was that after he awoke in the hospital on board ship after the attack, he couldn't remember anything clearly. The AK-47 slug had nicked a rib and taken a chunk out of his side. He was under heavy painkillers for weeks, which further twisted his hold on reality.

And nobody official had *ever* debriefed him about the attack. As far as the Army was concerned, *nothing* happened. When he finally got his shit together enough to start asking questions, he was told he was the only survivor in the Vietcong ambush. But his nightmares and eventually his memories told a different story.

Consequently, as he healed physically, his psychological state disintegrated. Finally, he was able to track down a captain in his company whom he had gotten along with and learned that his squad was lured into attacking the village and was subsequently ambushed by the VC. The toll of civilians dead was 53, U.S. soldiers eight, VC one—nothing compared to My Lai's 400-plus civilians but certainly nothing the Army wanted to come out; a double embarrassment at that. And the Army's solution was to keep Aaron quiet, which wasn't all that hard to do. What the hell was he going to say about it? I took part in a war crime? I shot down a young girl and an old woman? And once I realized, I tried to stop it? Riiiight!

Still, it took years for the whole picture to come out in his mind. And by that time, he noticed that an inordinate number of people around him—family, friends and colleagues—had had bad things happen to them.

Somehow, in his twisted brain, he came to believe he was cursed. Or the people around him were. Or something.

The longer he went without telling anyone, the more impossible ever owning up to it seemed to be.

Fifty minutes after leaving Jack Springs, they pulled up in front of a smudge-yellow house with an attached two-car garage in Commerce City. It was a warm night and both windows were down. As Toby turned the engine off, the muffled explosion of a powerful gunshot from inside the house pierced the air.

Toby and Aaron looked at each other. "Aw shit," Toby said, eyes wide. He picked up the mike, got Boulder Communications and asked the dispatcher to call Commerce City P.D. to report a gunshot inside the house at 6440 East Seminole St. and to ask for backup. A weak light was on inside the house, but no one appeared in the windows, although they were hard to see through the bushes.

Toby opened his door and started to slide out. Aaron's gut clinched and he grabbed Toby's arm. "We should wait," he said.

Neighbors, hearing the shot and seeing the police car in front of the house, started coming outside.

Goddamnit," Aaron said. Feeling the need to do something, he let Toby's arm go and got out, waving the neighbors back inside.

Toby and Aaron were looking at each other across the roof of the car. Aaron said, "We've got vests?"

"In the trunk." He popped the trunk and both crouched behind the upraised trunk lid. They slipped into the vests and velcroed each other in.

"Somebody might be dying in there," Toby said.

Aaron's eyes shifted anxiously to the closed door and the dark windows. "I go first."Toby started to argue but saw the look on Aaron's face, nodded, slipped the pack set into his belt, pulled the .45 Colt

Commander from his holster and racked a cartridge into the chamber. Aaron pulled his .357 and looked at the house. The front door opened on the right.

"We'll X it," Toby said, referring to the method of entry.

Aaron felt his butthole pucker, thinking: Don't freeze. Do not fucking freeze. You can't let anything happen to him. He felt the probing of Toby's dark eyes and snapped out of it. "You kick, I'll go left-to-right, low."

Toby nodded. He would knock, then kick the door open if no one responded. Aaron would go in and Toby would follow and cover the blind side of the room. Most often, the first guy in took the hit.

"Let's go," Toby said, his eyes jumping with excitement. Whatever had been bothering him earlier was forgotten in the heat of the moment. They ran in a crouch, with their guns trained on the windows. When they got to the house, they flattened against the cinder-block walls on each side of the door. Toby flipped the screen door open and Aaron pinned it against the house with his body. Toby pounded on the door.

"POLICE!" he shouted. "COME OUT WITH YOUR HANDS WHERE WE CAN SEE THEM!" Sirens wailed in the distance.

"POLICE!" Toby shouted again. "COME OUT WITH YOUR HANDS IN PLAIN SIGHT!" There was no response. Toby looked at Aaron and nodded. He tried the handle; it was locked. Toby stepped out and kicked the door. The frame splintered. He kicked again and the door sprang open. Aaron stepped through, crouching, and saw the chrome snout of a gun barrel dead center on his face. His gun was a little too low, so he screamed, GUN!" and rolled to his right. Before he could aim, the man holding the gun stuck the barrel up under his chin and pulled the trigger. His body jerked as if he were trying to stand while the top of his head erupted in a fountain of viscous red/gray froth and splintered bone. His body collapsed back onto the edge of the chair, then tumbled sideways to the floor.

"Well, fuck me," Toby said, his voice hoarse, crouched in the doorway with his gun up. They could hear tires screeching in the street outside. With Drusky's body twitching, they moved to get a better look and snapped their eyes on another body, against the wall. "This is not good," he said.

"It could be worse," Aaron said, putting his hand on Toby's shoulder. "We might have shot someone, or one or both of us could be dead. It could be *way* worse." Or you could be dead and I'd be alive, he thought. By the time he'd finished speaking, his voice was quivering.

"STEP OUT OF THE HOUSE WITH YOUR HANDS IN THE AIR!" came a sharp voice over the loudspeaker. Toby looked to the street and at Aaron. "We need to get out there, give me your gun. I'm going to put them on the table and step out. You need to follow pretty quick."

Aaron said, "I don't suppose you made a courtesy call to the Commerce City cops telling them we'd be doing this.

Toby shrugged, a little sheepish, said, "Ah, that would be a negative," and stepped into the doorway, hands empty. Aaron followed. Three patrol cars were in the street and officers crouched behind them with a variety of weapons leveled across the hoods and trunks.

"Call an ambulance," Toby shouted. They stepped outside, arms raised. "We've got two down, although I doubt if the paramedics are going to do much good."

"Both of you, on the ground. NOW!" came a voice from the street. Aaron and Toby complied, stretched out with hands extended. Slowly, the officers began emerging from behind their cars. A young cop, stocky, with a shaved head, said, "Cover them, Ernie. Frank and I'll check the house."

As much as Aaron knew it was necessary, it still pissed him off to be put in this position. He also knew there was nothing he could do about it so he lay there, tasting the sulfur in his mouth.

A few minutes later, the cop in charge walked up to them and said, "Names." When they told him, he looked at a small notebook he held and said, "Okay, get up." His name tag said P. Garrett.

"The Jack Springs Marshal's Office? So who are you two, Wyatt Earp and Doc Holiday?" he asked. "And tell me this isn't the OK Corral."

"This isn't the OK Corral," Toby said. "We heard a shot as we pulled up. When we went in, the guy we were coming to talk to shot himself in the head."

"This guy a suspect in a case you're working on?" P. Garrett asked.

"He wasn't, yet," Toby said. "But I think he just made the top of the list. The other guy in there was already dead."

Garrett offered to shake hands. After they did, he said, "Call me Pat."

Four hours later, Aaron and Toby emerged from the Commerce City police station into the warm night air and acrid odor from the gasoline refineries south of the interstate highway. The mercury streetlights reflected off the refinery haze and made the sky look like bruised egg yolks.

Even though their guns hadn't been fired, they'd been subjected to the drill—statements, interrogations, paraffin tests. Harlan, who had been on patrol for Aaron, had been called and allowed to sit in on the proceedings. Aaron and Toby emerged smelling better than the Commerce City air, which wasn't saying a lot.

The worst of it was Harlan; Aaron had never seen him so angry. He chewed their asses over not waiting for backup. After he settled down, he told them to take the next day off while things shook down.

Just before they were cut loose, Garrett had filled them in. The crime-scene techs had found some pieces of wire that resembled piano wire. They were also told there were no wants, or warrants on the other dead guy in Drusky's house. The little .380 had his prints on it and the slug in Drusky's shoulder was a match. The techs had dug a 10 mm slug out of the wall behind where the other guy's body had fallen. The briefcase had $5,000 on top of a bunch of office paper so that it looked like it was full of money. Garrett said he figured a rip-off was coming down, although who was ripping off whom wasn't clear.

There was some discussion about jurisdiction, since it appeared that somebody was being paid off, and it might have been for Jeter's murder. The decision was put off until the DA's offices in the respective counties could be consulted.

"This shit is getting way too deep for me," Toby said. "I'm gonna call Earl and see if the S.O. will take this over now."

"Well, that's your decision," Aaron said. "No one can say you didn't make some progress on the case. The S.O. does have better resources for the kind of investigation this is turning into. Or maybe Adams County will take it."

Toby looked up at the sky, fanned a hand in front of his face. "How can people live in this shit?"

"This is the good stuff, just your standard power plant and gasoline refinery toxins," Aaron said. "About a half mile east of here, they got whole lake beds and injection wells full of old pesticides and nerve gas, shit like that. You get an easterly wind, imagine what it would smell like. Don't even *think* about the groundwater."

"No thanks," Toby said, a visible tremor passing through his body. "Let's get the fuck out of here."

Chapter 15

June 17

Dawn broke clear and cool on the mountain but the sun's bright rays were peeking over the ridge behind his cabin, promising to make short work of the chill. Roscoe was curled up on the Hudson Bay blanket he'd slept on for six years. As Aaron began the process of getting his legs in position to sit up, Roscoe rose and walked stiffly to the bedside. Before Aaron could react, he lashed the blotched purple tongue across Aaron's ear, depositing a good bit of drool.

Aaron wrenched away, "Goddamnit, dog!" Roscoe bolted for the door, butting the screen door open with his head, and ran outside. Aaron staggered up and found a piece of paper towel to swab out his ear. When he thought about what had just happened, he almost laughed at the ludicrousness of the scene, made more so because Roscoe wasn't normally much of a licker—except for one notable recent occasion. Where that had come from was a mystery. Maybe he was trying to comfort Aaron, who still had the scent of death on him.

He walked to the window looking onto the meadow and saw Roscoe sitting in the tall grass, his eyes bright and wagging his miserable excuse for a tail. He was watching the cabin door, probably wanted Aaron to burst from the door and chase him around the meadow. Aaron shook his head in appreciation for his friend. But he wasn't ready to run anywhere. Sitting most of the night in the Commerce City police station and having a couple of slugs of whiskey when he got home had seen to that.

He brewed a pot of coffee. When it was done, he mainlined the first cup and went to the fridge, where he got milk for his Shredded Wheat, the only conventional breakfast food he could stand besides two eggs over easy, hash browns and toast.

As he finished up, he carried the bowl to the window. Roscoe was lying on his side in the grass, apparently having given up on Aaron coming out to play. He ran the spoon across the bowl's metal surface, and one of Roscoe's pathetic ears flicked into an upright position. Aaron waited until the ear was back against Roscoe's curly crown, then did it again. This time the ear came up and Roscoe's body stiffened. Aaron felt bad for teasing him so he sat the bowl and spoon on the floor with a clank. Roscoe was up and running for the cabin. It was an old trick and worked every time. When Roscoe came inside, he held the bowl between his paws and licked it clean beyond any possible residue of milk and sugar that might have remained. He had flicked the spoon a good three feet away on his second lick. He spied the spoon, stepped gingerly over to it and sniffed. He gave it a lick for good measure, then returned to his blanket.

Only then did Aaron flash to the scene last night when he and Toby busted into the house and saw the guy blow his brains out. He shook it off, went to the stereo and pulled out the *Best of Keith Whitley* tape, slid it into the tinny boombox and pushed the button. For the next hour, Aaron puttered around the cabin, singing along with Keith—who was telling his lover not to close her eyes when they made love—while he swept, washed the breakfast dishes, and picked up until there was nothing left to do.

The sun was high and burning the dew off the wildflowers and grasses in the meadow, so Aaron went out and sat on the step, looked up at his mountain as if for the first time. It had been too long since he had been still enough to see the place he lived in the way he used to before.... For two years now, it had been his bunker—a refuge where he could withdraw into his own particular hell, unassailed by the world around him. But today, the sky was deep blue, unfouled by the pollution from down in the flatlands. Tiny prisms of color shone from the grass where the sunlight struck the dew. The ponderosa pine needles looked like gold tinsel as they swayed in the soft breeze. Three slabs of the Devil's backbone sat astride the steep hills that rose above the cabin. A large raven swept through the sky, scrawing dementedly. Aaron smiled, took a deep breath and inhaled the sweetness in the air. Yet, he shivered, thinking how close he had come to checking out just a short time ago. He could feel that chasm, yawning, from time to time, calling to him, calling him back. But so far the nightmare had not returned. And that was enough, for now.

He went back inside the cabin, but with nothing to do, he started feeling a little restless, so he decided to go to the office, hang out a little and see which way the winds were blowing.

As he stood in the doorway to leave, he slapped his thigh and Roscoe almost knocked him over trying to get past. Outside, Roscoe rumbaed around like he was having a fit.

"Let's go to town," Aaron said and Roscoe bolted down the path like a runaway locomotive.

As he walked into the Jack Springs Marshal's Office, Belinda was at the counter, giving someone directions into the phone. When she saw him, her eyes narrowed and a deep furrow creased down to the bridge of her nose. Puzzled, Aaron just said, "Hey."

Belinda snorted and turned away, the unruly strand of hair came from behind her ear and fell across her face. She swiped it angrily back into place and hung up the phone with a sharp thud. Aaron shrugged and walked to Harlan's office, where he sat behind his desk, granny-size glasses perched on his nose over the Denver newspaper, looking as contented as the Buddha. Harlan waved him in, took off the glasses and closed the newspaper. He reached for a can of Skoal, slapped it against the palm of his free hand, opened it and took a small pinch, which he deftly placed behind his lower lip.

Aaron lowered himself into the chair across from Harlan's desk. "What's wrong with Belinda?"

"She's a woman, Aaron, just in case you haven't noticed. Women don't need a reason to act that way, although I'm sure she believes she's got one. She hasn't elected to share it with me in any case."

"Well, you don't seem afflicted with the same problem, whatever it is," he said.

Harlan sighed mightily, held up four stubby fingers and said, "Let's see, I've got two deputies with a death wish," he ticked one off and folded it into his palm, "high blood pressure," he ticked off another, "bad eyesight," one finger left, "but there's one problem I no longer have."

Aaron's first thought was uh-oh, Harlan's been fired. Couldn't be that, though: he was in too good a mood. "And that is…?"

"I'm no longer constipated," Harlan said, grinning and wiggling that finger back and forth.

"Well that's damn good to know, Harlan."

Harlan shrugged his shoulders and spread palms in supplication. "You asked."

"I did, at that," Aaron said, a chuckle working its way up from his belly.

A look of forced patience spread across Harlan's face. "If you are ever so afflicted, you won't think it's so funny."

Now, Aaron appreciated a good dump as much as the next guy, but his campfire coffee usually assured his regularity. "So, how did this miracle cure come about?"

"My dear wife of 35 years found this concoction at the health food store," Harlan said, shuddering and grimacing. "You mix it with water and drink it down real quick. If you don't drink it fast enough, it gets like three-day-old oatmeal, without the flavor." He appeared to be thinking about something else and the smile returned. "Can't argue with the results, though. Say, I thought I told you to take the day off."

"I'm not working. I just stopped by to shoot the shit—no pun intended. Any newspapers pick up the story?"

"The Post got the basics, a suspected murder/suicide in Commerce City. That's all the Commerce City police released, though I don't expect much interest when the details come out. That murder down in Boulder is getting all the media attention—not that I mind one little bit."

Harlan's aversion to the media was legendary. When cornered by a reporter, he would sweat and stammer, coming off like a country bumpkin, although he was anything but. The only newspaper he ever liked was the Mountain Miner, where Aaron had worked. But it had been bought out by the newspaper in Black Hawk, which rarely even sent a reporter to Jack Springs since the merger. After all, the big money was in Black Hawk, hundreds of millions of dollars in the casinos.

"Anything on follow-up investigation?" Aaron asked.

"The Boulder and Adams county DAs are meeting this morning, although I get the impression they like the scenario that these two yahoos conspired to murder Jeter. It makes things nice and tidy."

Aaron understood the tendency to clear cases like this—the suspects are dead so there are nobody's rights to worry about, no need for an expensive trial, no black marks for the cops or prosecutors for fucking up the case. He just hoped somebody in the investigating agencies would take enough of a look to be sure the dead suspects were the only ones responsible, which seemed a little far-fetched. Not that there was much he could do. He'd just have to watch and wait.

Harlan cleared his throat and interrupted Aaron's ruminations. "About last night, are you OK?"

"I'm fine."

Harlan said. "If you start having problems, let me know. As long as you're okay, I want you to work tomorrow, then take Sunday and Monday off."

When he walked past the dispatcher's console, Belinda never looked up from the book she was reading, but he thought he could see a snarl forming on her lips so he walked a little faster and got the hell out of there.

Damn women, anyway.

Chapter 16

June 22

Five days of absolute and unrelenting boredom later, Aaron's shift ended. After the bizarre murder and its apparent resolution, it was almost as if the good folk of Jack Springs had subconsciously colluded to claim the title of peaceful mountain hamlet.

He would have welcomed a little action to relieve the boredom and as a distraction from this *thing* with Belinda. To make his mood even darker, the Front Range was in a heat wave that left even the normally cool mountain town feeling scorched. Hell, here it was midnight and the thermometer on the tourist information kiosk across from the office read 80 degrees. The weather had been hot enough that Roscoe had refused to leave the cool shade beneath the cabin.

To add insult to injury, the Miller moth invasion was so bad you had to use a snow scraper to get the guts off the windshield before you could wash it. They rattled the windows, swarmed the streetlights and batted people in the eyes.

It was a virtual prescription for mayhem, yet the town remained eerily calm.

While never particularly superstitious, Aaron had begun to feel a growing sense of dread. In his experience, the lack of trouble for an extended period of time portended something particularly shitty was barreling down the mountain like a logging truck with smoking brakes.

Pulling up to the office at the end of his shift, Aaron saw Toby for the first time since the night of the shooting. He lifted a briefcase out of the cruiser, stopped and waited on the sidewalk as Aaron parked the Cherokee and retrieved the PAC radio and shotgun. Even in the weak street light, he could see that Toby looked exhausted.

"Hey," Aaron said.

"Hey," Toby acknowledged, nodding.

"How's the investigation going?"

Toby stepped over and sat on the cruiser's hood. Up close, he looked like more was bothering him than exhaustion. "Let's talk out here," he said. "Belinda's been acting kind of strange. Hardly gives me the time of day."

"You get the time of day?" Aaron asked, wrinkling his forehead.

Toby shrugged, too tired to reply. "We got the background on Drusky and Hoest, after the FBI stepped in and threw their weight around. Turns out that Drusky had been a contractor for various unnamed government 'agencies' until about 10 years ago, and then did a spell as mercenary. His autopsy revealed that he had been tortured and raped at some point in the past, and that he had colon cancer at the time of his death. The FBI said he'd been imprisoned in Columbia for two years during his mercenary period. They couldn't or wouldn't say what he'd been put in prison for.

"Karl Hoest was thought to have hired Drusky to infiltrate the Free Riders. There's no information on how they hooked up."

Toby yawned so hard his jaws popped, but he went on. "Hoest had been a cop and private investigator before he became a corporate fixer. This time around, he'd been hired by an off-road-vehicle industry group to quiet Jeter. Apparently, the bad publicity caused by Jeter had become a major embarrassment to the industry group, which is preparing a big push to open more public lands to off-road vehicles. They're lawyering up and will be meeting with the task force to give an official statement tomorrow.

"With Drusky and Hoest dead, there's no way to figure out how the murder plan had been hatched." He yawned mightily.

"Oh yeah, the wire found in Drusky's home was piano wire but not the same type used to murder Jeter. In fact, there was no physical evidence linking Drusky to Jeter's murder."

The news unsettled Aaron. Before he could say anything, Toby said, "Listen, Aaron, could you take the briefcase inside and set it on my desk. I've got to get home and get some sleep."

Uh-huh, Aaron thought, and that way you could avoid Belinda, you chicken. "Sure, get some sleep. I've got to take my equipment inside anyway." He'd already decided to confront her and had been steeling himself for the ordeal. He stuck the PAC set into the holder on his belt and picked up the briefcase. When he entered, Belinda was sitting behind the communication desk with her chin resting in her hand, reading something he couldn't see. Her hair was pulled severely into a bun, highlighting her high cheekbones. Her dark eyes flicked up then back down to the book. So, it was going to be the ol' silent treatment.

Instead of shuffling past, he stopped in front of the desk, and thudded the butt of the shotgun into the floor. She looked up slowly, as if she was considering coming across the desk and slapping him silly.

She slowly raised her head and performed an eye roll, which, if eye-rolling were an Olympic sport, would have been 10s across the board. "Yes?" letting the "s" linger on her tongue like the hissing of a viper.

He screwed up his courage and said, "Okay, goddamnit, I've had enough. Are you going to tell me why you're pissed?"

"Who says I am?" her voice rising in pitch while her brows arched innocently.

"Oh, that's a *good* one. You haven't said a civil word to me since last week. You look at me like you want to cut my balls off with a rusty knife. If you're not mad at me, maybe we better call a priest to perform an exorcism."

Her face relaxed and she appeared to be picturing something pleasant. Then she surprised him by smiling sweetly. "Just one, and not with a rusty knife."

"What?" Then he realized what she was saying. "Oh, I get it. What the fuck did I *do?*"

The smile was gone and she slapped her hand hard on the desk top, the sound like the clap of a gunshot. "Well, if somebody did that, maybe it would lower your testosterone to the point you would be smart enough *not* to crash into a house like you did without any backup!"

A lopsided grin twisted Aaron's face to the side. "You were worried about me?"

"How could I be *worried*? It was over before I heard about it. I just don't like to be around stupid people, and you, Mr. Hillbilly Hemingway, are *muy estupido*."

Aaron raised his hands in a peace gesture. "All right, all right, I admit it was stupid. If I promise not to do it again, can we at least be civil to each other?"

Her lips tightened. "Maybe, maybe not, we'll see." She dropped her eyes back to the paperback book. Aaron picked up the PAC set and shotgun and was walking to the equipment locker when he heard her say, "'Cause if you do it again, I might just kill you myself."

Aaron almost laughed but managed to restrain himself. Instead he smiled but kept his back to her so she couldn't see.

Sheeiit, she likes me, he thought.

Zuni, N.M.

Trey Carrington was footsteps away from inviting Fiona Donnegan to go to Gallup with him for dinner when his mobile phone, which was hooked into the horn on his Land Rover, began to bleat. Damn, he thought, what lousy timing. He'd been watching her, waiting for the chance to get her alone so he could ask her without attracting too much attention. The redheaded wench was so popular she was almost never alone. He'd been getting mixed signals from her and was therefore unsure what her answer would be. Now everyone was looking around the dig and Fiona glanced his way, too. And now, this goddamn phone call.

Carrington rarely got calls on his phone. Only a few people had the number. So even if he could stand to ignore it, it would have been unwise to do so. He turned on his heel and made an undignified beeline to the Rover. When he got there, he reached inside and grabbed the phone off its console.

"Professor Carrington," he answered.

"My dear friend Trey, this is Hazziz. There has been a worrisome development."

"How did you get this number?" Carrington demanded. He heard a sigh on the other end of the line.

"There are ways, Trey. There are ways. For a person such as myself."

"Yes, I suppose there are." The man was a fucking spook, for somebody, or more likely for anybody who had the money. "What's this development you mentioned?"

"Ted Fuller has been asking about you, particularly your current whereabouts," Hazziz said.

Carrington's legs felt like Jell-O. He opened the door to his Rover and slid into the seat. A number of possibilities flooded his mind, none good. When he had stolen Fuller's research and sold it to Hazziz, he'd made $2 million in cash. But the money was only secondary. He'd done it for the thrill; he wanted to see what it felt like to get away with something like that.

And he'd destroyed the data on Fuller's computer because Fuller was a sanctimonious prick and had begun to question Carrington's competency to be his dissertation advisor. His research had definitely created a buzz in the department, but only Hazziz had understood the military significance.

When that stupid cunt killed herself, he knew it was time for a major change of scenery. So he had nothing to lose by stealing the research and selling it to Hazziz. But in recent months, he'd been keeping an eye on the increasing frenzy of news stories about the illnesses so many veterans had come down with and speculation on the causes. First was nerve gas and second was germ warfare. He was aware that there were civil and criminal cases against American companies who supplied Saddam Hussein with the components of his arsenal. And he knew that the research he stole from Fuller might have been used against the soldiers. That was some serious shit.

He didn't know what else his family—wealthy Boston, liberal Episcopalians and dyed-in-the-wool pacifists—could do to him, but if it ever got out that he had sold something that was used against U.S. troops, they'd find a way. Maybe even renounce their pacifism long enough to put a hit out on him.

Since Fuller was asking about him nine years later, it was most definitely something to worry about. Hazziz had as much, if not more, to worry about than Carrington did. Realizing that, a wave of paranoia seized him. What if Abdul Hazziz had been busted and was trying to entrap him?

Hazziz spoke up. "This must be most distressing news, my friend. You haven't spoken in several moments."

"Not at all," Carrington said. "In fact, I can't imagine why I would care. Thank you for your concern, though. I have business to attend to."

"A wise move, I'm sure." Hazziz hung up before Carrington could. He was close to panic, so he called someone in the department he knew he could trust. Her phone rang five times as Carrington muttered, "Pick up, come on, pick up." When the answering machine kicked in, her message said she was out of town until July 7. Two fucking weeks away! Carrington slammed the phone into its carriage, all thoughts of seducing Fiona Donnegan gone from his mind.

Chapter 17

June 25

Since the dispatchers had slightly different work schedules each week and Belinda was off Thursday and Friday of that week, Aaron had gotten a breather from having to deal with her. It was Saturday and they were scheduled to work the same shift. He wasn't sure how he felt about it.

On Friday, Toby had filled him in on the latest developments, or non-developments, coming from the makeshift task force. The gist of it was that officials with the industry group admitted they had hired Hoest to "quiet Jeter down," and that he came with recommendations from other groups and corporations where he had performed similar tasks without any significant problems. On the advice of their attorneys, they declined to identify those giving the references. They were adamant on one point, though: They certainly never had extreme measures in mind when they hired Hoest to accomplish the task. And they claimed to have "no knowledge whatsoever" of Henry Drusky.

That very day, the task force had disbanded and called the crime solved without finding any evidence that either Hoest or Drusky had actually committed the murder. Likewise, they found no compelling evidence of anyone else's involvement. And never looked very hard for it, either, Toby added. He blamed the FBI for that, because once the corporate connection had been verified, the federal agency took control of the investigation, much to the chagrin of the other agencies.

It offended Aaron's sense of justice, too, that once powerful political/money interests were involved, the dynamic of the investigation changed. He didn't know why that still pissed him off after seeing it so often over the years, but it did and probably always would. That was the problem with being an idealist: it was like playing Russian roulette with five chambers loaded.

These thoughts were swirling around his brain when he walked in to the office and saw Belinda sitting behind the communications desk. It was immediately apparent that something was different about her—she looked smaller somehow, slightly deflated. It caught Aaron off guard and took the fight out of him. He nodded and said, "Hey." As he started to walk past, she put out her hand and held his arm.

"Listen, you want to come over for dinner tomorrow night? I'd like to talk to you but this isn't the time or place."

Aaron turned and looked into her eyes and saw the fiery Belinda was not at home. He wondered what he had gotten himself into, but there was only one way to find out. "Sure. What time?"

She smiled weakly, "About eight. I'm working graveyard tomorrow so..."

"Okay, I'll be there." Then he walked back to get his gear out of the locker, a fluttering in his chest, the cause of which he couldn't pin down.

Chapter 18

June 26

Belinda lived three blocks from the Annex in a house that had been converted to a real estate office on the first floor. A set of wooden stairs climbed the back of the building to a west-facing screened-in porch. The stairs creaked as he climbed. The sun had just fallen behind the peaks. Crepuscular rays of sunlight shined like the eyes of God down the valley, painting a gold filigree border around a flock of cumulus clouds that floated lazily in the sky. At the top step, he knocked on the screen door. "Anybody home?" he asked.

"Oh, shit," came her panicky response. "Is it time already? I'm sorry. Come on in." She came onto the porch, wearing a sweatshirt and cutoff jeans and an apron that had multiple red splotches smeared across it. Flour covered her forearms and a red smear of tomato paste slashed her forehead. Her hair was tied back beneath a red bandanna and her feet were bare. Aaron started to walk into the kitchen but she blocked his path.

"Don't go in there," she said. "I was trying to make a pizza from scratch. It's a disaster area," she glanced down at her clothes, "as I'm sure you can see." She looked like she was about ready to cry. "I *hate* to fucking cook." She stuck her lower lip out and rested her fists on her hips, elbows out, as if daring him to challenge anything she had said.

In an uncharacteristic moment of mental acuity, Aaron knew he was on exceedingly thin ice. He stood there looking at her trying to decide how to proceed but he felt a belly laugh forming in his gut. He tried to control it, flexed his jaw muscles trying to squelch the smile that was forming across his face. The effort backfired and his body started to shake. He turned away as if he was looking around the porch. "Nice view you've got here," was all he could think of.

At first Belinda looked confused but soon she flopped down onto the overstuffed couch, her elbows on her knees, her face covered by the palms of her hands. She, too, started to laugh. Aaron sat heavily on the opposite end of the couch. Soon, they were both laughing. Tears streaked down their faces. Finally, the laughter subsided to the occasional giggle. The whole time, they hadn't even looked at each other, feeding, instead, off the contagious laughter. When Belinda let out a big sigh, their eyes met and he could feel another round coming on. Belinda, sensing it too, jumped up and said, "I'm ordering a pizza and I'm going to take a shower. You better be here when I get out, buster, if you know what's good for you."

"Wouldn't miss it for the world," Aaron said.

The pizza arrived and Belinda came out wearing a clean, gray sleeveless sweatshirt and white baggy shorts, her hair damp and hanging to her shoulders. They didn't talk much while they ate—finishing off a large Canadian bacon, pineapple and jalapeno pizza and noisily sucking down their ice-laden 24-ounce Cokes. She set her soda carton down, tucked her feet under her legs on the couch. "I'm going to tell you some things about my life and if I see even a hint of pity coming from you I'm going to throw your *wetto* ass out of here. *Comprende?*" Her eyes, once again dark and shiny as a raven's wing, flared.

"*Wetto*?" Aaron asked.

"Whitey," Belinda said, shrugging unapologetically.

"This is not about feeling sorry; it's an explanation of why I have been so mad at you and Toby."

Aaron nodded.

"My family came from Chiapas, Mexico to the United States before I was born to escape the *Mano Blanco*—the White Hand. They were thugs hired by the landowners to stop the land-reform movement. The trouble was, the thugs didn't particularly care who belonged to the movement itself; all peasants were suspected. They'd wipe out whole villages just to make a point. My mother told me that's what happened to our village two years after she and my father came to the United States. My whole family had lived in that village for many, many years. You understand? Those bastards wiped out my family line, except for my mother and father.

"But my parents, like good campesinos, kept their eyes on the future, worked shit jobs and saved enough to buy a bodega in East L. A.," she said, her voice halting with emotion. She took a deep breath, exhaled slowly. "During my junior year in high school, some goddamn crackheads killed them both during an armed robbery." Her eyes welled with tears. She wiped them with clean napkins from the pizza delivery. After a moment, she continued.

"They were very strict with me, but you couldn't escape the gangs in East L.A. and I had some girlfriends who had their own gang. They were my only family after *mi madre* y *padre* were killed so I dropped out of school and sort of joined up. It was just like, one day we were friends and then, it was something more. We were for-real bad-asses, not gang hanger-ons like the *putas* who rode with the *vatos*."

So far, Aaron was more fascinated than anything. "Let me guess, you called yourselves Las Vidas Locas." He nodded at the tattoo on her arm. She rubbed her tattoo. "*Si, mi grupa*," she nodded.

"You don't need to know the details, but I got busted. One of the juvie correction officers, Kathy Escalante, took me under her wing and helped me get a GED and then a scholarship to community college. Because of Kathy, I got an associate degree in criminology. On the night I graduated, Kathy never showed up and I found out she had been killed in a riot at the youth facility."

Aaron was growing uneasy at the direction her story was going and started to fidget but kept his mouth shut.

"By then, two of my *hermanas* had also been killed and I got out of L.A. One thing led to another and here I am. But as you can imagine, I have a very hard time getting close to people. So, when I heard what happened in Commerce City, I start hearing this little voice in my head that says, "See, you get close to someone then they die. I *know* it's irrational, but hey, that's what happens. I don't want to lose any more friends, or whatever." She looked away. A cool breeze was coming through the porch screens; she shivered, crossed her arms and hugged herself.

Aaron was stunned at the parallels between their lives but his mind was going a hundred miles an hour. Belinda undoubtedly knew about the reason for his self-exile from Jack Springs. But she couldn't know much about his life before coming to town in the first place. No one there knew about it. Only Earl McCormick knew, not about the massacres in Nam of course, but the rest of it. And he had kept it to himself. Aaron felt like he should tell her but didn't know where to start. He knew he couldn't burden her with the whole story. It was something he was destined to carry himself.

They sat silently for a while before Aaron spoke up. "Thanks for telling me that. I had no idea, obviously."

She stood up and said, "Get out of here so I can get ready for work. And don't you go getting the wrong idea about this. Just because I don't want you to get your ass killed, it doesn't mean…"

Aaron stood. "Not in my wildest dreams would I think…"

She started shoving him toward the door. "Go, go."

"I'm gone," he said, looking over his shoulder and thinking: Spooky, fucking spooky is what it is. Belinda shook her head and shut the door.

Chapter 19

June 30

In the days following the pizza party, Belinda and Aaron's relationship had returned to normal, maybe a little better than normal. So a tenuous bond had been created. He had taken to stopping by the office more than usual and unless she was busy they talked, though he worried sometimes there was a quality of walking on eggshells when they did, as if she expected the bond to be broken by a casual remark, an errant thought spoken aloud. He guessed that it made sense to her way of looking at things—it didn't always take a catastrophe to bring the world crashing down around your shoulders. So far, so good, though.

One night he had bought his sandwich from Fat Jack's deli and went to the office to eat and chat with Belinda. It was during that conversation she'd become intrigued with Aaron's description of the mountain man and agreed to visit Sam with Aaron.

Since a busy weekend was coming up, they had decided to drop by before their shift started.

As Aaron and Belinda approached within shouting distance of the cabin, he put his hand out to stop her. "Sam has a loaded M1 carbine next to the door. I don't want to surprise him." He paused, and shouted, "Sam Hite! Hey, Sam. You home?"

Sam stepped into the doorway, pushed the screen open and took the top step. He wore a white dress shirt with the sleeves rolled into thick cuffs under his blue bib overalls. His long reddish gray hair looked combed and was tied back into a bushy ponytail. His beard looked brushed and trimmed. Aaron was puzzled—it almost seemed like Sam was expecting them, or expecting someone, anyway.

"Hoss," Sam said, nodding. Then he craned his neck a bit. "And who's this ravishing young lady you got with ya?" Aaron said, "Sam, this is Belinda. She's one of our dispatchers. After hearing me talk about you, she decided she wanted to meet you." As they approached the steps, Sam stood to the side, swept his arm toward the doorway, his bushy eyebrows waggling. "Why don't you step into my humble abode?"

Things went downhill from there.

The old fart fawned all over Belinda and swore if he was 50 years younger that he'd ask for Belinda's hand in marriage and wouldn't take no for an answer. Belinda, in turn, flirted shamelessly, to the point of asking Sam, "So, just how old *are* you?" Sam laughed so hard that tears streaked down his weathered face into his beard, while Aaron stewed in annoyance and jealousy.

When he finally stopped laughing, Sam turned serious and asked, "So, Hoss, I guess it was those ol' boys down in Commerce City what done in that feller." It wasn't a question but there was a hitch in Sam's voice that suggested something was not being said.

Aaron shrugged. "The official investigation is closed," Aaron said. He was a little surprised at the terseness of his answer and wondered if it wasn't the residue of his insecurity in the face of Belinda's flirting. Maybe, he thought, but quickly admitted that he was still unhappy with the neat package the feds had come up with once the politically connected money boys were involved.

Sam had picked up on it, though. "But?" he asked, his forehead wrinkling.

Belinda picked up the tension in the room, took a subtle step back and glanced at Aaron and Sam.

"Everything points to them," Aaron said, "but my gut tells me there was someone else involved—one of his cohorts or maybe even Jeter's wife. If so, they got away with it."

Sam nodded. There didn't seem to be much else to add, so Aaron said, "I hate to separate you love birds, but it's time I got back. *Some* of us have to work today."

Belinda stayed silent but threw Aaron a flinty look as she gathered her bag and jacket. Once outside and a few steps from the cabin, she said, "Hey, asshole."

Aaron, a pace ahead, stopped and turned into Belinda's fist smacking hard into his arm. Aaron hopped a couple of steps backward, grabbed his arm, and said, "Ow. Shit, that hurts. What'd you do that for?"

Belinda walked past him and left him standing in the road. "Think about it," she said, over her shoulder.

Aaron was thinking, all right: *back to square one.*

Chapter 20

July 1-4

Aaron hadn't been to a Jack Springs' Fourth of July celebration in three years. But from the talk in the office, it sounded like the holiday had become progressively more rowdy, which was kind of scary when he thought about it. Worse, the Fourth was on Monday, so the partying would last four days. Typically, they could count on a diminished level of good judgment and sobriety each day.

The Indian Pow Wow would be going on at the same time. A couple of hundred Native American dancers and musicians, fry-bread and jewelry sellers, the support staff and their families would be in town, as well as hundreds of people from the surrounding area, the locals and the tourists—a slumgullion stew of humanity

The only hope for sanity was if the weather got *really shitty*—high winds, rain and sleet, hail—and lasted all four days. The forecast, however, was for hot weather and clear skies.

Back in the good old days, as Aaron understood it, the Marshal's auxiliary would have been activated to help keep the peace. The problem was that the volunteers were pretty much among the worst troublemakers in town the remainder of the year.

One unusually clear-headed town councilman asked whether it was really a good idea to *let these people carry guns* in the name of the town, strictly from a liability standpoint, of course. His dissembling was intended to avoid getting on the men's bad side, as they were not known to be among the town's more stable citizens. Neither were they susceptible to the councilman's nuance. When Harlan made the announcement, some of the hottest hotheads threatened to "string the cocksucker up." The councilman decided to leave town over the holiday and Harlan had somehow unruffled the auxiliary members' feathers. After that the auxiliary had quietly faded away. In order to deal with the crowds, Harlan canceled all time off and requested three officers from area agencies to work evenings.

So the forces of order were ready.

Friday night the crowds had arrived from the north, south and east, like high-running mountain streams filling a lake in the heart of town. The through streets were clogged with traffic, the side streets with people. Early on, families of every stripe wandered and gaped at the locals, the shops, historical markers. They stood in line for frozen yogurt and take-out food. Things were fairly tame for the first couple of hours. Then alcohol began to lubricate the inhibitions of the hardcore partiers, the noise level rose, the families retreated and things got rowdy.

Aaron was taking a break, eating a sandwich in the Annex, and listening to the radio calls. Since he had sat down, Belinda had not slammed any books shut or phones down, snorted and given him any dirty looks. All she had done was ignore him, which he reckoned was progress of sorts. The phone rang and Belinda picked it up. "Uh-huh, uh-huh, got it." She looked over at Aaron. "Trouble's brewing at the Jackass. Alvie's got somebody in a headlock…with a pool cue. He said to tell us to come and get him or he's going to crush the guy's larynx." Aaron sighed, set the half-eaten roast beef sandwich in the Styrofoam carton, jumped up and headed for the Jackass, all of one block away. "Belinda, get somebody else over there with me until we know what we got." He heard Belinda call for Lila June. As he cleared the doorway, Belinda yelled, "I'll put the sandwich away for you."

It was the first thing she'd said to him since his most recent transgression. He grinned, thinking maybe she's over her snit. He saw the cruiser lights flashing as it parted the sea of revelers standing in the street in front of the bar; he started to jog.

By the time he got to the Jackass Inn, Lila June was looking at a guy face down on the floor with Alvie's knee planted in his back. As good as his word, Alvie had a pool cue beneath the guy's chin. Lila

June squatted next to him, saying something. The crowd was forming up around them and Aaron tried to see if anybody else was thinking about getting involved. It didn't look like it.

"Sir, I said I'm going to have to cuff you before you get up. Will you cooperate?" Lila June asked. Aaron stepped inside the crowd and started moving people back. He heard the guy gurgle something.

"Alvie, let off the pressure so he can talk," Lila June suggested. Alvie was the Jackass Inn bouncer/bartender, six-foot-five, with long hair and a beard, and arms as big as most men's thighs. As usual, he wore a ratty Harley T-shirt, a leather vest, greasy jeans and had earrings of small crescent wrenches dangling from his ears. He was an intimidating-looking individual. Aaron wondered what the guy had done to raise Alvie's ire.

Alvie said, just a little louder than a whisper, "I'm gonna let you up, motherfucker, and I *hope* you get stupid."

"Alvie," Lila June said.

"Okay, okaaay." He slid the pool cue out and stood, slapping its shaft into the palm of his hand. Lila June knelt down, slipped the cuffs on the guy and started to help him up. Aaron stepped to them and grabbed an arm. They lifted and the guy got to his feet. He had a mullet haircut like that guy Billy Ray Cyrus of Achy Breaky Heart fame, cutoff jean shorts, unlaced work boots and a Myrtle Beach T-shirt with dozens of cigarette butts stuck to it. He didn't say anything, just looked at Lila June.

"What'd he do?" Aaron asked Alvie.

"He pissed me off, is what."

"We can't charge him with pissing you off."

"Just get him out of here then."

They walked him to the cruiser, checked for wants and warrants, and let him go when his name came back clean. The entire time, he had not said a word but had glowered at Lila June.

"That was way strange, Fishboy, WAY too strange."

"It was, and I'm not sure why."

"I'm not sure I want to know," Lila June said, and shivered a little in the warm night, remembering the way the guy's eyes bore into her.

By the time the dust had cleared Tuesday morning, the consensus was that the while the fireworks had been spectacular, the partying had been a little off compared to recent years. For one thing, there had been no serious crimes committed. Over the four days, there had been seven arrests for drunk and disorderly, 28 citations for the same and 17 arrests for DUI. Those numbers were considerably lower than the previous year, when there'd been several aggravated assaults and felony menacings. No one had an explanation for it—hey, some years were diamonds and some were coal.

It had been busy enough that all the law enforcement personnel were exhausted, but otherwise in good spirits. All except for Lila June, who had asked on July 4 for the remainder of the day off. Harlan thought she looked a little peaked, so he let her go home.

Lila June returned to work the following night seeming a little off her game but recovered enough to make it through the graveyard shift.

Chapter 21

July 6

That evening, Lila June was lying in bed watching the orange and purple of sunset segueing into the neon blue of security lights from the businesses nearby, which shone in her windows mercilessly unless the shade were drawn, which she was too tired to do. She was wearing an old Denver Bronco jersey and a baggy pair of basketball shorts and listening to Charlie Pride ask if anyone knew the way to San Antone on the Denver oldies country station.

She hadn't slept well the past few days and it had caught up with her. She needed to get a couple hours of sleep before her shift started. A nightly ritual, she reached into the drawer of the nightstand and touched the cool steel of her back-up piece. Such a comfort—one of the things they don't teach a southern belle.

Lila June yawned, closed her eyes and drifted into a light sleep. Sometime later she was awakened when something went bump in the front of the house. It was an old building and was always making odd noises, from groans and squeaks to knocking pipes. But her brain had catalogued all those noises into an area that says "normal" and does not send out a warning. The bump she'd just heard was not one of those normal noises or she wouldn't have awakened. She crooned, "Hello, is somebody there? Hello?"

She almost gagged at the un-cop-like ridiculousness of her action. It was something her mother would do. But she couldn't help herself.

So she crooned again, "Helloooo."

Heavy footsteps pounded down the hall and her heart tried to crawl into her throat, but she had the presence of mind to grab her .38 snub-nosed Chief Special from her nightstand. As the gun cleared the drawer, the door burst open and a man wearing a Black Sabbath T-shirt, cargo shorts, a ski mask and holding a K-Bar marine combat knife loosely at his side stood in the doorway. Almost as alarming, the creep was vibrating like a guy wire in a high wind, even to the point that Lila June thought a high-voltage hum was emanating from his body.

Suddenly, the revolver in her hand seemed awfully small and she wished she had her small-frame Glock .45 because she figured the creep was wired to the gills on meth or crack. In one of her clearest memories from the academy, an instructor explained that only suspects on Angel Dust were harder to bring down. But still, he was across the room and had a knife. She had a gun. Maybe she could talk him into surrendering. No way was this asshole going to walk out of there free.

Whatever she did was going to have to be quick. "Drop the knife, shitbird. You're under arrest." Her voice sounded reedy and scared, she thought. Certainly not intimidating. She was reaching for her phone when he took a step forward and said in a hoarse voice, "A gun? That's no fair, sugarpot. I didn't bring no gun." He took another step.

That patronizing tone was a big mistake. "What you should've brought was some body armor, dimwit," Lila June said, and pulled the trigger.

The intruder screamed as he doubled over and slapped a hand to his thigh. A dark, wet spot was growing on his shorts. Then a shiny red streak was running down his bare leg. He jerked his head up looked at Lila June. His lips were pulled against his teeth like a rabid dog. He took a step toward her, staggered, took another and raised the knife. His breathing was hard and sharp. The smell of decay reached across the room and hit Lila June like a slap.

A voice was telling her, "Shoot him, shoot him." But she was paralyzed with horror at the macabre scene playing out before her. The voice was becoming more insistent and she felt the tension growing in her finger. But then, as if someone was dimming the stage lights in his brain, the knife slipped to the wood floor with a thud. She kept the gun pointed at him as he turned and staggered away, leaving, a trail of bloody footprints in his wake.

Lila June kept the gun pointed at the doorway as she listened to his progress toward the front of the house. She heard a starter grinding but the engine failed to catch. The starter continued to crank so she set the gun on the bed, turned on the light, picked up the phone and speed-dialed the office.

"Marshal's office. Can I help you?"

"Belinda, this is Lila June." Her voice was shaky. "A guy with a knife… a guy with a knife, I just shot a guy coming into my bedroom with a knife. He's outside trying to start his car."

"Are you hurt?"

"No. He never touched me. I think I just heard the engine catch."

"OK, I'll send Aaron. Stay on the phone."

Belinda called Aaron, who was patrolling alone, on the radio.

"Aaron, Lila June just shot an intruder at her place. She said he's in the parking lot, he may have just got his vehicle started."

"Okay, I'm on my way." He knew her house; it was less than a half-mile away just off the highway to Boulder. He hit the siren and light bar to clear traffic from his path through downtown and goosed the Crown Vic down the highway toward the reservoir.

"Any word on a vehicle?"

"Lila June, can you see his vehicle?"

"No. The engine died but it just started again." Hearing a big engine roar and tires spinning in parking lot gravel, she told Belinda, "He's pulling out right now."

"Aaron, the suspect is leaving."

The cruiser had just hit eighty and shifted into fourth when Aaron came in sight of the road leading back to Lila June's house. As he slowed to make the turn, a jacked-up old Dodge Power Wagon shot out into the road and turned east along the reservoir. Within seconds Aaron was on the truck's bumper but backed off as the suspect began to swerve wildly across both lanes.

He keyed the mike. "I'm in pursuit. We're next to the reservoir and headed into the canyon so call the S.O. and tell them he's … Whoa! Shit," he yelled before dropping the mike, as a westbound car had to swerve, tires screeching, into the eastbound lane to avoid a head-on with the truck. Aaron swerved into the westbound lane to avoid it.

The road was clear once more and Aaron swung back into the correct lane while blindly searching the floorboard for the mike.

"Aaron, come in! Aaron, are you okay? Come in! Please!" Belinda was panicking.

The suspect had increased his speed, but Aaron kept it steady at 70 mph, hoping the guy might slow down and not take anyone out in a head-on. He jerked the coiled mike cord and the microphone landed on the seat. He grabbed it, keyed the mike. "I'm fine. In pursuit."

The pickup stopped swerving; it was headed full speed into the last curve just above the dam.

Aaron's eyes grew wide as he pictured what might happen. Before that picture had faded from his mind, the truck sped straight into the gravel parking area and through the fence that kept people off the dam, launched into space draped with a long section of cyclone fence, and dropped like a rock into the deepest part of the reservoir. Aaron pulled to a stop, grabbed the mike and told Belinda what had happened, then jumped out in time to watch the tail and headlights grow dimmer and begin to flicker like aquatic fireflies as the truck descended into the watery grave.

With the suspect gone, Belinda had ended the call from Lila June to alert the Sheriff's Department that a hot pursuit was headed down the canyon. When Lila June stood up and started toward the door, she saw the blood—a fucking lake of blood—on the floor. Her head grew light and her guts quaked. She turned and lurched for the bathroom next to the bed. She barely made it to the toilet bowl. But strangely, as she kneeled there the nausea passed and was replaced by a feeling she couldn't quite describe, except to say it felt pretty goddamn good.

Chapter 22

July 9

Since Lila June was in law enforcement, the Boulder District Attorney's staff had conducted the investigation into the shooting. They learned that Lila June's assailant and the driver of the truck was Joe Jack Albreath, 31, the same guy Lila June and Aaron had pulled out of the bar Friday night. He had worked at the auto-body shop next to her house for a couple of months two years earlier and had been fired for erratic behavior and suspected drug use a month before Lila June was assaulted.

Her shot had hit his femoral artery and the guy was bleeding to death trying to get away. His autopsy showed water in his lungs so he was alive when he hit the water. Drowning was the official cause of death.

While toxicology tests were pending, the coroner said he suspected Albreath had consumed enough drugs to blunt the pain and shock and allow him to drive about two miles before he lost control or passed out from shock.

He also had a rap sheet for rape and attempted rape, possession of dangerous drugs, assault and drunken driving, but had served only minor sentences on reduced charges, probably to avoid having the victims testify in open court. In fact, he had just been released from an 18-month sentence in Adams County Jail two weeks before he entered Lila June's home with the knife. He had to have known that she was a law enforcement officer. So why would he come into Lila June's home with only a knife? Probably the drugs, it was agreed. Whatever, in this case it had been a fatal mistake.

Albreath's fingerprints were on the knife and his blood was splattered along a path leading from her bedroom to the parking lot. Since Lila June had not used the gun in the performance of her duty, she was treated as a civilian and the Boulder District Attorney ruled at the end of the second day of the investigation that she had shot in self-defense. She was scheduled to return to work on Monday.

Chapter 23

July 10

After a hectic but strangely satisfying month on the job, Aaron was hoping for a lull in the action. Just a hang-out and take-it-easy kind-of lull. When he had gotten home from work Saturday night, there was a message from Professor Ted Fuller on the machine asking about Aaron's progress in tracking down Trey Carrington. The problem was that Aaron had gotten so swept up in his day-to-day life that he had put no effort into finding Carrington. He returned the call late Sunday morning and admitted he had gotten sidetracked.

"Well, that's just great," Fuller said. "What happened to righteous indignation when you interviewed me?"

Aaron started to tell him about the murder case and shootings he'd been involved in but dismissed the thought. He'd had plenty of time to start digging but hadn't even considered what his next move should be.

"You're right. I'll get back on the case. Did you pick up any information I could use? It'd be helpful if I had a direction to move."

"I've been asking around," Fuller said. "I suspect someone in the department knows something, but no one will admit anything. A few just mention he had a place in Wyoming but didn't know where it was."

"Well, it's a place to start. I'll let you know what I find."

The question is, Aaron thought, how do I, with limited assets, find someone who doesn't want to be found? An enclave for the wealthy in Wyoming? That probably meant Jackson, Wyoming, where rich assholes had been flocking like starlings for years. It wasn't quite what you'd call a lead but it was a logical step.

The answer, he realized, was to get some assets.

July 11

As soon as Aaron had finished off a monster cup of cowboy coffee Monday morning, he called Mahoney, the attorney who had hired him, and got an OK for $250 in expenses. He also told him he might as well send a summons for Carrington to the office in case they got a hit on the location. Then he called Pete Magpie and asked if he knew the name of an investigator up around Jackson. It seemed farfetched on the face of it, but Pete had contacts in every cranny of Indian Country. Two hours later Aaron had a name and phone number.

The guy, Mitch Firestone, was in and Aaron told him a little about the lawsuit and why he was looking for Carrington. Firestone replied, "Yeah, I know all about the shit falling out of the sky. I got Agent-Oranged in 'Nam. Of course, it was our government dropping the chemicals that time."

"Not so different this time," Aaron said, then told the investigator about the U.S. government's subsidy of Iraqi dual-use technology to develop their chemical warfare capability and Carrington's possible involvement with the encapsulated aflatoxin.

Firestone was quiet for a while then said, "Not much changes, does it?" Aaron told Firestone he could pay him $250 to do a little digging around to see if Carrington was in the area. Firestone said things were slow so he'd give him four hours at half his normal rate, which was a C-note an hour. He said he'd call a friend at the Jackson PD for criminal records, do a public records search for property and utility hookups, and check with a reporter friend to see if Carrington's name showed up in the newspaper.

Aaron had told him thanks, said it was a good deal.

"Well, it ain't often you get a chance to make life a little miserable for one of these scumbags, so it's hard to pass up. By the way, tell Pete thanks for the referral."

That afternoon, Aaron drove to Denver to see Tye.

Zuni, N. M.

The past two weeks had been hell for Trey Carrington. Time and again he'd been tempted to try to find out what was happening with Ted Fuller. But ultimately he realized that Dolores Chappelle, the long-time secretary to the microbiology department chairman, was the only person there he could trust.

Somehow, probably because he shamelessly flirted with the wrinkled old crone, he'd broken down the barriers she'd erected to keep most faculty at bay in her despotic control of the office. Carrington doubted anyone else had ever tried that ploy, and when he, the newly arrived Golden Boy from Princeton, tried it she had melted like butter.

In the meantime Carrington had been edgy and withdrawn. The only possible distraction could have been making some progress with Fiona Donnegan. But she'd become very elusive, rarely alone and seemed to have eyes in the back of her head. Whenever he saw her alone and started to approach, she always managed to slip away. And she'd started wearing a wicked-looking hunting knife on her belt. What was up with that?

Carrington had even returned to Albuquerque but was too distracted to do more than drive and look.

Today was the day Dolores was set to return from her vacation and Carrington drove into Zuni to make the call. She'd answered on the second ring.

"Professor Corliss's office."

"Dolores, this is Trey Carrington." He listened for any hesitation or strain in her voice.

"Trey, you rascal, why am I not surprised to hear from you?" Her voice softened and was ripe with affection. "Have you gotten yourself into a pickle again?"

"Why do you ask, Dolores? I could be calling just to once again hear your sexy voice?"

"After all these years? I think not. Besides, it would be too much of a coincidence, wouldn't it?"

"What do you mean?"

She told him of returning early from her vacation and being approached by Ted Fuller, who asked if she had any information on where Carrington might be. When she said she had no idea, hadn't heard from him in years, Fuller had spilled the beans. Some small-town cop who doubled as a process server was trying to find him to serve a summons to appear for deposition. Apparently, no one had any idea where Carrington was.

Dolores, hearing questions about one of her favorites, had subtly pumped Fuller for more information but all she had gotten was the guy's name and where he worked. Hearing no note of accusation, Carrington asked her if she could give him the information so he could contact the man and maybe work something out without getting the department or Ted Fuller involved.

She easily told him and made him promise not to wait nine years to call again. "I might be dead by then," she said.

He winced. Despite his sexy chatter with Dolores, which she had never reciprocated, Carrington knew his relationship with her was as a kind of surrogate mother, because the cold-hearted bitch that brought him into the world had never had any physical contact with him since he was cut out of her womb. His hypocrite mother, who never turned her back on the needy of the world, never found a humanitarian cause she didn't like, returned from two years hospitalization for post-partum depression hating her son and wishing him dead.

So he was disturbed to think Dolores was not immortal. "I promise to call you soon," he told her, surprising himself because he felt like he meant it.

Carrington hung up, equally alarmed and reassured. But one thing he knew for certain was that he was not going to sit around and do nothing with this thing hanging over his head. He couldn't take that chance.

He knew a guy dumb enough to put someone in the hospital for a couple of months for a few thousand dollars, yet smart enough, he hoped, not to bring down any worse heat by killing the guy. He looked up a number in his personal phone book and made another call.

July 12

The next morning Aaron had the answer. "Nada, zip, zilch," Firestone said. "If Carrington is anywhere near here, he's playing hermit in a cave deep in the forest."

Aaron thanked him and said the check would be there at the first of the month.

So much for momentum. He called Professor Fuller and left a message, telling him he'd run out of ideas.

Chapter 24

July 13-18

After hitting another dead end with Carrington and during an inexplicable period of lawfulness in town, Aaron's thoughts turned once again to the fair—but irascible—Senorita Mondragon. Most of those thoughts came in the form of a monologue that would convince Belinda to agree to a (potentially) romantic interlude with him. At the same time, he was torn. Getting closer to her could bring up all the fears that had dogged him so long, the fears that have driven him to put the gun in his mouth that morning not so long ago. That he was even considering romance was little short of a miracle. But in the past six weeks, he'd made it through three potentially deadly situations without getting anyone killed. Joe Jack Albreath didn't really count; he was a dead-man-driving by the time Aaron caught up with him. So the fears were somewhat ameliorated.

On the other hand, if what they both believed was true, he and Belinda getting closer would be like mixing nitro and glycerin. All it would take was a little shake and their world would go BOOM!

Hell, he couldn't even say for sure why he liked Belinda. She was not always an easy person to be around—her emotions were right there on the surface. You always knew how she was feeling, if not why. She was not beautiful by contemporary standards. Her mouth was a little too large, the sharp cheekbones and dark eyes gave her face a severe look—until she smiled. Her body showed few soft curves, but instead was lean and muscular. Good legs, good shoulders, a flat stomach. OK, he had to admit it was a great body. And strong hands, long dark fingers.

Of course, they'd had that flirt thing going but she always stopped it before it got too far along with a "That don't mean…." But he had seen the glimpses of affection, maybe the small battles to keep that wall in place.

Finally, Aaron realized why he liked Belinda: because she liked him. He felt it the minute they first met. The instant approachability, not the normal distance when two strangers, particularly a man and a woman, meet for the first time. It was connection on a cellular level, pheromones or something.

In the end, all the mind-bruising debate was for naught. It was Belinda who popped the question.

Chapter 25

July 19

It happened after he mentioned that Earl McCormick had been making noises about bringing him into the Sheriff's Department as a mountain patrol officer when his stint with the Marshal's Office was done. Belinda got this look in her eyes and said she heard about a band that was supposed to be pretty good playing at a roadhouse down toward Blackhawk and she wanted to go but didn't want to deal with all the drunks if she went alone, so maybe they could go together, not a date or anything but sort of a premature celebration.

Aaron tried to think of some witty (wise-ass) answer but he figured he'd screw it up, so he just smiled and said, "Sure."

Still, he was as nervous as a brook trout in a beaver pond as he trudged up Belinda's stairs. Before he had a chance to knock, she yelled, "Come on in." He stepped inside as Belinda was coming out of her bedroom.

Like a mountain breeze, she swept into the living room wearing oxblood cowboy boots, a white off-the-shoulders blouse with puffy sleeves and a long Mexican fiesta-style skirt. Her wavy black hair cascaded down on her shoulders, with the troublesome lock of hair clipped above her ear by a silver and turquoise barrette. Dangly silver Kokopelli earrings flashed through the dark curls.

"Don't just *stand* there with your *mouth* open," she said in that singsong cadence he liked so much, "or you might catch a fly." She laughed and twirled once like a flamenco dancer, clacking the heels of her boots on the wooden floor. The skirt billowed and revealed her dark, shapely legs.

This was a woman who, up until tonight, wore three "uniforms"—blue-jean shorts, T-shirt and flip-flops if it was warm, jeans, sweatshirt and running shoes if it was cool, and her work uniform.

All Aaron could think of was that she looked hotter than a habañero pepper. And he blurted "habañero before he knew he had done it.

"*Que?*" she asked, as if hearing the mutterings of a mad man.

Aaron recovered. "I said, let's roll, Starsky."

She punched him on the arm. "That's *not* what you said."

"Well, that's what I meant to say."

Roscoe was unconscious in the back seat of the Subaru—suffering from his night of prowling about the mountainside above the cabin. His legs were straight up, like a cheap wood table turned on its top. They twitched in abbreviated running motions as Aaron and Belinda approached.

"Your dog is not normal," Belinda said.

"You'll get no argument here," Aaron said.

They slid into the car and Belinda scratched Roscoe's fuzzy belly, eliciting a big sigh, but he didn't awaken. They drove south on the Peak-to-Peak Highway toward Rocky's Roadhouse.

Cars and pickup trucks lined the highway before the roadhouse was even in sight. The parking lot was full so Aaron drove past and turned into a gravel road that ended fifty feet in at an old mine claim, where he parked. Somewhere among the sharp curves on the highway, Roscoe had rolled over on his side and was still sleeping while Aaron and Belinda sat for a moment in the car.

"What was that dog of yours doing, that he's so pooped out?" she asked with a smirk.

"Out all night looking for big critters to tango with, I reckon," Aaron said, grinning.

"Oh," she said, apparently thinking of something else. "I thought…"

"Ahhh," Aaron said. "It's possible, I guess, but there aren't any neighbors for a couple of miles and he's always home in the morning. I think Sadie broke his heart and he's given up on romantic entanglements."

"Don't you worry?" she asked.

"About?" He wondered where this conversation was going.

"Roscoe being out all night like that?"

"Yeah, but what can I do? He's never been penned up or anything. And I've never seen any indication he's been in a serious fight. He comes in muddy but never bloody."

Belinda just shook her head and she started to roll up the windows.

"I'm going to leave the windows down for him," Aaron said. "He'll be all right." She shrugged, got out, and stood waiting for Aaron. He joined her and they started walking on the highway shoulder toward the bar.

Rocky's always had an eclectic crowd, drawing locals and tourists who wanted to experience the "real thing." But the band, Levi Strange and the D-Ranged, would insure the crowd would be even more hats and boots than usual, whether the wearers had ever sat on a horse or gotten any cow shit on their boots. Whatever remained of the real cowboys would certainly turn out because the band was a bunch of good ol' boys who played music for the love of it. They had no dreams of a recording contract, but there was a purity to the music that was rare by the standards of the day and drew legions of devoted fans.

Rocky's was a ramshackle red wood building, positioned at the back of a large lot that had been bulldozed into the side of a hill. The front held a construction yard, with heavy equipment lined up behind a tall fence topped with razor wire. Tucked against one side of the construction yard was a garishly painted hair and nail salon called Myrtle's Curl Up and Dye.

Aaron and Belinda threaded their way through the lot beneath the blue sky suffused with gold dust as the setting sun filtered through the dust from the parking lot. As the front door to Rocky's opened, a shock wave of thumping bass and drums pounded a rock and roll backbeat out into the dusty parking lot. It wasn't a visually appealing scene, but it was sure different from the shiny happy places that were popping up in Colorado like boletus mushrooms after a heavy rain. Rocky's looked like something swiped from a different time and place. On the wall over the door a banner said, “Levi Strange and the D-Ranged.”

Belinda waited at the door, and then they stepped into the dimly lit building. To their left were a few pool tables. A horseshoe-shaped bar was directly across from the door, with a couple dozen tables, a large dance floor and bandstand to the right. It was smoky and noisy, as a roadhouse should be.

The band was fiddling with their equipment. Most of the patrons were standing around scoping out members of the opposite sex, swigging beer and pounding a few shots in order to lubricate their tongues and dancing muscles. Aaron and Belinda took a table near the bar and ordered long-necked Bud Lights from a pretty waitress. They were quickly delivered and Aaron paid, leaving a five-dollar bill on the tray for a tip.

“Well, Mr. deputy-sheriff-to-be, here we are *cel-e-brating, no?*” Belinda said, raising her beer bottle and one perfect eyebrow in a toast. They clicked bottles, grinned and took a drink.

The band filled the stage, the jukebox was turned off and the house lights dimmed. Except for the lead singer, the band looked not much different than the cowboys who came to see them. Big hats, Levi’s or Wranglers, Bar None western shirts and pointed-toe, high-heel boots. The lead singer was dressed more as a showman—no hat but a white satin shirt with an embroidered coyote howling at the desert moon.

When he stepped into the spotlight, the crowd quieted.

After a moment, he waved "Howdy all you cowboys and cowgirls out there!" The crowd erupted in yee-haws!

"Are y'all ready to scoot your boots, kick a little shit, polish some buckles?" People cheered. He stepped up to the microphone.

"Ya know, folks, we get around a lot, play different parts of the country. And every once in a while, someone comes up to me and says, 'Levi, y'all are just a bunch of rednecks. You ought to branch out a little..." he paused for effect, "...musically speaking."

"And what'd ya tell ‘em Levi?" the band members asked in unison. The drummer started a light roll on his snare drum.

"I'm glad y'all asked that," he said, his voice rising as the drummer popped his bass drum, then after a pause switched to a light 4-4 beat.

"I tell 'em, well, it might be true that we're a bunch of redneck cow chasers. But we like *all* kinds of music:" he paused while the drummer picked up the volume, "bluegrass," (cheers), the snare drum rat-tat-tatting like a machine gun... "country" (more cheers), the drummer was in danger of drowning Levi out. The bass player was thumb-slapping the E-string in time with the drummer..."western" (cheers and ye-haws) and.....(the crowd was hooting and stomping)...and...and...and... ROCK and ROLL!" to a roaring crowd.

The band exploded into the first verse of Johnny B. Goode and the crowd erupted and raced to the dance floor, which was immediately packed with dancers who looked like they were either walking on hot coals or wind-milling off the back of a bucking bronco. Whatever they lacked in technique, they more than made up for with enthusiasm.

With the crowd warmed up, the D-Ranged launched an up-tempo country set, which included Merle Haggard's "Mama Tried," Bob Wills and Texas Playboys' "Rose of San Antone," Felice and Beaudleaux Bryant's "Rocky Top," and Chris LeDeux's "Western Skies."

The crowd was happy, slinging down beers and dancing off the alcohol.

Belinda shot Aaron imploring looks, but he wasn't much of a dancer so he tried to ignore them. If worse came to worse, he would plead an old back injury.

Finally, when the lead singer called a young girl out of the crowd to sing Patsy Cline's "Crazy," he knew it was a lost cause.

Belinda grabbed him by the hand and dragged him out to the floor. "What, you think I'm going to let you take me to a *dance* joint and not dance with me?" She latched her body next to his and forced him to move around the floor. About halfway through the song, he got into the spirit and tried to lead.

Hell, this ain't so bad, he thought. And, as if it were a plot, at the end of the song the band went right into "Lyin' Eyes," by the Eagles. Belinda took him through the rudiments of Western swing and Aaron realized not only was he doing OK, he was soon twisting, twirling and shuffling around the dance floor with the best of them.

The set ended and the band promised to return in 15 minutes "or so." Belinda and Aaron wound their way through the crowd to their table. Belinda went to the bar and grabbed four shots of whiskey. The first two, they clinked and slammed. They didn't talk much, but Aaron was strangely content, not feeling the need to fill the space between them with small talk.

As promised, the band began playing after a short break, jumping right into Gram Parsons' "Return of the Grievous Angel," a snappy ballad about a drifter who always brought trouble with him.

If there were ever a singer who could communicate a tormented soul as well as Gram Parsons, it could only be Keith Whitley or Hank Williams. It wasn't lost on Aaron that they'd all died young, from alcohol or drugs, or both. Something about the song rang too true, as if Parsons had written it about him. A chill ran through his body. When the band started in on another Parson's tune, the "Streets of Baltimore," Belinda dragged him out of his seat and he was on the floor dancing again. Despite his unease, the shots of whiskey during the break had given him an odd toe-tapping energy, and somewhere in there, the D-Ranged played "Route 66" and "Six Days on the Road" back-to-back. Aaron and Belinda joined in the windmilling melee. The roadhouse was becoming a swirl of color, sound and smoke and the continued effects invaded Aaron's brain like an hallucinogenic drug.

Finally, the music was over and they made their way back to the table. As Belinda reached for her chair, she stiffened and a look of alarm came over her face. Aaron turned and followed her gaze to a guy at the bar. He heard her sigh as she sat down.

"Who's that?" he asked.

"Don't pay any attention to him," Belinda said, a hard bite to her words. "It's Wayne Jarvis, a guy I used to go out with. He's a cop over in Black Hawk. I met him while I was dispatching for the Gilpin County Sheriff. It didn't end well."

By the time she had told him this, Aaron heard someone approach and Jarvis stepped up and put a hand on Belinda's shoulder.

"Belinda, we need to talk," the voice said, tightly.

Her dark eyes flashed, and she tried to turn and face him. But Jarvis's grip must have been tight. Belinda sat motionless but turned her head slightly as if she couldn't believe what she just heard.

"Wayne Jarvis, I got nothing to say to you. Take your *chingando mano* off my shoulder."

"Belinda..." Jarvis said.

Aaron was pushing against the table to slide his chair back when he heard Sam Hite's voice.

"Let the lady go."

Aaron turned and saw Sam Hite's massive paw on Jarvis's shoulder. As Jarvis relaxed his grip, Belinda twisted away, stood up, and laid a right-cross against his jaw, knocking him into a chair, which tangled his feet and dropped him back on his ass. Before Jarvis could push himself up, Sam put his hand against Jarvis's chest and said something to him. Aaron grabbed Belinda and pinned her arms to her side. But she was still madder than a run-over rattler.

"You ever lay a hand on me again, Wayne Jarvis, and it won't be your jaw you have to worry about," she said. "It'll be your *cojones*." The table was quickly surrounded, and not a few of the onlookers were snickering.

Jarvis's face turned the color of his red hair. He slowly got up and dusted off. Then he wheeled around and stomped angrily to the door. Aaron let go of Belinda and she sat heavily back into the chair. He turned toward Sam, and with a little residual jealousy showing, said, "I could have handled it."

"I know you could have, Hoss," Sam said. "But I jest would've hated to see your evening with Missy end like that. Maybe I shouldn't have interfered."

Aaron hated to admit it but Sam was right. "Aw hell, I would have liked to take a poke at the asshole but you did the right thing."

Sam nodded and walked back into the crowd.

When Aaron turned back to the table, Belinda was rubbing her knuckles with a cold beer bottle. "Helps keep the swelling down," she said, matter-of-factly.

He raised his eyebrows a bit as that information sunk in. "Are you okay?" he asked. "Do you want to head home?"

"Hell no, we're going to stay. I'll be damned if I let that *cabron* ruin my evening."

They danced to several songs, but the luster had gone out of the evening so they returned to their seats and had a couple of shots of tequila. During the second drink, Aaron saw tears running down Belinda's cheeks.

"Maybe it is time to go," she said.

Aaron put his arm around her waist as they walked through the parking lot. Belinda rested her head against his shoulder. "I'm sorry about that," she said. "We only went out a few times until I realized he was an asshole, so I ended it. He started stalking me after that, sitting in front of my apartment and shit, so I quit the job. I just didn't want to deal with it. It wasn't even a romantic relationship. Just something to do."

"Don't worry about it, OK? I mean it. Not that I was much help."

Belinda shrugged her shoulders. They were quiet as they walked up the highway and turned into the deep shadows of the road where Aaron's car was parked. She halted, turned to Aaron and draped her arms on his shoulders. "I want you to take me home," she said.

Aaron was confused, said, "I *am* taking you home."

"No," Belinda said in a shaky voice. "I want to go to *your* home."

"Okay," Aaron said, "if you're sure."

"I'm sure." They continued up the road, Aaron's arm around Belinda's waist. Light from the construction yard and roadhouse, along with the passing cars, cast eerie dancing shadows among the trees on each side of the road.

As they reached the car, three men wearing camouflage and ski masks stepped silently out of the trees. The two on the outside had baseball bats and the one in the middle held a dark, semiautomatic pistol loosely at his side. Aaron pushed Belinda behind him and stepped toward the men. He raised his hands away from his side, palms up. The men came forward in a half circle and were raising their bats when Aaron heard a fearsome roar. Like a charging grizzly, Roscoe sprang from the car, hit the ground and launched himself into the air.

"Get him," the man holding the gun screeched in a surprisingly high-pitched voice.

Aaron bellowed, "NO!" just before a galaxy of fireworks burst in his head. A fine red mist was flooding his vision when the sound of his name being screamed and a gunshot penetrated the fast-closing darkness.

Chapter 26

July 20

During his first moment of consciousness, Aaron became aware of a throbbing pain in his head, as if someone had buried an ax in the side of his skull. Somehow, it seemed to be getting in through his eyelids.

Murmuring voices penetrated the fog, and Aaron was thankful that the sounds didn't hurt. Beyond all that, he was curious about where he was and why he was there. The red veil was still there but inch-by-inch was drawing open.

"Lights," he mumbled through the oxygen mask. He tried to raise his arm to block out the light but there were tubes in it. Somebody grabbed his arm and held it in place.

The pitch of voices became more insistent and someone said, "Dim the lights." Within seconds, the pain in his eyes diminished considerably.

After a few moments, he braved lifting an eyelid. When the pain stayed bearable, he opened both to a slit. Three hazy figures lurked in the background and one in green hovered over him.

"I'm Doctor Waring and I'm going to open your eyelid. If the pain isn't too bad, I'm going to shine a light very quickly into your eye."

"Ogay," Aaron mumbled.

The doctor did as promised and Aaron flinched when the light was flashed briefly across his pupil.

"The pupil is a little dilated but is reacting well. You're fortunate it was a glancing blow." As Aaron tried to focus, he could see the doctor was wearing a bandanna made from a small American flag on his head.

The remark brought back a sliver of memory that made Aaron wince but he brushed it away.

"Just open your eyes normally whenever you're ready," the doctor said.

Aaron didn't know if he was ready, but he sure wanted to figure out what the fuck was going on. With effort, he let the ocular muscles relax and opened his eyes farther. The pain was minimal but his focus was still fuzzy. He stared in the direction of the figures in the room until they came into focus.

It was Harlan and Earl. The memory slammed his heart like a jackhammer. He tried to sit up but found he was restrained. He struggled, the pain in his head came back and he collapsed, moaning, exhausted.

Gathering all the strength he could muster, he asked hoarsely, "Where are they?"

Harlan and Earl approached the bed. Aaron kept his eyes closed as Harlan began. "I-it's…" he cleared his voice, which was faltering. "Roscoe's at Doc Newman's, Aaron." Harlan let out his breath and said, "They worked him over pretty good. He bit one of them, had a lot of blood and skin in his mouth. From the look of it, Gus said some of the skin had tattoo ink on it. They crushed his backbone, probably to get him to let go, Doc said."

Aaron was spinning, as if he was being swept into a whirlpool.

Earl spoke up, more practiced at delivering bad news. "Aaron, Belinda was shot in the head. The neurosurgeons at Memorial operated on her for three hours. They got her stabilized but she's in a coma." Earl pulled out a sheet of paper and began to read, "The bullet entered her scalp just above the hairline at the parietal bone and traveled a path between the scalp and skull cracking her skull in three places. It exited at the back of the head without ever entering the brain cavity. There were multiple concussions. They opened the skull to relieve pressure of built-up cerebrospinal fluid. If she comes out of it, they don't think there should be too much damage to brain function. But there's no guarantee." He paused. "For what it's worth, the surgeon said Belinda's extremely lucky to be alive."

Aaron heard the words but they stayed at a distance. "What about me?" he asked.

"A moderate concussion. A glancing blow but still enough for 16 stitches. They want to keep you a couple of days for observation," Earl said.

Aaron lay back, let his body go limp and closed his eyes for a couple of minutes. The vertigo lifted. He heard Harlan and Earl discussing something. Earl cleared his throat and said, "I know this is not a good time, but we need to ask you some questions about what happened."

Aaron knew he had to go to that gray place in his mind where he had existed for so long to do what he had to do now. And he lay there, slipping back into the fog. It was easier than he expected. He could tell Harlan and Earl were getting antsy.

He opened his eyes and said, "Take me to see Roscoe, and I'll tell you on the way."

It was a hard sell, but after Aaron threatened to "pull out all the fucking tubes and wires and walk from Boulder to Jack Springs," they decided releasing him was the appropriate course of action. Dr. Waring even, with a wink, brought him a bottle of Percocets.

"I'm trusting you to wait two days to begin taking these, once the symptoms are gone. Don't make me regret my decision. The stitches are self-dissolving. If you start getting dizzy or blanking out, I want to see you immediately. If not, I'll want to see you in a week."

They started the drive in silence. Aaron could see in the rearview mirror dark circles under Harlan's bloodshot eyes. He looked like he had a monster hangover. Harlan, a simple man who hadn't experienced the worst his job as a law officer could dish up, *was* suffering.

Earl turned around and Aaron could see the stress there too: the tic at the corner of his eye, the vein standing out in front of his temple, the grim set to his mouth. But he'd seen too much as a cop to broadcast the kind of emotion Harlan projected.

Earl told Aaron that Sam Hite had found them right after it happened, in fact had been looking for them when he heard the gunshot. He said he never saw anyone, just heard the shot. When he got there, all three of you were on the ground. He ran back and called 911.

"They were waiting for us," Aaron said, his voice flat and emotionless. "Back in the trees. Full camo, ski masks. Two had baseball bats, one had a gun. They never said a word, but whatever they were going to do, Roscoe changed the plan. He'd been conked out in the car, and they must not have seen him. When they moved in on us, he came out of the car. Everything happened so fast. I think they hit me first, but I remember hearing the shot before I went out. That's it." The noise of his own voice was making his head throb.

"Anything you remember about their description?" Earl asked.

"It was pretty dark, but there was some light from the construction yard. They were big, none were fat or skinny. No voices, like I said. They might have said something like 'shit' when Roscoe came out of the car. I can't really remember."

Then something came to him. "We had some trouble with a Black Hawk cop right before we left. Belinda said he'd been stalking her when she worked at the Gilpin S.O. Sam kind of quieted things down, though. It never developed into anything too serious although Belinda popped him a good one to the jaw. He left before we did."

"Yeah, Wayne Jarvis," Earl said. "Sam had followed Jarvis out and said that he had driven south toward Black Hawk right after the tussle. After that, Sam went into the back room with some cronies, and just as he came out, he saw you and Belinda leaving. So he tried to catch up with you."

Aaron pondered the information. "I'd make Jarvis on this but these guys were waiting for us at the car. There's no way Jarvis could have found the car. He didn't even know who I was. If it happened in the parking lot, that's one thing. But someone had to follow us to see where we parked."

"We already talked to Jarvis," Earl said. "He was playing blackjack in a casino about the time you were assaulted. The dealer vouched for him."

"Unless Jarvis is the one who followed you," Earl said. "He could have still been stalking Belinda. Put some guys on to you. It's something we'll have to check out, anyway. We didn't have enough before to lean on him. This time we'll lean, hard."

"Then again, I don't know who else it could be," Aaron said.

"I think we can get something from the weapons angle," Earl said. "Why two baseball bats and a gun? Maybe a snatch but that seems unlikely, particularly with Belinda along. Why bring baseball bats if they were going to kill you? It would have been easier just to shoot you. For whatever reason, they were going to beat the hell out of you. If we can come up with a reason, we may be able to narrow down the suspects. Somebody was trying to discourage you from doing something they think you're doing. The question is, what is that?"

"I told you Earl, I haven't been doing anything …well… I was chasing Jim Bob, or whatever the fuck his name was, when he drove into the reservoir. But I'd backed way off, so it was more like I was following him. I guess if you're psycho enough, you could make some kind of case against me."

Harlan continued, "You weren't really involved in Tobias' investigation into the murder until the night you stumbled on that scene in Commerce City. So that shouldn't be it. I hate to say this, but we have to consider that they may have been after Belinda. And that brings us back to Jarvis."

They drove for a ways, a heavy silence hung in the car. After a time, Harlan spoke up.

"I don't know what you're thinking, Aaron, but Earl and I agree that all the stops will be pulled out on this. There's no goddamn way someone is going to nearly kill two of my employees, my friends, and get away with it." Harlan looked at Earl.

"That's right," Earl said. "We're gonna get to the bottom of this. I still want you to come work for me, as soon as you are cleared medically," he paused, "Of course, you can't work the investigation…" His voice trailed off as if expecting Aaron to explode. But Aaron stayed silent.

"And," Earl said, locking eyes with Aaron, "I don't want you digging into this on your own. If we're going to make a case, we do it by the book."

Aaron held his gaze for a short time and looked away without replying.

Right now, he was trying to prepare himself for what was coming and felt the fog slipping away—Roscoe hurt bad and Belinda in a coma with unknown brain damage—this was going to hurt.

Thinking of pain, he shook out a couple of Percocets, tossed them into his mouth and washed them down with bottled water. Earl and Harlan both looked at Aaron then at each other. Earl shook his head, as if dismissing whatever he was going to say. The only thing Aaron knew for sure was that a shit pile of hurt was waiting for him.

Zuni, N.M.

Trey Carrington was driving back to Zuni from Gallup when the phone rang. He picked it up and said, "Carrington."

"Professor, we put the hurt on that sucker, just like you wanted us to."

"You didn't kill him, did you?"

"No, sir," the voice said, adamantly. "We hit him upside the head with a Louisville slugger. It was a stand-up triple. He won't be botherin' nobody for quite a while, though."

"Good enough," Carrington said. "I'll put your money in the mail tomorrow. Don't cash it locally."

"Yes, sir," the voice said. Carrington hung up, with waves of tension rolling off his body. Maybe he could start devoting more attention to Fiona, finally bring her around. The more she avoided him, the more he became obsessed with her. But he reminded himself to check the Denver newspapers for a couple of days before incriminating himself by sending Kenny Tucker a check.

Chapter 27

July 21

Roscoe lay on his favorite blanket by the door, where he had been since Aaron brought him home. His breathing was irregular. He whimpered softly at times. His legs twitched like they did when he dreamed of chasing a rabbit. Aaron hoped that's what it was: good dreams. A battered old pickup pulled up the driveway and a few moments later Gus Newman was walking up the hill carrying his small doctor bag. Aaron sat back down and stroked Roscoe's fuzzy head, talked to him about nothing important, just to kill the noise in his own head.

Gus came to the door and Aaron said, "Come on in, Doc, it's open." Gus came in and squatted down, rubbed his hand along Roscoe's flank.

"It's a goddamn shame, is what it is," Gus drawled. "I'm sorry for him, and for you too."

"I thought hard about it," Aaron said. "You know, even if there was some way to accommodate him, Roscoe's been a free dog since I've owned him. He's been free to go where he wanted, to do what he wanted. Never been on a leash or on a chain. You can't raise a dog like that any more, Doc. I can't let him be carried around from spot to spot to do his business and to lie here on the floor between times. But I did have to think about it, because he's been my partner for seven years and I don't want to lose him. I asked myself if I'd want to live like that, and the answer is no. If that was me lying there and he needed to make the decision, it's what I would want him to do. And like I said yesterday, it's better done here at home, where he belongs."

Gus nodded. "Well, then, let's get 'er done." He looked Aaron in the eye to be sure he really wanted to. Aaron nodded. Gus opened his bag and pulled out a big syringe, filled it with colored liquid from a vial, shaved Roscoe's leg and found a vein. Aaron wrapped his arm around Roscoe's thick neck, buried his face against his ear, shut his eyes and whispered, "I love you, pardner. I'm going to miss you."

He kept his eyes shut and felt Roscoe's body relax. It was gentle, soft. The breathing stopped. And Roscoe was gone. He looked up after a few moments and Gus was packing up his bag.

"That's it, then," Gus said, his voice sympathetic, understanding. "You done the right thing. I've seen people go to god-awful lengths to keep their pets alive. It ain't fair to the animals."

Aaron nodded. "Send me a bill."

Gus nodded his head and said, "Okay," and left.

Aaron slid his arms under Roscoe's still-warm body and carried him to the upper meadow, where he had earlier dug a grave beneath a large ponderosa at a spot overlooking the valley. Roscoe's blanket was over his shoulder. He set Roscoe down on the grass and lined the grave with the blanket. Aaron lifted Roscoe from the grass, laid him gently on the blanket and pulled the flap over him. Tears blurred his vision as he covered Roscoe with good, mountain soil. When it was nearly full, he slid a section of stout welded-wire fence over the hole and rolled some large rocks onto it to keep the critters from digging up the body. With another layer of earth in place, he pulled a packet of wildflower seeds from his pocket and sprinkled them on the loose soil.

"May you rest in wildflowers, my friend," Aaron said, as an emptiness as wide and deep as a canyon engulfed his heart—an emptiness that grew even greater when he thought of Belinda. He pictured himself as a holograph, where a thousand points of light converge to create an image. But that picture was much dimmer without Roscoe and would be even more so without Belinda. He shivered, wrapped his arms around himself and rocked toward a state of catatonia.

Then the back of his neck prickled, and Aaron felt a presence, somebody or something watching him, and he raised his eyes to a high, dead branch in the large ponderosa that stood over Roscoe's grave. Sitting uncharacteristically silent at the top was a huge raven, black as a grave on a moonless night, his head cocked sideways as if watching the scene below. Aaron hated the idea that his most private feelings were being as spied upon and stood, grabbed a rock and hurled it into the branches above. The bird screeched indignantly, lofted itself with three beats of its giant wings, and slowly flapped away.

Aaron cast a glance in the raven's direction and walked down the meadow to his cabin, dreading what was going to happen next.

Aaron had believed that Belinda would look dead. Standing at the side of her hospital bed, the reality was better than he expected—but not by much. Her head was wrapped in a turban of bandages. He winced at the bruising and swelling, which was visible in the few bare areas on the right side of her head. Wires and tubes snaked away from her body to a saline drip, heart monitor, something measuring brain waves, all humming busily and steadily along. She was not on a respirator, only an oxygen tube taped below her nose that went sst… sst… sst, like a hustler with a lisp trying to get your attention from a dark alley.

Besides the rise and fall of her chest she looked, he thought, as if she had taken a time-out from the game of life and wasn't in a big hurry to get back on the floor. He held her hand, it was warm and soft. Her face remained impassive, unaware. The nurse told him it was okay to talk to her, that sometimes it helps bring people out of a coma.

So, when the nurse had gone, he began.

"First, I just want to say that I'm so goddamn sorry. I should have known better than to take the job and I should have known better to want to get close to you. The morning Harlan called, I was a heartbeat away from blowing my brains out to keep things like this from happening. If it wasn't for Roscoe, I would have done it. And now he's gone, too. All I wanted was another shot at being a normal, functioning human being. To have a reason to get out of bed each morning, and not just that but to look forward to getting out of bed.

"And it worked. Every day since I took the job I've looked forward to the day. And you have been a big part of that. I can't believe I held your hand that first time we met, through a minute of conversation, and didn't even realize it. How lame was *that*? You should have punched me out right then and there and been done with it. But you know, that was the first time I'd even touched a woman, I mean *touched*, in three years. And all of a sudden, I remembered how good it was. You know, that little tingle of excitement."

He could have sworn he felt her fingers move, but of course they didn't.

"And that time I was flirting with you on the radio and you used the squelch to cut me off. That was pretty quick thinking on your part and it started me wondering... Well, anyway. And the night we ate pizza. You were so funny with that smear of pizza sauce on your forehead..."

And on and on it went until the nurse came in and tried to shoo him home. She picked up pretty quickly that it wasn't going to work. "You're not going to leave, are you?"

He felt so goddamn helpless that he'd taken her suggestion to heart. If talking to Belinda might help her come out of the coma, he was going to tell her his life story. And over the next three days, that's what he did—leaving out his two years in Nam. The nurse had brought him a cot, so he slept in her room, ate in the cafeteria, and showered at the nearby YMCA. Leaving only for the doctor's examinations and Belinda's sponge baths. Harlan came by twice to see Belinda, and he'd called Earl twice to see if any progress had been made in the investigation. The answer was no, nothing. He felt like he should be angry but he knew Earl wasn't cutting any corners. The truth was, and he had been thinking about it every minute he wasn't talking to Belinda, that it just didn't make any sense.

Those guys were there to hurt him, not kill him. To punish him for something he had done or to stop him from doing something that he didn't even know he was doing. But all the obvious suspects—the punk with the machine gun they'd busted that first night, the cop from Blackhawk had rock solid alibis. The kid—Wentworth—was in a residential treatment center. The cop, he couldn't remember his name now, had been on duty before coming to the roadhouse and was playing blackjack afterward. The guy, Billy Jack or Joe Bob or whoever the fuck he was, that Lila June had shot was a dead man driving and Aaron's pursuit, except at the very beginning, was not close—he'd just been following. Aaron's name hadn't even been mentioned in the news story or DA's investigation of the incident so it couldn't have been that. He was angry and frustrated and felt helpless. So he did the only thing he could. He talked to Belinda.

"...and Harlan had just dropped me off at the newspaper and there was this wild-looking kid, hair chopped off and dyed in neon colors, multiple ear rings, huge sun glasses, and a pile of suitcases and a sleeping bag, sitting on the porch steps. I thought she was just another street urchin looking for the Rainbow Family gathering and I was about to walk past her when she looked up and said, "Dad?"

Just then the doctor came in, looked at Belinda's chart and said, "Sorry to interrupt but we're moving her to long-term care in a few minutes. Her vital signs are good. Physically, there's no problem. The swelling is going down. She's just someplace else right now. She'll come back when she's ready."

Aaron was ready to argue and the doctor must have sensed it. "Listen, this is good news. There's no guarantees, you understand, but it's my opinion that she will come out of it. When she's ready."

At that point, Aaron decided to go back to the cabin until they got her settled in at the new facility. He walked to her bed, grabbed her limp, cool hand and said, "I'll be back."

Chapter 28

July 22-23

He came home to an empty cabin. He sat and listened to the silence. It seemed bigger without Roscoe, although there were signs of Roscoe everywhere.

Needing to do *something*, he got up and started cleaning. First, he moved Roscoe's bed and food and water dishes into the lean-to on the side of the cabin. Everything he moved out seemed to expand the emptiness within him. Tears pooled but he kept on. They finally receded. He got the ancient vacuum cleaner and cleaned the worst of dog hair he could find.

He had a headache. He found the Percocets and shook a couple out, swallowed them with water. Next he boiled water in his blue enamel pot for coffee, dumped in some grounds and let it steep. He walked over and stood in the doorway while he waited.

A car pulled up and stopped in the driveway down the hill. A door slammed and Aaron saw Earl, in street clothes, walking up the path as if a thousand pounds were on his shoulders. Finally, Earl stopped at the foot of the stairs, his nose wrinkling.

"That what I think it is?"

Aaron nodded.

"It's against my best judgment, but how about a cup?"

"Come in, then," Aaron said.

Earl sat at the ancient Formica table that had probably been in the cabin for decades and Aaron poured the viscous brew through a filter into two blue metal cups and sat. "Hey, you've got a matching coffee set. Who'da thunk it?" Earl said, tried a grin, then dismissed it with a shrug. They both sat with their hands wrapped around the cups as steam rose in the cool morning air.

"So, they're moving Belinda."

Aaron nodded. "The doc said all the signs are good. She just won't wake up. Anything develop since yesterday?"

"Not a goddamn thing."

Aaron searched Earl's eyes, seeing some bad news lurking there. "And?"

Earl sighed uncharacteristically, shook his head slightly, "Aaron, Tyrone died three nights ago. Peacefully in his sleep, Maya said. They took his body to California to be buried near his family."

The news was like a final kick in the head at the end of a bad beating. By itself, it would have hurt like hell, but relative to the other pain present, it was more like gouging someone's eye out after you'd broken half the bones their body. Tye had looked weaker the past two times he'd seen him, but he was also excited about something, so Aaron had assumed he'd just worn himself out.

Earl pulled an envelope out of his back pocket and set in on the table. "Maya sent this to me to give to you. I don't know what's in it but she said you'd understand after you read it." He took a last pull on the coffee, stood and walked to the door. At the threshold, he turned and said, "Call Harlan. When you're finished with that job, I still want you at the Sheriff's Office."

"I'll call Harlan," Aaron said. "Thanks. I'll let you know."

Earl looked like he was thinking about something, wrinkled his forehead, reached around his back and pulled the black revolver out from under his windbreaker, stepped back to the table and sat it down with a thud. He then walked out the door and down the path to the driveway.

Aaron ignored the gun and picked up the envelope, which was blank. He held it in both hands, turning it over and over, as if he could learn its meaning through touch. Finally, he opened it.

The first sheet was a letter from Maya.

"Dear Aaron,

After your first visit, Tye started gaining enough movement in his hand that he was able to use this special computer that allowed him to write. It was really just moving the cursor over a letter and clicking the mouse. He started trying to write something about what happened to him in Iraq. It was working but I could see he was still frustrated because it wasn't coming out the way he wanted. But it was like, for those weeks, he had a reason to live.

I don't mean that he didn't love me and Preston, but I know that it tore him up to be so helpless. And that he saw that helplessness reflected in our eyes every time we looked at him. Somehow, you brought that reason to live back to him and he wanted to tell you what happened. So I enlisted this guy I met at Denver Community College—he's a writer and a black Gulf War veteran—and he and Tye worked on this together. They finished it two nights before he died. I read it, of course, and am now aware of how well his mind worked and how frustrating it must have been for him to be trapped in that body. I believe that he was happy when he died. And I'll always be thankful for that, and to you."

Love,

Maya

Aaron swallowed hard and unfolded the pages and read.

19/Jan./1991 Al Jubayl, Saudi Arabia

Corporal Tyrone Rexford stared gape-mouthed at the wide slash of stars glittering like a million diamonds in the inky night sky. He couldn't remember ever seeing the Milky Way before, not like this. In South-Central L.A., you couldn't even see the stars for the smog.

Behind him a sulfurous glow arose from the largest encampment of U. S. soldiers in Operation Desert Storm. He shivered from the enormity of it and wrapped his arms around himself.

Tyrone had been scoping a mile-wide section of the perimeter for hostile incursion. Three days earlier, the flyboys had started bombing the bejesus out of Iraq, but here, hundreds of miles from the Iraqi border, there wasn't much to watch out for. The Iraqi Republican Guard sure the fuck wasn't going anywhere with all the caps the B-52s and F-16s were busting on their rag heads.

His M16, equipped with a night-vision scope, was leaning against the rail, and his MOPP chemical-agent-protection suit was draped over it. He was supposed to be wearing it, but chem alarms had been going off all day and nobody had fallen over dead. The unofficial word was the alarms were faulty. And if this clusterfuck called the U.S. Army helped design them, it was probably true.

So Cpl. Tyrone Rexford was thinking of his wife, Maya, and his boy, Preston. And of the cops he had worked with on the North Metro Drug Task Force.

'They be sleepin' in after a night of takin' down junkies, pipeheads and dealers outside Mile High Stadium, where the Broncos play, while I'm standin' in this muthafuckin' bug-infested desert protectin' the oil of these ragheads, who wouldn't even piss on us if we on fire,' Tyrone thought, in the gangsta rap he'd grown up speaking. 'Or maybe they up on Speer Boulevard at the methadone clinic. Or Five Points, on the Hill, east Colfax, west Colfax, wherever the scum would be coa-fuckin'-lescin.' Bustin' heads and takin' names.'

Aaron, too, remembered those days: The Rolling 20 Crips, Bloods, Chingasos, a dozen different sets were riding high in Denver on an epidemic of crack cocaine, selling to the homies and honkies alike. Gang violence there was taking down two, three gangsters a week and that was a good week. In a bad week, there would be twice that many and a couple of kids cut down in a drive-by spray of 9s. Joining the task force at the height of the gang wars, Tyrone had acquired the nickname T-Rex; a natural contraction because the cops—like every one else, it seemed—had adopted the gangster culture though they nightly battled it, even despised it. But the nickname was one of those odd things that changes a person somehow, creates a life of its own. The brass had pulled out the stops trying to get on top of the gangs and their crack cocaine lifeblood, and T-Rex had been unleashed as the top predator in the Denver war, creating a legend for his fearlessness.

Aaron recalled that Tye's favorite tactic was jumping out of a plain-clothes junker, dressed like a homeboy in a plaid flannel shirt, baggy trou, a watch cap, and oversized work gloves, swinging a baseball bat like the Tasmanian Devil into the windshield, the headlights, the door glass of a gang-banger's car before anybody could even get out. His sheer guts had saved his life a few times, Aaron was sure, as the dopers were usually packing serious heat but seemed paralyzed by the sheer audacity they were witnessing through the dark-tinted windows.

Looking back, Tyrone could only shake his head in wonder that he had survived that craziness in South Central, where he was sometimes on the wrong end of the guns, and Denver where he was on the right end, only to be sent to this shit-hole. Even though no hostiles were within shooting range, and the only danger he faced here was dying of fucking boredom.

But thinking he had survived all that, he figured he'd survive this if he did his job, which was, at that moment, watching the perimeter. So Tyrone lifted his night-vision goggles and swept them along the "P", which the starlight illuminated almost to a greenish daylight. He couldn't resist lifting it to the heavens. Through the scope, the stars became almost indistinct, blocking out the dark sky with their light.

A memory tickled its way to the surface of his consciousness, something about African Bushmen. He dropped his scope and concentrated on the memory, then he had it: the Bushmen in South Africa believed the Milky Way was formed when the Creator tossed the ashes of a campfire into the sky to light the way for warriors and hunters far from home. That was it. He'd learned that in a college class.

It was strange how he could remember something like that when he recalled so little from his college classes and how unimportant those classes were to being a cop. The useful education came from the streets of his youth. But without that piece of paper he got from graduating college, he would have never become a cop. And football tied it all together. Without football he would never have got off the mean streets and got that piece of paper. Strange fucking world out there.

In the distance, Tyrone saw a smudge of light moving fast under the backdrop of the Milky Way, but there was shit flying around the desert continually so his brain was engaged with other matters. He was thinking, 'I sure the fuck hope them Bushmen are right because I am a hell of a long way from…' when an angry whine from the sky brought his thoughts to a halt.

He jerked his head up and scanned the sky, trying to lock on to the source of the sound. The smudge of dirty light was directly overhead, and a flashbulb went off in the sky. Something slapped his head like a cheap shot from a monster tight end and knocked him senseless to the floor. When he looked up, he saw a rain of fiery debris floating like tiny cherry blossoms down onto the desert.

"Oh man, I'm fucked, fucked, fucked," he chanted under his breath as adrenaline burned off the fog in his brain and he tried to decide whether to inject the atropine or put on his MOPP suit first. The atropine Syrette was in a pocket on the front of the suit so he tried to wrestle himself into it while flat on his ass. In his panic, he got his foot stuck in the folds. As his first leg slid in, ear-splitting sirens ripped the night and shouting filled the camp PA speakers, but with the sirens and speaker distortions, Tyrone could understand not a word of it. Not that he needed to—the speakers were telling him that a major shit- storm of bad news was coming down the pike. He got his other leg in, zipped the suit up and was pulling his hood down when a metallic odor hit his face like a brick. He pulled the Syrette from the pocket and slapped it against his thigh.

As the siren wound down, a panic-stricken voice screamed over the PA, "CONFIRMED NERVE GAS! CONFIRMED NERVE GAS! GO TO MOPP 4! GO TO MOPP 4!"

'No shit, Sherlock,' Tyrone thought, as he grabbed his rifle. He climbed down three rungs at a time, dropped the last six, hit the ground and rolled, coming up on his feet and sprinting in what felt like slow motion for a nearby bunker. The acrid taste in his mouth was so strong his throat nearly spasmed shut, but it stayed open enough to allow him to continue. He pounded on the bunker door, was admitted to the decon chamber, where a chemical spray washed his suit. He chucked it into a hamper, and jumped into the body shower, clothes and all, then collapsed through the air-lock door and lay gasping on the floor.

Two hours later, Tyrone Rexford had no noticeable symptoms—except for numbness in his lips—from whatever had been in the air. An All-Clear had been issued. Word then came down from the brass that the explosions were sonic booms caused by supersonic fighter jets and that no chemical agents had been released. They told their troops that the chem alarms had failed again.

"Yeah, that's for sure fuckin' right,' Tyrone thought, hoping to get the feeling back in his lips so he could clearly tell the first officer he saw to stick a sonic boom up his rosy pink rectum.

Aaron's hands trembled as he folded the sheets and placed them carefully back into the envelope. He made a pillow with his arms, but before he could lay his head down, he slammed his fists against the table so powerfully, the legs threatened to buckle. It wasn't enough, so he reached under the table and lifted it up and heaved it into the air, flipping it over onto the floor. He grabbed the chair and hurled it with both hands into the wall.

He stood there, shaking in rage and frustration. Rage at what had happened to Belinda and Roscoe. And now Tyrone. Frustration because there was nothing he could do about any of it. It was happening again. Just like always. In some ways, the thing with Tye was even worse. He even knew who Carrington was, knew that he might be responsible for what happened to Tye. Not that it could be proven because Maya had learned about the encapsulated alfatoxin way too late to have him tested. But it *might* be true.

The stitched-up wound on his head was throbbing. He looked at the overturned table and felt stupid. "I guess that showed 'em," he said to his empty cabin. He righted the table, picked up the chair and slid it into place. Neither was damaged to any extent, except the chair seemed to lean a little. His head still throbbed but he no longer wanted to destroy any innocent, inanimate objects. Instead, he laid his head on the table and cried.

When Aaron finally arose, he walked to the sink and took the beard trimmer off the charger. He put the thinnest attachment on it and began to run it through his beard, which had grown out considerably since he'd started working for Harlan. When that was done, he dug out an old disposable razor that had sat unused for years, lathered his face with soap and scraped the remaining beard off his face. Then he rinsed off and gazed at his chin, which he hadn't seen in a decade.

Changing the trimmer to the thickest attachment, Aaron went to work on his hair, favoring the stitches that were just above the ear on his right side, which was still swollen but shaved bare. When he was finished, about a half-inch of hair remained. He looked in the mirror. With his sunken cheeks and slightly protruding eyes, lopsided, zipper-stitched head and red eyes, the overall effect was of a medical experiment gone awry. All of the newly revealed skin was white but his forehead, eyes and nose were a bandit's mask of brown. Most noticeably, though, there was a leaden dullness to his eyes, as if the light within had gone out.

He wanted to be sure that every time he looked into the mirror he'd remember what he had to do—bring to some kind of justice to the people responsible for what happened to Belinda, Tye and Roscoe. Earl had had four days and come up empty. It was time to rethink the attack. Something was missing, obviously. He had to figure it out and go from there. As for Carrington, most of the puzzle was there. Just one little piece—his location—was missing. Aaron had no doubt, armed with this new incentive, this new purpose and will that he could be found. Before, it was more of a job. Now, it was personal. Turning his face from side to side in front of the mirror, he thought: that should do it.

He still had a buzz from the coffee and Percs and felt the stirring of hunger pangs. There wasn't much edible in the cabin at that point, but there was some bread and peanut butter. He made a couple of half sandwiches and gobbled them down. They were terrible, but the food gave him a little energy.

First, he called Professor Ted Fuller to see if he'd learned anything.

Fuller answered on the second ring. "Where the hell have you been? I've been trying to reach you for four days," he asked.

I guess you don't read the paper, Aaron thought, then realized there'd been surprisingly little coverage of the attack. Big media's eyes were on the Rainey girl's murder. Something was up, according to "sources."

"I've been out of commission for a few days," Aaron replied.

"You ought to get an answering machine," Fuller said.

"You've got me now. What's up?"

"I found out Carrington owns a place in Saratoga, Wyoming. Like I mentioned earlier, it's an enclave of the *uber*-wealthy just outside of town."

"How'd you find out?"

"Someone dropped a note in my mailbox."

Strange, Aaron thought. "Any idea whether he's there?"

"I don't," Fuller said. " I thought you, being a big detective and all, might be able to find that out yourself."

"I will. Just asking. I want to thank you, and I mean that. A friend who served in the Gulf just died a couple of days ago from some shit he picked up over there, might have been aflatoxin. So I have a renewed interest in dropping paper on this guy."

"I-I'm sorry," Fuller said.

Before he could go on, Aaron said, "Me too. I'll keep in touch," and hung up. Next he called Harlan. He didn't recognize the woman who answered the phone but asked if Harlan was in. She said he was not, so Aaron asked to leave a message. She connected him to Harlan's answering machine. He told Harlan he was going to take a couple of days off and try to serve a summons in an old case.

Aaron was thinking that a few days away, whether he was successful or not, might have a couple of additional benefits—it would help him clear his head and give Earl time to work the investigation.

So yeah, a trip to Saratoga was a good idea all around, and if he got lucky he could drop the paper on Carrington.

Aaron started packing a few things: a change of clothes, a bedroll, his .357—not essential for serving a summons but he knew he would never again be without a weapon close at hand, not after what had happened. It was too late to take off and he was still beat, as well as beat up. A good night's sleep would help so he rummaged around in the cabin and found a half bottle of Captain Morgan, shook out a couple more Percs and washed them down with the spiced rum, certain that sleep would come.

Chapter 29

July 25

A cool gray dawn found Aaron already sitting next to Roscoe's grave. No critters had discovered it; for that he was glad. It was just the shell of Roscoe down there, not his spirit, but Aaron didn't want it disturbed. It was the only physical connection he had to his friend.

"Well, pardner, we haven't found out who did this to you but I've got a job I need to do and I'll be away for a few days. Just thought I'd let you know." He dipped his head and headed down the hill. He finished up gathering his gear, hauled it down to the car, and came back up to check on Belinda over the phone. An emotionless voice told him, "Ms. Mondragon is in critical/stable condition." Aaron said "thanks" and hung up. He closed up the cabin and walked back down the hill to his car.

Aaron had passed through Saratoga once several years earlier but had little recollection of the town, except that it straddled the North Platte River and that it was the mailing address of Emma Sodenberg, someone who could have meant something to him once. It was unfinished business and likely to stay that way. But, at last, he had a reason to go and see her.

He drove to Fort Collins, caught U.S. 287 north and turned west up the Poudre River Canyon. About 20 miles up, the canyon opened into a wide valley. The sky was clear overhead but a haze was hanging over the mountain peaks ahead. Wide, lush meadows flanked the highway and the meandering river.

At the top, Cameron Pass rose abruptly and appeared to be swathed in a white shroud. As the road climbed, the gloom came rolling down to meet the car. Large, icy raindrops smacked the windshield like big messy kisses. A mile later, the wind picked up and blew wet snowflakes sideways across the road.

A couple miles later, snow was blowing so hard that Aaron was tempted to pull over and let the storm blow through. But he wanted to put as many miles between himself and Jack Springs as possible, and the storm looked weaker on the west slope so he kept going. A few minutes later, he was through the worst of it. The sky remained overcast as he came off the pass, and half-assed storms kept coming out of nowhere, throwing snow and then rain at the car. By the time he was in Walden, it was just cold, gray and windy.

Aaron filled up at the convenience store, paid for the gas and left. The highway to the north looked just as gloomy as where he had come from, and the last 24 hours came down on him like a blue norther. As bad as things were, the stinking weather in North Park was just rubbing it in. When he crossed, even the mighty North Platte River looked gray and sullen. Mountain squalls continued to blow out of nowhere as he climbed the gentle pass to the Wyoming border. But the farther north he drove the more the clouds came apart, revealing patches of blue sky. On the downhill drive into Riverside, the patches of blue became wider and wider. As Aaron crossed the Encampment River and turned north toward Saratoga, the clouds parted and sunshine fell upon the valley, a light so glorious it might have greeted Noah's Ark after forty days of rain. The rain-glistening alfalfa fields radiated aquamarine in the brilliance.

And just as quickly, his depression burned away.

Aaron drove slowly through the town of Saratoga. Well-preserved historic buildings, anchored by the three-story brick Wolf Hotel, lined Main Street. At the east end of town, he could see the bridge rise over the river. Old trucks and new cars shared the wide streets comfortably. People waved at each other. The town radiated an old-fashioned friendliness that was becoming rare in the West. Just past downtown, he stopped for gasoline, fished out Emma's phone number and a quarter. Doubt bombarded his mind as he walked to the phone. Would Emma be glad to hear from him? His heart pounded as he punched in the numbers. After three rings, it felt like a magnetic force was drawing the phone back to its cradle. At the very beginning of the fourth rang a young girl answered, "Hello?"

"Could I speak to Emma Sodenberg, please?" he asked.

"Oh," she said, sounding disappointed the call wasn't for her. "Who's calling, please?"

"Tell her it's Aaron," he said.

He heard her muffled yell, "MOM! It's that guy from down in Colorado you've been talking about." Aaron cringed as he waited.

Slightly out of breath, Emma answered, "Aaron? Good Lord, how are you? I haven't been able to find out anything for days. "

"Maybe a better question at this point would be where I am," he said.

"Oh, hell, you're in jail. Or in the hospital," she said.

"Well, not at the moment," he said, laughing despite himself. "I'm in Saratoga."

"WHAT? Are you serious?"

Aaron listened for that tone of voice, the restraint or false delight, that would tell him things had changed, that he'd waited too long to call. It wasn't there. Emma sounded happy to hear from him.

"I'm serious," he said.

"Well, then get your butt on out here, boy," Emma said.

After receiving directions to the ranch, he drove three miles north of town and turned east. Despite the recent rain, the county road wound its way through parched range land about four miles back toward the mountains. The road brought his car almost directly to the front gate of the Diamond S. The driveway lay in a slight valley, surrounded on three sides by the scrub-covered foothills of the Snowy Range. It split a large brown and green quilt of hay meadows, criss-crossed by shallow irrigation ditches. At the far end of the drive, nestled back into the hills, sat a rambling, white, one-story ranch house with a red roof surrounded by large outbuildings.

With a mixture of excitement and trepidation, Aaron drove across the Diamond S spread. Up close, the ranch looked more prosperous than he had pictured it. The house was stuccoed, with a large overhanging roof of red tiles that created a porch on at least two sides. Multi-paned glass windows spread across the south side. A large, natural-stone chimney rose from the middle of the roof.

He stopped the car, got out and walked up to the thick wood front door, which was cracked slightly open. From inside, a voice yelled, "Mommmm! He's here!"

From deeper in the house, Emma yelled, "Come on in."

Opening the door, Aaron Hemingway stepped inside to be ambushed by a teenage girl wearing an electric-blue, tight-knit skirt that barely covered her possibles and a floral-print bikini top. As he reflexively swept a look up down and up her body, he saw her long, muscular legs, a tiny waist and breasts trying to live up to the bikini top but not quite making it. Oh yeah, and the cutest little belly button—with a ring in it—that he had ever seen.

Her face, somehow, didn't match her body. It was full and not unpretty, but kind of plain. Her eyes hinted of sadness and vulnerability, as if she were aware that fate had played a trick on her by giving her this particular body with an unmatched face. Her hair was mousey brown and limp, cut straight just below the ears, parted in the middle and kept off her face with pink plastic clips.

She raised a slender hand and said with an enthusiasm likely strained by his gaunt look and stitched-up head, "Hi! I'm Ariel. That's Are-E-L, not Air-E-L. Nice to meet you."

He grabbed her hand and said, "Nice to meet you, Ariel. I'm Aaron." It was a nice hand, warm and strong, with long slender fingers, but it gripped his tentatively.

"Yeah, I know," she said, dropping the handshake. "Mom's friend from down in Colorado. Well, gotta go. See ya later." She wheeled around and sashayed out of the room.

Emma, who had stepped into the room in the middle of the drama, said, "You done good, Aaron. Since her father died, she's been on a bloody campaign to capture the attention of every good-looking man over the age of 30. I'm sorry to say it works way too often." She shook her head slightly, as if saying, 'What can a mother do?' "Oh, and I didn't know about the outfit, by the way. If that skirt was any shorter, she could use it for a tube top. She probably will in a couple of years."

Emma stood there, tilting her head to the side, looking for something behind the gaunt, beardless face and short hair.

"I heard about what happened. I'm so sorry. How *is* your friend?"

"Except for the coma, they tell me she's in good shape. Funny thing, those comas."

"And you, how are you?" She extended her hand and laid it on his arm. It had been three years, but Emma looked good, looked every bit a ranch woman with wide shoulders, a narrow waist and long, almost gangly, legs like a young girl who'd outgrown her body, which the years never really managed to fill out.

The looks were deceptive, though. When Emma moved she had the grace of a racehorse. Her thick-black hair was streaked with gray and parted in the middle. It was cut straight and fell to her shoulders when she let it down, which she usually didn't. Today, she had it pulled back in a band and then pinned straight up over the back of her head. A fine veil of fringe hung down the back of her neck. She had big brown eyes and and thin but not unattractive lips.

She looked tired, though. Beneath the ruddy complexion, a few more wrinkles than he'd noticed three years ago encroached on the corners of her eyes. She'd lost weight, and she didn't have much to spare to begin with. She was wearing a sleeveless denim shirt, with the tails tied above her belly and low-slung jeans tucked into the tops of cowboy boots. The Sodenberg women apparently had a thing about showing off their navels.

They sat across from each other at the rectangular, oak kitchen table. Rays of sunlight shone through the south-facing kitchen window as puffy clouds skittered across the sky. Bundles of herbs and red peppers hung from heavy beams and posts around the kitchen, exuding a heady aroma.

"So, Scribe, what brings you to the Sodenberg spread?"

He told her about the lawsuit and Carrington.

She furrowed her brow, looked dubious. "I guess I'm just a little surprised, is all. After what you've been through." So he told her about Tyrone.

"Well," she said, her eyes softening and showing something like forbearance, "that explains it then." She added, "Knowing you." She sighed, put her hands on her hip. "So, what can I do for you?"

Emma fixed steaks, baked potatoes and salad for dinner. After dinner and dishes, they spent the evening drinking wine and talking about things other than the attack—their kids, the ranching business, what was happening in Jack Springs. Since the somewhat dramatic introduction, the rambunctious Ariel disappeared into her bedroom, never to reappear. When Emma went to check on her, Aaron gobbled a couple of Percs and soon became sleepy.

Emma made up the guestroom and he retired to his bed there.

Chapter 30

July 26

The next morning, Aaron borrowed some of Emma's deceased husband's work clothes and an old straw cowboy hat and one of the beat-up ranch pickup trucks and drove through town. He slowed to admire the river while crossing the bridge over the North Platte. It was wide and wild at this point, and an island just upstream had been turned into a park of some kind. A walking bridge crossed over a narrow channel on the east side of the island and homes and businesses right above the water on the west bank. A car honked behind him and he drove on, looking for the road that led to Mount Baldy, the enclave where Trey Carrington reportedly lived.

As he crested a high hill overlooking the mesa, Mount Baldy came into view. From a distance, it didn't look to be a fancy place like you might expect given all the millionaires and billionaires who lived there. The homes were ranch-style, or log homes, nice but not fancy and tucked into rows of large trees. It was obviously intended as a place where the wealthy could come and pretend they were just regular folks. The only thing that belied that impression was the security force that patrolled the split-rail perimeter fence and the wooded lanes 24 hours a day, Emma had told him. She believed there was no way he could sneak into the area.

Aaron's plan was to bluff his way in by pretending to be a handyman hired to do some repairs to Carrington's house. He wound up the side of the mesa and after a couple of miles saw a small, glass and steel security guard shack under a massive, free-standing log and stone crossbuck over the entrance road. As he stopped, the driver-side window next to the guard hut, a heavily bandaged hand slid a glass panel back. A man with a severe military hair cut, heavy brows and a square chin leaned out.

Aaron nodded at the hand and said, "Ouch, that musta hurt."

The man asked in an incongruously high-pitched voice, "What's your business here?" No Mister, no Sir. Just fuck off. But the cartoonish quality of the voice, like someone who had inhaled from a helium balloon, set off a mild alarm in Aaron's head.

He shrugged, said, "I was just looking for a stream up on the mountain and got a little turned around. Sorry to bother you."

The man shook his head dismissively. "Keep turnin' it around and get goin', bud," he said. "Don't know nothin' about no stream up there."

Aaron glanced again at the man's bandaged hand, his left hand. He wanted to hear more, so he leaned out a little farther and said conspiratorially, "Y'ever get yerself any of that rich poontang—" he tilted his head toward the compound—"*in there?*"

Donald Duck did not like someone challenging his authority. His voice raised an octave and his face flushed pink. "I said, get goin' and I mean it."

At that moment, Aaron remembered what the man carrying the gun the night of the attack said—"Get 'im"—as Roscoe charged, and remembered the guy was holding the gun in his left hand. Roscoe was trained to go for the gun hand.

A tide of rage was welling in his gut but he held back, thinking: Don't, not here, not now. He backed out and looked over at the shiny, copper-colored early Bronco square-back parked inside the gate. He drove away without looking back. As he drove he searched for places to park and watch the road. If the security force worked three shifts a day, Donald Duck back there would be getting off between 4 and 6 p.m. He was almost sure he had found one of the assailants. But maybe one was enough, because it was fairly certain now Carrington was behind the attack.

One way or another, he would have the answer within 48 hours.

After returning Emma's truck, Aaron told her he couldn't get in to see Carrington and didn't have time to wait him out. Said he was going back to Jack Springs and take the job Earl had offered. Emma took his leaving good-naturedly and told him not to be a stranger. Instead, he drove 70 miles into Rawlins to pick up a few things.

Since there was only one road in and out of Mount Baldy, Aaron decided to wait at the point where it intersected the first county road. The rest was up in the air. He couldn't afford to ask around about the guy, even his name. So he had to follow him and find out where he lived, who he lived with, what his schedule was.

To be safe, Aaron arrived at the intersection at 3:30. He had his copy of *Black Cherry Blues* but was too antsy to read. The traffic began picking up as what looked like a steady stream of workers left Mount Baldy. As the traffic thinned out, Aaron saw the distinctive Bronco approach. Even though Aaron was in a different vehicle than he'd been that morning, he slouched down in the seat. Two cars were behind the Bronco, so he let them pass before he pulled out. Donald Duck stayed on the county road through Saratoga without stopping and drove west into the high desert. Aaron dropped way back but was able to keep the Bronco in sight. About four miles west the Bronco turned north. Aaron held his speed and saw the Bronco pull up and stop next to a dingy clapboard house. Aaron drove past about 200 yards, made a U-turn and pulled over. He looked around and realized there was no other house in sight. He waited there an hour, but he wasn't going to be able to sit there much longer without attracting attention so he drove past the house, saw there were no other cars parked there and continued into Saratoga.

He saw a sign for Bubba's barbecue pointing down a side street, followed it and drove up to a yellow house with Bubba's sign on it. He bought a beef sandwich and a Bud Light, and sat at a picnic table next to the river. Nearby were three latter-day hippies who, according to their conversations, were Greenpeace canvassers and weren't having much luck in Saratoga, a town where trout were important but whales apparently were not. They glanced at Aaron a few times, probably gauging his hostility. Sensing none, they resumed complaining.

Aaron listened, took a bite of the sandwich and had a long swallow of cold beer. Behind him, the river gurgled, popped and splashed, with the rejuvenating redolence of moving water. From the west, a warm breeze carried the scent of sage. The sun had fallen behind a bank of puffy clouds on the western horizon and was putting on a light show of blue, orange, gray and purple.

Sitting there, he could almost kid himself life could be good again. Almost. Then he thought about Belinda and Roscoe and shelved such nonsense. He was almost certain Donald Duck was the one holding the gun that night, but he had to have confirmation that it was Carrington who put him up to it.

If so, then he had some decisions to make. Big decisions, difficult decisions. Because if Nam had taught him anything, it was that there is a line that shouldn't be crossed. In war, enemy combatants are fair game, whether they're shooting at you or not. Civilians, even if they are enemy sympathizers, are not. In law enforcement, lethal force should only be used when the officers or innocent bystanders are in danger of being seriously injured or killed. In a perfect world, that's the way it should work. In the real world, with all the vagaries of human existence at play, things were never that simple. Reality in those situations was a virtual Chinese jigsaw puzzle of variables, including training, mental stability, fear, fatigue, and character, to name a few. But there has to be a standard.

At the time they destroyed the village, he had taken pride in abiding by the military standard. And then he killed two civilians, not even fighting-age men but a young girl and an old woman, neither of whom could probably aim or even lift a rifle.

And that's what had fucked him up so bad, because he wondered if for those first few seconds of the massacre he *knew* but didn't *care*. For those few seconds, he, like everybody else, had just wanted to kill. But then he came back to himself and realized what was happening. A lot of the "cherries," especially the draftees, liked to brag that they just wanted to kill gooks. They couldn't wait to kill some gooks or slopes and any of the half dozen other denigrations that reduced the Vietnamese to something less than human. But Aaron'd never been like that, never said anything like that. He just wanted to kill the enemy, the combatants. He took pride in that. And in the end, for those few seconds, he became like those who just didn't care.

He believed now that the reason he had become a cop was to put himself back in the crucible, to test himself, to prove that it *was* just a mistake—those few seconds. And it worked. In 15 years as a cop, he shot three suspects, killing none. Each had been ruled, and in fact were, justified.

So here he was, thinking of diving into a gray area, taking revenge by killing someone who wasn't actively trying to kill him. But he reasoned that Carrington, whose crimes went beyond the recent attack, had a penchant for getting away with things, maybe due to wealth or power. Whatever the reason, Aaron didn't want that to happen this time. He wanted Carrington to pay for his crimes. And he wanted to be the one who made it happen.

He had to where find out where Carrington was. And then he had to make certain this joker didn't warn anyone before he had a chance to do it. He could think of only one way to make sure of that: kill him. But there were problems with that, too. He'd just have to play it by ear.

Aaron drove to a state wildlife area north of town along the river. After he arrived, he realized he didn't have any alcohol. Rather than go back to town, he resigned himself to a sober night. He kept the windows rolled up to keep the mosquitoes out and tried to read *Black Cherry Blues* until he couldn't keep his eyes open. He climbed into the back and let the drone of 10,000 mosquitoes put him to sleep.

Chapter 31

July 27

The next morning, before the sun had topped the Snowy Range, he drove past Donald Duck's house. The Bronco was still there, so he drove back into Saratoga and waited just inside the town limit. About 6:45, the Bronco passed and drove east toward Mount Baldy. He got his Wyoming map out and saw there was a east-west section road a mile north of Donald Duck's house. He debated whether it was better to take a chance being seen on foot out in the middle of nowhere than have his car seen near Donald Duck's house. The section road won. And when he got there, he realized it was perfect. There were washes and gullies that would keep him out of sight most of the way, even a two-track that went back a hundred feet so he could keep the car out of sight from the road. Since there were no "No Trespassing" signs, he figured it was public land—probably U.S. Bureau of Land Management.

He parked at the end of the track and, staying in the gullies as much as possible, was inside Donald Duck's house, which was unlocked, 40 minutes later.

As Aaron searched the house, he learned that Donald Duck's name was Kenny Tucker, at least according to the mail strung around the kitchen. After a thorough search, he concluded that Tucker had no roommates, entertained himself with American Rifleman, Soldier of Fortune, dirt-bike magazines, pornographic videos and beer. The pile of wadded-up tissues on the floor by the bed (ugh) suggested he didn't get many visitors. His work schedule was on the dresser by the unmade bed. Starting tomorrow, Tucker would be on the swing shift, so whatever Aaron was going to do had to be tonight. He drove back to the wildlife area to wait and swat a few hundred more fucking skeeters.

Just as the sun went down, Aaron parked back on the two-track. He was impatient to get going but didn't want to get there until after dark. With nothing much to do, he tried to read *Black Cherry Blues* but the light was fading and the overhead light wasn't bright enough to read.

Finally, he estimated it was going to be fully dark in a half hour so he grabbed the athletic bag with his "tools" and set out, arriving at the ravine closest to Donald Duck's house before it was completely dark. He moved up into the cottonwood windbreak, hunkered down and waited another hour. A quarter moon was rising in the east. He couldn't wait any longer so he circled around so he could see the front of the house. The house lights were on and the front door was open, protected by a screen. The bare bulb in the porch light was dark. Aaron crouched behind another tree and watched Tucker drink a beer while he talked on the phone. When he hung up, Aaron pulled on some latex gloves, walked to the door, reached up and unscrewed the bulb in the porch light, then knocked. Tucker walked up, stood behind the screen door and said, "This better be good." He flipped the porch-light switch several times but it never came on.

"I work for Greenpeace and we need your help to save the whales," Aaron said.

As the door swung open, Tucker squinted into the darkness saying, "You've got to be fucking kidding—" Aaron drove a short punch into his solar plexus. Tucker doubled over and clawed at his throat, trying to get a breath. Aaron knocked him over with a kick to the head, pulled out a large zip tie, rolled him on to his stomach and locked his wrists behind his back.

Tucker started to buck. "Ouch, goddamn, that hurts," he said, gasping. Aaron pulled the Python, cocked it and placed the barrel to the back of his head. Tucker went as rigid as an oak plank.

Aaron asked, "You know who I am, dickwad?"

Tucker started to shake his head, thought better of it, and said in a whine, "No."

"What happened to your hand?"

"A dog..."

Aaron did a knee drop onto Tucker's back, who wrenched like he'd been shocked. "That's right, fuckface, it was *my* dog." Tucker went limp again. "And that is *my* friend you shot in the head." Tucker was listening intently. "I buried the dog, and my friend is still in a coma."

Tucker started to whimper. "I didn't..." Aaron pressed the gun harder into the skull.

"Uh-uh, don't even try to deny it, you piece of shit," Aaron said with a steely calmness. "But the thing is, you don't even know me. Right?" When Tucker didn't answer, Aaron tapped him lightly on the back of his head with the gun barrel.

"Right?" he asked. Tucker said no. "So somebody put you up to it. I'm thinking it was Trey Carrington who said, 'Hey boys, you want to make a little extra money?' Now, you're a fucking rent-a-cop, get to carry a gun, be tough, maybe a little militia tendency? Maybe even charter members of the local militia, huh?"

Tap, tap.

"No," he croaked.

"Oh yeah," Aaron said. "So you're thinking, sure, get a couple of the boys, go rough up some asshole down in Colorado, pick up a few grand for a couple of days' work. Piece of cake until the dog, his name was Roscoe by the way, until the dog came out of the car. Then it all went to shit. Were you trying to shoot Roscoe? Or did you just start blasting? Then Roscoe put the chomp on your gun hand and your boys crushed his spine to get him to let go."

Tucker started to gurgle something but Aaron tapped him on the head again. "No, it doesn't really matter about that now." As the words sank in, Tucker's bladder gave out.

"Aw, now you've gone and done it," Aaron said, a note of disappointment in his voice. "The thing is, you've robbed the world of a couple of beings that made this planet a better place. Sure, that happens all the time, right? But more to the point, you've robbed *my* world of them. And that was a big, no, that was a *huge* mistake. Now I'm going to ask you a question and I want the truth. It's very important that you tell me the truth, very important. And I better believe you, obviously."

Tucker went still again. "Is Carrington here?" Aaron asked.

"No," Tucker whined. "He's gone."

"Do you know where?"

"I think...he's in New Mexico, on some Indian reservation. Zuni is the town," Tucker said.

"What's he doing there?"

"He's some kind of archeologist," Tucker said. "He pays college kids to come and work the dig."

"College kids, huh? I bet he has a preference for pretty young women."

"He did mention something like that," Tucker said.

"Did Carrington say when he'd be back?"

"He said October, November, thereabouts."

"How did you find me?"

"Carrington said you were a cop in that town. He had your name. We just hung around for a few days. It wasn't hard to figure out who you were."

"Good, very good." Aaron said. "You know, Tucker, I believe you. The next question is what should I do about you?"

Tucker stammered, "I, I..."

Tap, tap. "I don't need your input on that one yet," Aaron said. Tucker went silent and stayed that way while Aaron thought. "O.K, here's the deal. I could kill you. But that could possibly alert Carrington and I don't want that to happen. The question is, if I don't kill you, will you warn Carrington? Let me tell you something about him before you say anything. Good ol' Professor Trey Carrington raped two college girls, that we know of. One of them got pregnant, and she committed suicide. She was a good Mormon girl and couldn't face her parents. He also almost certainly got richer by selling some real nasty stuff to Iraqi agents, stuff that could have and maybe did make a lot of soldiers in the Gulf War sick. One of those soldiers was a friend of mine and he died a few days ago.

"Do you know why he wanted the shit kicked out of me? Did he even tell you?"

"No," Tucker whined.

"Because I was trying to serve papers on him for a civil lawsuit. Trey Carrington did not want to answer questions about how some nasty germs got into the Iraqi arsenal. So what have we got here? A rapist, a traitor to his country. He uses people and throws them away with no more concern than stepping on a roach. And he believes he has the *right* to do it; that the rules don't apply to him. If you got any loyalty to Carrington..."

"I don't," Tucker said.

"By the way Tucker, I've got an ace in the hole. The cops down there in Colorado have some blood and tissue that was dug out of Roscoe's mouth, so they've got your DNA. If somebody drops a dime on you, you're facing attempted murder, and that's if Belinda lives. If she dies, it could be first-degree murder, considering premeditation and conspiracy.

"But don't worry about that because if I find Carrington where you say he is, you're off the hook." Aaron paused. "Now, don't go talking to your buddies about this. And if something should happen to Carrington, or he just disappears, you'd best forget all about me. In fact, if I were you, I'd get the fuck out of Dodge, so you're not even tempted. Because if Carrington gets word I'm looking for him, I'll be back. And you know what's going to happen then? You can answer this one."

Tucker whimpered but didn't answer.

Aaron grabbed him by the throat. "Answer me, you piece of shit!"

"Y-yes, I know." he sobbed. "I know!"

Aaron slipped a short length of pipe covered with garden hose out of his satchel with his free hand. "One last thing, Tucker. Do you think Carrington knows what I look like?"

"I'm n-not sure. I don't think so. He never gave us a description."

"One more last thing, Tucker, and this really is the last. Does Carrington know how your little party turned out?"

Tucker hesitated and Aaron nudged him with the gun barrel, "Uh, no, I just told him we worked you over real good."

"OK, that's all for now." He uncocked the Python and, just as Tucker was letting out a huge breath, he snapped the homemade sap against the side of Kenny Tucker's head a little harder than he intended. His body went slack. Aaron took his Buck knife out and slit the zip tie around Tucker's wrists. He put everything back in the satchel, turned Tucker over, checked his breathing and peeled back an eyelid. He'd have a bad headache, maybe a concussion.

But Mr. Kenny Tucker was incredibly lucky to be alive. Trey Carrington's luck had just run out.

Chapter 32

July 28-29

After leaving Tucker unconscious on the floor of his house, Aaron drove all night and was home early the next morning—still wired to the gills from what he had learned. He had a lot to do before he went after Carrington. But first he climbed the hill to Roscoe's grave.

Mist hung like a dirty veil over the meadow above the cabin. Aaron squatted next to the grave drawing wavy lines in the fresh earth with a twig.

"Listen buddy, I'm going to be gone for awhile. I feel bad leaving you, but I know you'll be all right without me. I wish I could promise you that I'm coming back. But I don't want to lie to you because I don't know.

"The thing is, I found out who did this to us. I'm the only one who knows, so I'm going to square things. I'll do my best to get back to you, but there's not much about the situation I know right now."

Aaron dropped the twig and placed the palm of his hand flat on the center of Roscoe's grave.

"So, if I don't make it back, maybe there's a place for people up there where the free-dogs run, you know, to be sure all you guys get your food on time, to pull porcupine quills out of your muzzles, cut the dingleberries off your hairy butts, things like that. If so, I'm a shoo-in for the job and I'll see you there."

He gave the ground a pat of reassurance. "*Hasta luego, mi amigo.*"

Once inside, he built a small fire in the woodstove so the cabin wouldn't feel so inhospitable, so empty. He needed to make a list of things to do, gear to take.

But another duty called to him: he had to see Belinda before he left and say goodbye—for now.

The new facility was the medical wing of what used to be called a nursing home but was now described as a senior residential community. It was new, clean and depressing only when you thought about its purpose: a warehouse for those nearing the end of the line. Belinda looked the same, with less medical equipment in her room—an oxygen bottle, an IV bottle of glucose and a heart-rate monitor. The green wavy lines were remarkably consistent—a good sign. Yet, after all the things he had told her a few days earlier, he couldn't think of what to say. It didn't seem right to tell her he'd found the man responsible for her being like this; that he was leaving to find him; that he might not come back. Neither could he lie.

So he squeezed her hand and tried to send these thoughts to her: I'm sorry this happened to you. I want you to be well; and I'll try to be here for you when you are. He repeated it like a mantra, hoping it would sink in, watching her eyes for a sign. None came and after a while he released her hand and left, the burden of his sadness not lessened by the fact that his feeling of helplessness was gone.

Over the last thirty hours, Aaron had told Sam and left a message for Harlan that he was going to Arkansas to look for his family. It was tough lying like that but he had to tell them something. Just disappearing would look…even more suspicious. He had called Earl to ask about progress in the investigation and had to leave a message. Didn't mention leaving. If there was one person he could never lie to convincingly—even in a phone message—it was Earl. They knew each other too well.

He had the rear window in the Subaru replaced and stopped by Pete Magpie's to tell him the bill for the job was coming. Pete tried to make sympathetic noises but couldn't quite pull it off, as his anthem was basically, "Shit happens." Aaron appreciated the effort, though.

By 3 a.m. he had the car packed and had lain down and slept. By 9 a.m. he was on the road.

He spent the first night in Chama, New Mexico, and slept in his car beside the Chama River. South out of Chama, he crossed the Naciemento Mountains and drove south again to the town of Cuba. At a gas station on the south end of town, an Indian couple sat on a pile of belongings in the back of a battered Chevy pickup. More piles were scattered around the rear of the truck beneath a for-sale sign. The couple looked old and sad and beaten.

After he filled the tank and paid, he looked at the old couple through the station window. They sat completely still. Never talked, never moved their eyes. He went outside and strolled over to the truck.

Aaron nodded as he approached. The woman looked away and the man nodded slightly but wouldn't meet his gaze. On one pile was a box with a derringer, looking something like a hand-sized, sawed-off over-and-under shotgun. He pointed, "That work?"

"Yep," the man said. "It's .44. It'll punch a hole the size of your fist in a 50-gallon drum at ten paces."

Aaron picked it up. It was a black-powder replica of an 1860s gambler's gun. He broke the action open, cocked the hammers back and looked into the barrels from the business end. It was spotless. Despite the coolness of the blue steel, the gun felt warm in his hand, as if it were a talisman, something he was meant to have, as if it had some purpose only meant for him.

"If you got the ball, powder and caps, I'll give you a hundred fifty for it."

The old Indian's eyes glanced quickly at his woman as if looking for a signal. She nodded, and a hint of a smile crossed her lips.

"Okay," the old man said and dug another box out of a pile of clothes. He handed both boxes over, and Aaron handed him three fifties. He was glad to be able to help them out. And he felt like he had gained an ally for what lay ahead although he had no idea what that was.

"You from Dulce?" Aaron asked. Dulce, pronounced dul-say, was the Jicarilla Reservation's only town.

"Yeah, I have to take my wife to the clinic in Albuquerque. Move down there for a while."

"Thanks for the gun," Aaron said. "Good luck."

"You too," the proud, sad man told him.

Outside Cuba, Aaron turned west on Highway 197 and headed for Gallup, New Mexico. The highway was wide and empty and rode the undulating landscape like a sinuous snake. He punched the Subaru up to 90, accompanied by the pleasing hum of the turbo. Together, they ate up the miles—little dots on the map labeled Torreon, Star Lake and Pueblo Pintado passing in blurs. He hit Highway 371 about 20 miles north of Crownpoint, just as the sun dropped behind the Chuska Mountains and he started looking for a place to pull off, have a snack and get some sleep. The wire fence along the highway was old and intermittent, not really holding anything in or keeping anything out. Every half-mile or so an old two-track road disappeared into the distance of the Navajo reservation.

He slowed in the next stretch and saw another side road coming up. It bisected some low hills where he would have some cover from the road, so he turned in and drove a couple hundred yards until he was behind a rise. There he stopped and sat watching the sky turn purple and orange in the haze from the Four Corners power plant. In the rearview mirror, he could see stars winking in the indigo creep of night.

For a long while Aaron sat and thought about the plan he had hatched, knowing it was mutable, that in the end he would play it by ear. Tomorrow, he would stay in Gallup, go in and look at some back issues of the newspaper, try to see if there was anything about Carrington. He knew he couldn't ask any questions that might link him to Carrington. He had to keep his options open. But he knew there were two, as it stood, the details to be filled in later. One was to kill Carrington and be done with it, take his chances on being caught. The other would be to maximize his chances of getting away with it.

In the first case, the details were few. Find Carrington, get him alone and take him out. The second would be trickier. Any murder on the Zuni Pueblo would be investigated by the FBI. That in itself was not a cause for much worry. Indian Country FBI postings were not given to the best and the brightest. They were for newcomers or exiles, greenhorns or deadwood.

But Carrington was from a wealthy family. He might have become the family black sheep but the wealthy don't like it when somebody gets away with killing one of their own. It reveals the façade of their own invulnerability. So yeah, Carrington's murder would get bumped up a notch or two. If his body could be made to disappear it would be better. But bodies have ways of turning up, even in the remotest areas. And moving a body carried the risk of being discovered with it.

The main thing Aaron had going for him was that only one person had any idea he was looking for Carrington: Kenny Tucker, who had a couple of very good reasons for keeping quiet. A number of others—including Emma, the university cop Delorio, Professor Ted Fuller, the lawyer Mahoney, Harlan and Earl McCormick—knew Aaron had wanted or tried to serve legal papers on Carrington, but none were privy to the knowledge that Carrington was behind the attack. If and when news got out that Carrington had been murdered, a few might realize Aaron hadn't been around Jack Springs at the time.

But with Carrington's background, who knew how many rapes, the stealing of Fuller's research and likelihood of it ending up in Iraq's biological warfare arsenal, Aaron would be way down on the list of suspects, if on it at all. And what were the chances that the only crimes he committed were the ones Aaron knew of? Slim to none. Enter another group of potential suspects.

Only Earl McCormick might put it together. Earl had to be wondering at Aaron's leaving town instead of bird-dogging the investigation, and could, at some point, wonder about his absence around the time Carrington disappeared. If he even found out about it. Too much coincidence.

These ruminations came to an abrupt halt when he realized the curtain of night had fallen. Only a smudge of gray lighted the western horizon. There was no moon. Eerie night sounds—a whoosh of wings, a tiny shriek, scratching sounds—emanated from the desert around him. He rummaged around and found a small flashlight in the glove compartment and moved everything he could to the front seat, leaving only his cooler, a small travel bag and bedroll in the back.

He flopped the rear seatbacks forward, laid out the bedroll and sat in the back of the wagon with his legs dangling off the rear bumper. A few cars and trucks zoomed past on the highway, but the Subaru was effectively out of view and the noise was minimal thanks to the rise of hills. The darkness was complete, except for the rear overhead light.

Aaron opened the cooler, reached in and found a cold can of Bud Light in the melting ice. He popped the top and drained it in two swallows. He let out a satisfying belch then found a snack can of freestone peaches, peeled off the top, chewed and let the cool fruit slide down his throat. As he put the empty cans back in the cooler, he felt in his gut rather than heard the deep rumble of an unmuffled engine, the rise and fall of the rpms indicating it was off the highway, the increasing volume indicating it was getting closer. Soon, bright beams of light pierced the night off to the side. He couldn't imagine what kind of vehicle it was, but a scene from the movie *Road Warrior* was playing in his head. He thought about killing the light inside the car but decided anyone out prowling the desert at night would be less likely to investigate if the car didn't appear to be abandoned. If they had already seen him, leaving on the light would make it seem like just a weary traveler who had pulled off the road for the night instead of someone up to some mischief. He felt the engine's rumble in his chest and saw the lights, which appeared to be mounted above the cab, casting unearthly shadows across the already eerie landscape.

The engine slowed and backfired, then the vehicle turned and the lights were pointed at his car, all but blinding him. With one hand, he worked the .357 from the travel bag and, with the other, found the bottle of whiskey. He uncapped it and held it high to take a swallow so whoever was in the vehicle could see. He turned away from the vehicle, which was probably 20 or 25 yards away, and ignored it. After a few moments, he took another drink, capped the whiskey, stretched out and turned off the overhead light. The noisy engine continued at an idle and the lights still spotlighted the Subaru. This went on for what seemed a long time.

Then the engine roared and the vehicle lurched forward. Aaron picked up the Python, slid out the rear, faced the lights and pointed the revolver into the night sky. When it kept coming, he fired a round into the air. The noise was like a thunderclap and drowned out, for a few seconds, the noise from the engine. Flame from the barrel shot about two feet into the air. An oversized dune buggy with fat tires jerked sideways then swung hard away to the west, rumbling across the sagebrush and cacti until it was out of sight. In a couple of minutes, the sound all but died and he could hear a pack of dogs yapping and howling in the direction the vehicle had traveled.

What the fuck *was* that? Aaron wondered, as the jackhammer in his chest eased off. Time to boogie. He transferred his gear to the back, closed the liftback, got into the front seat and started the car. He turned on the lights, made a U-turn and drove back to the highway. About ten miles down the road, he saw a large mound of gravel just off the road, checked the rearview mirror for headlights, and pulled behind it. In another two minutes, he was stretched out in the back, the magnum close to hand, waiting for sleep to come.

He thought once again of Belinda, lying there, head swathed in bandages, tubes and wires snaking out of her body into bags of fluid and beeping machines. The rise and fall of her chest under the sheets was the only sign the bright fire of her life force still smoldered. He thought of holding his face to Roscoe's ear, telling him goodbye as the drug took him away from the pain. And he thought of Tyrone, imprisoned in a stranger's body for five years, waiting, and likely wanting to die.

These thoughts chased away whatever doubts may have fluttered in his breast. Maybe life could be good again, or maybe not. But it would never be good if he didn't make Carrington pay for what he had set in motion. And it had to be him, Aaron Hemingway. He wanted to be looking into Carrington's eyes when he realized there would be no hung jury, no acquittals, no appeals for his crimes. And that he, Aaron Hemingway, was his judge, jury and executioner.

Holding onto that thought, he fell into a deep, dreamless sleep.

Chapter 33

While Aaron had been buying the derringer, Harlan Silbaugh was sitting in his cramped office and looking out at the desk where Belinda Mondragon had worked. Since the attack, he'd spread the work out among his other employees, getting a reluctant OK from the town council to pay a limited amount of overtime until another full-time dispatcher could be hired. At the moment, Lila June was working a four-hour shift and handling the task admirably. He would have liked to have kidded himself that Belinda might return, but he couldn't. He called the facility—The Kensington—twice a day but she was still in a coma. And when he could track him down, the doctor reiterated that they wouldn't even know the extent of the damage until she regained consciousness.

But no matter who was working, there was an emptiness in the office since she had been gone. He saw Lila June answer the phone. The intercom buzzed. He answered.

"Marshal, Lt. McCormick wants to talk to you," Lila June said, watching him through the window.

"Put him through, Lila June."

"Yes, sir." The phone rang, Harlan picked it up and said, "Earl."

"Harlan, how's things in your neighborhood?"

"Quiet," Harlan said, "and a little lonely without... well, you know."

"I do," Earl said, "and I wanted to ask you about that, particularly about the departure of your star deputy."

Harlan was a simple man and tended to trust the people around him, so when Aaron said he was going to visit his family back in Arkansas, well, he didn't really question the decision. After all he had been through, what with losing Roscoe and the injury to Belinda, it didn't seem all that curious. Except...well, if Aaron was most people. But Aaron was Aaron.

Earl continued, "Doesn't it seem just a bit out of character for him to just let matters drop, when we have made absolutely no progress on the attack? Is this the same guy that you and I know so well? To head for the hills and lick his wounds?"

Now that Earl had put words to it, it felt like a slap upside the head from a particularly vicious nun. "Well," was all Harlan could say with his ears ringing so loudly.

Earl stayed silent, waiting for Harlan to answer. Finally, Harlan said, "It does seem a little peculiar, for him."

"Yeah," Earl said, "and it makes me damned nervous. You got any idea how we could get in touch with him?"

"He never left a number, or anything," Harlan said. "Matter of fact he said he was going to Arkansas to look for his family, like he didn't really know where they were."

"Perfect," Earl said.

In the pause that followed, Harlan had a thought. "There may be somebody who might know something," he said. "Aaron and Belinda had been visiting with Sam Hite. They seemed to have gotten fairly close."

"You're talking about the guy who found them after the attack, who was, I seem to recall, a suspect in the murder up there in the park?"

Harlan added, "He was a logical suspect but never a serious one."

"Great," Earl said, his tone a mixture sarcasm and relief. "Maybe you could give him a call."

In the Cherokee, Harlan was able to navigate the four-wheel-drive road to Sam Hite's cabin. He was glad of that because he sure didn't want to walk up that road, or approach the cabin without warning. Sam was known to be a little quick on the trigger. As he stopped, the big black wolf dog with yellow eyes came outside and sat on her haunches, eyeing him as if he were a side of beef. He leaned out the Jeep window and called out, “Sam, Sam Hite? You in there?”

After a while, a voice creaked from inside, “I surely am, Marshal.”

Sam, dressed in a red, woolen union suit, with his feet stuffed into unlaced combat boots, opened the flimsy screen door and stood on the step. His red beard and hair were wrapped like a briar patch around his head. Dark circles hung beneath his eyes as if he were suffering from a monster hangover.

Sam glanced down at his clothes. “You’ll have to excuse the casual nature of my attire. I been under the weather a mite, and of course I wasn’t expectin’ no company.”

“That’s all right, Sam. I was wondering if I could talk to you about Aaron?”

“Hoss? What about Hoss? He ain’t got himself in another fix, has he?”

“Well, he took off and...we just...you know, we’re concerned is all. I was hoping I could have a minute of your time.”

“Surely, come on in. I’m needing some coffee and you’re welcome to join me.” When he saw hesitation, he noticed Harlan’s eyes were locked on Sadie. “Don’t worry none about her,” he said, tiredly. “She’s jest like a big old pussycat.” He squatted down and scratched her behind the ear. Her tail wagged once but she kept her eyes on Harlan. “See?” Sam said, rising with effort in a cacophony of creaks and groans.

Harlan got out and stepped lightly as Sadie remained in that position. Sam held the door for him and they went in.

Harlan was alarmed at the deterioration of the mountain man’s normal robust demeanor. “Are you all right, Sam? No offense, but you look like warmed-over dogshit.”

Sam winced, “That would be a great improvement over how I feel.” He shuffled toward the stove, grabbed the coffeepot and hand pumped some water in it. After setting it on the woodstove, he threw a handful of kindling in the firebox. He grabbed a whiskey bottle with a black label off the shelf and set it on the table. “Nothin’ a shot of ol’ George in a cup a coffee won’t help.” He motioned toward the table, “Sit, sit, yer makin’ me nervous.”

Harlan sat down. “What’s wrong?”

"What's wrong?" he turned with astonished eyes. "I find three friends bludgeoned, shot, and bloody. One's dead, the other's in a coma. And you ask 'what's wrong?'"

Harlan's face turned crimson. He raised his hands in supplication. "I'm sorry, I thought you might be sick."

Sam's eyes were like embers in a dying campfire. "Oh, I'm sick all right. Wouldn't you be? I been sittin' up here stewin' and drinkin' and tellin' myself if'n I'd'a been a mite quicker, they'd be okay."

The fire faded from his eyes as he realized who he was talking to. He dropped into his seat like a sack of beans. "I 'pologize to ya, Harlan. It's not your fault. I been sittin' here wantin' to kill somebody with my bare hands, jest rip their scrotum out and watch 'em bleed to death, and instead I'm feelin' sorry for myself. I jest needed somebody to take it out on." He shook his head in disgust.

Harlan started to tell Sam it wasn't his fault; that they were all feeling that way, but Sam waved his hand, dismissing the attempt.

"Anyway, what can I tell you about Hoss that you don't already know?" Sam asked.

"For starters, I was wondering if you know where he is?"

Sam's bushy eyebrows moved together. "He came by one day and tole me that he was goin' to Arkansas to look for his kinfolk. You think mebbe he was prevaricating?" "Not necessarily," Harlan said. "But, you know, I never heard mention of this family in Arkansas. I know his mother and father have passed on. He didn't talk about them much. But Earl McCormick thinks it was out of character for him just to take off, with the investigation into the attack still going on and Belinda in the hospital. I'm not sure I agree. Seems to me burying that dog just took all of the fight out of him."

Sam said, "I agree with Earl. He wouldn't look me in the eye when he tole me. I can tell you one thing, though. It wasn't buryin' Roscoe that changed him. I saw him for a short time before he went up to Wyoming and he was hurtin' and angry. When he came back he was quiet-like."

Harlan was surprised, but he realized that he hadn't seen Aaron in person since the night of the attack. All their communication had been over the telephone. At the time he just took it for grief.

"So, he was lookin' for some fella to serve legal papers on?" Sam asked.

"Yeah, it was some work he was doing before he came to work for me. Something about sick Gulf War veterans. All he said was he heard the guy was in Wyoming. He didn't even say where."

Sam waggled his eyebrows. "I remember he said something to me about Saratoga. Seem to recall he mentioned he knew somebody there."

"Ah," said Harlan, making the connection. "Emma Sodenberg. I think I'll give her a call." He got up to leave. "By the way, you probably said but I can't remember, what was it that made you follow Aaron and Belinda that night at the bar?"

Sam's expression relaxed almost into a smile. "It was jest a dog thing," he said. "Nothing of any consequence."

Chapter 34

July 31

A blood-red sky bled through Aaron's eyelids and announced the dawn. He closed them tight for a moment, remembered the strange encounter of the previous evening and felt for the comfort of his magnum. It was right where it was supposed to be, cool to the touch, a comforting solidity. He reminded himself to clean it tonight. And that reminded him of the derringer he now owned. This morning would be a good time to test-fire it.

First, though, he had to get rid of the dry mouth. He grabbed the bottle of Gatorade he had bought in Cuba and took a long swallow. The fire in the sky was quickly fading, so he shook off the sleeping bag, flexed his legs and arms, pushed up the lift back and slid out. The air was clean and dry, but the ground was largely barren, covered with swaths of red gravel and seams of black. Only a few shrubs, which looked like stunted sagebrush, grew in the parched earth.

He slipped on his boots, rolled up his sleeping bag and pulled out the derringer, the lead, powder and caps. After shaking two lead balls and two percussion caps out of their containers, he held the powder horn over the up-pointed barrels. He wasn't sure how much gunpowder to charge the barrels with, so he filled each barrel about a third full, dropped in the lead balls, tamped them down. The lead balls were slightly oversized and fit snugly in the barrel. Then he slipped a cap, which looked like the ass end of a .22 cartridge casing, onto the perforated nub at the back end of each barrel.

He stood and walked toward the large gravel pile that hid him from the highway. About 20 feet away, he the raised the derringer, cocked one hammer, aimed and fired. The gun bucked moderately and the slug plowed into the gravel about four feet left of the spot where he was aiming. Dark smoke was hanging in the air between him and the target. The whole thing had an unreal quality, as there seemed to be a slight delay between the hammer falling and the powder igniting. Likewise with the slug. It was almost as if he could see it come out of the barrel and slam into the gravel, like he was watching it in slow motion.

He fired the second barrel. It was pretty much the same. So he walked back to the car and poured half again as much powder in each barrel, tamped a lead ball into each, removed the spent caps and stuck on two more. Turning to the gravel pile, he walked to the same spot and fired again. This time the kick was more pronounced, sending his hand up a good six inches. The smoke was even thicker and there was no illusion at seeing the ball fly through the air. As soon as the powder ignited, a pile of gravel erupted outward.

That's better, Aaron thought. He fired again. Yeah, definitely better. A close-quarters weapon. About 15 feet, preferably less. He walked back, put the derringer and ball, powder and caps into their respective bags. If he could find a holster, the derringer would make a concealable back-up piece.

He packed up the car and headed south. Just outside of Thoreau, he saw a sign in red, white and blue lettering saying "Guns, Guns, Guns" on the side of a van parked in a packed-dirt patch near the interstate on-ramp. A flea market was in the process of being set up. Tables were erected next to the van and a man was arranging his wares. Aaron pulled into the lot and parked. He got out and walked toward the van. The proprietor wore long sideburns, and a mesh-topped, black NRA cap that didn't hide his bald pate, suspenders holding his work pants up to a small beer belly, and he had just swung into a metal folding chair when Aaron stopped in front of the table.

"Good morning, friend," the man said in a high, wheezy voice, his eyes flickering quickly away from Aaron's damaged head. He reached for a Coke can and dribbled a stream of tobacco juice into the can. "What can I do for you this fine morning in the U. S. of A—a promul*gatoire* of its citizens' right to bear arms?"

"I need a holster for a .44-caliber derringer," Aaron said.

The man waggled his briar-patch eyebrows. "Concealable or open?"

"Concealable," Aaron said.

"Of course," he said, slapping the heel of his hand against his forehead. "What the hell's the point of wearing a derringer in the open? You'd probably end up having to shoot someone to stop them from laughing at you. You caught me before I had my second cuppa joe. Anyways, let me rummage around in the truck." He was back in two minutes holding a pancake holster with a wide clip on it. "You can wear it inside or outside the pants. It's padded so's you can carry it in the small of your back without too much discomfort. It's not much good if you have to pull her out quick-like, though. Fifteen simoleans, if you don't tell anyone what a good deal I gave ya'." He winked. "I wouldn't want anyone to think I'm getting soft brained in my old age."

Aaron said, "Deal."

The gun seller scratched his bare chin absently, his eyes scrunched as if considering something. "Listen, I'm not trying to get into a man's business, you understand. But my gut tells me this derringer is going to be a working tool for you." He looked for a reaction.

"I think, generally speaking, a gun, like any tool, should be up to the job required," Aaron said, hedging his response.

The man nodded, "Well said, friend. These days a man can't be too cautious. What I'm getting at is…well…what kind of caps and powder do you have?"

"I couldn't tell you," Aaron said. "I just bought the derringer and it didn't appear to have been fired. The powder and caps came with it but I don't recall there are any names on the containers."

"OK, the accessories that come with new guns are not top of the line, as a rule. I'm going to make a couple of suggestions, and," he grinned, "maybe do a little more business."

"Sure, Aaron said. "Let's hear it."

He went back into his van and returned with a round tin in one hand, a black plastic jar in the other.

"These are CCI No. 11 Magnum caps. They'll hit the charge faster and hotter. And this is Black Mag 3 powder. You can use a third less and have the same charge as Pyrodex, or you can use the same amount and turn it into a magnum load. It's cleaner and produces less fouling. Forty-five George Washingtons for all three, the holster, powder and caps."

Aaron hesitated for a moment, then thought, aw, what the hell. "Sold," he said, handing over the money. The man wrote out a receipt and handed it to Aaron. At the top of the sheet it read, "Uriah Watkins, Armorer."

An hour later, Aaron pulled off Interstate 40 at Exit 22, crossed an oily wash named Rio Puerco and a dozen or so railroad tracks, then hit Old Route 66, where he turned west into Gallup. His first impression was dinginess. Colors were washed, faded, or tinged with soot. Only the new pickup trucks, of which there were many, had their original luster.

It got worse in the center of town, which wasn't hard to understand, with a dozen diesel locomotives idling in the massive rail yard not 50 feet from the highway. Attached to the locomotives were mile-long chains of coal cars, some empty, some full. Others, piled with scrap metal, stacks of lumber, automobiles, and all other manner of industrial detritus, sat idly on track sidings. A smudgy yellow haze hung over the Rio Puerco valley.

Although it was early, groups of Indians had gathered on street corners and were passing brown bags back and forth. Others, often alone, looked on wishfully. The street was lined with pawnshops, Native American craft shops, drive-up liquor stores, gas stations, car washes, restaurants and motels. The town felt like a living replica of the Depression, a no-man's-land way station for Dust Bowl refugees headed to California. The only clear signs of modernity were the cars and trucks, and the inevitable Wal-Mart.

It made sense because Gallup was the economic hub of a wheel that included a half-dozen reservations, none of which allowed alcohol to be sold. Aaron knew that while alcoholism was a problem on those reservations, these Indians were only a tiny fraction of the Indians living in the Four Corners, but they were a highly visible, concentrated fraction. He thought about his friends Pete Magpie and Toby Echohawk as an antidote to generalizing about Indians and alcohol. Pete didn't drink at all. Toby, who could drink a beer now and then without any obvious deleterious effects, said he liked the taste but not the buzz.

Up ahead, Aaron saw a convenience store and pulled in. In the console was a bag full of quarters. He grabbed a handful, walked to the pay phone on the front of the building and called the facility where Belinda lay. In the four days he'd been gone he'd called every day but at different times so the operator wouldn't begin to recognize his voice. He also knew that the calls weren't logged, and since he was calling from a pay phone, there'd be no way to check from the other end who was calling and where they were calling from. The automated voice told him to deposit $3.25. After clinking in 13 quarters, the phone rang.

"The Kensington."

"Yeah, I'd like the medical wing."

After five rings, someone picked up.

"Yeah, hello. I'd like to check on the condition of Belinda Mondragon," Aaron said, knowing that this was the only information hospitals or other medical facilities usually provided on patients unless the callers were family members.

"Ms. Mondragon is critical-stable," the woman said. "There's been no change. I'm sorry," a little warmth creeping into her voice. Maybe she remembered his voice from the earlier call. He'd have to call in the evening next time.

"Thank you," Aaron said and hung up, both relieved and disappointed.

He pulled away with a heavy heart but he knew he had to get focused. Every move, now, had to be calculated until he decided the play. Heading west on Old 66, he saw a motel sign for the Economy Inn. The paint was a little fresher than most others along this strip, so he was tempted. Of course, he could look for a seedier, no-questions-asked, hot-pillow dive. But he knew from experience that cops gave these places a little extra attention, simply because those staying in them might just be trying to avoid attention. He'd be damned if he was going to sleep in the car another night, making it three nights in a row without a shower.

Well shit, he decided, I might live to regret it but I'm going to give the Economy Inn a try. He pulled in front of the office and the parking lot was mostly empty, but even so, he could see it was a more respectable place than the others he had passed, and that gave it the anonymity he needed. He swung out of the car and went in. Behind the counter, a dark woman swathed in a translucent blue sari looked up from a desk. She stood and turned toward him. Her name tag said: Rumnit Chatterjee, Manager.

She smiled and asked, without so much as sweeping her eyes across his rumpled clothes or his four-day growth, "Do you need a room, sir?"

Aaron was immediately disarmed. "That would be good," he said. "I'm going to die if I don't get a shower and some clean clothes on." It was both the truth and a subtle way of telling her he didn't *usually* look this bad.

"Please don't die here. A shower is just minutes away." She smiled at her little joke, raised her brows slightly and asked, "Single?"

"Yeah, it's just me," Aaron said.

"That will be $31.50. Cash or charge?"

"Cash," Aaron said, shaking his head in wonder. "Thirty dollars? It must be the off-season."

This time she really arched her brows, not understanding. Then she relaxed and a smile tugged at the corners of her mouth. "Ah, a joke, I think. It's always the 'off season' in Gallup, I'm afraid."

Aaron handed her the money and she handed him a registration card. Fearing she was going to ask for identification, he gritted his teeth and signed his real name but made it even sloppier than usual. But he did reverse two of the numbers on his license plate. It wasn't much but it was the best he could do under the circumstances. So much for operational security.

She picked up the card without looking at it, took a key off the wall and handed it to him. "Room 10." She pointed to the juncture of the L-shaped building. "It is our quietest room."

"Thank you," Aaron said, and returned to his car.

After unloading his gear from the car, he took the long-awaited shower, spending 15 minutes under the hot water. He scraped four days worth of stubble off his cheeks and ran his fingers along his wound. The stitches were still prickling from the scar, but the wound had begun healing. He slipped on a T-shirt and shorts and channel surfed until he found a station playing country music videos. It was always interesting to see the faces behind the songs he sometimes heard on the radio.

Aaron watched a dozen or so videos of performers whose main attractions seemed to be pretty faces and sexy bodies but little of what he thought of as country music and then he yawned mightily. The encounter with the strange vehicle in the desert had taken a toll on his sleep. Nevertheless, he reached for the telephone directory with the intention of looking up the library and the local newspaper, where he hoped to learn something about Carrington's archeological dig. He was having trouble focusing on the print, so he laid the book on his chest and was soon asleep, the sound of pedal-steel guitars helping drown out the rumble of idling locomotives.

Earlier that day, Harlan had picked up the telephone and called Emma Sodenberg. A feminine voice answered. "Emma, this is Marshal Harlan Silbaugh."

He could hear a muffled, "Mom! This guy thought I was you and his name is Marcel Arden Seeball." Harlan turned red at the mistake. He could hear the phone being jostled. "Hello? Who is this?"

"Emma, this is Harlan Silbaugh."

"Harlan? Oh Lord, what's happened now?"

"Nothing's happened, exactly, Emma. It's just that Aaron took off and we're not quite sure what he's up to. I wanted to ask you what happened when he came up to see you."

"He was looking for Trey Carrington, one of the millionaires that lives up on Mt. Baldy."

"Who's that? I never heard the name of the fellow he was looking for."

"Trey Carrington. I know nothing about him personally. Aaron wanted to know if he could get in up there to find Carrington and serve a subpoena on him. I told him probably not. There's heavy security and nobody gets in without a pass or permission from a resident. He borrowed my truck and was going to try to bluff his way in. When he came back, he said he couldn't get past security. He said no more about it but that he had to get back to Jack Springs. He was definitely acting strange, though. He told me thanks and left as soon as he got his gear together. I just put it down to all the things he's been through."

"I'm sure that's right, Emma. It's just that a couple of days after he got back, he called to say he was going to Arkansas to look for his family. It just seems a mite peculiar."

"It definitely does *not* seem like the Aaron that I know," Emma said. "The fires of justice were burning brightly when he told me why he was looking for Carrington."

"Is there anyway you could find out a phone number for Carrington?"

"A girlfriend of mine works in the lodge up there. I could call her."

"Would you do that for me?" Harlan asked. "If you get something, give me a call. If I don't hear from you, I'll assume you couldn't." He paused. "Actually, could you call me either way?"

"OK, I'll call her now. She should be at work." Emma hung up.

Harlan started thinking about the frozen yogurt next door at Fat Jack's deli and was pushing his chair away from the desk when the phone rang.

"Marshal Silbaugh," he said.

"It's Emma, Harlan. I got the number." She read it to him.

"Thanks, Emma."

"Keep me posted."

"I'll do that." Then he called Earl McCormick and filled him in. "I'd prefer that you call him. I'm not much good at being, uh, sneaky."

"I'm real good at it," Earl said, hung up on Harlan and dialed the number. It rang five times before someone picked up the phone and said in a clipped, accented voice, "Hello, Mr. Carrington residence."

"I would like to speak to Mr. Carrington," Earl said, using his cop voice.

"He no here."

"Do you know when he will return?"

"Two month."

"Do you know where I could reach him?"

"No."

"How long has he been gone?"

"Two month."

"Who am I speaking to?"

"Handyman. Getting house ready for winter. Goodbye." Then he hung up.

Well, that's that, Earl thought, as he dialed Harlan to tell him.

When Aaron awoke from his nap, his mouth tasted as if he had been sucking on an old sock. He swung his legs off the bed, staggered to the window and peered out. The sky was an odd-hued mishmash of black, gray and pastels. He had slept into the evening. He remembered that a soda machine was a couple doors down so he slid some change off the dresser, walked down and grabbed a root beer out of the machine. He drank half of it before reaching his room. Sitting at the small table in the room, he cleaned the derringer and reloaded it. He slipped it into the holster he had purchased. Then he ran a cleaning rod with a cloth patch through the barrel of the .357.

He dressed in jeans, boots and a T-shirt and clipped the holster inside his above his right hip. He covered it with a light, flannel shirt, left untucked and unbuttoned.

After three days in the car, he decided to walk the few blocks up Coal Street to the bars. He wasn't sure why he was going out into a scene like he'd witnessed today. Maybe some perverse sense of raising his own state of being by associating with the unfortunates he was sure to find.

He wasn't disappointed. The first two bars he passed were dimly lit hellholes, with wet-brain drunks spilling out on the sidewalk. The alleys he passed reeked of urine and vomit. He had changed his mind and decided to just walk around downtown when he came upon another, which didn't have drunks loitering outside. He opened the screen door, squinted and walked in.

Eight or nine people, mostly men, were at the bar and three of the six round tables were occupied in the middle of the room. On the far side of the room, a mixture of cowboys and blue-collar laborers were quietly drinking in three booths with high-backed seats, cigarette tips winking like fireflies. Neon Bud and Coors signs gave color to the haze of cigarette smoke that hung, unmoving, near the ceiling. A large, silent TV screen showing a rodeo drew no interest. The clack of pool balls came from behind a partition off to the left. A buxom, middle-aged blonde with a helmet of big hair that looked like it could withstand a tactical nuclear strike was wiping down the bar.

Three seats were open at the bar and Aaron took one next to a geezer with greasy hair hanging over a deeply creased face. A cigarette with half an ash intact dangled from the guy's lower lip. His left arm was wrapped protectively around the half-filled glass of amber liquid. His ring and pinkie fingers and half his palm were missing, leaving a claw sporting long, dirty fingernails. He never looked up. Aaron began to question the uplifting nature of absorbing the local culture. Instead of leaving, he thought, what the hell, I'm here, I'm thirsty, and I'm going to have a drink. He ordered a Bud Light.

As he tipped the longneck high, the bar door opened and a lean, long-haired man with a face of quilt-like scars and a Bowie knife strapped to his right leg stepped inside. As he surveyed the room, a cue ball slammed into the partition like a gunshot. Aaron flinched but none of the other patrons seemed to notice the noise. The scarred man turned so he could see into the poolroom.

"Goddamnit!" the bartender yelled. "I told you guys to take it easy in there." She slapped a bar rag on the counter as the ivory ball rolled out of the room, across the floor and came to rest against the scarred man's knee-high moccasin.

A tall redneck, dirty hair sticking sideways like frizzy wings out of his Caterpillar cap and overalls covered with drilling mud and streaks of grease, moved into the doorway. He looked down at the cue ball and then up at the scarred man, as if he were expecting him to bend over and pick up the ball.

The redneck's bloodshot eyes took in the newcomer. A malevolent smile crossed his face. From where he stood, he could not see the Bowie knife strapped to the man's right leg. What he could see—the faded, torn jeans, the ragged fatigue jacket draped over the man's barb-wire-taut 6-1 frame—gave him no reason to fear.

A weak chin and protruding Adam's apple bobbed as the redneck worked a plug of chewing tobacco around in his mouth, getting ready to speak. He puffed up his chest.

"Say, Injun, why don't you make yourself useful and hand me that there cue ball. I'd get it myself but, unlike you welfare warriors, I've been working for a livin' and my back's a little stiff."

The scarred man turned to face him, bringing the Texas toothpick into full view. It was as long as a man's forearm and resting in an elaborately beaded sheath trimmed by leather fringe, each strung with a turquoise bead. It was secured at mid-thigh by two thick leather thongs—one around his waist and another just above the knee—a business-like arrangement that suggested you didn't want to see the business that would bring it out. Voices in the bar quieted to a few whispers. Two other roughnecks, long brown beer bottles in hand, moved in behind their friend, who leaned against the door frame and, buoyed by their presence, said, "Lordy, lordy, boys, I think we done stumbled on Frankenstein's Injun here!"

The redneck's eyes swept the rest of the bar patrons, who were Anglos and Hispanics, as if he expected some appreciation of his taunt. Instead, he saw what might pass for a few flickers of grim amusement.

"Fella, just go back to your pool game," the bartender said, her voice tense with annoyance. "I don't want any trouble in here." She dropped her hand out of sight behind the bar.

The scarred man looked down at the cue ball as if he had picked up a dog turd in the gutter. A whisper of a smile crossed his lips.

When he looked back up, his eyes had turned feral and cold, and locked onto the redneck's—the predator's challenge. A deathly stillness enveloped the room.

The redneck looked around the bar and swallowed, still fueled by a bully's courage but less sure now. He said, "Say, chief, are you hard of hearing or just stupid?" The scarred man's eyes never blinked, never wavered, the pupils so large you could not determine his eye color.

The redneck was, in that moment, reminded of the huge, coiled diamondback he had stumbled on in the mudshack that time out on the drill pad: the one that looked like it was measuring him for a coffin. He had blasted it with double-aught 12-gauge, hacked it to pieces with a shovel, stomped it flat, and it still took four hours to quit twitching. As the seconds of silence stretched out, the redneck could see that rattler's eyes in this broke-down Injun. His sphincter muscles were quivering, and his Adam's apple bobbed up and down as he tried to swallow the lump growing like a tumor in his throat.

Finally, without looking down, the scarred man's moccasin nudged the cue ball across the floor away from where the redneck stood. All eyes except the scarred man's followed the cue ball's slow progress as it ticked like the second hand on an old-fashioned time bomb across the uneven wood floor. Just before it banged into the wall, the other drinkers turned their eyes back to the bottles and glasses before them, ducked their heads into a defensive hunch, as if sensing something they didn't want to witness. The redneck's buddies felt the change in the room and began edging back into the poolroom.

When the redneck looked back at the scarred man, his alcohol-induced bravado betrayed him. "Fuck it, man. J-jest f-f-fuck this shit! This is nuts!" He loped like a bum-legged jackrabbit for the back exit.

A collective sigh of relief was audible in the room. Aaron, who had been watching the scarred man's eyes, motioned to the seat next to his. "Buy you a drink?"

The man nodded and sat. "Merilee, give me a shot of Beam. Since this gentleman is buying, make it the black-label bottle." His voice had the breezy, scary quality of the Hispanic actor James Edward Olmos, a grave, inflection-less whisper.

This close, Aaron could see a quilt-like array of scars that gave the man's face the look of a cubist painting—nothing was quite aligned. The scars were soft pink and faint against his dark face. The man knocked back the whiskey, sat the glass down gently and turned to Aaron. "I thank you for the drink." He held out his hand and they shook.

"Name's Carlos Corrigan," he said in a gravelly whisper.

"You're welcome. Adam, Adam Hathaway," Aaron said, using one of his old Denver PD undercover names. "That's quite a knife you got there."

Carlos almost grinned. He unstrapped it, set it on the bar and nodded, "Go ahead. It's a true Bowie knife, more than 140 years old." Aaron slipped it easily out of the sheath, held it up to the light, turned it this way and that. He set it down and picked up the sheath. "I'm no expert, but I'd say this is some amazing beadwork."

Carlos nodded. "My neighbor, a 92-year-old Navajo woman, did it, said a knife like this deserves a proper home."

"She did it up proud," Aaron said and placed it on the table next to the knife. Carlos put them together, wrapped them in the leather thongs and set them on his lap, out of sight.

"Does this kind of thing happen often?" He pointed his chin in the direction of the rednecks in the pool room.

"Not often," Carlos said. "And when it does, it rarely gets physical. I've cultivated a line of defense that makes me look tougher than I am. The knife's an important component of that. It's usually enough."

Aaron recalled the steely glare in Carlos's eyes and wasn't ready to buy the part about "look tougher than I am." He just nodded and said, "I'll agree that it is effective."

"Mostly, people do double-takes and walk way around me. Sometimes a kid'll come up and ask about it."

"That must be hard," Aaron said.

"Not so much, " Carlos shook his head dismissively. "We all have scars. Mine are just more obvious than most."

"Amen," Aaron said and raised his beer bottle. Carlos chunked it with his whiskey tumbler, then threw back the amber liquid.

An older couple slid out of a booth in the rear. Aaron looked around and no one was moving to take the seat. He nodded toward the empty booth and asked, "Got time for another?"

"That I do," Carlos said. They ordered refills and moved to the booth, studiously ignored by the bar's other patrons. They settled in and their drinks were delivered.

"Before you ask," Corrigan raised his chin slightly and turned his face from side to side, "A bear did this."

"Holy Christ," Aaron said. "How did you survive something like that?"

"She wasn't trying to kill me," Carlos said. "She was sending me a message."

"Where were you, up in Alaska?"

The man shook his head. "No, I was in New Mexico, a little north of Chama."

"Shit, I was just up there a few days ago. A black bear did that?"

"No, it was a griz."

It dawned on Aaron what he was hearing. "A grizzly in New Mexico?" Aaron asked, then immediately regretted it as Carlos's eyes turned hard.

"I know a griz when I see one," he said flatly. "And I saw this one real damn close up."

"I wasn't doubting you," Aaron said. "It just took me by surprise."

Aaron could almost hear the gears turning in Carlos's mind. Then they locked eyes and he could see some debate had been resolved.

"I guess a man who buys a stranger a drink is worthy of an explanation," Carlos shrugged, almost imperceptibly. "They thought the grizzlies in Colorado were gone by 1955, until another was killed just north of the New Mexico border in 1979. So they had escaped detection for a quarter of a century. Yet that bear was 14 years old so there were at least two generations born after 1955. And the necropsy revealed it had borne cubs, so there had been a male around at some point during that time. And potentially another generation after that. There's been a number of sightings since but nothing has been confirmed with physical evidence. The one that got me had cubs."

Aaron was dumbfounded. "How the hell could they stay that well hidden?" "There's two theories," Carlos said. "One is that they live in the deep canyons on the west side of the South San Juan Wilderness. The canyons are steep and littered with blown-down timber, making them almost impregnable. The other is that, unlike most grizzlies, which are aggressive, these bears have adapted by becoming reclusive, like black bears. I got between this one and her cubs. Even black bears will attack in that situation."

"What happened to the bear?"

"Nothing. I said it was a black bear and refused to tell Fish and Game where it happened."

"Why not tell the truth?"

"Because I didn't want it killed. It was my fault. I should have known better. I did know better. But I was drunk when it happened." Carlos broke eye contact and Aaron knew that part of the conversation was over. Just then a body hit the partition between the bar and pool room, hard enough to rattle the liquor bottles across the room.

The bartender threw her rag down and came around the bar with a stun gun in her hand, the muscles in her jaws working like she was breaking in a fresh piece of DoubleBubble chewing gum. She marched into the pool room and shouted, "Out, and I mean right now." She must have given the gun some juice because a crackle like rustling cellophane erupted. The roughnecks' heavy boots pounded the wood floor like a heavy-metal drum solo as they stampeded through the front door. The bartender walked back to the bar without comment.

The drama helped avoid any potential unease at the abrupt end to Carlos's explanation of his wounds.

Aaron couldn't say exactly why, but he trusted Carlos Corrigan. After the bartender brought another round of drinks and walked away, he asked, "You from around here?"

"I been spending some time here," Corrigan said, without elaborating. "And you?"

"I'm just passing through. I thought I'd go down to Zuni, look around." It was as if someone had tightened a noose around the conversation.

Corrigan looked thoughtful, like he was making a decision. "The people down there are, uh, interesting. They are polite enough but they don't take to strangers much. You know, they don't even have a motel or hotel in town so there's no outsiders hanging around. Some of the old folks can't or won't speak English."

"You sound like you admire them for it," Aaron said.

"I do. They're trying to keep their culture intact. That's no small chore in today's world. Unfortunately, though, three-fourths of the houses with electricity have 200-channel satellite dishes. You can imagine what that's doing to the kids." Corrigan shook off the thought, then smiled. "There's a good bunch running the newspaper down there, though."

"The tribal newspaper?" Aaron asked.

"No, it's independent of the tribe. And it's run by high school kids."

"No shit?"

"No shit."

After that, it was a tough conversation. There was some bond between Aaron and Carlos Corrigan, but both had to dance around whatever they were keeping from each other. Finally, it wore out. They'd both finished their drinks. It was decision time, Aaron knew. Order again and they'd have to talk about some things that he knew he didn't want to talk about and highly suspected Corrigan felt the same way. Either that or bullshit each other. What'd be the point? He picked up his beer bottle, shook it, and said, "Well, that's about it for me. Thanks for the information about Zuni. He reached across the table and they shook hands again. "Maybe I'll run into you here another time."

"If you come back in, that's a good possibility," Carlos said. Aaron started for the door, stopped and turned back. "What's the name of that newspaper down there?"

"The Shiwi Messenger," Corrigan said. "Shiwi means 'The People,' the Zuni."

Aaron wondered how Corrigan knew so much about the Zuni but didn't ask. Instead he said, "I might stop by and see them. I used to be a newspaper man myself."

A police cruiser was creeping past as Aaron walked out of the bar. The cops were looking at him, but it didn't feel like they had any *interest* in him, they were just doing what cops do—checking people out and looking for any reaction. With the derringer on his hip, the sight of the cop car sobered but didn't shake him. No quick turn of the head, no stiffening of the spine, no change in body language came from inside the car. He watched them pass, then turned and walked down the sidewalk. The cops kept going.

As he walked, he noticed that every surface—asphalt, concrete, brick and glass—had an oily sheen. The crowds had arrived since he had gone in to the bar. As he negotiated through groups of men and women, young and old and every age in between, who stood and sat passing brown bags in every recessed doorway, alley, and darkened street corner, talking quietly, angrily or drunkenly, he became aware that the sheen carried with it an odor, which the reptilian part of his brain identified as the stench of misery and desperation.

For as long as anyone remembered, throngs had gathered on the streets of Gallup to smother the pain of their existence slowly. But often, the pain ended quickly on the highway, railroad tracks, or some lonely hillside on a freezing night.

This may be as close to an actual place you could call hell as I've ever been, he thought, except for Nam, of course. Two months ago, before

Harlan offered him a job, he was, at best, on his way to ending up in a place just like this. Now, he knew that depending on how this mission turned out, he might be wishing he had. A chill breeze blew down the stinking street and slipped down his collar, shivering his soul.

Chapter 35

August 1

The next morning when Aaron pulled back the curtain the sky was considerably clearer of pollution than the day before. Activities at the railyard, while never shutting down completely, had apparently dropped off overnight. And a light westerly breeze had moved the remaining haze east toward Albuquerque.

He dressed, pulled on a DeKalb Seed ball cap to hide his stitches, packed some gear and paid Ms. Chatterjee for another night. Then he drove back down Old 66 until he found a decent-looking café and ordered two over easy, hash browns, toast and coffee. A quick scan of the *Gallup Independent* produced nothing of interest so he called the facility to check on Belinda. Her condition was unchanged.

Back at the Economy Inn the night before, Aaron had decided to change his plans. Instead of trying to find out about Carrington through the Gallup newspaper, he'd go to Zuni and ask for some back issues of the kids' newspaper.

By 9:30 he was driving south on New Mexico 602, climbing out of the valley into the dry pine foothills. Thirty miles later, he came to a T in the road. To the left, the sign said Ramah and El Malpais. To the right were Black Rock and Zuni Pueblo. He turned west on N.M. 53. As he entered the Zuni Pueblo, Aaron recalled that in New Mexico the word Pueblo refers to what most Indian tribes call a reservation.

However, most of those Pueblos had a collection of historic adobe buildings also called a Pueblo.

A few scattered homes with livestock pens, a garden, and maybe small hayfields were set back well off the highway. A mile or two farther was Black Rock, which appeared to be a collection of adobe-style apartments with playgrounds, carports, and lawns.

If this was reservation housing, it was certainly a world away from any Aaron had seen. There were no junk cars, no litter. The houses looked to be well built and well kept. It looked like suburban Santa Fe. He kept driving and a few miles up the road entered a breathtaking basin surrounded by a horseshoe of forested, red-rock mesas under a boundless blue sky. The most notable feature, however was a huge free-standing mesa reposed in the middle of the bowl, like a geologic hub in a great wheel of land, its spokes having melted away in time.

Ahead, the highway disappeared into a swath of green, as more buildings were scattered along the highway. Finally, the shape of the town itself emerged from the groves of cottonwood, elm and alder.

One of the first structures was a new adobe-style building. The sign out front said A:Shiwi Cultural Center and Museum. A smaller sign said "Information." Perfect, Aaron thought, intending to ask where he could find the newspaper office.

It was cool and a little dark inside the cultural center. Glass cases lined the walls with jewelry, artifacts, pottery, and other accessories of ancient and present Zuni life. Colorful rugs hung in spaces on the walls. A long, glass counter was in the wing to the right.

A middle-aged woman with a maroon blouse sat behind the counter. Her thick black hair was pulled into a long braid. She wore an elaborate squash-blossom silver necklace inlaid with large pieces of jade. She was concentrating on some paperwork when Aaron stepped to the counter. She looked up and smiled. "May I help you?"

"Yeah, could you tell me how to find the newspaper—the…Shiwi, uh..."

Her dark eyes twinkled. "Messenger. Surely. Go out the front door, go left until you're in the parking lot. It's the small brown building at the rear of the parking lot, with lots of young people about."

"Well, that was easy," Aaron said.

"Sometimes it is," she said, nodding and smiling.

The ramshackle house sat about 30 yards away. A pair of old couches, a table and several kitchen chairs were crowded onto a small porch. Scrawny elm trees were scattered around the porch and yard. Teenagers covered nearly every horizontal surface. They were involved in an animated discussion, punctuated by frequent giggles and peels of laughter. A sign saying "The Shiwi Messenger" hung from the eaves of the porch.

As he approached, a girl wearing bib overalls, a jersey shirt and white, high-top Converse sneakers looked his way and stood. Her long hair was parted in the middle, with long bangs covering her forehead.

"Is there something I can help you with?" she asked, a bright smile spreading across her wide, pretty face.

"I was wondering if I could get some back issues of your newspaper," he said, glancing at the rest of the group. They were caught up in whatever story was being told and oblivious to his presence.

"Oh sure," she said. "The papers are free but if you feel like making a *don-a-tion*…? She arched her eyebrows innocently.

Aaron grinned. "Sure, how about a dollar each?"

"Oh, no, that's too much. Fifty cents would be good."

"Okay, it's a deal. Seventy five apiece."

Up to this point, she'd been speaking very properly and sounding quite mature. That was about to end.

She rolled her eyes and said, "Oh, brother," stretching it out breathily in mock impatience. Then she giggled, and her hand flew automatically to cover her mouth. "My name is Amanda Delona," she said, waiting for Aaron to introduce himself. Already feeling guilty about the deception, he said, "I'm Adam Hathaway. Good to meet you."

"Good to meet you, too, sir. Come in."

They entered the house. Like the porch, the front room was replete with couches. She led Aaron to a short hallway between the living room and kitchen with floor-to-ceiling cubed shelves. She pointed to a cube near the middle. "This is our last issue. They go across and then down." A rust-colored mutt, curled up in an overstuffed chair, raised his head. "And that's Barks-a-lot," Amanda said, causing the dog to thump his tail two times before laying his head back down.

"Does he?" Aaron asked.

A wrinkle of puzzlement crossed her forehead. "Oh, you mean does he bark a lot? He did when we first got him out of the dog pound. But he's hardly barked since."

"Ah," Aaron said and turned back to stacks of papers, pulling the most recent issue, scanning it and seeing a story that almost buckled his knees. The headline read: "Zuni teens to visit archeological dig." He scanned down and saw today's date in the third paragraph of the story.

After giving the welcoming speech and assigning his college students to guide four small groups of visitors on a tour of the site, Trey Carrington retired to his Paradiso motor coach, where he congratulated himself on his brilliant scheme and watched small groups of students being herded around. Of the seventeen high school students from Zuni, eleven were girls.

Though dressed in the baggy uniforms the kids in town generally wore, he could see through the smoky window that three or four had matured sexually enough to make their clothes fill out in the right places. The prettiest one, however, looked to be 12 or 13 and had yet to bud. He noticed she never looked up while he was addressing the group. Her face bore a striking similarity to the junkie hooker in Albuquerque but this one was just what she seemed: pure, lovely innocence.

He just *ached* at the shyness, the giggles, the averted eyes and the constant blushing. It was hard to find innocence like that in today's world.

The little one was in the group passing by the motor coach, and she glanced shyly at his window and covered her mouth with her hand as Matthew was telling his group that's where the professor lives. While that window was covered with a reflective coating so he could watch without being seen, Carrington felt an exciting connection with the young one, making him squirm in his seat. He hoped that she was one of the ones who would return. He decided he'd have to learn her name and pay special attention to her. A mild buzz of excitement swept through his body. He turned away from the window for now. This was going better than he ever imagined.

Of course, he would never have thought of it if that redheaded bitch Fiona Donnegan hadn't turned on him, wasting the weeks that he had spent cultivating her. It had been an accident, really. She was warming to him, slowly, but surely. He had meant simply to pat her on the leg but misjudged and rested his fingers on the inside of her thigh. Misunderstanding, she had stood bolt upright and started to walk away when he grabbed her by her shoulders and turned her to face him, so he could explain. It was then he felt the tip of the goddamn hunting knife she carried poking him in the groin.

What he had really wanted to do was to lace his fingers behind her neck and press his thumbs into her trachea, watching her face turn red then purple as the oxygen was depleted to her brain, just enough acuity remaining to realize: YOU DO NOT DENY TREY CARRINGTON! But he knew that knife was sharp as a razor. He'd watched one of the boys dry-shave the hair on his arm with it, and she was pressing the point hard into his nut sack, even making little jabbing motions as if inviting him to try something as she glared defiantly into his eyes. Swallowing his fury, he told her to get out, right then, or he would have her charged with assault. She said, "Gladly, you sick fuck," packed her things and left in the ridiculous Jeep with the big tires. Fortunately, most of the other students on the site were in Albuquerque that night.

But, looking back on it, he thought it a fortuitous development, because he came up with the idea of inviting teens from the Zuni Pueblo to tour the site. Carrington knew that if he could interest some of those young girls in working the dig, it would be a whole different ball game than with the likes of the she-bitch, who he planned to track down and punish in the near future for her insolence. Just the thought of such sweet revenge lifted his spirits.

In this ebullient mood, he could not feel the tiny fissures opening in the thin shell of self-control he had maintained for the past several years. And even if he had, he might have ignored it. For such is the spiral of madness.

"Sir, are you all right?" Amanda asked.

"I just got a little dizzy. I'm okay now."

"Would you like to sit down?"

"No, no, I'm fine. Thanks, I'll take the past twelve issues." He dug out his wallet and counted out nine dollars.

She took the money and asked, maybe a little wary now, "Are you a first-time visitor to Zuni?"

"Yes, I am, he said. "I travel a lot and I've learned that the local newspaper is a good way to learn about a place."

"Yes it is," she said. "And there's a very good free publication up at the Shiwi Cultural Center that tells more about our history pre-Messenger times."

He thanked her, shook her hand and walked back to his car, still a little shaken. It wasn't finding Carrington so easily that spooked him but realizing that he should warn someone about his sexual predation, now that he could be looking for victims among the Zuni school kids. But whom? And how could he convince someone without tipping his hand and ultimately blowing his chance to get away with killing Carrington? Sitting in the car, he read the entire article. Carrington was proposing that the Zuni kids come out and be instructed in recovery techniques by the current group of college students. Then, when the college students returned to classes, Carrington himself would direct their work on weekends, until late October, when he would shut the site down until next summer. Of course, there would be a modest monetary stipend at the end for any Zuni student who finished the work, the story reported.

Aaron sighed with some relief. His first reaction had been to get a rifle and go out there, sit on the side of the mountain and just blow Carrington's shit away. Or to walk into camp, put the Python's barrel in his ear, say "Nighty-night," and spread his brains across the desert landscape.

He might do it that way yet. But the direct approach would increase the chance of getting caught. But even more important than that, it would rob him of the chance to see Carrington's eyes as he realized he was going to die. In some ways, that was more important than not getting caught. Because Carrington had robbed him of a future, just as he had Roscoe and Belinda.

For now, however, he had some breathing room. He got out of the car and went back into the cultural center to grab the publication Amanda had mentioned. It was sixty tabloid-sized pages of small print. He'd have some homework to do tonight.

Harlan had taken to visiting Belinda as often as he could, which was nearly every day so far. He did it because she was his employee and he felt that having someone there who cared about her might help her recover. In trying to find any next of kin, he'd struck out. Her last job had a contact name for emergencies but when he called, it was disconnected. He called information to see if there were other listings with that name but came up empty. So, with Aaron missing, Harlan was it. Belinda was truly alone.

Everyone at the Kensington recognized him, and he spent a good half-hour chatting with the staff on every visit. That morning as he was walking past the receptionist, whose name was Mary, she said, "There's been no change, I'm afraid. Her brain function is good, and her vital signs are good. But she's just out there, somewhere. It's sure nice of you to visit her. She hasn't had many visitors—just you, and the gentleman who calls every day."

Harlan stopped in his tracks. "Somebody has been calling?"

"Just like clockwork. He must be a traveling salesman or something."

"What makes you say that?"

"We have caller ID on the phones, sort of a trial run to see if we want to use the service, and everyday it's from a different place. And it's always from a pay phone, because the screen identifies the city and state and phone number, but there's never a name like a person or a business."

"Has he called today?"

"Yes, this morning about 9:15."

"Do you remember where the call came from?"

"It's a place in New Mexico that's in that song. In fact that's where he called from yesterday, too, now that I think of it."

"What song is that?"

"Oh shoot, I can't remember its name, either." Her face flushed in embarrassment.

"Listen, Mary, there's no way you should have remembered. You didn't know it was important."

"It is important, then?" she asked.

"Yeah, but not for the reason you might think. If I'm right, it's the man who was with her when she was hurt. He's...well, we're worried about him." Harlan left it at that. "I'll be in Belinda's room for a while," he said. "If you remember, tell me when I leave." He took his wallet out and handed her his card. "And if you remember it after that, give me a call. If he calls again, please write down the place he's calling from."

"I will. Do you want me to say something to him when he calls?"

"Not yet," Harlan said.

That evening, after sleepwalking through his day at the office, Harlan drove up to see the mountain man. He had debated off and on whether to call Earl to relay the information he'd gotten that morning at the hospital, because he was nearly 100 percent sure it was Aaron calling. But he didn't know where he was calling from, only that he'd been traveling, and not—from the sounds of it—to Arkansas. He decided he'd wait until he had something concrete before pulling Earl into it. And even then, he wondered what good would it do if they found out where he is?

Aaron was up to something—that seemed certain. But neither he nor Earl could afford to send somebody down there to find him. That's what he wanted to talk to Sam Hite about.

This time, the mountain man was fully dressed and looked much better. The wolf dog wasn't around.

Sam motioned to Harlan, saying "Come in, come in," as he stepped back inside.

"Where's that pussycat of yours?" Harlan wanted to know.

"I 'spect she's denning up somewheres," Sam said.

Harlan stopped inside the doorway. "I've got some information but I'm not sure what it means."

"Hell, sit your bones down and spill it out," Sam said.

"I called Aaron's friend, Emma, up in Saratoga, and she pretty much confirmed what he told us. He went up there to serve that subpoena. The guy wasn't there, so he came right back. I got the guy's phone number and Earl called up there looking for him. Whoever Earl talked to said Carrington—that's the guy's name—has been gone for two months and won't be back for another two months. He said he didn't know where Carrington was.

"But this morning at the hospital, I found out somebody's been calling every day to check on Belinda's condition. They got that caller

ID and said he's been moving around but the last two calls came from someplace in New Mexico. The woman couldn't remember the name but she said there was a song about it. She couldn't remember the name of the song either. I'm going to check with her tomorrow."

"Gallup, New Mexico. Route 66," Sam said, remembering the song from the night of the attack because the band had played it.

"What the hell is he doing in Gallup?" Harlan wondered.

"That's the question, ain't it?" Sam said.

"No, the question is whether you'll go down there and try to find out."

Sam let out a low, soft whistle and dragged his fingers like tines of a rake down through his beard. "You ask a lot of a decrepit old man."

"Decrepit, my ass," Harlan said. "Remember you're talking to the guy who has to drag you out of the Jackass Inn when you're on a toot and are fixing to take on half the people in the bar."

Sam flicked his wrist as if shooing away a mosquito. "All right, all right. It was just a figure of speech anyway. But I am old—76 in November." He paused, twirled the end of his mustache. "What the hell am I supposed to do if'n I find the lad?"

Harlan looked across at Sam, wondering just how much of what he'd been thinking he should share with this wild man. He decided on a middle course and hoped Sam would read between the lines. "Sam, I'm going to leave that up to you. This is strictly between me and you. Do you understand what I'm telling you? I just want him back here safe and sound."

Sam's eyes widened as it sunk in. He nodded, "Yes, sir, Marshal. I believe that I do."

When he returned to his motel room, Aaron read the back issues of the Shiwi Messenger and saw two additional articles about Carrington's dig. One mentioned the location of the site as on the southwest corner of Corn Mountain—the giant mesa in the middle of the valley. The other reported that Carrington routinely bought dinner for his students at the local cafe every Friday evening. After that, Aaron sat at the small table in his room with the History of Zuni publication spread out. He was on page 22, with 38 to go. He had picked it up with the hope of learning something he could use in snaring Carrington but got caught in the history of the Zuni people.

The Zunis, he learned, were geographically isolated and historically unique, and remained one of the more tightly knit, traditional Indian tribes. Their lands once encompassed about 14,000 square miles in western New Mexico and eastern Arizona. They had been far enough away from the troublesome Rio Grande Pueblos that the Spanish invaders for the most part ignored the Zunis. The original Zuni Pueblo was so large that, viewed from afar, it became the source of the Spanish legend of the cities of gold, later renamed by Coronado as the Seven Cities of Cibola.

When the United States took over the territory in 1848 after the U.S.-Mexican war, the Zunis sided with U.S. troops against the Navajo, their traditional enemy, in order to protect their agriculture and trade routes from attack.

He learned that the area atop Corn Mountain was large enough to contain the town of Zuni but that no building or any other activity was allowed there, because it was a sacred site, having figured in the Zuni's survival of the Great Flood in ancient times. In 1680, the Zunis took refuge on Corn Mountain, also known as Thunder Mountain, as the great Pueblo Revolt against the Spanish swept what is now New Mexico.

Even today, their 450,000-acre reservation was uncrossed by a major highway and appeared to be forgotten by much of the world.

Some Anglo anthropologists thought the Zuni were an offshoot of the Anasazi, formed when Ancient Ones abandoned Chaco Cañon. Their own creation story, however, said they ascended from a lake in what is now eastern Arizona.

He learned that the El Malpais lava fields, estimated to encompass 800 square miles, had had several trade routes through them. Some of those routes may have been established by the Anasazi themselves, before there were any Pueblos, the anthropologists surmised.

Aaron decided to ask Corrigan, if he saw him again, about the lava fields. Failing that, he would try to find a book about El Malpais. The place fascinated him. It sounded like a good place to get lost, or to lose someone, in.

Aaron returned to the bar later that evening and drank three beers slowly, but Corrigan never showed. A similar crowd was on the street when he walked back to the motel. Trying to figure out his next move, he decided the next couple of days might be well spent exploring the area around Corn Mountain and looking at approaches to El Malpais. It would be good to get away from Gallup and the ghosts of industrial civilization, maybe find some decent place to camp. Then on Friday night show up at the café in Zuni, do a little reconnaissance on Carrington, and follow him back to the dig.

Finally, the beginning of a plan. The first step would be getting a vehicle that blended into the scenery better than a Subaru wagon. And he had an idea how he could find one.

Chapter 36

August 2

Dawn broke with sheets of rain slapping the window as Aaron climbed out of the shower. He dried off, got dressed, opened his wallet and found the receipt from the gun dealer in Thoreau. For some reason, Aaron thought Uriah Watkins was just the guy to help him find a vehicle.

After asking for directions in Thoreau, Aaron found Watkins' home a couple miles from town on a gravel road. It was a small gray clapboard house set back in a grove of cottonwoods. The fields around the houses were weedy. The yard was hardpacked dirt and gravel. Behind the house was a cinderblock building with no windows and a large, metal, oversized door, which was open. The "Guns, Guns, Guns" van was parked next to the door. As Aaron was driving up to the building, Uriah Watkins walked outside wearing a work apron, safety glasses and a bothered look on his face. When he turned to swing the big door shut Aaron could see a handgun on his belt.

Aaron stopped about 50 feet away and stepped out of the car. Watkins squinted and Aaron said, "It's the derringer guy."

Watkins waved him over, turned back and opened the door. When Aaron stepped up, he saw Watkins' camo ball cap had New Mexico Militia embroidered on it. Watkins said, "A man can't be too careful in this business, or any business." He smiled, "But I guess you know that."

"It's a good rule of thumb," Aaron said.

Watkins stepped aside, swept his arm toward the gun shop, and said, "Come on in."

"Okay, but I'm not here about guns."

"Step in anyway, I've got work to do."

When Aaron walked inside, an industrial gumbo of odors, none of them unpleasant, hit him. Among them were Nitro gun solvent, gunpowder, overheated oil and hot metal. Along one wall was a glass case with a variety of handguns displayed. On the wall behind the case was a vertical display of various assault-style weapons. All were held against the wall by a two-inch-wide strip of steel. A walk-in gun safe dominated the back of the room. To the right were workbenches, tools, lathes.

Watkins asked, "So, what can I do for you?"

"I need a vehicle, preferably an older work truck."

Watkins' eyebrows arched into half moons. "I'm in the gun business, friend, not the truck business." He paused, searching Aaron's eyes for trouble. Seeing none, he said, "Tell me more, maybe I can figure something out."

"I need to use a truck, something that will blend in locally. It's just for a couple of weeks. Nothing illegal will be done with it. I'll pay two bills a week and leave my car for security."

"Nothing illegal? You sure?"

"I'll tell you this much. I need to look some areas over without being noticed. Think of it as surveillance. You don't want to know any more, but if I need to do something illegal, I'll use my car.

Watkins narrowed his eyes. "Four hundred in advance?"

"Sure, in advance."

"Let me make a couple of calls."

Aaron went out and sat in his car. About 15 minutes later Watkins came out looking pleased. "There's an old Navajo fella down the road who had a stroke and he needs the money. His Missus don't drive. He's got a '75 Ford, three-quarter-ton flatbed. Got a gun rack in the back window, a lariat hanging off of it and a toolbox on the bed. Nobody would look at you even the first time, let alone twice. I told him I thought you were being honest with me, but he said, 'Who cares? I can barely walk so they can't pin nothin' on me. I'll just say somebody stole it.'

"Perfect," Aaron said.

Twenty minutes later, Aaron was chugging down the road, headed for the Zuni Mountains to look for a campsite. Things were coming together. He had found Carrington, more or less, on his first foray into Zuni without tipping his hand, then the truck, which was solid but a little loud and rode like a Conestoga wagon.

Just what he needed.

After a little searching, Aaron found a good campsite in the Cibola National Forest north of Ramah. On the way up the road, he had also found a sweat-stained, lop-sided, old straw cowboy hat, something he had been thinking he needed to complete his "cover." It didn't seem to have anything living in it, and it fit. He pitched the tent to lay claim to the site but left the rest of his gear strapped down in the bed of the truck. He took off to do some exploring.

When he reached New Mexico 53, he drove east to San Rafael, just outside Grants, along the north edge of the Malpais. On his return, he noted the possible entrances, although the lava beds themselves were rarely in sight due to pine trees that bordered the highway. He stayed on 53 into Zuni then turned south on Pueblo Road 36. After it climbed out of the valley, the thick piñon-juniper forests that blanketed the Pueblo for as far as he could see swallowed any signs of civilization. Aaron drove to the Pueblo's border then turned around. But the road never came near the base of Corn Mountain, where Carrington's dig was supposed to be. Back in Zuni, he bought a reservation map at a gasoline station and found the route he needed, but it was getting late so he stopped at the grocery store for supplies, then headed back to his campsite.

On a dark stretch of highway, he realized he had forgotten to call about Belinda. Instead of turning up the Forest Service road, he continued on a couple of miles to the little town of Ramah. He saw a phone, stopped and tried it but it didn't work. Getting back into the truck, Aaron pounded the heels of his hands on the steering wheel, shaking the cab of the truck. He covered his temples with his hands and rested his elbows on the steering wheel. Is this what I've become, he wondered? So swept up in the hunt that I've forgotten the reason for it?

By agreement the previous day, Sam Hite would check in with Harlan before leaving for Gallup, and Harlan was thankful he did because he wanted Sam to know that Aaron hadn't called yet. It was possible he had moved on. In the new day's light, the idea of trying to find Aaron wasn't as appealing as it had been the day before.

About three in the afternoon, Sam walked into Harlan's office. "What's the word?"

Harlan said, "He hasn't called so far. I'd say let's wait another day and decide."

"Naw, I think I'll head on down there anyway. The idea of seein' me some different country has got my britches itchin'. Maybe Hoss is someplace where there ain't no telephone."

Harlan walked to his filing cabinet and got a copy of the photograph used in Aaron's identification card. He handed it to Sam. "What would he be doing in a place with no phone?"

"Huntin', to my way of thinkin'," Sam said.

When Aaron got back to the campsite, he spread his bedroll out on the back of the truck. He was feeling too claustrophobic to sleep in the tent. He put the bag with the Python up against the thin mattress next to his waist where he could grab it quickly. After taking a couple of hard pulls on the bottle of whiskey, he fell into a fitful sleep.

Chapter 37

August 3

In the nightmare, Aaron was wandering the woods looking for Roscoe, calling out his name. He knew Roscoe was there, somewhere. If he just kept calling he would find him. Finally, he wandered out onto an open hillside. Below were men with shovels, digging into the grassy meadow. Alarmed, Aaron ran down the hill, but the hillside became quicksand, sucking him down. He tried to shout but his breath was so thin all he could muster was a soft whisper. His heart was ready to burst as he at last managed to get a lung full of air. He screamed "NOOOO—" his body wrenched and he felt himself falling. He hit the ground with a thud, knocking the air from his lungs. He rolled on his side, opened his eyes and found himself looking at the left rear wheel and tire. The sun was coming up. His clothes were soaked in sweat. Tremors were passing through his body like aftershocks. He closed his eyes and lay there for a few moments, pushed himself off the ground and got to his feet. It was like the nightmare about the massacre in Nam, but in a different setting.

After rolling up his bedding and stashing it in the tent, he fired up the one-burner Coleman stove and put on a pot of water. When the water boiled, he dumped a handful of grounds in and turned it off to steep. While waiting for the coffee, he got out the derringer, loaded it using the new powder and caps, and walked to a dead pine tree on the edge of the campsite. He raised it and fired twice. The report was instantaneous; the kick harder. And he hit the spot he was aiming at.

That's more like it, he thought, walked back to the truck, poured some coffee in the blue enamel cup and took a sip. It was too hot to drink, so he dug around and found the cleaning kit for the derringer and ran the brush down the barrels a couple of times, then cleaned the chambers between the hammers and barrels. He loaded it again, pushed it into the holster and set the rig on the bed of the truck. Then he drank the coffee and thought about the day. He flung the last inch of coffee in a wide arc over the ground and picked up the map he'd bought in Zuni. There was a road from town that led past Corn Mountain, or Dowa Yolanne as it was labeled on the map. From the description in the news story, he thought Carrington's dig was on the southwest corner of the mesa. But rather than ride around out there looking, and thereby taking a chance on being seen, he was going to wait in the market parking lot across from the café this evening and hope Carrington would show up with his students for their weekly feed. If so, he'd get his first look at Carrington and try to follow him home. Even if he stayed well behind, he should be able to see where Carrington turned off the main road.

Before anything else, he was going to check on Belinda. He set his stove, water jug and cooking gear in the tent and packed the rest in the truck. If he took 53 to Grants, a town about the same size as Gallup, he could call from there in anonymity. And the route would give him a chance to look over the Malpais lava field a little more closely.

Along the road to Grants, there were only a few areas where the Malpais was visible—most of it in the few miles before the highway intersected Interstate 40. There was one obvious trailhead about 10 miles south of Grants and a couple of other possibles. He'd watch more carefully on the way back.

He turned east on I-40 and drove a couple of miles to the main Grants exit. A sprawling truck stop metastasized on the north side of the highway, so Aaron pulled up to the pumps and filled the tank. He went inside to pay and, looking around, saw a bank of telephones between the entrances to the restrooms, as well as a selection of paperback books for sale next to the cashier.

He paid for the gas and parked the truck behind the restaurant, re-entered and found two books—one a hiking guide to the Malpais and the other a natural history of the region. Opening the latter to the table of contents, he saw that a large section was devoted to the Malpais. He bought them, walked to the telephones, deposited a handful of change and punched in the number. The voice answering the telephone sounded familiar. He asked about Belinda. She hesitated, then said, "There's been no change. She's critical but stable. I-I'm sorry."

Aaron said thanks and hung up. But he heard something in her voice he didn't like. It was nervousness, yeah, sure as shit. It could mean a couple of things—either there *was* some change and the woman didn't want to tell him, or she was waiting for the call because somebody had asked her to. The first seemed unlikely, as the facility was legally required to give factual basic information on a patient's condition. The second was more likely. He knew a call that short couldn't be traced, but Caller ID had become a lot more sophisticated, and if the facility had it, it could possibly tell them where the call originated. If so, Harlan or Earl could now place him in the vicinity.

And that meant Carrington would have to disappear, completely. It would complicate his plans, but not too much because Aaron was already leaning heavily in that direction. He just didn't know how he was going to do it. And he would have to speed things up. Earl might want to send somebody down but Aaron doubted he could justify it, or that he would contact law enforcement to look for him. But in case he was wrong, he couldn't take as much time as he might have otherwise.

The smell of frying bacon coming from the restaurant, however, convinced him that he had enough time for breakfast.

Just minutes after Aaron called the hospital, the receptionist called Harlan. "Marshal Silbaugh, this is Mary, from Kensington medical wing. That young man just called. This time it was from Grants, New Mexico. I got the phone number here."

Harlan could hear the excitement in her voice and hoped she had been calm when Aaron called.

Mary gave Harlan the number. "By the way, there's been no change in Ms. Mondragon's condition."

"Thank you, Mary," Harlan said, thinking that Mary was a gentle soul who was getting a charge from her undercover work for him. He chuckled and pulled a road atlas from the shelf behind his desk. Grants was about a hundred miles east of Gallup. Then he called security at the phone company and requested a location for the phone number Mary had given him. He was put on hold for a couple of minutes. The security guy came back on the line and said, "It's a pay phone located at Tex's Truck Stop in Grants, New Mexico."

"Tex's Truck Stop." Harlan wrote it down.

"That's it. It's on I-40 on the western edge of town," the man said.

"Thanks for the help," Harlan said.

About an hour later, Sam called. He was, without knowing it, following Aaron's route and currently in Cuba, New Mexico. Harlan passed on the information about Aaron's last phone call. Sam looked at the map, "I could be there in two hours," he said, "not that he's going to be waiting around."

"Unless there's a motel there and he's staying in it," Harlan said.

"We'll know in a coupla hours," Sam said and hung up.

A large breakfast, several cups of coffee and 90 minutes later, Aaron was still at the restaurant table reading. The waitress had left him alone for quite a while but the lunch crowd was showing up, so Aaron put a ten-dollar bill on his ticket, grabbed the books and left.

As he pulled onto the Interstate, he reviewed some of the salient information he had just read: Malpais was Spanish for badlands or bad country, the first lava flow was three million years ago, the most recent eruption came around the end of the first millennium A.D. Some of the flows were in distinct areas but most overlapped like pancakes, with the oldest on the bottom, the most recent on top. Each exhibited some unique, as well as similar, geologic and ecologic characteristics. In appearance the flows varied from undulating black glass to crumbled charcoal briquettes. He particularly wanted to look at the Zuni-Acoma trail, which he had noted on the way to Grants.

The road back was not busy and there were no vehicles in the trailhead parking area. The trail guide described hiking in the Malpais as being incredibly hazardous, with the razor-like substrate capable of shredding a pair of running shoes within a couple of miles. Except at either end, the trail was not a worn path but the most negotiable route between man-made rock cairns strewn at various distances along the seven-mile length.

Most interesting to Aaron was the description of deep, narrow crevices and intact lava tubes, both of which formed as masses of hot lava cooled.

Aaron got out of the truck and put the Python and a water bottle in a butt-pack, strapped it on. A high thin layer of cirrus clouds gave the sky a washed-out look but did not portend any rain, so he started down the trail—a two-track across a fairly large meadow. A half-mile in, a wooden post up a thirty-foot embankment marked the trail as it wound through scattered, crumbling lava in a ponderosa grassland.

For the next mile, the terrain became more rugged, the lava thicker. Aaron stopped and glassed the trail ahead and saw a small upright formation that he thought might be the first cairn. He turned and looked southwest. In that direction the terrain could only be described as twisted, jumbled, cracked, and burnt, yet with pockets of vegetation spread sparsely throughout the lava—an alien, inhospitable landscape. Truly a badland. Across this terrain was an elevated northwest/southeast ridge.

Buzzards circled high in the sky as a reminder of the possible fate of the foolish or careless or unprepared in this harsh land. It was not the kind of place where people with strong survival instincts explored casually. It seemed to be, however, a good place to hide a body. And it was as far as he intended to go today.

Sam Hite's butt hurt, his back hurt and his legs were almost asleep when he pulled into Tex's Truck Stop in his road machine, a black 1988 Chevy Suburban that he kept at a storage lot in Boulder. It would have been an understatement to say he was a mite cranky. When he remembered that Aaron had been here, he forgot about the pain and circled the entire lot twice. But there was no sign of Aaron's car.

The Chevy Suburban and its smoked windows upped his status on the road and gave him a measure of anonymity, which was good because Sam did not look like a normal, senior-citizen traveler in most of America.

The thing about places like New Mexico, which still had more than its share of "characters," was that while people would notice someone who looked like Sam did, he wouldn't particularly be remembered unless he was strolling naked through some high-end yuppie suburb of Santa Fe.

Walking into Tex's Truck Stop, Sam never raised an eyebrow in the room. He could have been a long-haul trucker, a biker or just one of the many denizens who inhabited the rural interstate corridors. Sam looked around and saw the bank of phones, the restrooms, the restaurant and a young girl behind the counter. She didn't look so young when Sam got closer. Her eyes were hard, as if to ward off the attention of every mother's trucker who thought he was God's gift to young womanhood. She was chubby, her hair lank, had chipped blue polish on chewed-down nails.

Her mouth was unexpressive when she looked up and asked, "Can I help ya?"

Nobody was at the counter or on their way to it, so Sam slid his hand behind the mat of beard and fished Aaron's photo out of a pocket on his bib overalls. "I'm lookin' for my friend. I was wonderin' if'n you'd seen him?"

The girl looked up suspiciously. "You carry a picture of your friend around with you, Gramps? That's kinda strange, if you ask me."

Sam rested his thick, furry red forearms on the glass counter and leaned forward. The girl held her ground but managed to lean about fifteen degrees off plumb. Her eyes were no longer hard, however. Now they looked worried.

"Young Missy, I am not asking your opinion of anything I do. I asked if'n you'd seen my friend here. He's shaved and cut his hair since this was taken." He set the photo on the counter and stood straight, to give her room. She leaned forward, picked it up and tilted it at different angles.

"Well, I think it could be the guy who was here. But this guy, he had an old straw cowboy hat on. He bought some gas and a couple of books, made a call, then went in the restaurant. I think he was in there for a while, 'cause he just left a few minutes ago."

"Did you see his car?"

"Well, he didn't have no car, that's for sure. He had an old truck." She dared a smug grin, having got one up on the intimidating old fart who got in her face.

Sam never noticed her expression. He was thinking, Aaron's driving a truck? He had been counting on spotting Aaron's car. Now he wasn't even on square one. "What did the truck look like?"

She sighed, signaling her impatience. "It was red, it was old, and it had one of those flat thingies on the back instead of a box."

"A flatbed?" Sam asked.

"Yeeaahhh, it was a flat bed."

"You say he bought some books? Do you remember what books?"

She snorted and rolled her eyes. "Like, I'm sure I'm going to remember some fucking books."

Sam nodded, "Thanks anyway, Little Missy. I hope you didn't hurt yer noggin permanently thinking on that so hard." Her bubble gum was popping like firecrackers and she flipped him the bird as he turned and walked out. Sitting in his Suburban, Sam chastised himself for getting his hopes up. But Aaron driving a truck instead of his car meant something significant, but what? He started the Suburban and, without a reason he could name, pulled onto the I-40 west toward Gallup, hoping he would find an answer there.

Now that Aaron had the truck, he was more comfortable driving around Zuni. He wanted to get to know the Pueblo as much out of curiosity as for strategic reasons. So he drove around aimlessly, taking this road to see where it went and that one to see what was out that way. He found a road up to the rim of the north mesa and got a bird's-eye view of the town, the basin and the rolling forests beyond.

Already, he was seeing it differently. Instead of the trees, now there was forest. Instead of points of ingress and egress, he was seeing the nooks and crannies in between. But the thing he noticed most was how few sharp edges were in this land, as if eons of sun, wind and rain had polished away the hard angles. From the land to the faces of the people, there was an impression that harmony was important here.

Why had Carrington chosen the Zuni area? Was he looking for refuge or was he drawn to the area by innocence to be found there, a fresh set of easy victims? That reminded Aaron of the newspaper story about the amateur archeologist's willingness to take some Zuni kids under his wing. Again, he reminded himself that any danger would likely be weeks away and that Carrington would no longer be around to make good on the offer. But picturing him circling like a shark around the scent of sweet warm blood ran cold fingertips up Aaron's spine.

As the shadows grew long, Aaron found himself in front of the Zuni Café, where Carrington would later be holding court for his students. Being on the hunt had sharply increased his appetite, and even though he'd had a late breakfast, he pulled on his hat and went inside for some grub. He was hankering for a burger smothered with cheese and green chili. What the hell, he'd get some fries, too.

Three tourists in shorts and sandals, with colorful shirts depicting beach scenes and expensive cameras slung over the corner of their chairs, occupied one table. Two Zuni mothers with four young children had another. In the lull between mid-afternoon and dinner, the Zuni Café was three-quarters empty. Aaron took a table in the back corner, where he could see the whole room. His waiter was a moon-faced teenage boy with a burr haircut and big, thick-lensed glasses that had slipped down his nose a ways. When he asked if they had any "real-hot" green chilies, the kid flicked his eyes toward the kitchen, shrugged and said, "Yeah, I guess so. But they're pretty hot."

"Good," Aaron said, pointing to selection number four. "That's what I want." The kid wrinkled his forehead, wrote it down and pushed the glasses up on the bridge of his nose before he walked away.

About ten minutes later, the kid shuffled out of the kitchen with the burger and a pile of French fries on a platter. It looked great, maybe a little overdone, but Aaron liked it better that way than bloody. It was the way he was raised. He'd never seen bloody beef on a rancher's table. It was always well done. The fries were crispy. He had ordered a large Coke to help cut the grease.

The green chilies smelled strong, which suggested they were hot, a notion he suspected even more when he saw a couple of broad, grinning faces, one with thick glasses riding on his nose, peering over the swinging door to the kitchen. He acted like he didn't notice, but they were watching, he thought waiting, for him to take the first bite. In his peripheral vision he could see their eyes tracking the burger as he raised it to his mouth. He bit a big chunk out of the burger, chewed a few times and could feel the tingling on his lips migrate to the back of his throat. A few fat beads of sweat rolled down his nose. He swallowed, raised the ice-filled glass of Coke, took a sip, and turned to the kitchen door and nodded. In a peal of giggles, the two faces shot out of sight like prairie dogs in a hawk's shadow.

Machismo aside, he slathered ketchup on the fries and used two fistfuls to cut the burn. By the time he finished the second bite of burger, the endorphins were kicking in and the rest went down easy.

As he ate the last of the fries and drained the now-diluted Coke, the young waiter and a woman who was probably the cook were sliding three tables together in the middle of the room. They put a small 'reserved' sign on the first table. Aaron left a three-dollar tip and was at the counter paying his bill when a shiny-green, mid-70s Land Rover pulled up and stopped, followed immediately by an ancient International CarryAll station wagon. The driver of the Land Rover bounced out of the vehicle. A couple of college-age girls got out the passenger side.

Five more students evacuated the CarryAll like they expected it to burst into flames. The Land Rover driver was already up the steps and coming through the door so Aaron pulled his hat down to eye level and stood aside. In the millisecond of recognition, he was watching a red and black horror film in which he walked over, grabbed Carrington by the hair, pulled his head back to 45 degrees, rammed the Python under his chin and pulled the trigger. Instead, he remained still, letting Trey Carrington pass. The erstwhile professor was short, 5'7"-5'8" maybe, thick, unruly blond hair, with a ruddy but unlined face, and a small cleft in his chin. Carrington stepped to the table and clapped his hands once like he was calling his troops to order.

It was all Aaron could do not to stare because there was something odd about Carrington's face, as if parts of it were blurred. It took a moment to sink in: a thicket of long hairs protruded from each nostril. Likewise his ears. Aaron shook his head at the bizarre affectation, staring hard enough that someone might notice. He had to get out before he did something that drew attention. This was the guy he was going to kill? He was a fucking leprechaun, for chrissake. Aaron forced his clinched limbs into movement, climbed down the steps, walked to the truck and got in. Unless they lingered a long time over the meal, it was going to be light when he followed the crew back to the dig.

Still, Carrington had never even looked up, so full of himself he was, so insulated from his past deeds that no shadow of worry crossed his face. Through the side window, Aaron could see the group was gathered around the table and Carrington was gesturing, gesticulating and generally holding forth to his captive audience on matters of great import and subtle wit. Aaron's hand was frozen at a point between reaching for the Python and starting the truck: Boom—right through the window and haul ass. The truck won.

Aaron pulled across the street to the market, where he bought some coffee, baked beans, bottled water. Shit, he couldn't even think what else he needed so he just grabbed a couple of things on the way to the cash register.

When he got back to the truck, his eyes locked onto Carrington's every gesture like a laser sight. A Zuni Tribal Police car pulled through the lot. The cop gave him a little eyeball and pulled out. A thin Zuni face, white sidewalls, sunglasses, serious expression, sensing something was funny about the picture but unsure what. So Aaron picked up his book about the Malpais and tried to read. But the images in his brain were not letters, words, sentences and paragraphs. They were of Roscoe on his death blanket and Belinda in the bed with tubes and wires sprouting from her body and feeding into machines that beeped and buzzed and whined out the sad tale. They were of Tye and the tears in his eyes when Aaron had visited that first time.

Aaron slouched down, pretending to read. The Zuni patrol had been by a couple of times so Aaron was relieved, after a little more than an hour, to see Carrington's group getting up from the table. Once outside, all of the students piled into the CarryAll while Carrington alone got into his Land Rover. The students pulled out and Carrington followed shortly. Aaron stayed back a block or so. Carrington turned into the Zuni Post Office. As Aaron drove slowly past, he could see through the window that Carrington was emptying his post office box. He noted its approximate location, kept going and pulled into the Shiwi Cultural Center parking lot.

At the rear of the lot, the lights were on in the Shiwi Messenger office and a dozen kids were in the front yard. They appeared to be playing the knot game, in which the players hold hands, raise them high and fold into a huddle and then try to get untangled. If so, they weren't having much luck.

Where in the world would you find teenagers today playing something like the knot game besides right here, he wondered?

He was amazed but drew his eyes away and again slouched in the seat hoping nobody would recognize him. Nobody even looked his way. As a disguise, the truck worked like a cloak of invisibility.

Within a couple of minutes, Carrington drove past. Aaron pulled out and followed until the Land Rover turned south onto a side road between Zuni and Black Rock and headed toward Corn Mountain. He slowed and let the Land Rover get a mile down the road before following. The road was long and straight and Carrington's Land Rover was raising a big plume of dust so Aaron let him get another mile ahead.

About four miles farther, the dust plume was moving to the east. No cars were on the road. A few driveways presumably lead to small homes well back into the pinion and junipers, so Aaron continued until he saw a pall of dust lingering over a side road. He drove on a half mile, made a U-turn and pulled the binoculars from his bag. There were still no cars around as he approached the road to the dig, so he glassed the area but saw no structures. He kept driving and, once back on Highway 53, headed toward his campsite.

His plan was progressing. He now had two points of information: the location of the dig, and a way to get in touch with Carrington anonymously— the Zuni post office. It was a start. The other answers were out there. He just had to find them.

Sam Hite had been cruising motels and bars in Gallup for most of the day and felt like a damn fool. If Aaron was driving an old truck instead of his car, well, it was *possible* the car was parked at a motel or on the street, but not likely after such a thorough search.

He was still convinced that Aaron was in the area, and almost as sure that his presence here had something to do with the attack and the fella he was looking for up in Saratoga. Damned if he knew what it was, though. And what would he do if he found him? Kidnap him? Or help him in whatever damn fool scheme he was up to?

All these questions were making Sam powerful thirsty and he tried to recall if any of the drinking establishments he'd passed looked fit for a man such as himself. He remembered one up on Coal Street that looked to be worth investigating.

Before he got into his cups, however, he needed to find a flophouse, and he needed to call Harlan and fill him in.

Back at the campsite, Aaron decided to build a fire. It wouldn't be much work and a fire was always a source of comfort while camping. The Coke had not done much to slake his thirst so he checked the cooler and found three cold beers, popped the top on one and leaned against a log near the fire to read more about the Malpais.

An hour later, darkness forced Aaron into the cab of the truck, where he read by the overhead light. What he learned was that early attempts to explore the lava had often ended tragically. The foolhardy were lost when the thin ceiling on a lava tube collapsed beneath them; a stone arch over a deep crevasse crumbled; or by simple slips and falls that sent bodies into traumatic contact with razor-sharp lava. More recently, ATV riders found their air-filled and even solid rubber tires were no match for the lava. And not all the danger came from the earth. Lightning strikes sometimes came out of clear skies, exploding trees and turning sulfuric lava rock into showers of glowing shrapnel.

Aerial surveys had located narrow cañons full of grasses, small sinks and seasonal streams, slopes covered by pine and aspen. This life was made possible by the porous nature of degraded lava, which soaked up moisture like a sponge and then bled it into springs that bubbled to the surface. Thousand-year-old Douglas firs and junipers, the oldest trees in the Southwest, could be found there.

Within the Malpais were formations called kipukas where lava encircled areas but left the ground surface essentially undisturbed. Within these kipukas were remnant meadows of native plants, forests and animals. The largest of these was the Hole-in-the-Wall kipuka in the southwest corner of the lava fields. At least five others, all smaller, were clustered to the west of the Hole-in-the-Wall. Another half-dozen were scattered throughout the remainder of the Malpais.

While humans had not been able to conquer the badlands, it had become a refuge to 51 species of mammals, including bears, pumas, elk, deer, coyotes and antelope, nearly 200 species of birds, 34 species of reptiles, and an unknown number of insects including scorpions, tarantulas, black-widow and brown-recluse spiders. Some speculated Mexican wolves and jaguars might visit the area periodically, although no evidence of that was present.

The idea that such a unique place existed at all in the late 20th century was staggering. It was a true wilderness and would remain that way because it was too inhospitable to be of human value. After years of wandering the vast wilds of the San Juan Mountains, Aaron felt an undeniable affinity for the Malpais.

He set the book down, his head spinning like he'd been sparring with Mike Tyson. He switched off the dome light and was enveloped in darkness. His mouth was dry as an old, sun-bleached bone, so he got out of the cab, felt his way back to the cooler, and pulled out one of his last two beers. The ice had melted; the beer wasn't as cold as he liked it but it was cold enough.

The whiskey bottle was down to a couple of shots so he was going to have to travel to Grants or Gallup tomorrow and stock up. Seeing a glow from the fire pit, he finished the beer, walked over and urinated on the coals. He was worried about a wind coming up and spreading sparks so he grabbed the water jug and poured a half-gallon on the coals, causing steam and ash to billow out of the pit like a dirty-robed genie. After the mess cleared, he held his hand over the coals. They were still warm but would die out soon.

At the truck, he rolled out the sleeping gear, hopped up on the flatbed. He grabbed the whiskey and, seeking numbness, drank all that was left in one gulping swallow. That big shot of alcohol went off like a bomb in his stomach and he stretched out on the sleeping bag, feeling the kinks being worked out of his back. Above him, the Milky Way was bright and thick like a white superhighway across the universe. He thought of Tye, saw him trudging down that road going home.

Sam had found an old-fashioned motor court comprised of small, stuccoed cottages arranged in a horseshoe shape like those in the historic post cards of Route 66. Hell, the truth was that back in the day most of the motels in the U.S. looked just like this one. He half expected to see a 20-foot-high, concrete teepee in the courtyard. It could have been worse, he was thinking, as he flopped on the bed. The sheets were clean, the water was hot and the tiny refrigerator worked. He was tired already, feeling every one of his 76 years. He'd jumped at the chance to do something, anything, to make up for the helplessness he felt after finding Aaron, Belinda and Roscoe.

Aaron was the only one he could do anything for, so he came. Hell, if Aaron had found out, as Harlan and Earl had feared, who had attacked them, Sam would help him punish the son-of-a-bitch. The more he thought about it, though, the more futile it all seemed. There were just too many "ifs." It was a wearying effort. He yawned mightily and closed his eyes.

After a two-hour nap, Sam showered and dressed for the evening in a black Sturgis rally T-shirt, black leather vest, old jeans and motorcycle boots, got into the Suburban and drove back downtown to find the bar he had spotted earlier. The sign above the door simply said, "Bar." Neon signs for Bud and Coors hung in the window. That was it.

He opened the door and stepped inside, letting his eyes adjust to the darkness. Bar to the right, tables and booths in the middle, an empty poolroom and silent jukebox to the left. A pall of tobacco smoke hung in the air. The first seat at the end of the bar was open. In the second seat, an old man in work clothes and a ball cap so dirty you couldn't read whatever might have been written on it leaned over the bar with his arm wrapped protectively around his drink.

"Ya mind?" Sam asked. The old man didn't look up. Sam said, "Don't mind if'n I do," and sat. He looked at the bottles behind the bar and saw an old friend—Eagle Rare 104-proof sippin' whiskey. It was a comfort. Only a serious drinkin' man's bar stocked the brand.

The big blonde bartender walked up. "Help ya?" she asked.

Sam looked at her and thought she was a fine specimen of a woman. "Eagle Rare, straight up and too tall, darlin'."

She rolled her eyes but couldn't disguise the smile that was tugging at the corners of her mouth. "Whatever you say, wild man." After she walked away, with a little extra swing in her considerable butt, the old guy in the next seat said in a raspy croak, "The good stuff, eh?"

"The whiskey or the bartender?" Sam asked.

The man's dark face turned toward Sam, broke into a smile and started laughing— "ack, ack, ack"—until he was consumed by a coughing fit. He hunched over the bar and slapped the top like a referee at a pro-wrestling match. Sam thought about pounding the old man on the back but he looked so frail he was afraid he'd break something. By then, the coughs had subsided to a bubbly wheeze so Sam left him alone.

The bartender set his drink down, winked, and sashayed away. A crumpled pack of Lucky Strikes sat on the bar, and Sam's neighbor picked it up, fished out a cigarette and lit up. He took a deep drag and blew a column of thick smoke toward the ceiling, where it hung like an overcast sky.

"Why, the whiskey, of course," the man said, grinning through bad teeth.

Sam downed his shot, grimaced, wiped his mouth with the back of his hand and nodded in agreement. "Yeah, the good stuff. Can I buy you one?"

"It's tempting," the old man said, licking his lips. "But nope, I've had my allotment. One drink. I nurse it until closing time." He grinned again.

The man went back to his silence. Sam ordered another drink. "And what might your name be, darlin'?" he asked the bartender when she returned.

"I'm Merilee," she said. Nodding toward Sam's neighbor, "And this here is Cyrus Bowlegs. That's the longest conversation Cyrus has had in this bar in at least six months. And you are…?"

"Sam, Sam Hite," he reached across the bar and shook her hand lightly. "Well, me and ol' Cyrus here share similar tastes in whiskey."

Somebody called for a drink and Merilee scooted away, glancing once over her shoulder as if trying to reassure herself that Sam wouldn't disappear in a puff of smoke while she was gone.

Sam looked at Cyrus and asked, "There ever any excitement round here?"

Cyrus turned his head and squinted. "I've outlived three wives, four children, a grandchild and five doctors. Every night when I make it back here, climb up on this stool and take my first sip of whiskey, why, that's about as much excitement as this old ticker of mine can stand."

"Amen," Sam said and raised his glass toward Cyrus in a toast. After he set the glass down, he thought, what the hell, it can't hurt to try. He reached in his vest pocket and slipped out the photograph of Aaron.

"Say Cyrus, I'm lookin' for a friend of mine. He's been in Gallup recently, although I have no idea if he's ever been in this bar, or if'n he's still around here." Sam laid the photo on the bar.

Cyrus pulled it over, leaned over and squinted, shook his head. "I can't see it too good. Merilee, could you hand me that flashlight?"

She reached under the bar, grabbed the flashlight and set it in front of Cyrus. "Here you go, Mister Chatty," she teased.

He picked up the flashlight and shined it on the photo, looked over at Sam, "You say this is a friend?"

"That's right," Sam said, nodding. "I'm afraid he's got his self into some bad business down here. I'm tryin' to see if he needs any help." Sam paused. "These days, he's shaved his beard and cut off most of that hair."

Cyrus looked again. "Maybe," he said, straightening up and turning on his barstool towards the back of the room. "You might try talking to Carlos back there in the last booth." He turned back to the bar, slid the photo across to Sam and hunched over his drink.

"I thank ya," Sam said, got off the stool and walked to the back of the bar. The booth was dark. He could see someone sitting there, but it was a little like staring at a photo negative—the shape of his body was darker than its surroundings. There was a stillness to the man that spooked Sam more than a little, and he was not a man to be easily spooked.

It was strange, as well, that he could walk into one bar in a town chock full of liquor establishments and get on Aaron's trail. He was just going to have to bite the bullet on this one. He'd come here to find Aaron and if this man could help him do that, he would dance with the devil.

Sam could feel the eyes on him as he approached. "Excuse me. I'm lookin' for a feller, a friend, and Cyrus up there at the bar said I should talk to you."

The man didn't say anything for a few uncomfortable seconds, then, "Have a seat." His voice was little more than a flat whisper but easily heard in the quiet bar.

"'Preciate it," Sam said, sliding into the dark booth.

"What do you want with this man?" Carlos asked.

Sam considered. "I don't guess he would want me tellin' the particulars of his business. Truth is, I'm not absolutely sure what he's up to. But he may need some help. Some friends of his have asked me to try and see that he gets home free and in one piece."

Carlos might have nodded; Sam wasn't sure. The presence of a human body generates noise: wheezing, grunts, breathing, shifting in the seat. Nothing from this guy but feral silence.

As Sam's eyes adjusted to the darkness, he could see something was different about the guy's face. It was hard to focus on, like camouflage. He let the silence run, however. He reckoned if he became talkative, the guy would clam up for good.

"You got a picture," Carlos said. It wasn't a question. Sam passed it over, and Carlos pulled out a wooden match, struck it against his thumbnail, and picked up Aaron's ID photo. The flame threw more light on Carlos' face and gave Sam a start, but beyond shifting his eyes he didn't react.

"Tell me why he's here," Carlos said.

Sam paused, but he didn't have much choice if this guy was going to help him. He leaned forward and lowered his voice. "Somebody attacked him, his girl and his dog. His dog is dead, his girl's in a coma."

"That's it?" Carlos asked.

"If you want facts, that *is* it," Sam said. "The cops haven't been able to come up with any good suspects." He left it hanging.

"And he might have," Carlos said, nodding.

"He's also got a different vehicle than he left home with. He owns a Subaru wagon, but I learned he's drivin' an old truck."

"Better to blend into the local scenery," Carlos said, nodding again. "I may run into him. If not, I'll do a little looking around. If I see him again, I'll offer to help. You should go on home. There's nothing you can do down here."

"And you can," Sam said, waiting for an explanation.

Carlos wondered how much to tell *him*. The old guy was asking for a favor, so Carlos had no need to qualify his offer. On the other hand, he trusted the old man, just like he trusted the guy in the photograph—what was his name? Adam Hathaway. Probably not his name, but Carlos didn't know whether he needed that now.

After another timeless silence, Carlos began, so softly he might have been talking to himself but with remorseless intensity. "I lost someone, too. She was 12 years old. I never even found out what happened to her, let alone who did it. But I learned there was a major poaching operation in the area where she disappeared. I traced the poacher to this area two years ago. When I find him, I intend to ask him some questions. Let's just say the cops hereabouts know me and are tolerant of my efforts. So, like I said, maybe I can find your friend, maybe I can help him. You probably can't. This is a different world here. An outsider wouldn't get much help."

Sam didn't realize he'd been holding his breath but, as Carlos finished, he let it out in a whoosh and drew in another. He knew for sure this poacher fella would be talking his ass off when Carlos found him. And he had no doubt that would happen, however long it took.

"Well, that's good enough for me," Sam said, nodding. He stood and started for the door. Before he'd gone three steps, Carlos said, "He told me his name was Hathaway. I might need to know his real name."

Sam honestly couldn't think of any reason not to tell him. "Aaron Hemingway," he said. "Like the writer. And thanks for whatever you can do." Then he turned back and shuffled through the door into the bleak street as if his boots were filled with buckshot instead of flesh, blood and bones.

Chapter 38

August 4

When the morning sun warmed his face, Aaron opened his eyes, eager for the day to begin. Things were moving and that excited him. He cautioned himself not to get in a hurry and make a mistake. A worry from the day before crossed his mind: somebody knows where I am. If they had been recording where the calls came from, the most recent was from Grants, 100 miles east of Gallup. He thought it might be a good idea to drive to Albuquerque and make it look like he was on the move. After that, he would have to stop calling, or just keep driving farther every day to sustain the illusion. And that wasn't really an option.

He crawled out from under the bag, still wearing his jeans, socks and T-shirt from the day before when he got a whiff of himself. Ugh! He resolved to do something about that. The air was cool. At this temperature, there was no way he was going to try to clean up here at the campsite. He popped the toolbox lid and grabbed the Carhartt vest.

He was antsy to get things moving, so he peeled up the top of a couple of cans of peaches, swallowed them for breakfast.

Once he got to Albuquerque, he'd find a truck stop and use the shower. After that, he would go downtown for liquor and food and try to find a laundromat to wash his clothes. He had just enough gas to make it to Albuquerque. He packed his valuables, stowed sleeping and cooking gear in the tent, and headed off the mountain.

Driving the truck at top speed—55 miles per hour—he made it to Albuquerque in two hours.

He found a TA truck stop downtown where Interstates 40 and 25 crossed, filled up and took a shower. Although there was a laundromat in the truck stop, Aaron decided against using it and drove around, finally finding a Doozy Suds on University Boulevard. While his clothes were drying, he called the facility for a report on Belinda. A different voice from the one he was used to hearing told Aaron, after a longish hesitation that there was "no change in Miss Mondragon's condition."

Two buildings down, Aaron stumbled across a bonus—a costume and classic clothes shop. He bought a sleeveless, faded denim jacket, a dark wig that gave him hair down to his collar and a pair of wrap-around, mirrored sunglasses.

Sam checked out of the motel late that morning. After talking with the mysterious Carlos, a couple of things were clear: Aaron was up to something, and Sam could do nothing more to help him. But he had a nagging sense that if he told anyone that Aaron had talked to someone in Gallup, it might come back to haunt all of them in some undefined way. He'd have to trust the man, Carlos, to help Aaron if he could.

On the way out of town, he stopped at a pay phone and called Harlan.

"I couldn't find him or anybody who's seen him. I need to check up on my dog so I'm comin' back."

"That's just as well," Harlan said. "He just called the Kensington from Albuquerque, so I guess he's on the road. What I can't figure is why he'd tell people he was going to Arkansas to look for his family, then end up in New Mexico."

"'Tis a mystery," Sam said.

"And maybe better left that way," Harlan said.

"Amen," Sam replied.

Driving on the highway alone, with no radio, often got Aaron's mind working. The problem was how to lure Carrington into the Malpais. A key might be that Carrington considered himself an archeologist. His obvious vanity, selfishness and greed, and his humbling exile from academia, were all possibly useful.

Aaron had to come up with something in the lava fields that would draw Carrington out. Something he couldn't resist, something that would make him willing to be secretive in his pursuit and to overcome any suspicion at the circumstances. What the hell that might be still eluded him.

He already had an outline of how it might work: send a letter, ask for a phone number, nothing specific on paper. The only problem was that it was going to take time and patience, two things he currently lacked.

The question still remained: What was the bait?

Chapter 39

August 5

Aaron's eyes blinked open as soon as the sky became light. A plan had come to him when he reread the section about early cultures in the book about the Malpais.

Around 10,000 B.C., the area around the Malpais had been inhabited by Folsom Man, a nomadic people who wore furs and skins and who had developed a distinctive spear point by chipping tiny flakes of hard rock like obsidian and flint until they were razor sharp. They were successful big-game hunters and gatherers. This was at the end of the latest Ice Age after mammoths and mastodons had been hunted out but giant bison still roamed the landscape. The Folsom people used large spears to bring down the bison, which were about twice as large as the current version and very dangerous due to long tusks that projected several feet forward from the jaw. In order to be more effective, Folsom hunters sometimes used the atlatl—a wooden launching device that gave the spears more velocity and killing power.

While various archeological evidence of Folsom Man existed, the spear points were the main artifact of the period. Aaron recalled that one of the articles from the Shiwi Messenger he'd read mentioned that Carrington's archeological dig was at a suspected spear point-making site and that his students were looking for the flakes and broken spear points that might be found there.

No bodily remains of Folsom Man had ever been discovered. So, what if a Folsom hunter had wandered into the Malpais and died in one of the ice caves, where the remains had been minimally preserved in the freezing air? It could have happened, and although none had been found, who'd been looking?

It would be a discovery of astounding proportions in the world of archeology. He hoped Carrington could be lured into the Malpais to see the mummified remains of a hunter who happened to possess a large spear with a Folsom point and an atlatl.

The only plausible scenario he could come up with was to pass himself off as a low-level pothunter who knew a big-time find when he saw it but didn't know how to capitalize on it. It wasn't like a pothunter, who sold his wares on the black market, could exactly waltz out of the Malpais with a desiccated body over his shoulder, throw it into the back of a truck, and then call around looking for a buyer. And he had nothing at all to gain by discovering such a relic. The federal government would control it until a commission could decide what to do with it. There would be no reward, only notoriety, which in turn meant scrutiny—the last thing a pothunter needed.

But if the lowly pothunter had heard of an archeologist, one who reportedly had plenty of money, he could offer the find for a nice but not exorbitant sum of, say, $25,000.

The archeologist could arrange, surreptitiously, to have the body removed and protected from the elements, then sell it at an appropriate profit. Or maybe simply announce the discovery and revel in the glory.

On several levels, it sounded dubious. He'd thought about it long and hard the previous night and could come up with nothing else. The only thing he hadn't decided was whether to try and lure Carrington to go into the Malpais alone and either follow him or be waiting for him at some prearranged spot, or to lead him there. In the first two scenarios, the chances of being spotted trying to follow Carrington or simply losing him in that jumbled landscape were high. If he waited at a pre-arranged spot, Carrington would probably become lost and miss the hookup altogether. He might also become suspicious of a suggestion to go into the Malpais alone and say no.

If Aaron offered to lead him in, there was a chance that Carrington would recognize him. If that happened it would force Aaron to kill him on the spot and increase the chance of being caught. Kenny Tucker said that Carrington had never shown him a picture and didn't seem to know what Aaron looked like. The Denver papers had carried brief stories about the attack but no pictures. So Carrington probably didn't know what he looked like.

From any angle, leading Carrington in looked like the best chance. It was still a long shot, but Aaron also knew that the easiest person to con was often another con. And what was a sociopath like Carrington but the ultimate con?

Aaron tidied the campsite and headed to Zuni. Right before reaching the highway, he slipped the wig on and pulled the hat down over it. He added the sunglasses, glanced in the mirror and realized he looked like a pervert at the rodeo.

He arrived at the post office just as an older woman wearing a postal uniform unlocked the door. The building was large and had a lot of boxes. The counter was around the corner from the boxes. He couldn't assume a misaddressed letter would get to Carrington, but if the box address was in the same area, it decreased the chances it would get stuck in the wrong box.

He noticed that the old-fashioned boxes had glass windows, so he walked to the area where he remembered Carrington's box was located. Some were empty but 886 had a couple of letters in it. Aaron lifted the sunglasses and peered through the window.

All he could see was the return address on a magazine but it was from the American Archeological Association, and that was enough.

The noose was tightening.

Coyote Cañon, Navajo Reservation

Despite last night's liquor, Carlos Corrigan had awakened with a perfectly clear mind. These days, he never got drunk, never had a hangover. No matter how much he drank. What the booze did was take the edge off the pain in his soul.

He wanted to get an early start and be in position before the traffic picked up at 7 a.m.. So he pulled out of the collection of dilapidated mobile homes, Bureau of Indian Affairs plywood cracker-boxes and hogans in Coyote Cañon that he called home. Seventeen miles to the highway, another seven to Gallup and he was on schedule to do that when a fan belt broke in his beat up old Dodge van 10 miles south of Gallup. He hiked a couple of miles to a nearby convenience store/gas station and called NAPA auto parts for a replacement. It took two hours to get it and 30 minutes to put it on since the engine was encased in a metal shroud inside the van that was removed to allow access to the engine, leaving little room to work.

While he was replacing the fan belt, he didn't see the red Ford flatbed driven by a guy with a beat-up straw cowboy hat drive past.

When Carlos finally arrived at the Zuni Pueblo, he backed into a pull-off at the junction of Highways 602 and 53. From there he could monitor all the through-traffic in a 1,500-square-mile chunk of land because every car, truck and motorcycle traversing the the triangle between Zuni, Gallup and Grants had to pass this point.

Carlos was still very good at sitting and watching, because, before being washed out as a drunk, he had been a special agent of the U.S. Fish and Wildlife Service for 14 years. Thousands of hours of surveillance instill habits that are easily revisited.

Three hours after leaving Zuni, Aaron read the letter aloud: "I have found something very valuable, archological speaking, in the Mal Pie. If you are interested, send a phone number by Agust 8 or I will fine some body else."

Luther Elliston
General Deliver
Gallup, New Mexico

Aaron had printed it with his left hand, purposefully misspelling some words to stay in character, and was wearing latex gloves to handle the envelope and paper. He addressed it and would drop it into a box outside the Gallup Post Office. On the way out of town, he pulled off his wig and glasses. If he were going to spend a few nights in the Malpais, he'd need some additional gear. He thumbed open his wallet and surveyed his cash. It was getting short but he had enough to finish this. First it was back to Albuquerque, then it was time to journey into the Badlands and find the kill site.

Trey Carrington was as excited as he'd been in a long while. Shortly after the Zuni teens had visited his camp, he'd gotten confirmation that eleven kids would participate in his archeological "education" program. The little one with whom he had become so taken had signed up for the project. Her name was Vera Ortega.

Upon realizing Vera—such an adult name for such a sweet young thing—would be coming to the dig in September, Carrington could hardly contain his excitement and quickly hatched a plan to see her sooner. He had rented a room in the community center in Black Rock and would give a party for the kids from Zuni. In preparation, he had sent his college students to Gallup to buy decorations, balloons, bags of chips and cases of soda. The names of the Zuni students would be taped to the chairs and he had placed young Vera front and center.

The party was tonight and Carrington was becoming so worked up that he could barely write out a program. But finally it was finished. He would give the opening remarks, and then ask his college students to address the importance of archeological study, getting a good education, going to college and whatnot.

Then he would give the closing remarks, being sure to single out young Vera for attention. He had sent the college students ahead to prepare the room and hadn't been aware of the strange looks they'd given him in the days preceding the event. Before leaving for the program, Carrington had showered—studiously avoiding any undue scrubbing in the groin area for fear he would lose control and diminish his delicious desire and the resulting animal magnetism he knew he projected at such times. He had trimmed and groomed his nose and ear hair and put on the khaki pants, shirt and jacket he had had cleaned and pressed in Gallup just for the occasion. He looked in the mirror, combed and mussed his hair a bit. Then he got into the Land Rover and drove to Black Rock.

Everything was ready in the room. The bunting, ribbons and balloons were hung. The bowls were full of chips, the coolers full of ice and cans of soda. The nametags were in place. The college students were standing in small groups, hands in their pockets, keeping their eyes away from Carrington. Not that he noticed. He clapped his hands loudly and most faces turned to him. "Excellent job, people."

The clock on the back wall said 6:55 and the first few high school students showed up. Carrington watched for Vera as the Zuni teens made their way into the room. A small measure of disappointment gnawed at his gut as Vera hadn't shown, but he tried to hide it behind a generous smile, as if each of them were equally important.

Carrington was near panic as he counted the tenth Zuni teen entering the room. Closely following the tenth, however, a short, dark-haired child with long bangs, bright eyes and a heart-melting smile stepped inside.

His heart soared as she entered. He clapped loudly again and told the students to find the chair with their name on it. The room broke into motion as the students responded. Vera was the last to take her seat.

"Welcome, young people, welcome," Carrington said, fondly, his eyes surreptitiously probing the baggy clothes Vera wore for body curves and other signs of sexuality. But from her high-top Converse shoes to her baggy jeans and oversize T-shirt, there were none. He forced himself to look out at the other students and began his spiel about how they were embarking on an exciting new chapter in their lives—the world of scientific discovery. All he saw was either the tops of their dark heads or blank looks. His eyes crept, uncontrollably, back to Vera, whose hands were covering her mouth, while her face became increasingly crimson. The room itself was strangely quiet, but a small tinkle of giggles escaped from behind her fingers. Her body was beginning to tremble.

With a slight knit of his brow belying the smile on his face, Carrington said, "Well, Miss Ortega, you appear to have found a measure of humor in these proceedings. Would you care to share your thoughts with the rest of us? Humor is good for the soul, you know."

Vera hunched even more, as if she were having a stomach cramp, but she shook her head, declining.

"Come, come, Miss Ortega, tell us what is so humorous. You're among friends here. I assure you it is okay."

With every eye in the room on her, she slowly began to raise her head. Her eyes were open but she still held her hands protectively over her mouth. Finally, she was facing Carrington, eye to eye, and she dropped her hands.

"Isn't that better?" Carrington nodded and smiled. "Come now, Vera. What's the joke?"

Vera took a deep breath, let it out and said, "That hair in your nose, it looks so *fun-ny* I just can't stop *laugh-ing*." A chorus of titters came from the Zuni teens and a couple of guffaws from the knot of college students, which were nervously cut short.

The words struck Carrington like a shock wave from an atomic blast. His face felt irradiated. His white-knuckled hands gripped the lectern, trying to maintain control, because he wanted to step around and strangle the little bitch. How *dare* she? In all of his years of teaching *no one* had *ever*… All eyes were on him, waiting to see what he would do.

Even little Vera was terrified now. The black rage in Carrington's eyes was sucking the air right out of her lungs. She wanted to cry, she wanted to run, but she was paralyzed.

The terror on her face actually jerked Carrington back from the edge of complete dissolution. A tiny thread to his survival instinct was still intact. To act now would be the end. He couldn't respond in any way. So he did the only thing he could: he turned and walked silently from the room.

It was a remarkable show of self-control because Carrington was already planning various scenarios against the little brown-skinned twat. The only thing that made it possible was picturing the look on her face as he took his revenge. She could have had affection, innocent touching, expensive gifts and pleasure and assuredly found her way out of this Third World hellhole to a finer existence.

But not now. The pleasure would now be all his. She would have pain and terror and ultimately death. Just thinking of it, the arousal was becoming painful—he needed release.

Fortunately, there was an option, a poor one but one that would provide immediate gratification. He'd heard that there was a prostitution ring operating out of a truck stop just east of Gallup, and that some of the hookers might be young Indian girls. There would be no sex with those diseased little whores—there were other ways to find release. For now, that would have to do.

Chapter 40

August 8

After three days of fruitless surveillance, Carlos decided his first stop would be at the Zuni Tribal Police station. He needed to talk with his buddy, Sgt. Eddie Othole, and see if there was anything going on in the area that would help him focus his attention. This dead-ass surveillance was beginning to seem like a waste of time.

Eddie was at his desk grimacing at some papers he was holding.

Carlos knocked. Eddie looked up and waved him in. Carlos sat quietly until Eddie let out a breath and set the papers down. Carlos could see some photographs among what appeared to be a police report.

"That bad?" Carlos asked.

"Yeah, that bad," Eddie Othole said, his face darker than usual, his mouth grim. He reached into the pile, removed a photograph and slipped it across the desk to Carlos, who felt the bile rising into his throat. The picture showed a woman's naked body with large bruises on her torso. Her left arm and right leg appeared to be resting at unnatural angles. Her eyes were gone and several fingers on one hand appeared to have been chewed off. The top of her head showed patches of broken skull and brain matter. And what appeared to be a length of tree branch protruded from her vagina.

"A Zuni woman, a girl really, who was working out at the truck stop east of Gallup, was found beaten to death last night in a ditch near Ft. Wingate. I had McKinley County copy me the report and photographs. She'd been missing for three days." Eddie Othole nodded at the photograph. "What kind of a monster would do something like that?"

Carlos slid the photo back. "A very angry one." Nodding toward the photograph, he said, "She one of yours?"

"Not officially. She'd been living outside the Pueblo for two years."

"Any leads?"

"Not yet," Eddie said, shaking his head. "They've got video cameras on the filling areas and on the registers. They're gonna be looking at those. But none in the restaurant itself or the parking areas. Her car was in the parking lot, so someone maybe grabbed her there. In that case, the videos won't tell us much."

Carlos knew that a crime of this enormity was unheard of within the Pueblo boundaries, due to the strong cultural and religious taboos against violence. But even a Zuni who lived outside the Pueblo was still a member of A: Shiwi—the People—and the murder would be taken hard by the tight-knit community.

"I hear you been sitting down at the crossroads for a few days," Eddie said, putting the papers in a drawer.

Carlos shrugged. "Just keeping in practice."

"Yeah, sure," Eddie said, weariness lining his face. "Listen, Carlos, you're going to have to excuse me. She's got some people down to Fence Lake. I have to break the news to them."

Before Eddie got up, he asked, "Was there something you needed?"

Carlos nodded. "I just stopped by to see if you've had any strangers hanging around town."

Eddie stood and walked over to the hat rack for his Stetson. He sat it on his head. "No one so strange that they've been brought to my attention." A flash of memory crossed his face. "Well, one of our patrol officers reported some white guy in a red, mid-'70s Ford 250 flatbed was sitting in the market parking lot reading a few days back, which is unusual but not illegal. He left after an hour or so."

"Okay," Carlos said, remembering what the old man had told him. He nodded. "See you around. Hopefully under better circumstances."

"Yeah," Eddie said. "Better would be good."

Renewed by this bit of information, Carlos drove down to the crossroads and resumed his vigil. He was thinking he might as well give it another day. He had told the old man he'd try, but there was a limit. Hellfire, Hemingway could be in Montana by now. For the first five hours, there was even less traffic than usual on the road. Maybe he was getting old, but this sitting-in-a-car-seat shit was hard on him. His neck was a little stiff so he rotated his head. As he did, he caught his reflection in the mirror. He studied his face, side to side, straight on. And it never got any better—not that he expected it to. What they'd done to him after the mauling was nothing resembling cosmetic surgery. They had cleaned the wounds, filled him up with antibiotics and Demerol, and simply sewn him back together. The odd thing was that the wounds were almost superficial. The bear's claws had not hit bone or eyes or seriously damaged any facial muscles. The skin on his face was neatly flayed. Almost as if the bear were being gentle. He laughed at the thought. It was almost too weird to consider. Still… He shook it off. Luck of the draw. That was all.

Picturing again the brutalized body of the young Zuni woman, his mind flashed for the thousandth time to the night his daughter—Mattie—had run off. During that summer in the cabin, she had developed a knack for finding wounded and orphaned animals. A few, very few, had recovered but most died. And she always got hysterical when she had to bury them. He'd put up with it because he knew what she was really doing—trying to defeat death. Since she hadn't stopped her mother from dying, she didn't want anything else to die. If nothing else, it gave her purpose.

Yet three of her "patients" had died that week, and she had cried and cried, finally becoming hysterical. That's when he told her: no more. Her hysteria had then ratcheted itself up to fury. Mattie had screamed that she hated him and run out. He was drunk at the time, as he was most evenings after his job as caretaker on the upper Chama Land and Cattle Ranch was done. Too drunk to go after her. Too drunk to care.

It was the last time he saw his daughter. Three years ago, almost to the day. A year after that he'd had the run-in with the grizzly during a renewed search for her…for clues.

There was another possibility to Mattie's disappearance that he didn't like to think about—not that any were good. But he couldn't help but wonder if the grizzly had killed her. After the initial weeks of searching, he hadn't come up with any evidence but a freshly abandoned bear pit, which put him onto the fact that there had been a poacher in the area. Through his contacts at the U.S. Fish and Wildlife Service, he'd learned the poacher's name. He was making another sweep when the bear nailed him.

The idea of his daughter dying in a grizzly attack was almost more than he could stand. But so was any other explanation. He felt the spasms in his diaphragm—*uh, uh, uh*—that proceeded one of his rare breakdowns. The photo must have really gotten to him. The pressure was building in Carlos's chest when he saw a beat-up, red mid-'70s Ford flatbed approaching from the east on 53. As the driver slowed to make the turn onto 601, he shot a quick glance at the van with the dark windows and Carlos got a good look at the driver's face. Although the he wore a battered, sweat-stained straw cowboy hat, Carlos was certain it was Hemingway.

That quickly, the spasms were gone. He was thankful for the reprieve.

Aaron had searched the Malpais for three days before deciding where he would kill Carrington. If anything, there were almost too many good spots. He had found collapsed tunnel ceilings, sinkholes and long, deep crevices. He chose a crevice that paralleled a ridge formed by magma butting up a sandstone bluff. Except for the first stretch, the hike was a difficult, sometimes-treacherous three hours from the trailhead. The ridge itself was tall enough to be seen from the trail. The chances of another human being in the area were hardly worth considering.

The plan was coming together. But none of it would matter if Carrington didn't respond to his letter. Which is why he was on his way to Gallup—to see if Carrington had taken the bait. Ideally, he *should* wait another day. But the suspense, now that everything else was in place, was killing him. Funny, Aaron thought—the suspense is killing *me*.

Carlos closed the gap a few miles from Gallup and stayed three car-lengths back as they got into town. He followed Aaron to the post office, where Aaron parked and went inside. Carlos parked a half-block away. He pulled binoculars from beneath the seat and watched. Aaron came out in less than a minute and, from the expression on his face, got what he'd been expecting.

Carlos realized he could just go up to Hemingway and explain about meeting the old man, offer to help. But Hemingway seemed to be content working alone—understanding correctly that his chance to get away with whatever he had planned was better that way. So the offer would probably kill the deal.

Piece of cake, Aaron thought, as he came down the steps, letter in hand. He climbed into the truck before opening it. He pulled out a small, folded slip of paper with a telephone number on it.

He started the truck, drove down Old 66 looking for a phone with enough space around it for privacy and found one next to a car wash. He rehearsed what he was going to say, took a deep breath, dropped a quarter and dialed. On the seventh ring, somebody picked it up.

"Professor Carrington."

There was something odd about Carrington's voice, Aaron thought. It sounded strained and a half-octave higher than he remembered. Aaron wondered if it was suspicion. He decided he had to play it out. "Yes sir, this is Luther Elliston. I wrote you that there note," he said, cranking up the hillbilly drawl. For several moments, Carrington said nothing. Then Aaron heard a sigh.

"Just what did you find that could possibly be valuable, Mr. Elliston."

"Well, sir, I do believe it's worth a lot to *somebody*, but not to me. I'm just a pothunter. This is way out of my league. I'm asking $25,000 to show it to you."

"Twenty five thou...Do you plan on telling me what it is?"

His voice sounded hoarse, like he'd worn it out shouting. "No sir, not until I see you in person."

"Forget it. You're wasting my time."

"Hold on, now. Let me think here a bit." He's gonna bite, is what Aaron was thinking. "Well, I guess since you don't know where it is, it'd be okay to tell you. You can't find it without me."

"That's right, I can't."

"It's a… a mummy."

"A mummy?"

"Not like King Tut or…It's the dried-up body of an Injun in an ice cave in the Malpais lava fields."

"You're calling me about some goddamn drunk Indian who crawled in there and died?"

Carrington's voice was becoming higher, almost brittle with incredulousness. Aaron knew he was going to lose him.

"What kind of a fool—?"

"There's an atlatl with a perfect Folsom point layin' next to him," Aaron said.

After a long moment of silence, Carrington said, "Really?"

All life should be so easy.

Carlos watched Aaron call from across the wide street. Just after hanging up, Aaron gave a little fist pump. All right, Carlos thought, looks like we're in business.

Trey Carrington sat there looking at the phone in his shaking hand as if it were an alien object. Slowly, he lowered it into its holder on the dashboard. The past three days, since the episode, as he'd come to think of it, had been like nothing he'd ever experienced. He felt like a disembodied spirit hovering at treetop level, watching himself going through the meaningless motions of life.

The only thing that had penetrated this state he was in was the letter. It was just so damn strange he couldn't get it out of his mind. And now this phone call. His mind and body were both back in one place again. It was a shaky arrangement. He felt like his nerve endings had been sanded. Noise, light and touch affected him just under the threshold of pain. But at least he was functioning again. He needed to be able to function, to make plans for an exit—a non-suspicious exit.

Like manna from heaven, this stupid hick had given him one. If it were true.

They'd haggled out the details. Meet early tomorrow. Take the pothunter's truck. Carrington wouldn't have any money on him, but he'd agreed to pay the $25,000 as soon as they returned, if he was satisfied with the worth of the discovery.

The best-case scenario was that it really was a Folsom specimen. If so, it would be a seminal discovery in North American archeology. All he had to do was find it and announce the discovery. Let the government handle it. Fly off to New York and bask in the glow. Forget about little Vera, let her rot right here where she belonged. He could already hear the strident squabbling as academics battled to protect their turf.

If the "mummy" was of more recent demise it would just be a wasted day. If there was no "mummy," it meant the pothunter was up to something. Trey Carrington was no fool, however. He would be ready for that, too.

Aaron made a quick stop at a liquor store, then, seeing another pay phone, he realized he hadn't been near a phone to check on Belinda in three days. He was torn every way he could be—what if it were good news? He was so far into this…thing, it had taken on a life of its own. Would his conviction waver and cause it to backfire in his face? What if it was bad news? Would his rage do the same thing? What about his worry that the calls would somehow tie him into Carrington's disappearance? He just wasn't up for a drive to Grants adding 200 miles and taking four hours out of the day. So it would have to be from Gallup.

Weigh all of that against his belief, his hope, foolish though it may be, that having somebody out there caring about her, checking up on her was like one more thin lifeline to keep her from…to keep her with us. He owed her that much. It was his foolish belief that he could escape the goddamn curse he'd carried from Vietnam that got her hurt in the first place.

For all the arguments against calling, he could feel this obligation was tipping the scale. He went back into the liquor store and got change, dialed the number he knew so well.

"Kensington medical wing." The voice, for the first time, was a man's.

"I want to check on the condition of a patient. Belinda Mondragon."

There was a pause. "Uh, sure, Mondragon you said? Could you hold on a second?" The man who'd answered the phone put him on hold and Aaron thought he'd just made a mistake. "Shit," he said under his breath, looked at the receiver as a wave of paranoia rocked him. He set it in its cradle, said, "Shit, shit, shit," and walked unsteadily to the truck to try and figure out what had just happened. Once in the cab, he began to worry that his initial take might have been wrong, that something might be going on with Belinda. And that was even worse.

He could see where this line of thinking was going to take him: emotional gridlock. He couldn't let it happen. He was in this all the way now and had to see it to the end. He couldn't let himself be distracted.

Well, what's done is done. But, it did convince him to try something he'd been mulling over those two dark nights he'd slept in the Malpais. So he drove to a Radio Shack and picked up an item he'd likely have no use for, using more of his dwindling supply of cash than he should have.

From the Radio Shack, it was a short hop to 602 southbound. He knew it was going to be a long, tense night.

Carlos Corrigan realized he was getting into this drama maybe deeper than was wise and wasn't sure why. Was it the chance at vicarious revenge? Maybe it was the challenge of staying out of the play but helping influence the outcome. Or getting caught up in the excitement of the chase. Probably a little of each. He liked Hemingway okay and could relate to what he was feeling. But the truth was he was bored. There hadn't been any information on the poacher he was looking for, Buster Bodeen, in some time. He had followed Hemingway to the liquor store and watched him make another phone call, a strange call from his actions. What the hell was that all about? Maybe he did have some help. If so, fine.

He followed Hemingway to Radio Shack and Carlos wondered again if he was reading the whole thing wrong. He decided to give it one more day. He stayed with him down 602 but this time he was hanging way back. He'd close the gap just before the intersection with 53 and try to keep the old truck in sight until he found where Hemingway was holed up.

When Carlos topped the hill coming into the Pueblo, Hemingway wasn't in sight, but Carlos spotted the old truck headed east. He followed and was able to stay close because several cars had gotten between them and didn't look to be interested in passing. Just before the town of Ramah, Hemingway turned up a gravel road into the Cibola National Forest.

Good choice, Carlos thought, as the whole watershed was laced with four-wheel-drive tracks. A lot of good places to hide. The only problem was all the roads were dead ends. One way in, same way out. That wasn't a problem for Carlos—he knew exactly where he'd be waiting early in the morning.

Whatever Hemingway had planned could be days away. But Carlos, who had hunted men for 14 years, could feel the momentum building; he thought it would be soon.

He had some sleeping gear, food and water in the van, so he'd hang around Ramah, find a place to pull off and sleep for the night. Tomorrow he'd be ready to rock and roll.

Chapter 41

August 9

Aaron had barely slept, worrying about the phone call and what it could mean, but also thinking about Belinda. Thinking about the way she looked the evening she had invited him over for pizza, with flour on her face and arms, the tomato paste on her sweatshirt and a smear over her eye, or the night they went dancing, with her dark hair let down, her bare shoulders and her red boots. And those flashing brown eyes. But the one picture that kept popping into his mind was the unruly lock of hair that kept falling over her eye, particularly when she was angry. Which he recalled was pretty often.

Aaron was haunted by thoughts that Belinda would blame him when she recovered. He had no doubt she would recover. He couldn't hold it against her because, hell, he blamed *himself.* She was just one more casualty in the trail of carnage that lay in his wake.

With all the turmoil swirling around in his brain, he was up plenty early to meet Carrington at the Bonita Cañon turnoff, which was a mile from the Zuni/Acoma trailhead. The location wasn't ideal but it was off the reservation so the FBI would be less likely to get involved. Carrington's Land Rover would be found fairly easily and a search would focus on Bonita Cañon. Then, possibly, across the road into the Malpais.

After pondering what could go wrong for much of the night, he decided just about anything. The worst thing would be if Carrington figured out that Aaron was packing. He came up with a solution minutes before it was time to leave.

His gear was already stowed in the truck. He wasn't hungry but knew he had to eat, so he opened a can of Chef Boyardee cheese raviolis and ate them cold. Then he spent a few minutes fiddling with one of his Power Bars.

He was wearing jeans, work boots, a T-shirt and a light denim western shirt, unbuttoned, the sleeves rolled up to just above the elbows. The straw cowboy hat was pulled down to cover his scar. No way he was going to wear the wig out there in the badlands. It would parboil his brain.

He dropped the empty can on the passenger side floorboard and got ready to meet his destiny.

Carlos Corrigan spotted the truck about 9:30 turning east on 53. Traffic was light so he stayed a couple of miles back. The highway here dipped and curved slightly but there were plenty of long stretches where he could keep Hemingway in sight. Like the road between Zuni and Gallup, there weren't a lot of places to pull off.

Carlos sped up as Hemingway approached the Malpais because there were two roads right at the boundary. One went north into the Cibola National Forest, crossing the Zuni Mountains to I-40 and Grants. The other was the Chain of Craters Scenic Byway, which went south and circumnavigated the entire west side of the Malpais, joining Highway 117 at its southern tip.

Carlos half-expected Hemingway would turn onto one of these roads, as there was only one other road intersecting the highway until the outskirts of Grants. Either would be a problem because traffic was virtually nonexistent on them, and it was impossible for another vehicle not to be noticed in that barren country.

Hemingway cruised past without slowing at all. It was eight miles to the next road, so Carlos dropped back again. He would put on a burst of speed at four miles and should close the distance right before Bonita Cañon. That was easy to do because Hemingway never went faster than 55 mph. Probably all the old truck could do.

He kept to the plan and caught sight of Hemingway about 300 yards ahead. The truck's brake lights came on, the left-turn signal blinked and the truck pulled into Bonita Cañon. Carlos drove another hundred yards and pulled onto the shoulder then down into the barrow pit. It was decision time because if Hemingway kept going up Bonita Cañon, there was no way in hell he could keep following.

When Aaron got to Bonita Cañon road, Carrington was leaning against the front fender of his Land Rover. As he pulled up, Carrington made a point of checking his watch. They had agreed upon 10 a.m. as the meeting time. Aaron's watch showed 10:02. It could be off; he hadn't been paying much attention to the precise time since he'd been in New Mexico. He's playing me, Aaron realized. But that was okay. Play now, pay later, motherfucker. Before getting out of the truck, he tried to calm himself. What he wanted to do was shoot the arrogant prick in the guts and watch him die slowly. He knew he had to get out of the truck right now or the situation would deteriorate.

So he slid calmly out of the truck and walked over to Carrington. He was shocked by how different Carrington looked: his hair was lank, he hadn't shaved in several days, and he had dark circles under his eyes as if he had been on a monster drunk. Nevertheless, Aaron offered his hand. "Perfessor Carrington." Carrington nodded but never looked down at the extended hand. Aaron flexed it a couple of times like he was working out a kink.

"There's been a change of plans," Carrington said. "I'm going to follow you in my vehicle." When Aaron withdrew his hand and started to object, Carrington flicked his wrist in dismissal. "It's non-negotiable. Where are we going?"

"Just up a ways," Aaron said, thinking it hadn't taken long for that part of the plan to go south. Having Carrington's vehicle parked there could be a problem because it was technically within the El Malpais National Monument. There was nothing to be done about it now. He walked back to the truck, got in, turned the truck around and pulled onto the highway.

Carlos was surprised when two vehicles pulled out so quickly and headed east. One looked like a well-kept, early-generation Sport Utility Vehicle. The other was Hemingway's truck. Carlos closed the distance in time to see both vehicles pull over into the parking area for the Zuni/

Acoma trailhead. The highway was visible for a couple miles in either direction. So he kept driving.

Aaron slid to a stop in the gravel at the west end of the parking area, which was little more than a wide spot in the road. He grabbed his butt pack, snapped it on, locked the truck and walked over to where Carrington had parked— thirty yards farther. As he arrived, they both heard the sound of a vehicle and looked up to see an old Ford van with tinted windows passing by.

As Carlos drove past, both men cast a quick glance over. He could see their eyes but the glances never lingered or looked particularly startled.

When he realized who was with Hemingway, he said, "I'll be goddamned." It was the archeologist—Cavanaugh…Christianson… Carrington, yeah, Carrington. He kept driving until he was around a bend and couldn't be seen, made a U-turn and pulled into a narrow arroyo that cut into the hillside.

Carrington pointed at the pack and said, "Open it." Like he was in charge now. His breath smelled like vegetable soup gone bad. A vein was throbbing at his temple.

"There ain't no need for that," Aaron said.

"You want a shot at that $25,000, you open it. I'm not going out into that…" he tilted his head toward the lava "…with someone who's carrying a gun."

Aaron unsnapped the buckle, set it on the ground and opened it. He moved the contents around to show a water bottle, a small first-aid kit, a snake-bite kit, two Tiger Milk bars and two Power bars, a throwaway poncho, a flashlight and a pair of thick gloves. Carrington reached in and snapped open the first aid kit, closed it and dropped it back into the pack. He glanced up and down the highway.

"Turn and face me and raise your arms." Aaron did. His shirt was open, exposing the T-shirt. His sleeves rolled to wide cuffs just above the elbow. Carrington ran his hands from Aaron's armpits down to his ankles. He ran his hands down the inseams. "Turn around, keep your arms up." He patted Aaron's waist and the backs of his legs. He raised the back of the shirt.

"Drop your pants," Carrington said. Aaron acted disgusted and submissive now, loosening his belt and unzipping his jeans, dropping them to thigh level. Carrington turned away. "OK, Mr. Elliston, let's go earn your $25,000. Lead the way." He slung the daypack over his shoulder.

Aaron resisted the urge to smile as he re-stuffed his pack. While he was bent over, Carrington grabbed his straw hat, lifted and quickly set it back on his head. "Just checking," he said, then gave a short gasp. "That's a nasty scar you have there. How did it happen?"

Aaron was unprepared and said the first thing that entered his mind. "I fell in the rocks out there." He jutted his chin toward the lava.

"Sure," Carrington said, wondering how a scar that straight could be caused by a fall into the lava. "As I said, lead the way." He began to wonder why Elliston had lied.

Aaron was still holding his breath as he stood, buckled on his pack and started walking. He exhaled a silent "whew" and sucked in a few quick gasps to get some oxygen in his lungs. He thought he was busted for sure, but beyond what had happened, Carrington seemed unconcerned. He set a brisk pace across the flat, hard-packed dirt field.

Carlos grabbed his binoculars and climbed the hill for a better look. By the time he got high enough to see, Hemingway and Carrington were on the trail into the Malpais.

That simplified things because there was no way he could go into the lava fields with the old boots he was wearing. He shook his head in admiration of Hemingway's plan—it was exactly what Carlos would have done. However, there was *still* a big obstacle to Aaron's getting away with it…

Half a mile in, they climbed up to the wood post and followed the trail as it wound through a wide belt of ponderosa pine grassland and the beginning of the lava. Shortly, they were at the first cairn. "It's about a mile and a half on the trail, then two miles cross- country." Aaron pointed west and saw the hesitation in Carrington's eyes. Rather than let the thought take shape, he got up and began walking. He heard the crunch of Carrington's footfalls in the lava.

They reached the lava bridge in about forty minutes. The sun was getting higher, the air heating up. At an average altitude of 7,500 feet, the Malpais was not as hot as people expected, but that didn't mean it was cool. He estimated it was already in the mid-80s. A bank of anemic-looking cumulus clouds forming on the southern horizon didn't promise much relief. Aaron took off his hat and ran his thumb along his forehead, then flung a spray of sweat on to the lava. He snapped the hat back on his head as Carrington walked up.

"Water break," Aaron said and sat down. As he gazed toward the ridge, he was finally able to describe what the terrain looked like: an expanse of huge, black land-locked coral, an ancient, dead sea. A faint trail snaked southwest into the lava, but Aaron knew it soon played out. They'd be bushwhacking the rest of the way. Carrington's safari jacket was already soaked with sweat.

Aaron pointed to the ridge. "The picnic's over, Perfessor. We're going over there." He pointed west to the ridge, decided to taunt him. "It's not too late to back out."

Biting his lower lip, Carrington looked for a moment as if he were thinking about it. He shook his head and set his jaw. "We've come this far. Let's keep going." He took a long drink from his bottle. "But I do need to rest for a bit." He sounded like some of the fight had gone out of him, just as Aaron had hoped.

After a few minutes, they set out, Aaron in the lead again. Within 200 yards, the "trail" disappeared and they plunged into a landscape literally forged in the bowels of the earth. They would be winging it now, as there was no way to retrace Aaron's earlier route.

About an hour and a half later, Aaron reached the base of the ridge they would traverse, looked back and saw Carrington about two minutes behind. Keeping his back to Carrington, he pulled his butt pack around, unzipped it, then worked a piece of tape from beneath the rolled-up sleeve on his left bicep. He tugged it and the derringer and a short section of Ace bandage slipped into his hand. He dropped both into the pack and realized that the bandage was damp with sweat. He hoped the sweat hadn't worked its way into the powder. There was nothing he could do about it now. He turned and watched Carrington approach.

Trey Carrington looked up and saw the man he knew as Luther Elliston had stopped. He kept thinking about the scar and the lie, but his mind was still a little foggy and couldn't quite grasp what was bothering him. Being hot and tired wasn't helping.

Carrington came up, wobbly, and sat heavily on a cone of dark gravel well away from Aaron. His face was flushed, his breathing heavy. "How the fuck did you ever find this…this mummy?"

"I spend a lot of time out here," he said, curt and dismissive.

Carrington grunted and began eating a protein bar. He washed it down with water between bites.

"How much farther?"

"Not much, just over the ridge and down a ways."

Carrington stuck the water into his pack, dropped the candy wrapper on the ground and slung the pack over his shoulder. "Lets get moving. I want to see this fucking dead Indian."

Aaron started up the rock, thinking it was too bad there wasn't a way to make the son-of-a-bitch *really* pay for what he'd done. Tell him what was going to happen, then stretch it out a couple of days. But that just wasn't practical. This was going to be a quick strike—a surgical strike. Unless…

Shrugging off the thought, he climbed up the ridge, reached the top and started down the crest, watching as the crevice to his right— where he planned to hide Carrington's body—widened.

As Carrington reached the crest and stepped over it, Kenny Tucker's words came to him like a sucker punch to the solar plexus: "I hit him upside the head with a Louisville slugger." This guy was the cop he'd hired Tucker to fuck up! Fear flooded his bowels like a cold-water enema. But then he remembered: he had a gun, the cop didn't. Then anger replaced the fear. There was no mummy, no easy excuse to get the hell away from here. Now he would have to sit it out, watching from the hot seat as the investigation into the Indian girl's murder proceeded. He didn't think anyone had seen him, but he hadn't been in the best state of mind that night to be careful.

Even so, he wasn't sure his nerves would hold up. If he pulled out of town before the dig was scheduled to close for the winter with no good reason, *that* might get someone's attention. He *needed* this goddamn mummy.

Watching the cop move away, Carrington's anger blazed into rage. He reached into the pocket of his jacket, but he tripped over a jutting slab of lava and crashed to his knees and yelled "FUCK." As Aaron turned to see what happened, Carrington drew a small, dark semiautomatic, raised it and aimed straight-arm in Aaron's direction.

Carrington said, "You're the cop. The one Tucker roughed up."

Aaron's look of surprise was real as he saw the gun. "What? A cop? I ain't no gol-dang cop. I'm a pothunter." He took a step toward Carrington, who was still on his knees. The gun barked and Aaron was spun around, falling forward on his hands. The pain at his waist hurt like a bitch. Blood was seeping out of a long gash in his thick leather belt. The lava was gouging his palms, but it, too, could have been worse. It was more like sharp gravel than glass. He threw a look over his shoulder, and saw Carrington trying to stand.

He raised himself on his elbows and rolled onto his butt, and turned to face Carrington, who was about 30 feet away.

"You crazy motherfucker, I ain't no cop!" Aaron screamed. "I done tole ya, I'm a pothunter."

The force of his denial shocked Carrington, injected a sliver of doubt. He raised the gun, said, "Don't get up. You stay right there or I'll start shooting."

"Okay, okay, but I've gotta get something on this wound."

Carrington waggled the gun. "Not yet. What happened to your head?"

I knew it, Aaron thought. That fucking scar. "I lied. So what? I got in a fight at a bar. I was whaling on this dude when his white-trash girlfriend snuck up behind me and hit me with a pool cue. Ain't nothin' to be proud of."

Carrington appeared to be thinking about it. "Throw me your wallet. I want to see some identification."

Aaron shook his head in dismay. "Well excuse me all to hell for not bringin' my driver's license into the Malpais. I locked my billfold in the toolbox on my truck. Don't have no money in it anyways."

Carrington looked down momentarily at the torn, bloody knees of his pants. "I don't believe you."

"Yeah, well, tough shit," Aaron said and opened the buckle on his butt pack.

Carrington looked startled. "What are you doing?"

"What's it look like I'm doing? I'm gonna look at this hole in my side. I need to patch it up."

"Well, don't try anything funny." Carrington eased himself down onto a flat slab of lava.

"If I do, just go ahead an' shoot me," Aaron said, dismissively. He had to lure Carrington into the range of the derringer. With only two shots, he couldn't afford to miss. Carrington's little automatic wasn't much more accurate but he probably had six more cartridges in the gun. He couldn't believe he let himself be searched and never even considered that Carrington might be armed. So far, Aaron knew he'd fucked this plan up about every way it could be done. He wondered what else he had fucked up that he had yet to discover? He was lucky to still have a big advantage: Carrington didn't know about the derringer. All he had to do was lure Carrington to within 15 feet without getting himself shot.

For the moment, they appeared to be at an impasse, so he undid his belt and saw that it had taken the brunt of the damage. An angry gash in his waist had almost stopped bleeding so he spread some antibiotic salve on it, covered it with a 3x3 sterile pad, taped it down and cinched the belt tight over it. Carrington still had the gun halfway pointed at him but had pulled up a pant leg and was examining the damage to his knee. Just as he did, Carrington looked over and frowned. "Throw that first-aid kit over here," he ordered.

"Fuck you," Aaron said. "You tried to kill me. Why should I do anything for you?"

"I wasn't trying to kill you," Carrington said. "It was a warning shot. I wasn't even trying to hit you."

"Well, you sure are a piss-poor shot then." But he realized Carrington had given him an opening. He shrugged, grabbed the nylon first aid bag and flipped it in Carrington's direction. It landed about 15 feet away but skidded another five feet. Too far. Carrington got up, and, with the gun trained on Aaron, walked the 10 feet, picked it up and backed away.

"What are you so scared of, Perfessor? You afraid I'm going to spit in your eyes and blind you?"

Carrington ignored him but it occurred to Aaron that maybe Carrington was telling the truth. He probably could have shot Aaron down, if he'd believed Aaron was who he thought he was. So maybe there was some doubt. Or maybe Carrington wasn't ready to give up finding the mummy. Maybe it was too important to him to give up without knowing for sure it existed. What could make it that important? Aaron ran a scenario in his head: It was worth trying.

"The price is $50,000 now," Aaron said.

Carrington's head snapped around like he'd been bitch-slapped. "What?"

"I said I want $50,000 now for showing you the mummy. You shot me, remember? That's attempted murder."

"I told you I wasn't trying to kill you. It was an accident."

"It don't make no difference. You almost did."

Carrington shook his head violently. "You're out of your mind."

Aaron grabbed his pack and started to stand. "Forget it then. I'm going back and I'd advise you to follow. You seen what the lava can do."

Carrington stood and pointed the gun at Aaron and aimed it. "I'll kill you right now." Aaron knew, at that point, that Carrington's desire for the mummy had trumped his doubts.

"You'll never find it without me. A month, two months, a year won't make no difference. I been out here for the best part of 20 years. I walked right past a dozen times before I found it." He watched the agonized debate on Carrington's face as he balanced the competing arguments. Then he saw the brief flash of a quickly hidden smile as Carrington likely realized that he could still kill Aaron if he couldn't produce the mummy. Or maybe kill him in either case.

"All right. Fifty thousand. If it's as you described it."

Aaron sat back down. Carrington frowned. "What are you doing?"

"I'm going to have a candy bar and some more water. This getting' shot has made me hungry." Carrington looked down at his knees and the first aid kit and shrugged.

Aaron took the Power Bars out of his pack and sat them on the lava. He gave one a squeeze, frowned and picked up the other one, opened it and took a bite. "So Perfessor, who's this fella you thought I was?"

Carrington had set the gun down and was taping his knee. He looked over, annoyed.

"I mean just general-like. No specifics. I'm just wondering why I almost got killed."

Carrington was mumbling, but Aaron couldn't hear what he was saying. "What?" he asked loudly.

There was that grin again, like *so what if he knows?* "It was just some hick- town cop who was in a position to cause me some trouble. I hired a couple of guys to rough him up. The scar on your head looked like, well, he said he hit the guy in the head with a baseball bat. That's what your injury looked like. So I thought..."

"Remind me to stay on yer good side, Perfessor."

Carrington was working on the other knee. "You're smarter than you look, Luther."

Aaron smiled grimly, picked up the remaining Power Bar, squeezed it and put it back in his pack, and took a long drink from his water bottle. "Any time you're ready," Aaron said, thinking: now it gets tricky, because this was where he had planned to shoot Carrington and roll his body into the crevice. He figured he had about 10 minutes to come up with and execute a plan before the shit went all Dodge City on him. Then he heard the last thing he wanted to hear.

"How much farther?"

"Not much," Aaron said, his thoughts approaching warp speed. He needed to get the gun out of Carrington's hand, or at the very least close the gap between them. His eyes were searching frantically as he approached the high end of the ridge. This was new territory. He hadn't gone this far before. He felt like a hummingbird had burrowed into his heart; his breaths were coming short and fast. Then, as he topped the rise at the end of the ridge, he saw what he was looking for across the sandy wash at the bottom of the ridge—another wave of folded lava that had, somehow, come to an abrupt stop and formed an overhang that ran for several hundred yards in each direction.

Almost directly across from him, the overhang had collapsed, leaving a gap that could be negotiated to reach the top. It was a steep 15-foot climb up the ragged chute but it could be done, using the hands.

"Why have you stopped?" Carrington demanded, stopping as well, intent on maintaining a good interval between them.

"I'm just lookin' at payday, Perfessor, just thinkin' of that $50,000 and what I'm gonna do with it. The ice tube is right across the way."

"Really?" Carrington said, his voice a mixture of suspicion tinged with excitement.

"Yep," Aaron said. "The ice tube is beneath that slab of lava over yonder. A small section of the ceiling has collapsed down the ridge a ways. The mummy is a couple hunnerd feet down the tube." He looked back but Carrington still wasn't moving. "Let's get moving."

"No," Carrington yelled. "Just stay right there and keep your hands out where I can see them. I don't want to lose sight of you."

Aaron held his hands out and shrugged. "Whatever you fuckin' say, Perfessor, but this shit is gettin' old." Carrington's contrariness gave him an idea.

"Too bad," Carrington said, as he approached with the gun extended. When he got within about 10 feet, he told Aaron to go ahead.

When they were both in the arroyo, Aaron asked, "You got any gloves?" Carrington shook his head no. "Then I'm going to climb up first and throw the gloves down to you. You'll need 'em if you don't wanna tear up your hands."

Carrington looked at the chute and realized the dilemma it presented. Finally, he said, "No, I'll go first. I want you to stand on the far side of the arroyo while I'm climbing." Aaron shook his head disgustedly, threw down the gloves and stalked across the dry wash, smiling.

Carrington wiggled his hand into one loose, leather work glove, and stuffed the other in his pocket while keeping the gun in his bare hand. He made it about four feet up and couldn't go any higher. He cast a glance over his shoulder at Aaron and tried again and almost fell. He got his feet under him, threw a glance back at Aaron, put the gun in his jacket pocket then pulled on the other glove.

Aaron slowly unzipped his butt pack. Carrington made better progress with both hands, got up about eight feet and pulled loose a chunk of lava. He came close to falling but got another handhold, tested it and made it another couple of feet, so his arms were about half his body length below the top. Some of the lava he was standing on crumbled, leaving him in a three-point hold, trying to find another foothold.

Aaron reached in and grabbed the derringer, cocking both hammers, and started taking long strides across the wash toward Carrington. He closed the gap quickly. Carrington looked back and saw him coming and began clawing at the rock. More debris came loose. Aaron stopped and sighted the gun at the middle of Carrington's back.

"Looks like you got yourself in a fix there, *Pro*fessor." Carrington took a quick look, his eyes widened when he saw the derringer and he reached for his gun. But the glove was too thick. He fumbled it, and it discharged as it hit the lava.

By the time Aaron flinched, the slug had sailed harmlessly into the air. He stepped forward and reached down for the gun. It was an old Beretta single-action .32. It had automatically recocked when Carrington shot him and Carrington had dropped the hammer on a loaded chamber. When it hit, the gun had fired. The hammer had recocked after the last round fired. He thumbed it back, squeezed the trigger and released the hammer softly on to the firing pin. He put the gun into his butt pack, zipped it shut.

Chunks of decaying lava continued to dribble down as Carrington tried to solidify his purchase.

Aaron backed up, held the derringer at his side and said, "By the way, motherfucker, I *am* the hick-town cop you had roughed up. Your boy Tucker tried to rearrange my brain matter. I guess he forgot to tell you that he and his thugs shot my friend. She's in a coma. And they crushed my dog's spine. I buried him."

Carrington's head was cranked around so far he was going to break his own neck if he didn't relax. "That wasn't part of the deal," he whined. "That wasn't supposed to happen."

"Well, professor," he said matter-of-factly, "that's what happens when you hire some shit-for-brains miscreants who beat off to gun magazines to do your dirty work." He paused. "I think you should come on down now."

"No," Carrington said, shaking his head frantically. Aaron raised the derringer and sighted on the back of Carrington's head. He took a deep breath, let it out slowly, raised the barrel and fired. The lead ball exploded as it entered the lava, raining a wave of shrapnel down on Carrington who screamed and swatted at his head like his hair was on fire.

As his body began to slip, he scrabbled against the lava like a spider sliding down a mirror. But it only slowed his descent. About three feet from the bottom, a grapefruit- sized chunk came loose in his hand, and he wrenched his body around and flung it, hitting Aaron in the left shoulder. Aaron staggered back a couple of steps but held on to the derringer. Carrington's boot caught in a crack and he pitched forward into the air, arms flailing, and belly-flopped onto the lava-sand with an "*oof.*"

With Carrington's pathetic gesture of resistance, the thin veil of restraint that had kept Aaron from shooting him was gone. In its place was a blood-red flash of light in his head, unleashing the rage and hurt and fear and guilt that he'd kept dammed up for so long. As Carrington started to rise, Aaron took a step and kicked his skull like a football. It was a glancing blow but enough to roll Carrington onto his back. Carrington's arms were spread-eagled. He was trying to rise but his neck muscles weren't cooperating and his head was rolling side to side. Aaron stepped over Carrington's body and dropped onto his chest, pinning his arms to the ground with his legs. He jammed the barrel of the derringer into Carrington's mouth, who was gagging while trying to draw a breath.

Aaron pushed the barrel into the back of Carrington's throat as faces swirled through the red mist: Belinda's inanimate face in the hospital bed, the tracks of Tye's tears coursing down his dark face like silver ribbons, Roscoe's ragged breathing as Aaron hugged him and whispered into his ear as the drug took him away.

The wind moaned like a chorus of tortured souls across the stark landscape of a million years of fiery destruction, but Aaron knew the sound was coming from within himself. It was the same sensation he had experienced when killing the Vietnamese peasants in that ville half a world and lifetime away. All the rules were now out the window. Deep inside, every man wants to believe there is an unstoppable force within himself to wreak havoc if the proper conditions are met. And he was there, now. Almost.

By any reckoning, Carrington deserved to die. But a lifetime of dealing with the repercussions of that long ago action, did Aaron want to take a chance that this time was different? That somehow the irrefutable evidence of Carrington's transgressions would let Aaron off the hook for cold-blooded murder?

His finger tightened on the trigger, a feather's brush away from dropping the hammer onto the cap that would ignite the powder, launching the ball that would sever the brain stem an inch away, as Carrington lay paralyzed with fear. It felt so good, so right, but he couldn't shake the nagging realization that if he hadn't given in to the feeling on that hillside above the ville, so much would have been different in his life.

He thought of Cassie and Belinda and wondered if they'd be better off by his killing Carrington, or would they somehow be hurt? The latter seemed a real possibility. And with that admission, the black wind began to fade. His finger relaxed on the trigger.

Carrington's eyes were open, watching his fate being decided. He must have realized something had changed, because Aaron could see, even with the derringer still jammed into his mouth, a hint of cockiness there.

That wouldn't do, not at all. He jammed the barrel hard into Carrington's throat again. "See, Professor, besides my friend and my dog, a whole shitload of trouble has come back to haunt you today. I know about the research you stole and sold to the Iraqis. A good friend of mine came back from the war sick."

The cockiness was gone from Carrington's eyes; he was starting to gag again. "This friend, he'd been totally paralyzed for five years. Before that, he'd been fine for what, a year and a half, then something struck him down like a bomb had gone off in his brain. He died the same night your boys did their dirty deed. Did I mention it could have been from encapsulated aflatoxin?

"Another 50,000 of those poor bastards who fought over there are now sick. I wonder how many of those you're personally responsible for."

Carrington was blinking, his eyes darting wildly, as if he were looking for help that wasn't going to come.

"And the rapes," Aaron said. "The ones everyone knows about and the ones we can only guess about." Carrington started to struggle. Aaron lowered the hammer on the loaded barrel, raised the one on the empty barrel, said, "Bye, bye, Professor," and pulled the trigger. The click was somewhat muffled to Aaron but it must have sounded like a mallet on a steel drum to Carrington. His body arched like he'd been hit with a Taser, bounced Aaron off like a bronco. Then Carrington's bowels opened and a putrid odor flooded the arroyo like a poisonous cloud. He rolled into a fetal position and began to whimper.

"Now are you going to be a good boy?" Aaron asked, standing up. Carrington didn't respond.

"Get up. We've got a date with the sheriff." Carrington shook his head but didn't move. "Did you hear me? I'm going to turn you over to the sheriff's office. Would you rather I go ahead and shoot you?"

Carrington uncoiled his body, struggled to his feet. The shit had soaked through the seat of his pants and ran down the inside of both legs. But he didn't seem to notice. Aaron pointed and Carrington walked away like a whipped dog.

Before reaching the trail, they came upon a shallow pool of stagnant water. Aaron told Carrington to go down and clean off. He couldn't stand the thought of riding in the truck with that mess. Carrington stumbled through the process like a zombie. When he was done, the shit smell was weaker but the odor of dead fish had been added. Aaron shook his head, said "Get going."

The hike out was uneventful until they got to the parking area and saw that Carrington's Land Rover was gone. Carrington stared about, looked at Aaron accusingly. "I don't have a fucking clue," Aaron said, "so save your breath." As they approached the truck, Aaron saw something tied around the door handle. When he got closer, he could see it was a piece of leather fringe threaded through a turquoise bead. His eyes traveled over the hills across the road.

A hundred questions bombarded his brain but he knew there would be no answers today, maybe never. Still, a chill worked its way up his spine as if a ghost were lurking nearby. He shook the thought away.

What he wanted to do was to tie Carrington across the stake-bed like a dead deer in hunting season to further humiliate him and keep the smell out of the cab, but he needed to talk to the cops first, tell them he was bringing in a suspect. Having a cop stumble on him with a live body bound and gagged in the back of the truck would be a little tricky to explain without a heads-up.

So he taped duct-taped Carrington's hands and ankles, then taped his hands to the wing window post and tightened it. The odor was still nauseating but there was nothing to be done about it. He backed out, made a U-turn and headed for Gallup.

Aaron pulled the truck over at the pay phone in Ramah. The phone book was weathered and had pages torn out but the page with the number for the McKinley County Sheriff's Office was intact. He dropped in a quarter and this time got a dial tone, so he called and explained that he was an officer from Colorado coming in with a suspect and asked them to call Lt. Earl McCormick at the Boulder County Sheriff's office for details. He got directions to the jail.

On the way, some of Carrington's shock appeared to be wearing off. He stayed quiet but Aaron could almost hear the gears grinding in his head, planning what he was going to do when they got to the jail. Aaron couldn't wait to see his face when he sprung his little surprise on him.

No sooner were they inside the Sheriff's Office than Carrington started shouting. "I'm Professor Trey Carrington and this man tried to kill me. He's deluded, making unfounded accusations about some attack on himself. I demand to be set free and that you arrest him!"

It caused quite a commotion, and a number of officers wandered into the booking area to see what the ruckus was about. A stocky Hispanic officer whose nametag read Gilbert Solano came up to Aaron. Two others grabbed Carrington and held him. They got a whiff and groaned, held him at arm's length with their heads turned away. When Solano heard, he turned to look and the odor of shit and dead fish rolled over him. He took Aaron by the arm and moved him across the room.

"You Hemingway?" Solano asked. Aaron nodded. "I talked to Lt. McCormick, and he confirmed the details of the crime but he said he knew nothing about any suspect. In fact, he said he didn't even know where you are. He did confirm you are a Deputy Marshal in some mountain town."

Carrington had been listening intently and started spewing. "See, I told you. He tried to kill me. He put a gun in my mouth and pulled the trigger. He's out of his mind. I de—"

"If you just shut up, we'll get to the bottom of this. But I don't know, it's pretty hard to miss from that range, the gun being in your mouth and all."

Carrington's jaw jutted belligerently. "It misfired or something. That's why I messed myself."

Solano turned and looked at Aaron, his bushy brows arching.

Aaron shrugged. "He'd already shot me and he'd just nailed my shoulder with a chunk of lava. I was trying to gain a little compliance."

"Shot you?" Aaron unbuckled his belt and showed Solano the bloody bandage. Then he pulled his left arm out of the shirt and displayed the angry bruise on his shoulder. "Okay, just keep the rest of your clothes on."

"It's all lies," Carrington shrieked. "I demand—"

"SHUT THE FUCK UP," Solano said, and turned back to Aaron. "McCormick also said if you say this is the guy, he probably is. But…" Aaron held up his palm, then took the Power Bar out of his pocket and shook a microcassette recorder into his hand. He rewound it. Carrington's head snapped up.

"I made this a few hours ago. *After* he shot me and *before* I put the gun in his mouth." He punched the play button.

So, Perfessor Carrington, who's this fella you thought I was? I mean just general like. No specifics. I'm just wondering why I almost got killed.

(inaudible mumbling)

What?

It was just some hick-town cop who was in a position to cause me some trouble. I hired a couple of guys to rough him up. The scar on your head looked like, well, he said he hit the guy in the head with a baseball bat. That's what your injury looked like. So I thought…

Remind me to stay on yer good side, Perfessor.

You're smarter than you look, Luther.

Carrington had stiffened, but as the tape played on the deputies' grip tightened visibly. He croaked, "I want an attorney."

Solano told Aaron, "We'll hold him for 24 hours." He turned to the deputies. "Lock him up."

"Wait," Aaron said to the deputies leading Carrington away. They stopped and Aaron reached into his back pocket, withdrew a folded sheet of paper. "Professor Carrington, you are duly summoned to provide information in U.S. District Court case 97-1003 concerning the transfer of biochemical warfare technology to Iraq in 1988." That was more information than he usually provided when serving papers but he wanted these officers to know who they were holding. The officers holding Carrington tightened their grip at this bit of news. He walked over and stuffed it into Carrington's shirt pocket.

Carrington started struggling. But the officers locked their hands on Carrington's arms and marched him down the corridor. Aaron walked back to Solano.

"Luther?"

"Long story, " Aaron said.

"Well, I've got time to hear it," Solano told him. "I'm still a little uncomfortable about this situation."

Aaron left out a lot but in the end he'd woven a tale of running an elaborate scam on Carrington to get him to confess. There were gaps as wide as the Rio Grande in the story and Aaron knew Solano knew it. But in the end, none of that mattered because, dark intentions aside, Aaron had committed no crime or even coerced the confession. Since Aaron was essentially acting as a citizen, he wasn't even required to give a Miranda warning.

Aaron also filled him in on the Gulf War stuff. That hit home because Solano said his brother-in-law had fought in the war and had been sick since he got home. When the interview ended, Aaron got up and started for the door.

"Oh, I almost forgot," Solano said. Aaron stopped and turned. "Lt. McCormick told me to tell you that he wants you to give him a call. Immediately."

Aaron nodded and said thanks. "By the way, did he mention...?"

Solano smiled kindly, "Oh yeah. And he asked me to tell you your friend has come out of the coma. He'd just found out right before I called. Said that's all he knew." Aaron felt like the steel cable that had been holding him upright had turned to rubber. His legs nearly buckled.

"Thank you," he croaked and staggered through the doorway.

On the drive to the Economy Inn, Aaron wanted to shout with joy, wanted to dance with abandon, wanted to cry like a baby. Instead, he was in a state of stunned relief.

After dealing once again with the delightful Ms. Chatterjee, he took his gear to the room. He was tempted to jump in the shower and get the stink off, but he decided to make the call first, find out more about Belinda, and get the ass-chewing out of the way so he could relax the rest of the evening.

He picked up the phone, dialed, and Earl answered on the third ring.

"McCormick."

"Hey," Aaron said. "So, Belinda's okay?"

"Well, well, well!" McCormick was almost shouting into the phone. "If it ain't Harry-fucking-Houdini himself!"

"Okay, all right. You'll have plenty of time to give me an ass-chewing. But, please, tell me about Belinda first." He heard McCormick exhale the next round of castigations.

"Well, she's out of the coma and coherent, so it looks pretty good. But let's not get sidetracked. You're sure this is the right guy?"

"I'm sure."

"Tell me about it."

So he did, from the beginning, leaving out that he'd planned to kill Carrington. Earl wasn't fooled.

"You went down there to kill him." Not a question.

"That was the plan."

"What changed?"

"I don't know if I can explain it, Earl, but I began thinking that killing Carrington, except in the seconds or minutes of terror before dying, was like letting him off the hook. And I wanted the son of a bitch to suffer, Earl. I wanted him humiliated in public, then sent to prison where he can play hide-the-salami for some 300-pound Aryan Brotherhood psychopath. And I figured that standing trial on conspiracy to commit murder, the veterans' lawsuit, maybe even federal charges on the Gulf War shit would do that.

"But in the end, I just wondered if killing someone in cold blood, even someone who deserves it, a scumbag like Carrington, was something I could live with. It wasn't that I couldn't do it to him. I just couldn't do it to myself. And, besides, it wouldn't bring Roscoe back, or help me straighten out the situation with Cassie, or bring Belinda out of the coma—all the things I really care about."

"You know, we could have arrested the guy up in Saratoga and sweated it out of him. Offered him reduced charges if he flipped on Carrington. It would have saved a lot of grief."

Aaron could now hear the barely restrained anger that he knew had been there all along. "Carrington has been in some legal scrapes before this and his wealthy family got him off." He knew how lame that sounded. "Besides, I was in a different frame of mind at the time. I wanted to be the one who did it."

"Okay, but the thing I don't get was the tape recorder. You had it all planned out but you couldn't have known he would confess the way he did."

"Well, you know me. I like to hedge my bets. It was a long shot. It worked out. There's not much else to say."

Aaron heard Earl sigh, most likely in resignation. It wasn't the last he'd hear about it, he knew. "I've got enough for a warrant. I'll fax it down there first thing in the morning."

He could tell Earl was getting ready to hang up. "Have you seen Belinda?"

"No, I've been busy writing the warrant in order to keep your ass out of jail for unlawful detention. But Harlan was there when she gained consciousness. He said the old mountain man brought a puppy into the room and put it on her stomach. It started moving around and Belinda's hand came up and touched it. After a while, she opened her eyes."

"A puppy?"

"I guess Roscoe and that mountain man's wolf did the nasty and produced a litter. Most of them look like the wolf dog but one, a female, looks like, and I quote, a ball of belly-button lint with a purple tongue, one blue eye and a corkscrew tail."

"No shit?"

"So I'm told."

Aaron felt raw emotion closing his throat while his diaphragm fluttered. His eyes stung. Belinda, and now Roscoe's pup. He couldn't speak.

After a few moments, Earl cleared his throat and Aaron thought uh-oh, the bad news. "One more thing, though. After what you've told me, I can't bring you into the department before the election. If this gets into court before then and Carrington maintains you were planning on killing him, well…"

"Earl, I knew when I went after Carrington that the job wouldn't happen."

"You won't have to look too hard. Kuchera's planning on retiring. Harlan's going to offer you the job. He apparently and probably correctly reckons that having a vigilante on his force won't necessarily be a negative in a town like Jack Springs."

"Maybe, maybe not," Aaron said. "But right now, I've just got to get back and see Belinda, and Roscoe's pup. I can't think about anything else."

"It sounds like your head's on straight for a change. Call me when you get back." Earl hung up.

Aaron yawned mightily. The exhaustion of the day, the past two months, his life, could no longer be held at bay. The stink on his body could not wait, however. So he got up, staggered into the shower and let the hot water wash the stink and some of his cares away.

He dried off, slipped into cutoff sweatpants and lay back on bed, knowing there was still some business to be taken care of. Most important was finding Cassie and seeing if there was some way of undoing the damage he had done to her, their relationship.

But first, assuming that Belinda was willing to listen, he had a story to tell her, a story about 20 seconds in a young man's life, a young man whose biggest mistake might have been not those 20 seconds but trying to shoulder the burden of that story for 27 years all by himself.

The Gallup Independent, Aug. 15, 1997
By Willie Crudup
Staff Reporter.

An archeologist who had recently worked with college students at a dig near Zuni has been named as a suspect in the murder of a 19-year-old Zuni woman, according to Sgt. Wayne Lagerson, of the McKinley County sheriff's department.

Trey Carrington, whose background as an archeologist is somewhat murky, came to the attention of authorities when his 1975 Land Rover was found parked at the truck stop east of Gallup two days ago. Carrington was already in custody and awaiting extradition to Colorado, where he is wanted on a conspiracy-to-commit-murder charge.

Zuni Police Sgt. Edward Othole alerted the Sheriff's Department to the location of the vehicle after receiving an anonymous tip, according to Lagerson.

Jenny Chimoni, the victim, had disappeared from the truck stop on August 5. Her body was found on the side of the road to Ft. Wingate two days later. She had been beaten to death, according to the McKinley County Coroner. Ms. Chimoni was employed as a hostess in the restaurant at the time she disappeared.

Sheriff's investigators reportedly found some evidence that "suggests the victim was recently in Carrington's vehicle," according to Sgt. Lagerson. He declined to identify that evidence. Lagerson added that employees at the truck stop weren't sure when the vehicle was left there, but that it had been reported stolen at the time Carrington was taken into custody on the Colorado charge.

"It is a mystery," Lagerson said. "But if the vehicle had been found anywhere else, we would have been less likely to connect it to the murder. Maybe Ms. Chimoni had an avenging angel."

NOTE

The description of conditions in the old, downtown area of Gallup N.M. are accurate as of my first visit there in 1998. In two subsequent visits, the conditions were much improved. How it was accomplished, I don't know. Description of Saratoga, Wyoming was and is still accurate. It's one of my favorite places. Jack Springs, is physically and atmospherically based upon the town of Nederland, Colorado. It is my favorite place in Colorado. The only character not fictional is the veterinarian, who's a good friend, erstwhile fishing buddy and excellent animal doctor.

The biochemical agent encapsulated aflatoxin did not exist during the first Gulf War. Aflatoxin was discovered in Iraq's arsenal but was not encapsulated and there was no evidence it was used during the war. However, a mycoplasma, a bacterium, was encapsulated and ultimately found in thousands of ill Gulf War veterans. It was hard to detect due to the encapsulation but successfully treated with intravenous antibiotics. The only other time this organism was found was in hundreds of prison inmates in Huntsville, Texas, about five years before the first Gulf War. No explanation was ever given for how these occurrences took place. I may have given Caller ID capabilities it did not have in 1997 but doing so was necessary to the plot.